You, with a View

You, with a View

JESSICA JOYCE

Berkley Romance
New York

BERKLEY ROMANCE
Published by Berkley
An imprint of Penguin Random House LLC
penguinrandomhouse.com

Library of Congress Cataloging-in-Publication Data

Names: Joyce, Jessica, author.
Title: You, with a view / Jessica Joyce.
Description: First edition. | New York: Berkley Romance, 2023.
Identifiers: LCCN 2022044791 (print) | LCCN 2022044792 (ebook) |
ISBN 9780593548400 (trade paperback) | ISBN 9780593548417 (ebook)
Subjects: LCGFT: Novels.
Classification: LCC PS3610.O974 Y68 2023 (print) |
LCC PS3610.O974 (ebook) | DDC 813/.6—dc23/eng/20220916
LC record available at https://lccn.loc.gov/2022044791
LC ebook record available at https://lccn.loc.gov/2022044792

First Edition: July 2023

Printed in the United States of America
2nd Printing

Book design by Daniel Brount

Gram, I got all your signs that you were with me while I wrote this. I love you further than forever.

You,
with a
View

One

WAKE UP TO TWO MILLION VIEWS.

I don't know it at first. With my eyes closed, my hand traverses the obstacle course of cups, food wrappers, and ChapStick tubes on my nightstand to find my phone. All I want is to know the time.

Or maybe I don't. From the sunlight piercing my screwed-shut eyelids, it's embarrassingly late.

My fingers wrap around the charger cord, and I drag the phone across the nightstand, knocking the ChapSticks down like bowling pins.

Whatever. Future Noelle can deal with that mess.

I finally get a hand on my prize and illuminate the screen. But instead of the time, my bleary eyes snag on an avalanche of TikTok notifications. Even as I blink at the astronomical number, it keeps ticking, growing by five, by seventeen, by forty-two.

"What the hell," I croak.

Then I remember: my video.

My already sleep-weak grip fails me, and the phone drops onto my face.

The door flies open at my pained howl. Through watery eyes, I make out the general shape of my mom. "Noelle, what in the world?"

If this were a sitcom, this is where it would freeze: on me, twenty-eight years old, rolling around in my childhood bed, blinded in a freak iPhone accident after going viral on a social media app meant for teenagers.

The only thing that doesn't make me want to die inside is how many people have seen this video. My heart skips a beat. Maybe even the *right person*.

I knife into a seated position, my fingers pressed against my aching orbital bone as I fumble for my phone. From the doorway, Mom watches in bafflement, decked out in Peloton gear instead of a power suit. Must be Saturday.

"Are you okay?" Brown eyes that match mine slide to the bike in the corner of the room. On the wall, a neon sign cheers BE AWESOME.

I can tell she's dying to turn it on. I wish I could tear it down. Nothing like waking up to aggressive positivity every morning when you're a grown adult who had to move back into your parents' house after getting laid off from a job you didn't even like.

"Yes, Mom, I'm great." I sigh, a headache blooming. "Just dropped my phone on my face."

"Sorry, sweetie. Hey! Since you're up, I'm going to get a quick ride in."

She says all of this in one breath, already at the bike with her special, extra-loud shoes in hand. The number of times she's woken me clacking across the hardwood these past four months can't be counted on all my appendages. It's not her fault she turned my childhood bedroom into a shrine to her two-thousand-dollar bike, though. None of us anticipated I'd be here again.

"Do your thing." I burrow back under my duvet and pull up my account on TikTok, my heart pounding.

Right there, on my latest video posted just over a week ago, is the number of views: 2.3 million. There are over four hundred thousand likes and sixteen hundred comments.

Holy shit.

What the hell happened? When I fell asleep at nine last night, I held steady at a paltry eighty likes. And, most crushingly, no comments.

My expectations were low, but they should've been lower. I created the account last September on a bored whim, then started posting my photography after seeing other photography accounts take off, though no one gave a shit about mine.

But hope starts with a seed, right? At least, that's what my gram used to tell me with a wink.

I keep all of the advice she gave me tucked in my pocket for when I need it, which was often before her death, and near constant now that she's gone. She was a fixture in my life from the start, the person I turned to when anything happened, good or bad. It's unconventional to call a grandparent your best friend, but Gram was mine from the time I knew what best friends were.

It took two months after she died before I could look at pictures of her without instantly crying. I have a voicemail of her singing "Happy Birthday" that I can't listen to, even six months later.

But this video—the one that now has millions of views—is as much a love letter to her as it is a question to the universe. Or a plea.

When you find out your grandmother had a secret lover when

she was twenty, you want to know more. And when she's not around to answer the tornado of questions that kicked up the second you pulled those pictures out of a timeworn envelope in a box transferred from a dusty corner in her garage? Well, you have to find alternate means.

My dad was my first stop. I asked if he knew anything about Gram's romantic history, keeping it vague. I had to tread lightly—if he didn't know about the relationship, it might upset him. His grief was still as raw as mine.

"It was only ever Pop for her, and Mom for him. She always talked about how he was her greatest love," he told me.

His parents' relationship has always been a point of pride. Their love story set his own expectations sky-high, turning him into a hopeless romantic, and those expectations trickled down. It was a long-standing joke in our family—*if it's not like Gram and Grandpa Joe, we don't want it.*

Dad's eyes had narrowed with curiosity, maybe suspicion, at my ensuing silence. "Where'd that question come from?"

"Oh, nowhere," I said while a picture of her and another man burned a hole in the back pocket of my jeans.

So, Dad was out. And if he was out, everyone else in my family was, too. They'd just turn around and tell him.

I'd spent enough time on TikTok to know it was equal parts useless and transformative—insipid dance routines mixed with reunion videos that made me sob into my pillow at two a.m. If I posted the information I'd found and made it compelling enough, there was a chance someone would see it. There was a chance someone would *know.*

Maybe they'd know something about the collection of photos and the single letter Gram squirreled away for over sixty years. Maybe they'd know the handsome man in the pictures with wavy dark hair and a deep dimple named Paul—it was written on the back of the pictures in a steadier version of her loop-happy handwriting, along with the years: 1956 and 1957.

She married Grandpa Joe in 1959 after a whirlwind romance. I know their story by heart—Gram loved to tell it to me. But she never uttered Paul's name, not once, and that's strange. We played a game we affectionately called Tell Me a Secret constantly. I always told her mine, and she told me hers.

So I thought.

Before gathering up the nerve to look at the comments and confirm whether my answer is there, I decide to rewatch the video.

I press my thumb to the screen, and it starts up, playing the Lord Huron song I chose for maximum heartstring pullage. The text I added overlays each picture I hold up in the frame, the chipped mint polish on my thumb a stark contrast to the black-and-white prints.

There's a bite of grief looking at her face, which in its youth looked so much like mine. The architecture of our features is the same; people have always told us that. Twins separated by fifty or so years. Soulmates born in different decades.

The first picture is Gram and Paul standing in front of a house I don't recognize. The text on the screen reads: My grandmother passed away recently. I found these pictures of her and a man I never knew.

Then it's them at the beach, her looking up at Paul with a flirty grin on her face: The only info I have is his name is Paul and they knew each other in Glenlake, CA, sometime around 1956.

Next, it's a picture of them embracing, her cheek pressed against his chest, eyes closed: Her name is Kathleen, and I believe she was twenty in these photos.

The last is Paul sitting at a picnic table, his chin propped in his hand, gazing into the camera in a way that reveals who was behind it: This is a long shot, but if you recognize him, please reach out. Gram never mentioned him, but he looks important. I really need to hear their story.

There's a thread of commonality running through each picture: they were always looking at each other and smiling. Often in each other's arms. In many of the shots, Gram was looking up at Paul with hearts in her eyes.

And his heart clearly belonged to her. If I hadn't known it by the way he looked at her, the letter he wrote said it out loud.

I peel back the duvet to make sure Mom is still occupied. There's sweat dripping down her face, her attention laser-focused on the screen in front of her. I might as well not be here.

Perfect. I pull out the letter I stashed under my spare pillow, smoothing over a crease with my thumb.

July 1, 1957

Dearest Kat,

I understand why we can't elope. I truly do. I just want you to be well.

The end of our relationship won't stop me from loving you for the rest of my life. I don't know if that helps or hurts. The only thing I ask is that you remember what we promised each other: never forget our time together, and think of it with happiness.

I promised you it would be okay, do you remember? And it will.

Yours always,
Paul

I can say with certainty no one has ever loved me like that. So why did she say goodbye?

I've never put my face or voice in anything I've uploaded. Even my username is anonymous, just *user* and a random mix of numbers. But now Gram and Paul's faces are there, and 2.3 million people have seen it, and I don't feel bad. My grandmother loved this man, but I can't ask her anything. She can't tell me this secret.

So, if Paul is still alive, I hope he'll tell me for her.

I slip the letter back into its hiding place, then flip onto my back, picking my phone up to go comment diving.

But before I can get there, the duvet is unceremoniously ripped off my head. For the second time today, I drop my phone on my face.

"Fuck!" I yell, covering my face with my hands. My flailing legs connect with a body.

"Fuck back!" The familiar voice groans. "You got me in the balls!"

"I can't hear Cody's instructions!" Mom puffs over the instructor's shouts and her Lamaze-adjacent breathing pattern.

I uncover my face to find my younger brother, Thomas, doubled over, his forehead resting on my bed, hands tucked between his legs. His breathing pattern is Lamaze-adjacent, too.

In the middle of all the ruckus, my dad pokes his blond head through my doorway, a bright smile on his face. "Does anyone want eggs Benny? I thought we could do brunch since Thomas is here."

I rip my scrunched duvet out from under Thomas's head, yanking it back over my legs. "I would love everyone to get out of my room. Remember my rule about not being in here when I don't have pants on?"

"I'm almost done," Mom pants. "I'm about to PR."

Thomas groans.

God, same. My good eye strays back to my phone as a slew of notifications bubble up onscreen. I'm desperate to check, but I don't dare in a room full of Shepards who don't know about any of this.

Thomas rebounds, his sea-green eyes turning sharp with curiosity as he sees my lit-up screen. Looking at him is like looking in a mirror, minus the eleven months between us; we have the same honey-blond hair and dark eyebrows, but my eyes are the color of coffee dregs.

He nods his chin toward my phone. "What's going on?"

I flip it on its face. "Nothing."

"Your Tinder blowing up, Beans?" He smirks. "What a catch."

Dad has disappeared to start on the eggs Benedict, and Mom is busy celebrating the end of her ride, along with her PR. I take a risk, putting both of my middle fingers in Thomas's face.

"Knock it off, you two," Mom says, out of breath.

Thomas cackles, sliding out the door. If I didn't have chronic back pain, I'd swear I was fifteen again. Being in this house makes us both regress.

Mom jumps off the bike, an exhilarated smile on her face. She turns to the BE AWESOME sign behind her, pulling the string. It only gets illuminated if she feels it's deserved. It zaps on, the pink light turning her face even redder.

Her dark hair is damp around the edges of her ponytail, and her eyes go soft when they meet mine. Same as they always do lately.

"You good?" she asks, and it's not perfunctory, exactly, but we both know I'm not.

Still, I say my line with ease. "Yep."

Her quiet sigh indicates she doesn't believe me. Fair. I don't, either. "Well, it's eleven, so maybe you want to get out of bed?"

Be awesome, indeed.

———————

THE UNREAD COMMENTS WHISPER URGENTLY ALL THROUGH brunch. I shovel my dad's eggs Benedict into my mouth, nearly choking.

Just what I need, death by Canadian bacon.

I'm tempted to pull my phone out no less than one million times, but it'll invite questions I'm not prepared to answer. My family is nosy on a regular day. Since I had to move home, they've turned into helicopters, clearly concerned that I'm one job rejection email away from losing my shit.

I finish my breakfast in record time, slamming my fork down like I'm the winner of a Benny-eating contest no one else entered. "Done, see you."

"Why, do you have plans?" Thomas asks over the screech of my chair and around a mouthful of food.

"Why, does it matter?" I shoot back.

He lifts an eyebrow. "I just got here, and you're already ditching me?"

"Mas, you slither up from the city whenever Sadie has plans that don't involve you. I'm sure I'll see you in mere days."

"I don't *slither*," he grumbles, though his expression softens at the mention of his longtime girlfriend—and my best friend. The softness is replaced by mischief as he pulls a magazine from his lap, curled open to a specific page. "We didn't have time to discuss this."

"What, that *Maxim* still exists or that you're still subscrib—"

What I'm looking at sinks in, and I snatch the magazine from Thomas's hand with a gasp.

He leans back in his seat, grinning. "Your boy Theo Spencer is one of *Forbes* 30 Under 30."

I snort. "*My* boy? You're the one who had a crush on him throughout high school. He was a pain in my ass. On purpose."

"Keep telling yourself that," he says smugly.

I ignore him, and the two men bracketing Theo in the picture, instead staring at the face that's vexed me for years. That wavy dark hair, the barely there dimple that pops when he smirks. Those deep blue eyes shaded by stern eyebrows that curve into cockiness with infuriating regularity. At least, they did when I last saw him years ago.

We may have been voted Most Likely to Succeed in high school, but our paths diverged dramatically when we went to college.

Obviously. The man is in *Forbes*, and I'm in SpongeBob sleep shorts. I'm not sure what's more annoying—his latest accolade or the fact that he's still smoking hot.

"Good for him," I say in a tone that clearly conveys *fuck that guy*, if Mom's arched eyebrows are any indication. I toss the magazine at Thomas, smiling triumphantly when it hits him in the face.

Thomas's snort echoes as I drop a kiss on Dad's sandpaper cheek to thank him for the meal.

I hightail it out of there, using the fumes of my annoyance to speed out to the backyard. Specifically, to the hammock in the far corner, where I can dive into comments without interruption.

Forgetting Theo, his perfect face, and his Midas existence, I pull up the app.

In the grand scheme of things, none of this matters. I had the perfect childhood. I had parents and grandparents who loved me, who showed up to my millions of extracurriculars, who thought the sun rose and set on my and Thomas's existence, along with our cousins. Grandpa Joe was a sweet man with a booming laugh who used to tug on my bottom lip when I was pouting just to get me smiling again. Gram being in love with another man when she was young doesn't change anything about my life.

But now that she's gone, I'm desperate to know this story. She clearly found her way to ultimate happiness. How?

I don't know what my ultimate happiness looks like or how to get it. If it even exists. Without Gram here to tell me it'll be okay, and after the missteps that have moved me further from my Most Likely to Succeed path, I'm not confident I'll ever find it. I wish she could tell me *something*.

There are nearly two thousand comments, but the most popular ones are at the top. My eyes scan the first five, almost desperately, like I'm looking for a life-or-death test result.

Two things happen.

The first: my breath catches as I see a comment, three words long.

And the second: Thomas pops out of nowhere, yelling, "GOTCHA!"

I jerk violently, screaming as the hammock swings and dumps me onto the grass below.

But I saw the comment before I tipped over, and it made my stomach drop harder than falling.

User34035872: that's my grandfather.

Two

"YOU REALLY MADE THIS?"

I settle next to Thomas on the edge of my bed. After our tangle outside, he demanded to know what was up. We brought the party upstairs so I could walk him through everything privately. Now, I've got the stack of pictures in my hand, and Paul's letter is unfolded on my duvet.

"Yes, for the fifth time, I did."

Thomas looks up from my phone, his eyebrows raised high. "First of all, the production value is incredible."

I sigh.

He reaches over to adjust the frozen peas I'm holding against my head. "Seriously, this is great, Beans. That company did you a favor laying you off." He tilts his head, tapping the phone screen. "But we already know you're not utilizing your true talents."

I smack his hand away, ignoring his well-meaning jab. Photography is on the back burner indefinitely. "Few people's true talents lie in basic data entry. And if my talents *did* lie there, I'd ask you to go back in time to when you nearly drowned me in Gram's pool and finish the job."

"I was seven," he responds defensively. "It was an accident."

"Anything can be on purpose if you try hard enough."

"Okay, let's focus here." He absently fiddles with the thin gold hoop in his nose. "Gram really had a side dude?"

"He wasn't a side dude. She must have dated him before Grandpa, and he was clearly very important to her. They were going to elope, for god's sake. That letter makes it seem like she was the love of his life!"

Thomas grabs the letter from me, scanning it, then thumbs through the pictures. I watch how his expression changes carefully, from curiosity to surprise to something heavier. His thumb moves over Gram's smiling face, and he swallows as he sets it down, then picks up the letter again. "Where'd you find all this?"

"It was in one of the boxes in Gram's garage. Dad brought a bunch of them over, remember?"

"Ah, right, the boxes you've been raccooning through."

I elbow him hard. He elbows me harder, sending the peas flying out of my hand.

He's not far off, though. I've spent the past couple months picking through the boxes Dad brought home when he and my three uncles cleared Gram's house out. He came back from the task red-eyed and quiet, put the boxes in the garage, and hasn't touched them since.

Besides his assertion that Grandpa Joe was Gram's one and only, it's how I know he's never seen any of this. The letter and photos were stuffed at the bottom of a box in a big manila envelope. A *sealed* envelope. I mean, hello, suspicious. I get my insatiable curiosity from him.

Or maybe we both get it from Gram. Our Tell Me a Secret

game started when I was old enough to have any. We traded secrets like currency, always an even-steven deal. Mine started out small and inconsequential, growing as I grew, too. I talked to her about relationships, anxiety, school woes, and, later, my struggle to adjust to the disorienting letdown of adulthood. She ended up knowing everything—she was my secret-keeper, my living diary.

Given how our game deepened once I was an adult, Paul should've come up in conversation. I'm still the only one who knows she and Grandpa Joe went through a rough patch in the eighties, that the "errands" they'd sometimes sneak off for were actually an excuse to get it on in the car. She knew *every* juicy detail about my relationships. Why didn't I know this man existed? Did she not want to tell me specifically, or was it something about the story itself that kept her silent? Either way, it stings. It's a small betrayal to the rules of our game.

If there's a reason she held back, I need to know.

I take my phone from Thomas, scrolling down to the comment that still has my heart racing like a hummingbird's wings.

that's my grandfather.

Dozens of responses cascade below it, a waterfall of *OMGs* and *Y'ALL IT'S HAPPENINGs*.

The million-dollar question is what, exactly, is happening? This person could be lying. They could be telling the truth, but Paul could refuse to speak to me. He may not remember anything. User34035872 could have difficulty distinguishing between past and present tense, and Paul could actually be dead.

Thomas rests his chin on my shoulder. "What are you going to do?"

His voice is knowing, though, because he knows me. It's what he'd do, too. We're nearly identical, save for his irritatingly beautiful eyes and his propensity to be a shithead. We have a mile-wide impulsive streak, a competitive spirit bordering on homicidal, and a dedicated *it's fine!* optimism that gets us through when hasty decisions go south.

I touch the username, which brings me to a blank profile. No posts, no followers.

"Kinda sus," Thomas murmurs.

I pull up the send message function anyway, feeling a sense of purpose for the first time in months.

And I type out a message to Paul's alleged grandkid.

SADIE SLIPS INTO THE SEAT ACROSS FROM ME, SLIDING ME THE salad she ordered while I grabbed a table outside the restaurant. Overhead, the midday sun is pale in the rich springtime sky.

I pull off the top of the container with a happy sigh. "You're an angel, Sadie Choi. I Venmoed you."

Lovingly full-naming her doesn't offer the distraction I hoped for. Her eyebrows drop into a frown. "What did I tell you about your sneaky Venmo tactics? Stop paying me back for things I want to pay for."

I spear a bite of lettuce and chicken, my cheeks heating. "I can't have a twenty-dollar pity salad on my conscience, okay?"

Though she's wearing white heart-shaped sunglasses, I know her brown eyes are soft behind the lenses. "There's no such thing as pity between best friends. I love treating you, and I'm the one who invited you today in anticipation of good news from your interview. So, just so you know, I'm going to decline your payment."

"Just so *you* know, the interview was a bust." I give her a breezy grin that belies my panic. Sitting in that stuffy conference room while the hiring manager listed tasks boring enough to make my soul shrivel up, I wondered for the four hundredth time why the hell I can't figure out how to adult successfully.

Sadie pushes a strand of straight black, chin-length hair behind her heavily adorned ear. "All the more reason to treat you."

"If you want to treat me, give me copious amounts of free alcohol."

Her response is interrupted by my phone chiming. I look down, inhaling sharply, and anticipation dumps into my veins. It's a TikTok message notification.

"Saved by the bell?"

"Literally."

After several days of back-and-forth with who I've confirmed is Paul's grandson, every notification comes with a fight-or-flight chaser. In addition to exchanging messages, he's sent through several pictures of a man who matches up to the Paul in Gram's photos.

Yesterday I asked if Paul would be willing to speak with me. I nearly chickened out, and the silence I got in return made me question my brazenness. Though I wouldn't call Paul's grandson a prolific pen pal—his responses are short, leached of personality, very bot-like—his turnaround time has been quick.

Until now. Twenty-six hours he's let my request hang. I'm almost afraid to open his reply.

"Get it together, Noelle," I mutter as Thomas joins us, a plastic bag swinging from his fingertips. He and Sadie both work in downtown San Francisco, though Thomas works from home two days a week. When I lived—and worked—in the city, we met up often for lunch and happy hours.

Thomas slides into a seat, pushing his hair from his forehead. It's a lost cause; it's thick and getting surfer-boy long, so gravity always pulls it back. "Hey, kids. This lunch is officially the best part of my day thanks to you." He flashes a brilliant smile at Sadie, then turns to me. "And you're here, too."

I roll my eyes. Sadie technically belonged to Thomas first; they met during college and immediately fell head over ass for each other. But as soon as she and I met, it was clear we were the ones who were meant to be. Thomas and I have spent the past five years vying for Sadie's ultimate affection. I'm confident I'm losing, but it doesn't stop me from trying, if only to annoy my brother.

After leaning over to accept Thomas's kiss, her attention returns to me. She brandishes her fork at my phone. "Open the message!"

Thomas rustles around in his plastic bag, pulling out a sandwich and a bag of chips. "What message?"

"Paul's grandson wrote her back."

"Teddy?" Somehow his mouth is already full of chips, and they spray out in a disgusting arc.

Sadie's eyebrow raises. "Teddy?"

I've given Sadie the whole story, with updates texted as they happen, but I only found out his name yesterday. Something about learning it, knowing I was that much closer to uncovering a new secret about Gram, sent me on an emotional bender.

So I took a hike, literally. It's what I do whenever the grief threatens to wrap its hand around my neck and choke me. I hit whatever trail makes me think of her most—ones we hiked together religiously—and walk myself into exhaustion. Then I cry it out at the peak so there's no chance Dad will see. Watching his eyes fill with his own sadness *and* empathy for mine became unbearable quickly. Hours-long hikes are my escape and sanity.

After I returned from my six-miler at Mt. Tam, I fell into bed, exhausted in too many ways to count, and forgot to update Sadie.

Still, getting every detail matters to her. She's been obsessed with this story since I told her about it.

Thomas pipes up before I can appropriately grovel. "That's his name, allegedly. Could be a fake. Noelle gave a fake name."

"I did not!" I regret ever telling my brother any of this. "I said my name was Elle. It's a half-true name."

"Teddy is for chubby babies and little old dudes," Thomas says. "If this guy is supposed to be Paul's grandson, he's probably our age. He gave you a whole fake name."

Sadie puts her hand on Thomas's arm to quiet him down. "Open the message."

I narrow my eyes at Thomas when he lets out a scoffing noise, then open the app.

My message from yesterday is there:

I'm glad Paul saw the video and liked it. That means a lot. You said he was open to speaking with me? I'd love to talk to him ASAP. I'm in the Bay Area, not sure where you're located. We could speak on the phone or video chat, or whatever he's up for.

And underneath, Teddy's response:

We're in the Bay too. My granddad wants to meet with you in person. Are you willing/available to meet in the city? Send times that work for you if so.

"Oh my god."

I don't realize I've shouted it until everyone at neighboring tables looks over at us.

"What?" Sadie shouts back.

"They live here. I mean, Paul does, who cares about his grandson." I set my phone facedown on the table, overwhelmed. "He wants to meet with me."

"You have to do it." Sadie leans forward. Next to Thomas's swimmer's shoulders, she looks bite-size, but her excitement adds a good three inches to her five feet.

"This is a murder plot," Thomas says with equal parts assertion and disinterest.

"Counterpoint." Sadie holds a finger up in his face. "She could meet the love of her life."

"*Paul?*"

"His grandson." Exasperated, she leans back. "Dude, come on. Have you not paid attention to any of the rom-coms we've ever watched?"

Thomas gives her a meaningful look, flicking his eyes to me and back again. "Are you seriously asking me that?"

Sadie flushes, and I throw a balled-up napkin at my brother's head. "Gross. Come on."

They start bickering lovingly, so I pivot my attention.

My stomach pulls tight as I reread the exchange. Paul wants to meet me. This is exactly the outcome I wanted, though I never anticipated it would happen. It's like playing the lottery once and hitting the jackpot; it feels impossible, and yet you play because you know there's a chance, right?

"I'm going to say yes. I'm going to meet up with Paul."

When no one responds, I look up from my phone. Sadie has a

ring-laden hand over her mouth, her ecstatic smile peeking out from behind it. Thomas is watching me dubiously.

My thumbs fly over my phone screen as I reply:

What a small world! I'd love to meet with Paul. I'm available—

I pause, chewing on my lip. I'm available all the time, but that sounds pathetic, so I pull three times out of thin air.

—This Friday at 10am, Sunday at 2pm, or Monday at 10am. Please let me know the best place to meet.

I keep one eye on my phone for the next twenty minutes. Sadie and Thomas carry the conversation but go silent when I get another alert.

Friday at 10. We'll meet you at Reveille Coffee on Columbus at one of the tables outside.

"Friday's the day." I let out a deep breath, my heart racing. "And looks like Teddy will be there, too."

Sadie collapses against her seat. "God, I wish I could come with you."

"I'd go if I didn't have to work." Thomas, clearly disappointed, rubs a hand along his scruffy jaw. "Make sure you stay around people the whole time, okay?"

I give him a crisp salute before my eyes wander back to Teddy's message.

Tell me a secret, I hear Gram whisper to me, and my heart stretches in memory.

I blink up at the sky, wondering where she is.

Someone's going to tell me one of yours.

———

THE WEEK MOVES AT A GLACIAL PACE. MOM TALKS ME INTO trying the Peloton, and I last an entire thirty-minute class, then spend the next three hours determining whether I need to go to the hospital.

I also make a halfhearted attempt to look for jobs. The work I'm qualified for doesn't exactly light a fire under my ass, and I won't touch any photography-related jobs with a ten-foot pole. I'm not paying rent but am contributing to household expenses, and without an income, my paltry savings is drying up fast. I have an inheritance from Gram sitting in my savings account, but she stipulated in her will I was only to use the money for something that inspired me. Needless to say, it's untouched.

Also untouched: my camera. It stares balefully at me from my dresser. I haven't picked it up in six months.

I need to *do* something, but I'm frozen by my indecision and fear, and it's starting to eat at me.

Thursday night, Thomas shows up for dinner, and we linger at the table in the backyard long after our parents go inside, talking through scenarios for the next day. I stand with a groan as the conversation wanes, my scratchy eyes alerting me it's bedtime.

"Hey, listen," Thomas says. "Don't get your hopes up, okay?"

I pause mid-stretch. "What do you mean?"

"I know you miss Gram." His tone is careful. He was heartbroken when she died, too, but our grief isn't the same, and he knows it. "Just don't go in expecting this to take that away."

"I don't." My defensive tone gives me away, but he doesn't call me on it.

He runs a hand through his hair with a sigh. "Tell me how it goes tomorrow, okay? Call us."

"Fine," I say, still annoyed by his hawk-eyed observation. "'Night."

The earnestness of our conversation must have grossed him out—I wake Friday morning to Theo's *Forbes* picture staring at me, wedged next to my pillow.

Gah. Disgusting, my rational brain says. *Sign me up*, my lizard brain counters.

It's with that irritating thought that I get dressed. I lock up the silent house and drive into the city, my inner monologue moving so quick and loud it sounds like static played at full blast.

It's not until I'm parked and walking down Columbus Avenue in the heart of North Beach that my mind goes quiet. It's a power switch flipped off as Reveille comes into view, the black brick building looming ever closer.

I should probably order coffee first, give myself a minute to get my shit together, but my hands are shaking inside the pockets of my jean jacket. Caffeine will shoot me off into the stratosphere. Maybe once I see Paul, the anticipatory anxiety will ebb.

As I get to the café, I wonder if Gram's hands shook when she met Paul, or when she realized she was in love with him. When she said goodbye. If she ever felt anticipation so thick she thought she'd choke on it.

My mind is darting so quickly from thought to thought as I round the corner toward the outdoor seating that I almost miss them. But it's Paul seated at the furthest table, no doubt, his hair white, his age-spotted hands wrapped around a coffee mug. His eyes slide past the person he's talking to across the table—the broad back and dark-haired head facing away from me—and move past mine, then bounce back. Widen.

My heart stutters to a stop along with my legs. I lift my hand, tentative, shocked by his shock, but get distracted by the man sitting across from him.

The shoulders stretching across that broad back straighten, and Paul's grandson turns in his seat, his hand gripping the back of the turquoise metal chair.

And then my heart stops for real. Theo Spencer, the beautiful, infuriating centerfold of *Forbes* magazine, is staring right at me.

Three

"IS THIS A JOKE?"

We say it at the same time. That also has to be a joke.

Theo stands, and I catalog everything about him before I can process how I'm feeling: the worn-in Levi's with a button fly, god-damn him; the wavy hair rustling poetically in the breeze; his expensive-looking navy sweater, sleeves pushed up his forearms. The material looks so soft I want to rub my cheek on it.

No, I *don't*. What the *hell*.

"What are you doing here?" I demand as his expression cools from its initial shock.

Theo's eyes skim my body, but not in a sexy way. Like he or-dered Wagyu steak, and he got McDonald's instead. I regret the short corduroy skirt I'm wearing, and especially the Doc Martens. They're from high school.

When his gaze does a U-turn back down to my feet, one corner of his mouth hooks up, and I *know* he remembers the damn boots.

"Still wearing those shit kickers, huh, Shep?"

That voice. I hate it. It's like velvet rubbed the wrong way.

There's a texture to it that crawls up my spine, and a depth that sprinkles goosebumps on the back of my neck. I still remember sitting on stage at graduation, staring daggers at his back while *his* voice delivered the valedictorian speech instead of mine.

"What are you doing here?" I repeat.

One eyebrow raises, stern as ever. "I think it's obvious, isn't it?"

I don't want it to be true, but the truth is staring at me, wholly unimpressed: my high school adversary is Paul's grandson, and we've been talking all week without realizing it.

What force has brought him back into my life? Satan? No, that doesn't make sense—the same force brought Paul into my life, too.

My gaze moves up to the sky. *What are you doing up there, Gram?*

A throat clears and Theo and I turn at the sound. Paul pushes off the table to stand, his eyes—deep blue like Theo's—bouncing between us.

"I take it you two know each other?" he asks.

"Unfortunately." I hold up my hands, horrified. Even if it's true, it's his grandson I've just insulted. "I'm so sorry, I didn't mean that."

"Yes, she did," Theo says.

I shoot him a glare, and it's as effective as if we've actually hurtled back in time. We used to exchange endless jabs in class, on the tennis court where we both played varsity, at parties. Through unfortunate luck, we liked the same people, so our paths crossed constantly. Murdering him with my eyes is muscle memory. His returning smirk is, too. He loved riling me up.

I'm not going to give him the satisfaction. I'm an adult, despite my circumstances proving the opposite, and he's not going to get to me. Even though the dimple popping in his cheek—and the heat blooming in mine—says otherwise.

"Haven't seen that smile in a while, Teddy," Paul says with a grin the same shape as Theo's, dimple and all.

Like that, all expression drops off Theo's face. "I'm going to grab another coffee." He lifts his chin at me. "What do you want?"

"Nothing." The last thing I need is caffeine. Or to owe Theo Spencer anything.

He lifts his shoulder in a shrug, then walks off. Paul and I both watch him go before turning to each other.

"Sorry about that. We have some, um, history."

"So I saw," he says, his tone amused and thoughtful.

I hold out my hand. Steady now. "I'm Noelle, Kathleen's grand-daughter."

He takes my hand in his. His skin feels fragile, but his grip is strong. "Oh, I know, sweetheart. You look just like her."

My throat goes instantly tight. "Thank you."

"I was so sorry to hear she passed."

He stutters over the last word, as if it's from a language he doesn't know. It still feels foreign in my mouth, too, and like that, the connection between us is set. A gossamer thread from his heart to mine.

There's a handkerchief in his outstretched hand before I realize my eyes are welling. I take it, pressing it to my face. The hand-kerchief is timeworn and smells like fabric softener. Something about it makes me feel like I've been punched right in the ster-num. I miss Gram so much I can't breathe.

A gentle hand at my elbow guides me to a chair, and I plop down inelegantly.

I pat at my cheeks, pulling my canvas bag onto my lap. "I don't really know where to start."

Paul runs a hand down his checkered dress shirt. There's a

gold band on his ring finger. Looks like he found his happiness, too.

"What would you like to know?"

I let out a breath. "Everything."

He rubs a hand along his cheek, appraising me. "That's a tall order, Noelle."

"Is it? I know nothing. I don't know how long you were dating. Or how you met. Or *where* you met."

I reach into my bag, extracting the pictures Gram kept, along with the letter. When I slide it across the table toward him, he presses his palm over it. I can almost see him transporting back to that time when he picks up the letter, unfolding it carefully.

He looks up at me, eyebrows raised. "She kept this?"

"Yeah, I found it in a sealed envelope. The pictures were with it."

"Did you find others?"

I shake my head, then lean forward as he puts the letter down. "Were there more?"

He sighs, gazing down at a photo he's picked up. "Oh yes. We loved to write each other letters during our time together. I sent her several once she went home, though I'm not at all surprised she didn't keep them. I'm much more surprised she kept this one."

"Went home?"

He flips another photo toward me with a chuckle. They're perched on the edge of a stone wall, Gram leaning back into him with a wide smile, her eyes lowered coyly to the ground. "We met at school. This photo was taken there, at UCLA."

I frown. "My grandma didn't go to UCLA. She didn't go to college until her kids were older."

Paul's expression drops back into its previous sadness. "She did go. She just didn't finish."

Leaning back in my seat, I take that in while Paul continues to shuffle through the photos. It's another secret revealed, a small piece of what is a much bigger puzzle than I anticipated.

A bottle of fancy sparkling water is set unceremoniously on the table, interrupting my thoughts. I blink down at it, then turn to Theo as he slides into his seat. His jean-clad knee knocks into my bare one before he adjusts his position to put more space between us.

"What's this?"

He leans closer conspiratorially. He smells so good I want to yell, like firewood and a hint of something sweet. "Don't tell me I have to explain what water is, Shepard."

My gaze strays to Paul, who's watching us with mirth in his eyes. I press my lips together, swallowing down the fourteen rude things waiting to launch from my mouth.

"Thanks," I manage. "Let me pay you back."

"I'll survive," Theo says, his mouth quirking.

Right. He's the CFO at Where To Next, a travel app that acts as a concierge for anything from à la carte to full-service travel packages. Flights, places to stay, experiences, you name it. God knows I've used the app to book one of their screaming off-season deals. Once, Sadie, Thomas, and I stayed in a monster cabin in Tahoe for practically nothing. Theo is also a cofounder—he and two of his college friends started it—and must be sitting on a pile of money. I made the mistake of looking him up on LinkedIn once, not realizing he could see I'd viewed his profile, and read through a ton of gushy articles he was tagged in. I still remember the private message he sent me the next day:

Looking for something specific, or is this just run-of-the-mill stalking?

It took everything in me not to delete my profile. That I still get notifications for any mentions of him in the news will go to the grave with me.

I pull a five from my bag and slide it toward him. Then I push the bottle of water off to the side, turning my attention back to Paul. "I had no idea she attended UCLA. So you didn't meet in Glenlake?"

He shakes his head, taking in the spread of memories on the table. "We had an art history class our sophomore year. She hated me from the start. Thought I was a cocky SOB. Which I was." At this, he winks and I grin, charmed. "I didn't think too highly of her at first, though she was the most beautiful girl I'd ever seen. Whip-smart and she wasn't afraid to show it. I was intimidated by her, so I needled her a lot."

"Needled?"

"Tried to get a rise out of her," Paul says, grinning. "She didn't like that much."

I laugh, imagining it. "She was feisty."

"Sounds familiar," Theo says into his cappuccino.

I twist in my seat, raising an unimpressed eyebrow. "*Feisty* is the word you'd use to describe me?"

He blinks innocently, and I get momentarily distracted by his long, curled lashes, the tiny freckle underneath his left eyebrow. "Can confirm it starts with an *f*."

Releasing an impatient breath, I turn back to Paul. "Sorry, go on."

"We got off to a bumpy start until one of her best girlfriends started dating my fraternity brother. Once she was forced to so-cialize with me, we discovered we were both from the Bay Area. I grew up here in the city." He traces his finger over one of the photos. "It was a simple way to connect, but it led to us striking up a friendship that turned fond very quickly. We started dating not long after."

His hair moves in the breeze, and his hands are lined and spotted as they move over another photo. Despite the obvious signs of his age, he looks strong, at least a decade younger than he is.

Gram looked strong, too. She *was* strong, driving like a demon up until the day before she died, when we went on a hike at Tennessee Valley. She played tennis with me regularly, and whupped my ass at it, too, even though I kept up the hobby after high school.

And yet she died in her sleep three days before Thanksgiving. She had the ingredients for her famous pumpkin pie stacked up on the counter. She wasn't ready. I wasn't, either.

A streak of jealousy runs through me like electricity. Like poison. I begrudge Theo for being able to grab a cup of coffee with his granddad when I'll never see Gram again. It makes me want to grab onto Paul's hand, hold him hostage until he tells me every detail of their story. Every anecdote about her—that feistiness, the way she'd clap her hands when something really delighted her. Her loud, boisterous laugh that could make your ears ring if she did it in a small room. The other things I apparently don't know.

I want to twist my hands around his memories like I'm wringing out a towel so I can get it all in one fell swoop.

"What happened?" I ask. I can't help myself. "I mean, the pictures—that letter—you were clearly in love. Why did you separate? You said she left school. Why?"

Paul dips his chin, pinning me with a look equal parts stern and kind. "You're impatient to know it all right now."

"No, not at all." I backpedal like my life depends on it. I don't want him to stop talking because I've pushed too far.

It's only when Theo presses his finger against my knee that I notice it's bouncing. "You're vibrating."

I push his hand away, rubbing the skin he touched, then cover it with my palm so he won't see the goosebumps.

"I'd like to tell you the story, Noelle, but it's not going to happen all in one day," Paul says.

"Granddad—" Theo starts, sitting up straight.

Paul's gaze flickers to Theo, then back to me. A whisper of a smile alights on his lips, a secret one. "You want to know everything, and I'll answer any questions you have. But I'd like to request more of your time to do so."

"Of course. I have nothing *but* time." Shit. That doesn't sound like something a thriving person would say. "I mean, yes, I will absolutely find the time. Just tell me when and where."

"Let me check my date book when I get home," Paul says. "I do have a few things planned next week, and I don't want to double-book you."

"God forbid you miss poker afternoon with your frat buddies," Theo mumbles, but his voice is affectionate. It gives the texture of his voice a softer feel.

"Soon enough they'll all be dead. Got to get my time in with them while I can," Paul replies jovially. He turns to me. "Why don't we exchange numbers and we can chat."

"That sounds perfect." I input the number Paul rattles off into my phone, then call it so he has my number, too.

Theo leans forward to catch my eye. "Isn't it easier if I message you with logistics stuff?"

I spare him a glance. "Nope. Paul and I can take it from here."

"Right." Theo's phone starts shimmying with an incoming call.

I catch the contact name—Dad—before he turns it facedown, his jaw tight. Paul's eyebrows cinch together, his gaze lingering on his grandson's phone, as Theo lets out a sharp breath. "Are we done for the day? I have to get back to work, and I need to drop this freeloader off at home first."

I push down my disappointment, reminding myself this is the beginning, not the end. "Lots of *Forbes* 30 Under 30 things to do today, huh?"

As soon as the words are out of my mouth, I want to absolutely destroy myself. It's the LinkedIn incident times ten.

But Theo's reaction is nothing like I expect. He doesn't smirk or say something cocky. Instead, it's like watching someone's power switch get turned off. He just . . . shuts down.

"Bye, Shepard," he says blankly, swiping his phone off the table. His chair screeches against the concrete as he stands and stalks a few paces away.

I have very little time to wonder how I wiggled my way out of that one, or what exactly crawled up Theo's ass. Paul hands me the photos and letter, then takes my hand in both of his after I've tucked our treasures in my bag.

"I'm very glad you found me, Noelle," he says, his expression earnest, a mix of pleasure and melancholy. "I hope you get what you need out of this new friendship."

My throat pinches with emotion. "Me too. We'll talk soon."

Paul walks to Theo, his hands in the pockets of his perfectly pressed khaki pants. Theo's eyes slip past his granddad to me, and for an extended moment, we stare at each other. He breaks contact first, his hand slipping to Paul's back to help him down the subtle slope in the sidewalk.

I let out a breath, suddenly exhausted. Exhilarated. Scared

about what I might find out, and how that might reshape the picture I've painted of Gram.

I push that last emotion away and hike my bag onto my shoulder, preparing to make the trek back to my car.

But I swipe the fancy-ass sparkling water off the table before I go.

Four

I DECIDE I'LL LET PAUL MAKE THE FIRST MOVE WITH OUR NEXT date. I'm terrible at waiting, though, so by the time the weekend ends, I'm crawling out of my skin.

It's the only excuse I'll allow myself for digging out my Glenlake High senior yearbook: boredom. Restlessness. An excuse not to stare at my phone. It doesn't have anything to do with seeing Theo, which I'm still wrapping my mind around.

Of all the people in the world, *he* had to be Paul's grandson? Beyond a few accidental run-ins over the years, I haven't seen him in forever, and this is how he reenters my life? It feels like fate, but not the good kind. The *Final Destination* kind.

With a sigh, I drop onto my bed, flipping the yearbook open.

I typically suppress my memories from high school. Not because they were terrible, but because they were the last time I had my shit together.

Theo and I are both sprinkled heavily throughout the book. No surprise. Not only were we at the top of our class, but we played tennis all four years, and he also played varsity soccer. I was the queen of extracurriculars, though my favorite by far was photography.

I worked my ass off and got into UC Santa Barbara, but when I got there, it was clear I was a minuscule fish in a massive pond. Teachers didn't know my name, nor did they care. No one gave a shit that I was smart; they were, too, and they'd speak over me in class to prove it. I had a shitty roommate, I was lonely, and my freshman year GPA decimated my confidence.

As I scraped my way through school, I struggled to find my place. Even photography, which had always been something to escape into, felt like a slog. There were at least ten people in my photography electives who were better than me. It grated against every perfectionist bone in my body. I crawled over the finish line at graduation, but I was battered and bruised and incredibly disillusioned. Every label I'd ever given myself now felt like a lie. College, and my subsequent struggle to carve out a meaningful career path, all but confirmed it.

Meanwhile, Theo had flourished at UC Berkeley, where his parents were alumni. Our mutual friends loved to give me updates on him—his internships, the semester he spent abroad in Hong Kong, the cushy job he landed at Goldman Sachs. He was probably making money hand over fist. And there I was, fresh out of college, determined to find a way to make photography my main source of income. I started assisting a portrait photographer, who was brilliant but a total bastard, in hopes of eventually ditching my desk job. After a year of sacrificing weekends to Enzo, who vacillated wildly between tepid praise and molten admonishments, I was fired when I didn't get a specific shot at a wedding. No doubt the catering staff working that night can still hear him screaming "you'll never amount to anything" in their sleep. God knows I do.

Deep down, I feared he was right. There was plenty of evidence to support it. My photography aspirations flamed out after that, despite my family's insistence I keep trying. I took pictures, but only for myself. I stopped hearing my own voice in my head, or even Gram's. It was only Enzo's, telling me I wasn't special, that I'd never make it. I believed him. Maybe I still do.

Some people really do keep climbing. And some people, like me, peak in high school.

I flip to my and Theo's senior portraits, which are side by side. Shepard and Spencer: a match made in alphabetical hell.

He's intensely serious, in a mug shot kind of way. It's the same expression his dad wore every time I saw him. I don't think the man ever looked happy, and now I wonder if the dimple skipped a generation. What a waste. Despite the irritating package it comes with, Theo does have a beautiful smile.

The thought comes before I can squash it: *I wish I could photograph him.* In my head, I line up a shot from Friday: Theo watching his granddad, those eyebrows softened by affection. The phantom weight of a camera in my hands is heavy, and I clench my fingers around the lost-limb feeling.

My phone rings, breaking me out of my disturbing daydream, which is even more disturbing when I see who's calling.

I answer, chirping out a strangled, "Paul!"

"Hello, sweetheart," he says cheerfully. "I hope this isn't a bad time."

I look around my room, as still as the rest of the house. My parents won't be home for another three hours. "Not at all. I'm in a bit of a work lull right now, so this is perfect." I blaze right through that understatement. "I'm glad you called. I really enjoyed meeting you on Friday."

"Not nearly as much as I enjoyed it. I'm so tickled you know my Teddy. What a small world."

Too small. "It's been a long time, but it was . . . uh, interesting to see him again. He was always very ambitious in high school. I'm not surprised to see him doing well now."

"Yes, well," Paul says, a bit of the cheer draining from his tone. "Sometimes a little too ambitious for his own good, but we're working on that together."

That sounds . . . weird. "Right."

"At any rate, I was hoping you might want to come to my house for lunch and a chat."

I stand, wincing against the ache in my back. If nothing else, I need to move out soon so I can escape this mattress. "Sounds great. When were you thinking?"

"Tomorrow would be best if you don't mind. Can you come by at noon?"

"I'll be there." I was going to go on a hike, but I can do that . . . well, anytime. "Should I bring us lunch? I can stop by a great Thai place near me if you'd like."

"Oh no, I'll have lunch ready to go. Just bring yourself."

"You got it." I scramble for a pen in the desk Mom keeps in the room. "What's your address?"

He rattles it off, and for lack of any paper around me, I transcribe it onto my leg. It's in Novato, which is about fifteen minutes north of Glenlake.

"Perfect." I stare down at the address on my goosebump-textured skin. "I can't wait."

My mind swirls with questions after we hang up. Has he been here this whole time? If so, did Gram know? Did they speak at all after Paul sent that letter, or has it been over sixty years of silence?

The questions don't end. Not for the first time, I wonder how long it will take until I'm satisfied by the answers.

I wonder, too, what will happen if the answers aren't enough.

PAUL LIVES IN A SMALL RANCH-STYLE HOUSE ON A QUIET street shaded by oak trees. I pull up to the curb and sit for a minute, the car engine ticking in the silence.

I chose a dress since it's unseasonably warm for April, but now I feel overdressed and awkward. Though Paul has proven to be the nicest man ever, I'm nervous to see him.

There's another feeling, too, and my chest ticks like the cooling engine of my Prius. With the departure of Gram, I'm left without any grandparents at all. Grandpa Joe left us five years ago, and Mom's parents died when I was a kid. An entire generation who won't witness all of my future memories. I'm too young to have lost them all, but it is what it is. And yet here's Paul, a grandparent himself, inviting me into his life like I didn't barge in demanding answers to questions that may be painful for him. Inviting me into a space that's been empty for the past six months.

Maybe that's what it is—having something halfway and knowing it's not really yours.

I hope Theo knows how lucky he is.

I unbuckle my seatbelt and grab my bag from the passenger seat, looping it over my shoulder as I make my way up to the driveway. There's a Hyundai SUV parked there, along with the most beautiful soft-top Ford Bronco I've ever seen.

"Go, Paul." I stop at the driver's side door to peek in. The exterior is a sexy cherry red, the seats a buttery brown leather. The interior is spotless save for a water bottle in the cup holder and a bag of soil on the floor of the backseat.

I squint at it, then down at my dress with tiny flowers dotted all over it. It's garden inspired, sure, but I hope Paul's not going to put me to work. I have whatever is the opposite of a green thumb.

With one last lingering look at the car of my dreams, I make my way up to the front door. A generic-looking welcome mat lies in front of it, but otherwise the porch is empty. I frown, looking around. Given the soil in his backseat, I'd take Paul for a plant guy, but it almost looks like he just moved in.

It takes a few moments after my jaunty knock before the door swings open to Paul, who's wearing an adorable cardigan, pristine white Converse, and a wide smile.

He steps back to make room for me. "Hello, Noelle, dear! You're right on time, come on in."

Whatever nerves I felt disappear in the path of his sweet warmth. "Thanks, it's great to see you again. I was just admiring your Bronco."

His white brows pull together in confusion, then smooth out. His reply is a beat late, but no less friendly. If anything, he kicks it up a notch. "Ah, yes. Are you hungry? I thought we could eat first, then I have some things to show you."

"That sounds wonderful," I say, hanging my bag on the coat-rack in the foyer.

He leads me through the living room, bright and gorgeously furnished in a midcentury style. It's the type of interior design my dad, an architect, would drool over. I slide a look at Paul, wondering who this guy is, but my gaze snags on a wall made up entirely of framed pictures.

I stumble to a stop. Paul hears the commotion and turns, eyes widening. "Are you all right?"

"Just got distracted by these photos." I step closer to get a better look, devouring each one. The composition is stunning; the use of texture, of color, or the lack thereof—every photograph makes my chest ache and my index finger itch.

It's only when I get to a black-and-white portrait of a young Theo that I realize who the photographer is. Theo's standing in front of a bodega in what looks like Manhattan, grinning down at a handful of candy clutched in his fist. His knees are knobby and darker than the rest of his skin, as if there's dirt on them. His hair is curlier than it is now, wild on top of his head. He's in his own little world, about to indulge in all that sugar.

This portrait is a declaration of love. Showing joy for the sake of it, beautiful and uncomplicated and sitting in the palm of a little boy's hand.

I turn to Paul. His hands are tucked into the pockets of his slacks, his head tilted as he watches me.

"You're a photographer." He dips his chin in acknowledgment and my heart presses against my ribs, desperate to get back to the beauty of the photos. "You're incredible."

"Thank you," he says with a small smile. "I was lucky enough to make a career out of it. These are some of my favorites, but not all of them."

I point to little Theo. "I can see why this one is."

He takes a step closer. "How?"

"Besides the structure, it's obvious you think this smile is special. The background is shadowed to let him be the focal point, and that "Open" sign illuminated right over his head is like a wink to his expression here." Paul is quiet beside me, and I start to feel self-conscious. "I mean, I know—knew—Theo, so it's probably easier for me to pick it out because I know how serious he is, but it'd be obvious to a stranger this is someone you love."

He nods, an expression I can't identify crossing his weathered features. "Are you a photographer yourself?"

"No," I blurt. "Not really. I used to dabble in it. Took classes in high school and college, but nothing serious."

Paul looks like he doesn't quite believe me, which is fair. I'm giving him a half-developed picture.

My stomach, always here to remind me of the important things in life, lets out a threatening growl.

"Why don't we pop outside for lunch?" Paul says. "You can look at these all you want after you're fed. I'd be happy to tell you the story of each."

We both know the story I really want to hear, but I nod anyway.

We're nearly to the sliding glass door leading to the backyard when he turns, his expression innocent. "I forgot to mention—I got my days mixed up, so we're plus one for lunch."

Foreboding crashes through me as Paul opens the door, stepping out onto the deck. Before I can form a response, I see a naked back across the yard, curled over a large raised planter box.

"Teddy!" Paul calls out. "Look who it is."

I sense the awareness in Theo as his back straightens. The ravine running from between his shoulder blades to the waistband of his gym shorts deepens with the movement, muscles stretching and contracting as he looks over his shoulder. He stares at me, his expression unreadable underneath the bill of his Oakland A's hat. His shoulders lift in a sigh I can't hear, and he spears the trowel in his hand into the dirt with more force than is strictly necessary.

He only says, "Granddad."

"I got my days mixed up," Paul repeats. "I invited Noelle over for lunch and a chat. Why don't you take a break and we'll eat?" He turns to me. "Theo is planting some vegetables for me."

"I see that," I murmur as Theo stands, yanking his gloves off and letting them fall onto the ground. When he turns, I inhale so sharply I choke on air.

Paul pats my back. "Are you all right?"

"Bug," I choke out.

More like *body*. I want to know what kind of devil deal Theo made when he was born. Besides his questionable personality, he was built lovingly and with extreme care by whoever is in charge of those things.

His chest is broad, his skin honey-hued underneath the midday sun. He's sculpted in an elemental way that broadcasts he knows how to use his body, that the muscles and tendons underneath that smooth skin work for him however he wants them to. It's so intensely hot I want to run away from it until I find a cold body of water to submerge myself in.

It's fucking rude that he's so good-looking. It offends me.

I cross my arms over my chest while he takes his sweet time getting to us. My eyes are fully disconnected from my rational brain, which is screaming to *look anywhere but at his chest or his abs or his belly button. What kind of asshole has an attractive belly button?!* No, my gaze eats him up, and my lizard brain doesn't even care that he notices. His mouth pulls up into a tiny smirk.

"Did he give you the same story?" he asks me as he takes the stairs up to the deck.

"Mm-hmm." I clear my throat. That was basically just a grunt. "We've been ambushed."

"It's this old brain," Paul insists, but I see the smile he's failing to hold back.

A horrifying thought pushes its way past all the horny ones: Is Paul trying to *matchmake* me and Theo?

You can't matchmake the unwilling, but my god. I'm a visual

creature. I'm not sure how much shirtless stimulation I can take before I break in some way. That would be catastrophic.

Theo braces a hand on Paul's shoulder, pulling him close. He murmurs, "I know what you're doing."

Paul ignores him, gesturing to the dining table set off to the left of us. A cheerful bunch of yellow tulips stretch up from a mason jar. "I'll be right back with the food. You kids settle in."

"Do you want some help?" I ask, a little desperate.

"No, no!" He's already bustling inside, waving a hand over his shoulder.

With a deep, cleansing breath, I pivot back to Theo.

He's still shirtless.

I'm still affected.

"You can close your mouth now, Shep," he says with a lazy grin.

I roll my eyes, running a hand over my stomach, which is growling with all kinds of hunger. "It's because your shoulders are already red, Spencer. I'm appalled by your lack of sunscreen usage. Do you even know what UV rays do to your skin? You're going to look seventy by the time you're thirty."

He twists to eye his shoulder, humming in dismay. "I put some on a few hours ago."

"You're supposed to reapply every eighty minutes." I smile sweetly when he gives me a dry look.

Keeping eye contact with me, he swipes a bottle of sunscreen off the table and starts applying.

This feels like a test. I keep my gaze firmly planted on his face, but the sound of Theo's palm gently slapping his skin as he applies the sunscreen pings my most animalistic senses.

"What are you even doing here?" I ask.

"Planting vegetables." He doesn't say *you genius*, but his tone doesn't *not* say it.

"I mean," I say, infusing the same energy into my voice, "it's the middle of the day on a Tuesday. Why aren't you at work?"

In my periphery, his hand stalls. "Why aren't *you* at work?"

"I'm working from home today." The lie slips off my tongue like silk.

Theo's expression turns sharp with awareness, his grin sharp with it, too. "What do you know? Me too."

I believe that about as much as he believes me, but I don't have time to push. Paul walks out with a tray of food.

"Lunch is served!"

"You should put on a shirt," I say as I push past Theo to get to my seat.

He runs a hand over his stomach, grinning. "Nah, I'm good."

Well, that makes one of us.

Five

THEO KEEPS HIS SHIRT OFF THE ENTIRE MEAL. IT'S OB-
scene. My eyeballs hurt from the strain of not looking.

Paul picked up sandwiches from one of the best spots in Marin County. The homemade bread is crusty perfection, and at least half of it ends up in my lap, little sourdough snowflakes drifting from my mouth every time I take a bite. It takes everything in me not to pick up each fleck with my finger after I've demolished my sandwich.

Our conversation flows smoothly thanks to Paul, who asks about my job (I continue the lie and say it's great), what I do in my free time (I wing it, since *hike* and *doomscroll* aren't legitimate answers), and how I got into photography.

Here I can be honest and tell him how when I was twelve, I picked up an old camera of Gram's, which was collecting dust on her bookshelf.

Thomas tried to fight me for it, but I came out of our wrestling match victorious, albeit bruised like a peach. I started using it constantly so Thomas wouldn't have access, but it turned into a genuine love. An obsessive one.

Paul smiles at this. "I'm familiar with the feeling. Now that you're done with your meal, should I go grab what I wanted to show you today?"

"Yes," I say enthusiastically. Theo lets out a soft huff. Not a laugh. Something rustier.

Paul disappears into the house, and the silence stretches between us.

"So why aren't you doing your photography thing full time?" Theo asks finally.

I eye him, and the flake of bread caught in his chest hair. Disgusting. I want to pick that one up with my finger the most.

"Because you can't just *do things*," I say. "It's not that easy."

One eyebrow raises slowly, like a bridge lifting for a ship. "If anyone can just *do things*, it's you, Shepard. You've been just *doing things* as long as I've known you."

"You sound like an unhinged Nike ad." I lean back in my seat, tilting my face to soak up the sun's warmth. "It's easy to invest time in something you love when you have the money for it."

"You'd be surprised." I look over at him, indeed surprised by the bitter edge in his voice. He runs a hand over his chest, dislodging the crumb in the process (RIP), and shifts in his seat. "You specifically can do anything you put your mind to, is what I mean. You were always like that in high school. Singularly focused, especially with photography. Good at everything you tried. Not as good as *me*, but—"

I snort, my chest tight. I want to be that version of Noelle, but I'm so far away from her, she feels like a different person.

"I can tell you love it still, is all," he finishes.

I try to deaden my curiosity, but that's like asking me not to breathe. "How's that?"

"The deranged look in your eyes when you talk about it."

"It's just . . . not for me. I learned that lesson a while ago."

Theo's gaze turns sharp. I avert my eyes from his attention, that face and those shoulders, the skin, which upon closer inspection, is quietly freckled. I take in the backyard instead, needing space from his wordless probing. It's small, immaculate. There are several raised beds along the perimeter of the pine fence, several bags of soil open and sagging against them.

"Your granddad's house is beautiful." I focus on a hummingbird flitting around a tall plant with tubular red flowers. Wish I knew their name. "How long has he been here?"

Theo removes his hat and tosses it onto the table, running a hand through his hair. His temples are damp. That shouldn't be so hot. "Since February. He was in LA, but my grandma died last fall. He was getting lonely, so I moved him up here."

My heart sinks so fast the world tilts. Paul's gold band flashes in my mind. "I'm—I'm sorry. About your grandma."

Theo shifts, uncomfortable. "Thanks. It's not the same as what you're going through. I mean, it was very sad, obviously, but she married my granddad when I was a kid, long after he and my dad's mom divorced. Both of my biological grandmothers are still alive, but I'm not close to them. Not like I am with Granddad, anyway."

"Grief is grief. You don't have to qualify it."

"Some grief is different, though," he says, looking out at the yard. "You can be sad but be okay. If my granddad dies, you know—"

He stops, like it's too painful to think about. That *if* a stand-in for the other word he can't say out loud: *when.* I sense the same connection between him and Paul as what I had with Gram. That soulmate thing, the string connecting two people, longer than death, further than forever.

I want Theo to sketch out his family tree for me. I'm getting crumbs of so many different things, like the flakes still littering my lap, and it makes me hungrier. I know Theo is an only child, that his dad pulled him aside after every tennis and soccer match he attended, talking to him in low, intense tones while his mom watched. That he never looked happy with his son, nor with his wife when she intervened. Remembering that makes it hard to believe he came from Paul. Is that Theo's grandma's influence, the sternness Theo seems to have inherited, too?

I hate being curious about him. I've fought against it since the beginning. But I'm me and I need to *know* things, so I open my mouth to ask more questions. I barely inhale when he shakes his head, his expression shifting from melancholy to wry.

"Don't make this earnest and uncomfortable."

"No, totally. Emotions, right?" I pretend to gag. "Disgusting."

He doesn't respond, and a tiny, microscopic, very small part of me is disappointed. My blood runs faster in my veins when we talk. But surely that's just irritation.

Theo stands, swiping a t-shirt from the chair at the head of the table. He eases it over his head, making it look like porn somehow. My body pulls tight.

One thing is certain: I'll never figure him out. I don't want to, and he'd never let me anyway. So I busy myself with brushing the crumbs from my lap, letting them fall to the ground. The birds can have them.

PAUL EMERGES A FEW MINUTES LATER, A BANKER'S BOX IN HIS arms.

"*Wow.*" I gape as he lowers the box onto the table. "We're going to be here for a while, huh?"

To my right, Theo sighs. I give him a droll look over my shoulder, where he's parked himself against the railing, but he's not looking. He's been ignoring me since our near-brush with human emotion, grimly tapping out messages on his phone.

Paul takes Theo's seat next to me. "Some of this is your grandmother's. We saw each other once after we separated—before I sent the letter you found—and she gave me things for safekeeping."

"What do you mean, for safekeeping?"

He sits back in his seat with a hum. Birds sing around us, tucked into trees. Somewhere nearby, a lawn mower buzzes.

Finally he says, "It's no surprise you have so many questions, or that you don't know much about your grandmother's life prior to her marriage to your grandfather. Our relationship was not well received by her family, and when she left school, she didn't leave with many reminders of our time together."

"So you kept all this for her?"

"For us," he corrects gently. "When our relationship ended, it wasn't acrimonious. We wanted to make sure it'd always be a lovely memory."

"But she made it a secret," I say, watching as he begins pulling items from the box.

"No." Again he corrects me. It's still soft, but there's steel behind it. "Whatever life she and I wanted, planned, or talked about was never going to be. Kathleen keeping a box of reminders of how she'd defied her parents would've prolonged her grief. Her parents and brother knew the whole story once it was over. I imagine it was initially too painful for her to recount further, and by the time you came into the world, well . . ." He smiles. "Life goes on."

I look for pain or anger on Paul's face, but all I see is nostalgia mixed with affection, softened with time.

"Your letter to her mentioned an elopement," I venture.

"Yes, we did make plans to elope."

"But it never happened. Because of her parents?"

"It was . . ." He pauses thoughtfully, his gaze going to the sky. "Not just that issue, but her parents were certainly the biggest hurdle to overcome."

"Why didn't her parents like you?"

He laughs. "Where to begin? We had one mess of a dinner with our families where everyone made it clear where they stood on a variety of subjects, including whether Kat and I should be together."

"What were the other subjects?" Theo asks.

"Well, over appetizers, my mother got going on women taking a more prominent place in the workforce, which Kat's homemaker mother thought was shocking. She already wasn't thrilled that her daughter was at college. She wanted her to get her MRS degree." Paul eyes us. "Do you know that phrase?"

I nod. "They wanted her to find a husband."

"Right you are. I just wasn't the one she was supposed to find," he says with a little smile. "The most insurmountable thing, though, was that my father and I were outspoken about the US military taking action internationally. I even went so far as to say I'd be a conscientious objector if things in Vietnam ramped up. It wasn't something her career-military father or her brother, who'd gotten a Purple Heart in Korea, wanted to hear." He shakes his head. "In hindsight I should've bitten my tongue when the subject came up. Kat had prepped me not to bring up anything political in nature, but my temper got the best of me. That night was enough to set the path to disaster, though Kat and I didn't give up afterward."

"I see."

And I do. My memories of my great-grandparents are fuzzy. I was young when they died. But I do remember my great-grandfather was an old-school, solemn man who'd shoot puzzled looks at my wild hair and Thomas's pink T-shirts, even as he let us crawl all over him during Thanksgiving dinner. My tenderhearted, progressively minded dad had a complicated relationship with his grandfather. Gram did, too. But she loved him deeply, and he doted on her, even though it's clearer to me now that his love could be destructive. One of my most vivid childhood memories was Gram crying at his funeral while I clutched her hand.

My thoughts go to Paul's letter, his acknowledgment of their permanent separation. With this new context, it breaks my heart even more for both of them. "You said in that letter you would love her your entire life."

He nods. "I did, and I will." He places a stack of pictures in front of me, but I don't pick them up yet. "She was my first great love. I was hers, as well. But your grandfather was her last."

"Who was your last great love?"

"My wife, Vera. She passed last fall, but we had twenty-three wonderful years together."

I put my hand over his. "I'm so sorry for your loss."

He pats my hand, his blue eyes watery. "I appreciate that."

My curiosity over Theo's other grandma—his biological one—is gnawing at me. But, given that she and Paul divorced, I'm going to assume it's a story I don't have a right to ask about.

Theo takes the seat across from us. His hat is back on his head, shading his eyes and any emotion lurking there. But I notice a distinct lack of surprise.

"Do you know all of this?" I ask.

"A lot of it," he says.

"The marriage stuff, too?"

Theo says again, stoically, "A lot of it, I think."

"How?"

His gaze darts to Paul before he squints off into the distance. "Kathleen wasn't ever a secret in my family."

I chew at my lip, wanting to ask more, but sensing I'm somehow pressing up against a bruise of Theo's. His shoulders are tense, like he's waiting for my next question. Like it'll hurt to hear it.

I could push until he gives me answers or tells me to fuck off. God knows I want to know everything. But for reasons I don't want to examine too closely, I let it go instead. "Let's see what's in this box, huh?"

"Dig in, kids," Paul says, giving me a warm smile, as if I've passed a test I didn't even know I was taking.

I start flipping through the stack of photos Paul handed me as Theo takes another. My attention splits between the images in my hand and the way Theo's eyes scan each picture before he lays it carefully on the table and moves on. Occasionally his mouth will pick up in a half smile, and he'll flip the picture so Paul and I can see it. Most of them are goofy photos of Paul, but some of them are gorgeous shots of Los Angeles, the UCLA campus, or the group of friends that start to become familiar as I move through my stack.

Paul notices that I linger over a photo of Gram standing in front of a fraternity house. She has one leg crossed in front of the other at the ankle and wears a mischievous smile. It could be me in the picture; our legs are long and lean, our smiles equally wide, a little crooked. Her bottom lip is even snagged a little on her left canine, like mine does. In this picture, she's wearing *my* best-day smile. I know, deep in my bones, that when this picture was taken, she was happy.

It's the power of photography. To capture it and let it live past the subject's lifetime. To allow someone to look at it years later and smile along with them.

I press my thumb against the glossy paper, working against the moisture in my eyes and the lump in my throat.

"You look so much like Kat," Paul says. I blink over at him, pulled out of my memories and hers. He nods his chin at the picture. "It's almost uncanny."

Across the table, Theo's eyes trace my face.

"You and Theo do, too," I say. "I actually can't believe I didn't notice the resemblance when I found the pictures. I spent so much time looking at them while I made that video."

At this, Theo's eyebrow quirks up. Even after years apart, I know his *I'm about to be an asshole* tell. "Was my face fresh in your memory, Shep? Been staring at my LinkedIn profile picture every night?"

"Please don't project your fantasies onto me."

Paul chuckles and even Theo grins, his damn dimple popping.

Ugh. Even when he doesn't win, he wins.

I half stand and peek into the box, needing a distraction. There are more photos, ticket stubs, and envelopes yellowed with age. But my gaze snags on something even more interesting. It's a map, folded up carefully and perched on top of a yearbook.

I take it out like it's a precious artifact. Which, really, all of this is. "What's this?"

"Take a shot every time Shepard asks a question," Theo mutters across the table.

I shoot him my most innocent smile. "Oh, I'd *love* to see you play that game. We both know your tolerance is laughable."

I'm immensely gratified by the way his cheeks turn pink. One night we were at a party—not together, but . . . existing in the same space at the same time—and he puked Mike's Hard Lemonade all over his date's shoes. I had to help her shower it off because they were both too wasted to get the job done.

He recovers quickly, his voice dipping. "My stamina has improved significantly since high school."

I make a noncommittal sound. I don't want to think about his stamina now.

God knows Theo and I could go for days like this, but my attention is diverted. As I unfold the map, the writing looped over top of Washington, Idaho, and Montana stops me short.

Paul and Kat's Honeymoon Road Trip

Six

"WHAT IS THIS?"

"Je-sus," Theo mutters, but I don't miss the way his gaze lingers on the writing, or how his eyes widen once he reads it. His eyes jump to Paul.

"So you *don't* know everything," I say triumphantly.

Theo ignores me, his attention on his granddad. "You two had a honeymoon planned out?"

Paul nods. "Before things ended, we planned a road trip for the summertime. We were going to elope as soon as school was out and then go on our way. That was Kat's stab at the plan, but I had it in my head we'd go all the way across the country and back. Take all summer before we settled back in LA."

He says this with a fondness I can't understand. My heart hurts just thinking about it, knowing it never happened.

"That's a little more premeditated than the 'we were crazy kids in love who thought, screw it, let's do this' story you told me."

"The timeline was fast, Teddy," Paul says. "We had about a

month to plan for it—eloping, the honeymoon, our life after— before she had to leave. Your interpretation isn't wrong."

Theo and I exchange a look. I can't even revel in the curiosity lighting up his face now; I'm feeling it, too. He may know more than me, but we both want to know it all.

Leaning in, his eyes travel down to the map. Circles dot the western portion: Yosemite, Zion National Park, the Grand Canyon, and Sedona, among others. I trace the route with my finger, feeling the give in the paper where Gram traced the route with her pen.

A breeze picks up, winding under my hair, and I close my eyes, imagining it's her fingers whispering down my neck, the same way she'd do to help me fall asleep. I have no idea where people go when they die, but sometimes I swear I can feel her. Right now, I do.

The thought enters my mind like someone yelling it: *Go on this trip.*

My gaze flits up to the sky, and I shift in my seat, lowering my eyes to trace the route again. Curiosity and restlessness wrap around my heart like vines. What would it be like to follow in footsteps she never actually took? Would I be chasing a ghost? Or would she feel closer than ever?

"I want to ask you a million more questions," I admit.

"I'm an old man and don't quite have the stamina for lengthy storytelling anymore . . ." At this, Paul slides a look to Theo, whose eyes roll in reluctant amusement. Paul's grin turns sly, and his gaze bounces between the two of us before he focuses on me. "But I'm happy to give you answers. I'm afraid it'll just take some time, if you have it."

"I really, really do." Theo takes note of my wistful tone and raises an eyebrow, but I push on before he can ask questions of his own. "I'm curious about something you said last time—that you didn't get along at first. Obviously you ended up loving each other deeply if you were going to get married without Gram's family's approval. What changed?"

Paul laughs. "*Us*. We realized that first impressions don't dictate what the final impression will be. Once we opened ourselves up to truly knowing each other, it was easy to fall."

Again, he splits a look between Theo and me. In a rare act of agreement, we ignore it.

"You also mentioned there were more letters?"

"Yes, as I said, we enjoyed writing to each other. She wrote me sassy notes in class before we started dating, too."

I perk up, delighted. "You don't have any of those, do you? I'd love to see."

"Why, so you can take notes?" Theo murmurs.

"Don't need to. I'd say it right to your face," I murmur back with a sharp grin that curls his mouth into a wicked shape.

If Paul hears the exchange, he doesn't react. He pulls the box toward him with a hum. "Let me see."

I fold the map while Paul riffles through the box contents. Across the table, Theo is watching all of this with an inscrutable expression. His gaze lingers on me until I start squirming in my seat. When I wipe at my face, searching for errant crumbs, he smirks.

"What?" I mouth.

He shakes his head, and I watch, fascinated, as his lips pout around his response: "You."

Like a sparkler bursting from a single flame, my mind erupts with countless meanings for one word. *You what?*

The urge to ask him what the hell he means wars with the refusal to give him the satisfaction of knowing he's sent me spinning. But he reads it on my face, like it's written in a language he created, and that smirk turns into a full-out grin.

Time and distance will make you forget, but I've never had enough of either to forget the way Theo Spencer can aggravate every nerve in my body with the twist of his mouth.

I nod my chin, forcefully banking the heat he's stoked in my body. "What's on your agenda for the rest of the day? More vegetable planting? Some remote CFO-ing while you're elbow-deep in cukes and tomatoes?"

He doesn't respond, but I don't expect him to. I anticipate the way his smile falls, the way his gaze moves past me, and I feel a pang of . . . regret? No. I'm not going to feel sorry for him, even if I'm beginning to see that work is a wound for him. I'm sure his feature in *Forbes* soothes the ache.

"Oh, I have some zucchini going in, too," Paul says cheerfully, pulling out a stack of papers.

I match his tone, just to irritate Theo. Sure enough, he snorts when I say, "Sounds delicious!"

"When everything starts coming in in a few months, I'll put together a salad for us."

"That sounds really nice."

My throat goes suddenly tight at just how nice it sounds, to have someone who knew Gram in a way that feels new to me *and* who calls me sweetheart, whose *s*'s have a slight whistle to them, a sound brushed over with age. A grandparent, though I can't call him mine.

Paul holds up a piece of paper triumphantly, then hands it over. "Found one."

Theo rises from his seat and circles the table, sitting next to me. I give him a sidelong glance. "You really want to read this?"

He lifts a shoulder. "It's my family, too, right? Might as well."

Not quite as obsessive as my thought process, but he has a point. This is a tie that binds us, for better or worse.

With a sigh, I return my attention to the paper. But the hand-writing stops me short.

I didn't realize how emotional it would be to see Gram's writing again. It got spidery in later years, but this is still the hand that wrote her love for me on birthday cards every year, when I got my first period in seventh grade (she got me a cake, too, chocolate with red frosting), when my tennis team won district champs my junior year. She said it out loud, too, so often I still hear it sometimes when it's really quiet and very late.

I didn't keep most of those cards. After she died, we found every one we ever gave her stashed in a series of storage bins. I sped back to my apartment in the city, tore through my room, my roommate hovering in my doorway while I tried to find any cards she'd given me over the years. I finally found a few, and they're tucked into my nightstand now. But I regret every one I ever discarded thinking I had an infinite supply of them.

This note is a gift for so many reasons, and my blurred gaze moves to Paul. "It doesn't have to be today, but can I read anything else she wrote you? Her handwriting . . ." I swallow hard. "I miss it, and this makes me feel like I'm getting to know her in a different way."

It's too revealing, especially with Theo sitting right next to me, his gaze heavy on my face. But I can't care about that right now. I want it all.

"Of course," Paul says gently. "I'll organize them so you can read them in chronological order for next time. I'd be happy to tell you the story alongside them."

I give him a watery smile. "That'd be perfect."

Theo's knee presses into mine. "C'mon, get reading, Shep. I'm way ahead of you."

I huff out a breath, blinking away my tears. "It's not a contest, Spencer."

"Isn't it always with us?"

When I look over at him, his expression shifts from something undefinable into a challenging smirk.

"Because you make it that way," I mutter under my breath, then focus back on the letter.

Paul.

Incredible. Gram could have taught a masterclass on how to infuse deadly disdain into one word.

We've been in this class together for two weeks and you're already a nuisance. I wasn't sobbing outside, despite how you classified it. I was . . . misty-eyed, but this is how it is when I come back to school after the summer. I can't wait to get back here, and then I leave and—

I don't have to explain anything to you. I miss my family, but I'm fine. Two weeks from now, my father will be irritating me with calls and I'll be glad for the distance, so you'll never see this again.

A word of advice: if you see a woman who is actually crying, staring at her in bewilderment is a horrible strategy to make her feel better.

Kathleen

"You weren't kidding about her not liking you at first," I say with a laugh.

Paul grins, his dimple popping. "And yet, weeks later we were dating."

"Who could resist that charm of yours?"

He laughs, squeezing my shoulder. "I'm going to take a little rest now, but don't leave on my account. Teddy has hours of work to do."

"Great to hear," Theo says dryly.

My gaze flits to him and then away. "I should probably get back to work . . . ing from home. My work at home." It takes everything in me not to close my eyes over the mess I just made of that statement. "Thank you for taking the time to talk to me today."

Paul squeezes my hand with a kind smile. I still see so much of Theo in it, though the emotion is completely different. "Feel free to come by this weekend. We'll dive into those letters."

"I'll take you up on that."

Theo rises from his seat. "So, what, is this going to be a regular thing?"

"Don't worry, I'm sure this schedule mix-up is a onetime deal. No more unexpected run-ins." I wink over at Paul. "Right?"

He puts on a bewildered expression. "I'm still not sure what happened."

"Mm-hmm." Theo's skepticism is clear, but he doesn't say more. Still, he doesn't look pleased by the plans Paul and I have just made.

I don't care if Theo wants to share. I'm going to take every minute Paul will give me. It's one more minute I have with Gram.

DESPITE HIS APPARENT ALLERGY TO SPENDING TIME WITH ME (which is returned), Theo insists on walking me out. It's not until we step out the front door that I remember the Bronco.

I stop in front of it. "Oh fuck. Is this your car?"

God, I really need to learn to regulate my brain-to-mouth filter.

Theo nods. "That's Betty."

"She's gorgeous," I sigh, running a finger over the paint, daydreaming about driving her down Highway 1 along the water with my hair flying everywhere, all of my worries and sadness whipping out of my body into the salty air.

"Yeah." His voice is low and close. I turn my head, and he's right there, his gaze bouncing to where I'm touching his car.

But I swear it bounced from my face.

I let out a breath, realizing belatedly Theo is still talking.

". . . The first thing I bought when we started making money off of Where To Next. Anton and Matias—those are the other founders—" He says this like I don't know every goddamned thing about his dumb company. "They put down payments on their places in the city, but all I wanted was this car." He lifts a shoulder in a careless shrug, running a palm over its side like I imagine he would over a woman's hip. A craving in the midst of being satisfied. "Took me a few months to track the right one down."

"This is my dream car, you know." My tone comes out more accusatory than I want, but when Theo raises an eyebrow, I raise mine right back. I don't know what it is about him; I want to fight. I want that spike in my blood reminding me I'm capable of emotions that aren't heavy and flat.

"Was I supposed to avoid it, then?"

"You could've gone with something cliché, like a Porsche or a Maserati. A 1970 . . ." I trail off expectantly.

"'77," he supplies, amused.

"A 1977 Ford Bronco, perfectly restored in *cherry red*? Give me a break. That's *so* specific." I squint at him, only half joking. "Did I mention this to you in high school once or something? Is this some twisted gotcha?"

"That would be a long con, considering I had no idea I'd ever see you again when I bought it."

"Mm-hmm."

"Your crush isn't special, Shep. Lots of people have boners for Broncos."

"I bet you have a car club called Boners for Broncos, you big nerd," I say.

He pushes his hat up his forehead, and the sun hits his face, illuminating his eyes. There's a starburst of lighter blue around the pupil, and against the depth of the rest of his iris it looks almost silver, like moonlight touching the ocean. "Don't be mad just because I got something you wanted."

It takes all my willpower not to suck in a breath. He hit his mark, but I don't want him to know it's true. He's got *everything* I want: success, accolades, a life with direction. Even this car.

I hitch my purse up my shoulder, my heart beating hard. "I'd love to know where you get your attitude from. It's certainly not from your angel of a granddad."

He laughs, but it's humorless. "That's a gift from my dad." I don't get a chance to process or respond. He turns, lifting two fingers over his shoulder as he walks back inside. "Bye, Shepard."

"Yeah, bye," I mutter, taking one last look at his annoyingly beautiful ass. "Hopefully for good this time."

Seven

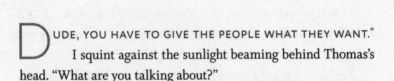

"DUDE, YOU HAVE TO GIVE THE PEOPLE WHAT THEY WANT."
I squint against the sunlight beaming behind Thomas's head. "What are you talking about?"

On the other side of me, Sadie says, "Your TikTok is still going off. Thomas has been watching it obsessively."

I sigh, turning my gaze back to the sky. Thomas and Sadie drove up to Glenlake for dinner, and we decided to take a walk while my parents cooked and danced around the kitchen like moony teenagers. We stopped at the neighborhood park, where we're now stretched out on the grass side by side. Thomas is on his stomach, head propped on his arms, while Sadie's on her back next to me, her fingers loosely twined with mine.

I'm grateful for their company. It's been two days since my visit with Paul, and even after updating them on everything I've learned, my mind is still spinning.

"I had to turn my notifications off," I admit. "My phone kept overheating."

"People want an update," Thomas says, laying his cheek on his forearm, his gaze sharp on me. "You need to tell them you found the guy and you know his grandson. Someone said, 'if you don't give us an update I will literally die.' They're gonna *die*, Beans. Come on."

"That's not my fault!" I laugh as Sadie squeezes my hand, her shoulder shaking against mine.

He props up on his elbows. "You're sitting on a gold mine. When people find out the grandson is your old nemesis, they're going to lose their shit. Do you know how many fifteen-year-olds wish they had this clout? You can't waste it."

"TikTok was a onetime deal. I got what I needed out of it. There's no reason to continue, even if someone's threatening death by curiosity." I pause. "Relatable, though."

He's quiet for all of three seconds. "Weren't you using TikTok to show your photography?"

Immediately, I picture the videos I put together, little montages of shots I took on random weekends, set to some indie song. "Kind of, I guess. I mean, not in any serious way."

Thomas snorts. "Yeah, that's the theme there, huh?"

"Mas," Sadie warns softly.

I whip my head toward him. "What does that mean?"

"It means you're afraid to fail at something you really love to do, so you've barely put any effort into it."

"I don't know if you remember this, but I did, in fact, already fail at something I love to do."

"No," he insists. "Enzo was a dick who was wrong about you, and you believed his bullshit. I'm telling you, this is a once-in-a-lifetime opportunity. Maybe if you keep going, it'll help you get more attention with your photography."

I gnaw at my lip, my heart beating hopefully against my ribs. It doesn't have the common sense my brain does, and pushing against it with my fingers isn't slowing it down.

"If you're going to keep seeing them, you should do it, Noelle," Sadie says quietly. "It might be kind of cool to document this whole thing on video as you go. Since that's how it started, you know?"

"Exactly," Thomas says. "And listen, if it'll give you confidence about your photography—which *is* great, by the way—then even better."

"All your compliments are freaking me out, please stop."

He grins, hearing the *thank you* buried there.

Would people be into it? Would they care about what's happened since that first video, follow me on whatever path this takes me down?

"Besides, what else do you have going on? You're unemployed. You have all the time in the world to do this."

"Back on familiar ground," I mutter.

He marches on. "Honestly, what you really should do is go on Gram's honeymoon trip and document *that*. People would lose it; you'd get some free promotion. Ride that viral wave."

I blink over at him. The voice that whispered to me when I saw the map won't quiet down, and now I wonder if Thomas heard it, too.

More than anything else I learned at Paul's—Gram going to UCLA, their planned elopement—that map has been digging under my skin. The route sketched itself out in my mind as I filled out online applications yesterday, and I ended up down a Google rabbit hole, researching each destination Gram circled and imagining what I'd see and do. I even dreamed about it last night. I was standing at the base of Zion's rich red cliffs, and I couldn't see

Gram, but I *felt* her there. She was standing right beside me, her touch against my hand as soft as the wind, and as fleeting. There was a creek running behind us, sage-colored shrubs rustling around us, and it felt like peace.

I woke up wondering if I was dreaming about it because I'm desperate for an escape from my hamster-wheel life, or if it was a sign. Thomas bringing it up feels like the latter.

His phone trills before I can formulate a response.

"Dinner's ready." He leaps up and holds a hand out for Sadie and me.

Sadie wraps her arm around my waist, squeezing me against her. "You'll figure it all out."

I keep hearing that, but I'm no closer to figuring anything out than I was a year ago. Or the five before that.

THOMAS ZEROES IN ON DAD'S FAMOUS CHEESY GARLIC BREAD as soon as we walk into the dining room. "Hell yes."

"Don't take it all this time," I say as he slides into his seat, Sadie dropping into the chair beside him.

"I had four pieces last time."

"You had *eight*." I look at Dad as he walks into the dining room, a stack of dishes in one hand. He stoops his six-five frame down to engulf me in a one-armed hug. "Why did you make him this way? He has a hole in his stomach."

He kisses my temple with a sweet laugh, setting the plates onto the table. Thomas and I can talk all kinds of shit about each other, but Dad never fully engages. "DNA is a crapshoot, honey. Mas, bud, save some for the masses, okay? I made extra pasta for you."

"Best dad ever." Thomas reaches up to pat him on the back while I take the silverware from Mom and hand it out.

When I'm done, she ruffles my hair and wraps an arm around my waist. We're exactly the same height, down to the centimeter, coming in at just over five-nine. I miss the days when she could engulf me in a hug, when I could press my cheek to her chest and listen to her heart beat.

"You are both perfectly made," she says with conviction. "And you, too, Sades, our almost-daughter."

"That's a subtweet about marriage," Thomas mumbles, grabbing a piece of cheesy bread. But he winks over at Sadie, who laughs. That proposal is inevitable, and probably more imminent than Thomas has shared.

Dinner is our usual chaotic affair. By the time I've polished off my second round, my stomach is seam-rippingly full and my defenses are down.

That must be why Mom takes the opportunity to pounce. "Hey, Jumping Beans, we didn't get a chance to finish up our conversation this morning."

"This morning," I echo from my food coma. Across from me, Thomas picks at his teeth with a fork. Dad is polishing off his beer at the head of the table, though he lowers it, splitting a curious look between me and Mom.

"How the job search is going," she says, leaning back in her seat.

Right. When Mom finished her prework Peloton ride, she stood in front of her BE AWESOME sign, asking hopefully, "Any update on the job front?" I want to get out of this house as much as Mom seems to want me to, though it's clearly more about my well-being than reclaiming her space. Dad has been tiptoeing around the subject, as tuned in to my emotional temperature as I am to his, but if I had something lined up, he'd be thrilled. He'd definitely cry.

Unfortunately, I remain empty-handed. "Oh. No, we did finish it up. I said 'could be better.'"

She lifts a dark eyebrow. "I got a work call and had to step away after that."

"That covers it." I shift in my seat, my cheeks flushing, though everyone in this room knows every detail of my struggle. Across the table, Sadie throws me her most supportive best friend smile. Not wanting to be the bearer of total bad news, I fib, "I'm working on a couple things. Trust me, I want to get out of your hair as much as you want me out."

"That's not it," Dad says. "I've loved having you here, especially given the way we ended last year." His eyes dim before he sighs, forcing a smile. "But Mom and I also recognize this is your safe landing spot for a bit. You'll fly away again when you're ready."

My throat tightens. It's a gift to have someone believe in you, especially when you're low on it yourself. "Thanks. It's harder than I thought it'd be. I assumed I'd be here for a month, two tops, then be gone."

"I was thinking," Mom says, laying down her napkin. "There's a position open at my company you may be qualified for, and I know the hiring manager. If you want to give me your résumé, I can put in a good word for you."

Thomas drops his fork slowly, squinting at her in horror. "Mom, no."

"What?" she asks, double-taking when she notices Dad looking at her in the same way.

"I don't think that's a good idea." Shame spreads, slow and hot. Dear god, I need to get my life together. This right here might be rock bottom.

"Why not? It's a great company. The benefits are wonderful.

It's in the city, and I'm sure you'd get a salary that would let you get back into an apartment with a roommate quickly."

"I love you so much, and it's a generous offer," I preface, holding my hands up. "But not only would I have to fling myself into the nearest pit of lava if my mother got me a job, we can *never* work for the same company."

She sits back, insulted. "Why not?"

"Because my title will be Marnie Shepard's Daughter, no matter what the role is. You're a legend there. The Oprah of sourcing." At this she perks up. Deep down, I am my mother's daughter; we love people gushing about our accomplishments. She's a kick-ass VP at a wearable tech company, and *everyone* knows her. "I appreciate the offer, but it will mean more if I do it myself."

Her work voice goes into full effect. "So, what are you doing?"

"Marnie . . ." Dad says.

"Grant," she shoots back, and a lengthy silent sentence follows.

Thomas looks between us, tennis match style. Next to him, Sadie mouths a word: *trip.*

The map flashes in my mind. Those locations circled by Gram's hand.

The words fly out of my mouth. "I—I may have a thing."

Mom raises an eyebrow. "A thing."

"A thing?" Dad repeats, hope in his voice.

Something like guilt gnaws at my chest, but I force it aside. Across the table, Thomas is catching on. He bites back a smile. "When I said I was working on a couple things, this is one of them. It's like a photography . . . thing." Someone grant me the ability to start saying words that aren't *thing.* "A trip. A, uh, two-week trip, um, across the western United States."

"A photography trip!" Dad says, his face lighting up. "How awesome, Beans."

"Is it paid?" Mom asks.

My brain scrambles for an answer. "No, but it could lead to paid opportunities."

It's been nearly two weeks since my TikTok went viral. Maybe Thomas was right. If I keep telling the story on the road, people could continue to latch on to it. I could take pictures along the way, use them to make jazzy clips with music and vibes, talk about the landmarks I visit. When done well, those types of videos do solid numbers, and I already have people waiting on me. I could finally do something with the online shop I'd been setting up before Gram died, link it to my TikTok account.

I could try again.

It's a hell of a way to do it, but I can't think of a much better reason to dust off my camera. I haven't been able to shake my restlessness knowing Paul and Gram never got to fulfill that trip. Maybe hearing the rest of the story from Paul and then going will soothe it. Maybe walking in Gram's planned path more than sixty years later will help me hold on to her. It could soften some of this grief, let me feel like I'm actually *doing* something in the process.

I think of that dream, of Zion. Of Gram standing next to me, her hand almost in my hand.

I press on, determined now. "Uh, the photos I take will be judged for quality"—I'm literally thinking of TikTok commenters now—"and based on that, I might have some really great options."

Dad is getting misty-eyed, and the guilt turns thick. No turning back now, though.

"Is this a group trip?" Mom asks.

"Yes." It comes out sounding like a question.

"Are you lying to me?" She leans back in her chair, her dark ponytail bobbing with the movement. Her arms are tanned and perfectly Pelo-toned. Strong enough to literally wrestle the truth out of me if she were like that.

"No! And Mom, even if it was a solo trip, that would be okay. I'm twenty-eight." I look from her to Dad, who's watching me with a tired smile, his blond hair and work clothes mussed. "I know I'm Benjamin Button-ing all over the place, but I am actually a grown human being who, up until four months ago, lived on her own."

"I know." I give her a look and she holds up her hands. "I do! I just don't love the thought of a woman traveling alone—particularly a woman who wears *my* heart on her body."

We exchange world-weary looks. "I hate that we have to think about it."

"Fuck, me too," she says, which shocks us into laughter. She's not much for the f-bomb, but when she says it, she really makes it count.

"This is incredible, Noelle." Dad reaches a hand across the table. I take it, my throat squeezing in tandem with his fingers tightening around mine. "I'm proud of you."

"Thank you," I manage, feeling equally hopeful and like shit on the bottom of someone's shoe.

"When is this happening?" Mom asks.

"In a couple weeks." Completely pulled that out of my ass. Hopefully it's enough time to get myself together and go.

"And how are you going to pay for it if it's not a paid thing?"

"I'll use some of Gram's inheritance." I've been holding on to it, waiting for something she'd deem worthy. This is it, I know it.

Dad nods, his eyes shining. "She'd love that."

I want to lay my head on the table and cry. What would he do if he found out about Paul? Would he care? Would it break him? Am I betraying him by not telling him about this, the way I feel betrayed by Gram for not telling me?

What a mess. What an absolute clusterfuck. And yet, now that I've decided, I have to see this through.

"Okay," Mom says, her expression twisting from doubt to cautious optimism. "Yeah, this could be really good for you, Noelle."

It could. And clusterfuck or not, I'm doing it.

Eight

WHEN I SHOW UP AT PAUL'S HOUSE ON SATURDAY, I bring guests. Thomas and Sadie wanted to tag along to see the map and anything else Paul is prepared to show, and Paul was gracious enough to accept us all for an early lunch.

He opens the door with his signature sunny smile, stepping aside. "Come on in, kids. I've set us up on the deck again."

I beam at him as Thomas and Sadie introduce themselves, though my stomach does a somersault. I'm revealing my plan today, and I have no idea what he'll say.

It takes everything in me not to run for the back. I want to pore over Gram's letters, and I need to take another look at the map. Maybe I'll take a picture of it or—best-case scenario—borrow it so I can take it with me. I'd also like to get details of the originally planned trip from Paul so I can plot my days out. The clock is officially ticking.

I'm so caught up in my to-do list that Paul and Thomas end up at the front of the pack as we walk in. When we get to the living room, Thomas gestures to the gallery wall, coming to a halt. "Noelle wouldn't stop talking about this after your visit. She said these are all your photographs."

"They are indeed. I've been freelance, have worked with *National Geographic* and other publications you probably wouldn't know. Took me all around the world for a time."

"When did you slow down?" I ask.

Paul gazes at the wall. "When Theo was born. He's my only grandchild, so I have a bit of an affinity for him." My heart softens at the affection on Paul's face as he continues, "I lived in Los Angeles from college on. My son, Sam—that's Theo's dad—moved up here when Theo was in junior high, and Theo's uncle, Mark, and his husband left for Arizona about a decade ago, so for a time it was just Vera and me."

Thomas smiles over at me, both impish and proud. "Noelle's a photographer, too."

I resist the urge to play it down or deny it altogether as Paul eyes me.

"I had a feeling. She told me she wasn't."

"I'm nowhere close to you," I say, gesturing at the display before us. Somehow, my hand ends up pointing right at that childhood portrait of Theo, and I stuff my hands into the pockets of my jeans.

Sadie weaves her arm through mine, shaking me gently. "You're amazing."

"She's downplayed her talents, then," Paul says with a sympathetic smile. Like he knows it's an achy spot. I swallow and look down at Sadie's long rainbow nails, bright and cheerful against my sun-starved skin.

"That sounds about right." Thomas sticks his hands in his pockets, rocking back and forth on his heels. "The funny thing is, when she was in high school, she wouldn't shut up about all the things she was good at."

"What's truly funny," Paul says, "is Teddy talked quite a bit about a very accomplished girl in high school. Now, it took me a bit of time to unravel all this after I met you last week, but I realized the name I always heard as *Steph* was actually Teddy talking about you and calling you *Shep*."

My heart plops into my stomach. "I'm sorry, what? He talked about me in high school?"

Next to me, Sadie inhales with barely concealed delight, her fingers digging into my arm. She won't let go of the idea that this is fate's way of bringing me the love of my life.

Maybe I'd play along otherwise, but the idea of Theo being the love of my life—or even the love of one single month in my life—sends icy fingers dancing down my spine.

"Yes, indeed. Theo spent every summer with Vera and me—"

"Wow, the whole summer?" Thomas interjects.

Paul nods. "Since he was six. It was a deal I worked out with his parents. He came to us the week after school ended and left the week before it began."

"That's intense. I'm surprised his parents let him go." I hold up my hands. "I mean, I'm sure it was great. It's just a long time to be gone."

"It was a good setup for everyone involved," Paul says simply, his gaze moving back to Theo's picture.

I always wondered where he went, though I pretended not to care. The momentum of the school year and all of the energy I expended to be the best—better than Theo—fizzled into a melancholic lack of direction during the summer. Sometimes I felt lost without something (or someone) to direct my ambitions toward.

Paul picks up the thread of the conversation, pulling me out of my memory. "At any rate, your name would come up during conversations about the school year. You played tennis as well?"

"Yes, I played number one singles on the girls' team. Theo was the same on the boys' team, but you probably knew that."

Paul nods. "I was his number one fan. Always have been, even though I couldn't make it up north to watch his matches but for every once in a blue moon."

"Some people tried to organize a head-to-head match between Theo and Noelle their senior year to raise money for charity," Thomas pipes up, "but the principal shut it down. He knew it would end in bloodshed."

I toss him a glare. "That was the official story. I think Theo was afraid I'd win, and he paid Principal Reyes off. He still owes me a head-to-head match."

"I actually would pay to watch that," Thomas says. "As long as bloodshed was guaranteed."

"Noelle would wipe the court with him," Sadie says loyally. "Respectfully. She's a beast on the court."

Paul laughs, shaking his head. "I have no doubt it would be entertaining." He sweeps an arm toward the sliding door. "Should we continue on with our current adventure? You and Teddy can discuss your match next time you see each other."

I'm actually shocked he isn't here now, although Paul did promise no more "mix-ups."

I have to squeeze my brain like a fist to crush my curiosity about what he's doing on such a beautiful Saturday morning. Is he still sleeping? Is he alone, or is there someone warming the other side of his bed?

Gah. Shut it down, Noelle.

I give Paul a carefree smile, towing Sadie with me. "Adventure time it is."

THOMAS AND SADIE TAKE THE SEATS CLOSEST TO THE DOOR, their backs to the house. They lean toward each other, heads bowed over the photographs I've already seen. Meanwhile, Paul digs through the box, presumably to grab the letters he promised we'd read.

I fiddle with a stack of photos, trying to figure out how to bring up the map. My plan. What I need from Paul. It's possible he won't care and say "here you go, good luck." But it's also possible he'll think it's odd, or he won't approve. In that case, do I go? Will he still tell me the rest of the story? I don't know how I'd feel going on their aborted honeymoon trip if I didn't have his blessing. It's a weird enough idea as it is.

Sadie keeps sliding me looks, then darting her eyes purposefully at Paul. I widen my eyes back at her, a clear invitation to chill out.

My clammy fingers wrap around a worn envelope with mementos—ticket stubs, old flyers from school, a note that Paul and Gram seemed to pass back and forth. I show it to him and he laughs softly.

"Even after we started dating, she wrote me notes in class." His thumbs smooth over the wrinkled paper. "Probably trying to distract me into failure."

"An elite tactic." Wish I'd thought of that in high school, though I have no idea what I'd have distracted Theo with. Cassidy Bowman's ass, maybe? God knows he looked at it enough.

A foot connects with my ankle under the table. "F—" I cut off my curse with a cough.

"Are you all right?" Paul asks, placing a hand on my back.

"Fine," I croak out, communicating with a glare that I *will* murder Thomas when he least expects it. He mouths *do it*, though he's talking about the map.

One corner of Paul's mouth pulls up, revealing his dimple. "Another bug?"

My cheeks blaze as I remember how I reacted to a shirtless Theo. As I remember shirtless Theo, period. "Yeah, I guess they love me."

Paul walks over to the corner of the deck, where a mini fridge is set up. Theo's been busy this week. There are railing planters lining the perimeter of the deck, all filled with flowers and herbs, and the raised planters Theo was working on earlier this week are now filled with greenery, the soil black with fresh moisture.

All of this had to have taken more than one day; is his schedule *that* flexible? Seems a little unusual for a CFO.

Paul sets a bottle of water in front of each of us. We all murmur our thanks, then lapse into silence. For a full minute, the only sound is Paul humming to himself and the crinkle of paper as he shuffles through letters.

Thomas and Sadie are full-on staring at me now. My heart is pounding with purpose and anticipation, and anxiety, too.

My gaze locks with Thomas's. He watches me with eyes the same color as Dad's, and I remember the look in *his* eyes when I came up with this ridiculous plan. The hope there, and the happiness. Like I'm finally pulling myself out of whatever black pit I sank into when Gram died.

It's not just that I want to go. It's that everyone *else* wants me to. If this doesn't work, it'll be another failure. And in some way, it'll feel like losing another piece of Gram, one I've regained since her death.

"Hey, Paul," I say, licking my lips, my attention still tethered to my brother. Thomas nods, just once. There's something like hope in his eyes, too.

"Yes?"

I turn, squinting up against the sun haloing Paul's head. "Um, I was hoping I could talk to you about something."

He lowers himself into the chair at the head of the table, his expression open but touched with concern. "Of course, Noelle. What is it?"

"It's about the map. Your honeymoon trip, actually."

"All right," he says slowly.

I open my mouth to just *say it*, but it gets stuck in my throat. I hate that I've become so afraid of not succeeding that even in this moment, I can't go after what I want. "Would it be possible to look at it again?"

"Sure." Paul pulls the box closer, tips it so he can look inside while seated. He pulls the map out and hands it to me.

Thomas and Sadie shift all of the various photos and mementos out of the way so I can lay the map flat. They don't say anything, but Thomas moves a finger over the writing at the top, his expression turning solemn. Since Gram died, he's shed his fair share of tears. She was the source of joy who lit us all up; the group text thread with my uncles' families is an ongoing testament to that.

Paul's chair creaks as he leans forward. His eyes lock onto mine. They're Theo's color but kinder, full of an emotion I feel echoing in the empty parts of my chest. He's known grief, and he's showing it to me.

I press my palm flat on the paper. "I want to go on this trip."

His eyebrows raise in surprise, but he recovers quickly. "Oh?"

I nod. "I'd love to borrow the map, but if you don't want to part with it, I understand. So maybe I could take notes or pictures of it—"

"You can have it, Noelle," he says gently.

"Oh. Wow, okay, thank you," I stutter out. "Could you tell me what your plans were? There are lots of places circled here, but I'd love to know if there are certain things you wanted to do, so maybe I can do them, too." I swallow, suddenly breathless with the weight of all of my emotions. Everything is sitting on my chest: relief, unbearable sadness, hope. All of them the same weight in different ways. "I'm going to take my camera. I'd love to take some of the pictures you would have. They won't be as good as yours, obviously, but . . ." I lift my shoulder in a helpless shrug. "I think this might help. Nothing else has."

Paul looks at me for a long moment, his eyes traveling over my face like I have my own map plotted out there. His fingers are intertwined, resting on the table between us. I fight the urge to reach across the table and cover his hands with mine, beg him to give me his blessing. Beg him to give me his stories before I go.

I hold my breath, my heart racing. I need this to work, for so many reasons all tangled up together.

His hands reach out to take mine, as if he knows I need the grounding touch. Finally, he says, "I have a better idea. Like I said, you can take the map. But I'd like you to take me, too."

Nine

I'T'S SO QUIET I CAN HEAR MY HEARTBEAT IN MY EARS. SO quiet that Thomas's and Sadie's surprised inhales sound like a hurricane.

I don't get a chance to process what Paul's just proposed, let alone respond. My attention is stolen by the sound of a slamming door, then a shadowy figure storming through the living room, head down, shoulders tight and high.

My heart picks up a frantic pace as Theo roughly slides open the screen door.

"I'm fucking done with them—" He looks up from his phone, and I swear his soul exits his body when our eyes meet. His heel slips, and he grips onto the doorframe to keep himself from falling on his ass, pressing his phone over his heart. "Jesus *fucking* Christ, what are you doing here?"

He's looking at all of us, but clearly talking to me.

Sadie turns in her seat, her eyes going comically wide. I've shown her pictures of Theo, but he is a million times more potent in person. "*Wow.*"

"Yeah, that's a universal reaction," Thomas murmurs, throwing Theo a wave over his shoulder. "Hey, man."

Theo runs a hand through his hair, giving my brother a distracted "Hi." He clears his throat, his gaze lingering on me before he turns to Paul. "I didn't realize you had company."

"I told you I was having Noelle over when we had dinner last night," Paul says. His expression vacillates between concern and amusement. "I knew you weren't paying attention. You had your nose in that phone all night."

Theo blows out a breath. "Sorry, I . . . was distracted."

"Are you all right?" Paul's tone is careful, and I scan Theo for signs of damage. Physically, he's as aggressively handsome as ever, wearing those old Levi's and a plain gray T-shirt that presses up against his body as a breeze picks up. Who can blame it? It's probably a great body to be pressed against.

It takes me three seconds and a subtle head shake to remember why I was looking at him in the first place.

Something is wrong, and it's not physical, but I knew that. He came ripping out here like a bat out of hell, talking about—

I'm fucking done with them.

Who are *they*?

I don't even realize I've said it out loud until Theo responds. "Sometimes it's okay to keep the questions inside your mouth."

"That's what I tell her," Thomas says.

"No one asked you," I shoot back.

"No one asked *you*, either," Theo says without heat. In fact, I see a brief flash of dimple, a lightning strike against his cheek.

I meet Sadie's gaze—she's been watching all of this with interest. "I told you."

I've spent at least three cumulative hours talking about our enemy vibes.

"You're right." Sadie nods. "But I mean . . ." *he's hot*, she finishes in silent best friend shorthand.

I raise my eyebrows. *You can't overcome that personality.*

Her mouth purses thoughtfully. *Can't you? Not even for one night?*

Theo looks between us, then directs stern eyebrows at me. "Stop talking about me."

"We weren't talking about you," I lie.

Thomas snorts.

"I'll come back later," Theo says, already starting to back up.

Paul starts to stand. "Do you need to chat?"

"No, no." Theo holds up the hand clutching his phone. It's lighting up like a July Fourth sky. "Didn't mean to interrupt."

Disappointment blooms without my permission, but before I can force it down, Paul says, "Stay, Teddy. You'll probably want to hear this."

Theo's midnight gaze moves to me. "Somehow I doubt it." My hand smooths over the map in reflex, and his attention drops there before bouncing back to my face. "You didn't have enough time with that on Tuesday?"

"I'm borrowing it."

"Why?"

I don't want to tell him, but he'll find out eventually anyway, especially if Paul wants to come along.

God, does he really?

I lift my chin, trying to project an air of confidence. "Because I'm going on this trip."

I expect him to make some derisive remark, but after the initial surprise, his face softens into something like understanding. "I see."

"And so am I." Paul smiles over at me. "If you don't mind, that is."

"I'm sorry, *what?*"

Ah, there's the reaction I was expecting. Theo's expression twists with disbelief as he stands to his full, distressingly attractive height.

Paul squares his shoulders. "We didn't get a chance to discuss it, since you walked in right as I told Noelle, but I'd like to join her."

Theo looks at me, eyes flashing, like this is somehow my doing. I hold up my hands. "I haven't even had a chance to process this. Turn your angry eyes elsewhere."

"Are you or are you not trying to drag my granddad on a multi-day, multistop trip down memory lane?"

I cross my arms, glaring up at him. "I'm not dragging *anyone*. I told Paul I needed to borrow the map to go on this trip, and right before you burst in here like the Hulk, he said he wanted to join me. I would love his company"—I smile at Paul so he knows I'm accepting his request before turning my murder eyes back on Theo—"but I'm not forcing anyone into anything. I'm doing this for myself. If Paul wants to join me, that's his prerogative."

Theo's mouth twitches.

I point at him. "Do *not* smile, I'm being authoritative right now."

"Uh-huh. Don't quit your day job, Shepard," he says.

Thomas chokes on his water, and I shoot him a look while Sadie elbows him in the side. But Theo's not paying attention anyway; he's facing off with Paul, his arms crossing over his chest.

"Why do you want to do this?" he asks. "Is this about Kathleen? Is this some wish fulfillment thing?"

Paul shakes his head. "Kat and I had our closure. I'd like to be there for Noelle if she has questions or needs support. In fact, I'd love to tell her the whole story as we go." He reaches over to take my hand, and I have to work extraordinarily hard not to burst into tears. The thought of doing all of this at once is an overwhelming mix of joy and grief. Across the table, Thomas sends me a quiet, understanding look.

Theo doesn't miss my struggle with emotions, but then again, he doesn't miss much.

Paul's voice dips as he continues, "And I've been kicking around one house or another since Vera died, Teddy. I'd like to get back out into the world, even if it's just for . . ." He trails off expectantly.

"Two weeks," I supply.

"Two weeks. I need this as much as Noelle does." He levels his grandson with a look. "And, I suspect, as much as you do, too. Travel's always done you good."

My heart leaps into my throat as Theo scoffs. Across the table, Thomas and Sadie are staring between the three of us, eyes wide. Sadie's go even wider when they meet mine, as Paul's implication takes root.

He wants *Theo* to come on this trip, too? I resist the urge to scream out "NO."

"I can't leave," Theo says into the bloated silence.

"Why not?" Paul asks. It's the most confrontational I've ever heard him.

"Because I—you know why." Theo gestures to him with a wild flick of his wrist. "And you shouldn't go, either. You're not thirty anymore."

Paul waves him off. "I'm healthy as a horse and you know it. Maybe I'm slower than I used to be, but I can still get around just fine. I walk three miles every day, and my father lived to be 104. If I called my physician right now, he'd say go." He tosses up his hands. "Hell, he'd probably ask to come along, too. There's great golf along the way."

Theo sighs deeply, running the hand not clutching his phone through his hair. His fingers grip the ends, a frustrated move.

"Well, I can't talk you out of it," he says finally.

"You're right," Paul says. He turns to me. "Are you sure it's all right with you? I understand if you want to go solo."

Theo frowns. "It's not all that safe, Shep."

"Thank you, I already got that lecture from my mom, and it doesn't matter anyway. Paul and I are going on this adventure together."

Theo scrubs at his jaw, his eyes closing briefly. "Yeah, that makes me feel so much better. I—"

His phone buzzes and he looks down at the screen. *Dad* flashes urgently across it. Seeing his name and the way Theo's expression caves in on itself is a déjà vu moment: we could just as easily be in our high school parking lot right now, me watching Theo's dad admonish him in that quiet, controlled way that was ten times more intimidating than shouting.

"Of course," Theo mutters with a grim smile. "Be right back."

He disappears inside, and I turn back to Paul, who's watching his grandson disappear. His expression is pinched with concern, but it smooths out when he feels my attention.

"I'm excited to do this with you." As soon as I say it, the matching emotion runs through my veins, like adrenaline but sweeter.

"I appreciate you letting me tag along. This'll be the perfect way to tell you our story." Paul pats the side of the box. "I'll bring along the letters and fill in what I can until you have the answers you need."

I can't describe the feeling in my chest. It's not happiness; it's sharper than that, even though it's warm and golden, too. It makes my eyes sting. I'll get their whole love story, an extended game of secret sharing. But I won't be playing it with Gram.

"Oh!" Paul says, perking up. "I'll bring my camera along, since you're bringing yours."

"Nice, like a photography trip." Thomas looks at me meaningfully. *Not such a lie after all.*

Paul's eyes are saying something, too. They shine with support, and I can't help thinking of the way Gram used to look at me the same way. Like she was just happy I was trying. "I'm eager to see your work."

"Well . . ." I let out a nervous laugh. This man is an accomplished photographer with a career I could only dream of. "Manage your expectations."

Sadie brings her intertwined hands up to her chin, grinning at me. "I *love* this idea. I'm so glad you're going together."

I reach up, fiddling with my earrings, which are, ironically, shaped like little cameras. From inside, Theo's voice raises, though I can't make out the actual words. "It's been a while. I'm *really* rusty, so let's just see where it g—"

"The universe is telling you something," Sadie insists, wincing at the slam echoing from somewhere in the house. "You need to listen to it."

I snort. "I'd love to know what the message is."

The screen door screeches open, and Theo's there, color flagging his cheeks. "I'm coming, too."

I'M SILENT DURING THE DRIVE HOME.

Thomas and Sadie chat in the front, but Thomas's eyes keep flicking to the rearview mirror, and Sadie's hand snakes back to squeeze my knee more than once.

It all happened so fast. One minute I was going alone, and the next I had two extra bodies I'll have to cram into my Prius. I guess the upside is that from a logistical standpoint, it makes what I told my parents less of a lie. Three people make up a group.

But one of those people is *Theo*.

He made the decision in anger. I could see it in his slightly shaking hands when he slipped his phone into his back pocket. I'm not even sure he saw any of us, or fully processed Paul's delight. But as soon as I saw Paul's smile, the stark relief in his eyes, I pressed my lips together so I wouldn't ruin his happiness.

I would do illegal things to go on a two-week trip with Gram. I'm not going to take it away from Paul and Theo, no matter how much Theo plucks at every single one of my nerves.

My only attempt to finagle my way out of it was to ask, "Are you sure you can get the time off work?"

His expression soured further, his eyes thundercloud dark. "Yes. It's done. Not a problem."

We left not long after, and I heard myself say from somewhere very far away that I'd follow up with them on details.

Thomas and Sadie invite me to spend the day in the city with them, but this is one of those times where I actually *want* to lie in bed and stare at the ceiling. So that's exactly what I do after I wave goodbye and trudge through the silent house. My parents are off gallivanting with friends somewhere; their social life is unmatched.

I flop onto my bed with a groan, closing my eyes.

When I'm awakened by my phone buzzing under my ass, it's dark outside.

It's a number I don't recognize. I'd usually let it go to voicemail, but my thumb is pressing the green button onscreen before my brain can catch up.

"Hello?"

"Were you sleeping?"

Theo's voice is sexy in person, but over the phone it's lethal. Thank god he balanced it out by being irritating.

"Okay, first of all, *hello*." I sit up, blinking into the velvet darkness of my room. "Second of all, how'd you get my number?"

"Got it from my granddad."

Paul's a traitor. Noted. "We'll skip to the third point, then: Why are you calling me? Couldn't you just text whatever you need to say? What kind of millennial are you? We're supposed to be afraid of calling people."

His sigh is all-suffering, leftover tension pulling it tight. "I want to make sure you're fine with all of this. You were suspiciously without words at the end there, and that's unlike you."

It vexes me that he knows me well enough to say that. "I . . . well, I was in shock. It's one thing for Paul to want to come, but you?" I pick up steam as my thoughts finally crystallize. "You weren't even into it. Are you going because you're running away from something, or do you not trust me on the road with Paul? Are you chaperoning us in case I lead us astray and we stumble off a cliff? I promise I'm not *that* inept."

I stumble to a stop with a grimace. *Maybe a little too revealing, Noelle.*

"I don't think you're inept at all," he says. I don't know if it's the timbre of it or the steel behind his words, but I actually believe him.

"Then what is it?"

He hesitates, reluctant. "My granddad was right. I need to get away from the city for a couple weeks. It's been a long time since I had any kind of vacation."

"And you want that vacation to be a road trip with your grandfather and old nemesis?"

He laughs. It's a soft sound, less stressed than before. "This isn't an episode of *Scooby-Doo*, Shepard. You were never my nemesis. You were my . . ." I hate how I hold my breath. "My motivation."

I have no idea what to make of that. It sounds diabolical, but everything he says does. It certainly doesn't sound like a compliment, though if anyone else said it, I'd take it that way.

"Well, whatever." I stand, letting out a quiet moan as my back cracks. "You could fuck off to Turks and Caicos or something, but road trip it is. Are you fine with me taking care of booking everything?"

"We should hash out some of the details together," he says. "That's the other reason I called."

"Okay." I drag the word through my annoyance. "I'll text you links to stuff, then, and you can yea or nay me."

"Granddad wrote me out a long-ass list of activities. I'm assuming you'll want to see it, so let's do it in person."

"In person?"

"Yes, like where I see your face and you see my face and we exchange words in the same room."

My heart prances like a nervous Chihuahua. "Who says I want to see your face?"

"You're gonna have to get used to it."

My mind gets busy sketching out a visual—the broad, angular cut of his jaw, those deep, probing eyes, and the mouth that doesn't let me get away with anything. That damn dimple.

"We can get it done in one night." His tone is so cajoling and soft it's almost a croon. It's a tone for darkness. For bedrooms.

He knows it, too. I can practically hear his smirk when I sigh. "Okay. Why don't I come to your place? Tuesday evening? I'd like to get everything settled as soon as possible."

"Oh." There's a beat of surprised silence. "You want to come to my place?"

Well, he's certainly not coming to *my* place, unless he wants to meet the parents, and a café isn't going to give us the room and time to plan. "We'll need reliable Wi-Fi and a place to spread out." I realize how that sounds a second too late and rush on to say, "Spread out notes and the map and stuff."

"Right." I'm gratified by how uncomfortable he sounds. "Fine. I'll text you my address." There's a short pause. "Do you like steak?"

My stomach growls shamelessly. "It's fine."

"I'll cook, then. Be here at seven."

He doesn't wait for me to respond; the line goes dead and I pull back, staring down at my phone screen.

It was a power move, and I hate that he got the last word just as much as I hate how hot it was.

Two weeks on the road with Theo Spencer. God help us both.

Ten

THEO LIVES IN COLE VALLEY, AN UPSCALE NEIGHBORHOOD in the middle of San Francisco. His street is quiet, lined with single-family homes, shaded by tall trees shimmering in a gentle breeze. Sutro Tower stretches at the top of the hill dead-ending the street, glinting in the setting sun.

It's not what I expected for him. I assumed he'd be in some fancy apartment, not shacked up in a home that looks unassuming, at least from the outside. It's Victorian style, painted slate gray with a brick façade. Near the arched doorway, bougainvillea crawls up the wall.

I park in front of his driveway as directed, a relief since there's no street parking to be found, then grab the canvas bag packed with my laptop, the map, and a spiral notebook crammed with *to-dos*.

My camera's in there, too. I grabbed it impulsively, shoved it into the bag before I could think too hard about why I wanted it.

My gaze travels up to the second-floor bay windows, spilling out golden light.

I'm nervous, and I'm pissed that I'm nervous, and I'm pissed that I'm wearing a dress, too. It's a casual black cotton one, but it skims my body the way I'd want a man's hands to. I thought about Theo's hands when I put it on, and I want to be pissed about that, too. Instead, I'm confused. What am I supposed to do about an attraction to a man I don't even like?

I stride up to the front door, knocking briskly. On the doorjamb is a Ring camera. I stare at it when he doesn't immediately answer, knocking again.

Theo's voice calls out from the Ring, "I didn't realize we were dressing up tonight, Shep."

"Don't take it personally. It has everything to do with not wanting to put in the effort to wear pants." I knock again, just to be a pain in the ass. "Will you open the—"

The door swings open, and there he is, phone in hand. He puts his mouth up to the speaker, his eyes on me, the tiniest smirk pulling at his lips. "It's nice."

His voice echoes all around—here in front of me, through the Ring. It sets my teeth on edge, that backward velvet feeling vibrating through me.

I run my gaze from the top of his tousle-haired head, down his shirt-and-Levi's-clad body, all the way to his bare feet. When I get back to his face, I widen my eyes in mock amazement. "I'm sorry, did you just compliment me?"

"Don't take it personally," he echoes. "I tell my accountant he looks nice all the time, too."

"It's a slippery slope to earnest compliments, Spencer."

He tilts his head, appraising me. "I don't expect you to let me get that far. You've never been one for accepting my compliments."

"You've never been one for giving them to me."

"Maybe you weren't listening."

"Trust me, I was."

I want to snatch the words back immediately. The truth is, I was always plugged in to everything Theo said and did back in high school; I wanted to say and do it better. I remember every bit of praise he ever gave me, however grudging, because I ate it up like candy.

I don't know how to exist in an earnest space with Theo, but he saves us both, stepping back to reveal a staircase that ends at a landing. His teasing expression smooths out into something careful. "I'll get some practice in on Isaiah, then, and get back to you. In the meantime, come in."

I take the stairs with Theo right behind me. There's an awareness between us as we walk up together, his quiet footsteps falling in sync with my sandal-clad clacking. I swear I feel his eyes everywhere, but when I look back, his gaze is focused over my shoulder.

I don't know if I'm disappointed or not. And if I am disappointed, what does that mean? I want him to look at me? To touch me?

Maybe being in Theo's house alone with him was a bad idea, but I need to numb myself to his irritatingly strong magnetic pull if we're going to travel together. So I straighten my shoulders and keep climbing.

"STOP BREATHING DOWN MY NECK."

"I'm not breathing down your neck. I'm *breathing*."

I exhale sharply. "Do it less, then."

"Breathe less?"

"Yes, breathe less, Spencer, that's exactly what I mean."

An amused huff hits the nape of my neck, but Theo doesn't say anything else. In the resulting silence, my keystrokes on my laptop sound like thunderclaps.

We're set up at the kitchen island post-dinner, and Theo's been curved over me for the past ten minutes, watching as I add to our itinerary. Distracting me.

As we ate on the back patio earlier, I eyed Theo between our fits of sparring, wondering what his life looks like. Not the one printed in *Forbes* or any of the myriad industry rags he's mentioned in, his *actual* life inside this house when he's not Theo Spencer, CFO. It was jarring to realize I actually want to know.

I refuse to think too hard about why that is.

Once dinner was over, we moved into the kitchen to get to work. I emptied out my bag, popped open my laptop, and let Theo spread out the map, trying not to notice the way his palms smoothed over the paper, how his thumbs circled the curled-up edges, coaxing them into flatness.

But I'm wine lubricated, and so is he. My eyes have been lingering, and over the past hour he's been slowly swaying his way into my personal space.

Now I'm painfully aware of how close he is, the way his body lines up against mine. I'm tall, but so is he, and so his chest brushes right up against my shoulder blades, his jaw grazing against my ear every time he leans in to look at my screen. When he pressed up against my back, complaining about one of the hikes I put down for Yosemite, I nearly turned around. To push him away or pull him closer, I still don't know.

But if he doesn't stop breathing down my neck, one option is inevitable.

"I'm not going to type faster with you staring at the screen," I say.

"Well, you sure as hell can't type any slower."

I turn my head until his face comes into my periphery, letting my finger descend onto the *f* key.

"Let me guess, the next letter is *u*," he says dryly.

"Sorry, you'll have to buy a vowel."

"Pretty sure I can solve the puzzle, Shepard."

God, he's annoying, and yet I have to press my lips together so he won't see my cheek rise in a smile. He's close enough to catch the barest twitch. Which means he's still too close.

I push my elbow into the hard slab of his stomach. "Seriously, I can't do this with you up my ass."

Theo's wicked, smoky snicker winds its way down my spine as he steps away. "Let me buy you a drink first."

"It would take more than one, trust me," I mutter.

We've got a robust plan filled out on an Excel spreadsheet now, although it took an exorbitant amount of back-and-forth to get there. Our first stop in Yosemite is fully booked via the Where To Next site, as is our overnighter in Las Vegas. We've plotted out our Utah and Arizona stops, too.

"We should do an Airbnb outside of Zion," I muse, clicking through the site.

"Sure, whatever."

"I bookmarked a few options. Do you want to look?"

He shakes his head, leaning an elbow on the counter as his gaze roams over the mess I've made. "You're the boss here."

Something like purpose flares in my chest. I am the boss, at least in this little corner of my life, and getting to fill that role over Theo feels unsurprisingly good.

Still, he's playing *his* typical role to perfection. "Funny, since you've fought me on every decision so far."

"Not every decision, but we're not camping with an octogenarian."

I sigh, toggling over to an adorable cabin outside the park. "I know I'm going to pick a place, and you're going to bitch about it when we get there."

Theo lifts a lazy shoulder. "You know my requirements."

"Yeah, yeah, enough rooms and beds for all," I mumble, exiting out of the site. I'll figure it out later.

Theo's quiet while I color code some columns. It's almost . . . nice. It's so nice, in fact, that I get suspicious as I finish up and save the document, then shut my laptop. I dart my eyes sideways, trying to look at him without him *seeing* me looking. But his attention is on something else, anyway.

"Why are you staring at my camera?"

"Because you brought your camera," he says.

"And?"

He rolls his eyes. "*And* I've gotten the impression that's not something you do."

I open my mouth to brush it off, to deflect or make some pithy remark about how he's taking notes on me. But something about the way he's looking at me—challenging, but without judgment—has me holding back a verbal bite.

Instead, I eye the camera, frowning at the smudge of dust marring the mode dial. I thought I wiped it off earlier.

My eyes slide from the reminder of my neglect to Theo. "I'm thinking about documenting our trip."

His brows lower in confusion. "I thought that was a done deal. You and my granddad are going to pal around with your Canons or whatever he's using these days."

"I meant like on social media. TikTok."

"Oh," he says, surprised. "You're going to post more videos?"

"I . . . maybe. The one I posted is still popular. People want an update on us." Theo straightens, and I hold up my hands. "I'd do a mix of stills and video, landscape stuff. I wouldn't put you and Paul in it, other than potentially narrating his and Gram's story as we go. I can give an update without even including you, actually."

Theo's mouth curves microscopically. "By all means, pretend I don't exist."

My gaze skims over him from head to toe before I can stop myself. *Impossible.*

"What will you get out of the TikTok thing?"

I square my shoulders, considering the question. "To tell a story, I guess. To remember it. To feel like the photos I'm taking serve some sort of purpose. To see if people even care."

He nods, and we get caught in a moment where there's no snark or deflecting. It lasts a second, maybe two. As long as it would take me to press my finger against the shutter release. As long as it takes me to capture an image forever.

I break away first, blinking down to the counter. "We never talked about how weird it must've been to see your granddad in some random video."

He snorts out a laugh, sliding a hand along the marble counter as he moves closer. "It was pretty bizarre. I signed up a while ago because we have a big presence there. Eventually I got sucked into this vortex of, like, an hour of mindless scrolling before I went to sleep every night. The night I saw your video, I'd taken a sleeping pill. Thought I was hallucinating."

I fiddle with my earrings. "I'll bet you never imagined it'd play out this way."

"No." His voice is quiet as he watches my fingers. "I definitely didn't have this on my bingo card."

I clear my throat. "So, are you cool with me documenting some of the trip?"

He blinks and rocks back on his heels, running a hand through his hair. "That's fine. Granddad will be into it."

My chest warms at the thought, and I see a sudden snapshot of my Sunday morning explorations with Gram. She'd find the most picturesque places—Muir Woods, Cowell Ranch Beach, Land's End—and watch me take a million pictures with a smile. We'd exchange our latest secrets over lunch, which, post-college, were either juicy details about my dating life or my anxiety over never accomplishing anything worthwhile.

We'd sit together at her iMac after lunch, which she only bought because I'd mentioned once I wanted a desktop but couldn't afford it. She never touched it except when I was uploading my photos or looking something up for her. We'd sit side by side, and she'd watch while I edited the best shots and ordered prints for her.

"Looks like you're accomplishing something to me," she said once, pointing to the screen.

"You're biased," I scoffed.

She shook her head. "You're already doing great things, Ellie. You're young still and figuring out what that looks like. Give it time."

She always told me how my photos painted stories without words, and that's what I'm attempting here. Paul's potential excitement feels like that memory revisited. Like an accomplishment in its own right.

"Shepard."

I startle out of my thoughts to find Theo watching me. It's clear by the volume of his voice he's been trying to get my attention, but his expression isn't irritated. I couldn't give it a name if I tried.

I rub at my aching chest. "Sorry, what did you say?"

"Are you taking pictures tonight?"

"Oh." I look over at the camera. "No."

He nods his chin in the same direction. "Then why'd you bring that?"

The challenge in his voice is back, as if he knows I packed it to use it, only to chicken out.

"Just in case you had some photogenic spot in your house where I could set up an impromptu shoot." My eyes roam around the sparkling room. Behind the massive, empty dining room table there's an honest-to-god fireplace. "Unfortunately, no dice."

Theo isn't impressed. "You're going to have to pick it up at some point if you want to do this." He motions to the map. "Why not now?"

My heart beats faster. It's a mix of fear, anticipation, and grief, a rejection even as my mind imagines the shot: the map spread out on the counter with Theo's hand pressed over it. I'd take only half of his hand in frame, get the tension in his wrist, the blanching of his knuckles and the way his fingers web out over Arizona and New Mexico. When I retouched later, I'd make sure the veins traveling down his hand looked like its own roadmap.

But I can't do it. Not yet, and not with Theo watching me.

"I haven't taken a picture in six months. Since my gram died. I—I'm not ready." The confession slips out too easily. His expression goes infinitesimally softer, like he's gone slightly out of focus behind my lens.

That was too much. I look at the clock on his microwave. It's nearly eleven. "I should go."

He doesn't say anything, though he looks like he wants to, and I'm grateful for it. While I stuff my things into my bag, Theo folds the map up with careful hands. I pull my bag straps apart so he can tuck it safely between my notebook and laptop.

Neither of us speak as we make our way to the door. I take

one last greedy visual sweep of his house. It really is beautiful, if very quiet.

Theo gets to the front door first and opens it, silently stepping back to let me by. He's distracted, his gaze far away.

"See you next Friday." I doubt I'll see him before we leave for Yosemite.

But Theo catches my wrist before I can get too far. His grip is startling—not too tight, and incredibly warm. I swallow a gasp.

"Listen, I—we should be on our best behavior for this trip."

I frown. "What does that mean?"

"Exactly what I just said." Some of the attitude is back. I'm relieved, honestly; things were getting too cozy. "You and I tussle a lot, but this trip means so much to my granddad. He's excited to do this with you, and I don't want us at each other's throats ruining the experience." I open my mouth to prove his point, but he holds his hand up. *Right* in my face. "For him *or* you. I know it means a lot to you, too."

This silences me, but only momentarily. "All right, best behavior. Got it."

The hand in my face slips down into the space between our bodies, hovering near my waist and brushing against my forearm. He clearly doesn't know how long his fingers are. "Truce?"

I laugh. "*Truce?* Are we eleven?"

Theo rolls his eyes, and this time the graze of his fingers against my skin is purposeful. They skim down my wrist, wrapping around my hand. He manipulates his hold on me until we're engaged in a handshake.

"I'll make an effort to put up with you if you'll do the same. It's two weeks in close proximity. I don't want it to get weird."

I eye him, utterly aware of his skin against mine, of the flex of his fingers as they wrap more solidly around my hand. Thank god it's dark out; I can feel how pink my face is, but he can't see it.

"History isn't on our side, Spencer." My voice comes out softer than I planned.

His reply is equally soft. "We're not the same people we were in high school."

"Trust me, I know." He appraises me, my subtext obvious. "You're right. It's fine. We can fake liking each other for two weeks. For Paul."

Theo lets go of my hand, smirking. "No one said anything about liking, Shep."

No, I remind myself sternly as I make my way to my car. *No one did.*

Eleven

TIME SPEEDS UP AFTER MY NIGHT WITH THEO. I FORGOT what it's like to be busy. To have something to look forward to, even if it's edged in anxiety that ebbs and flows when I think about picking up my camera. Or when I think about two weeks with Theo and the kaleidoscope of emotions he sends tumbling with a long look, that sharp tongue.

Thursday, the night before we're set to leave, Theo texts me.

I have to do something tomorrow morning. We're leaving at 3. My granddad is staying the night here. Can you find a ride?

No, *I'm so sorry our plans have changed and we're not leaving at ten after all, so that afternoon hike we're doing in Yosemite? Not happening. And also by the way, Paul isn't going to pick you up on his way down here anymore, will you be okay?* Just a bunch of robot words formed into a demand.

I don't respond, my blood boiling as I throw my entire underwear drawer into my suitcase. The truce Theo and I agreed upon is already crumbling—I'm going to *strangle* him when I get to his house. However the hell I get there.

Thomas is my saving grace; Sadie's on a work trip all week, and he's feeling emo, so he decides to stay in Glenlake for the night and offers to drive me to Theo's the next day.

My parents throw me a bon voyage dinner, decking out the dining room with streamers and a gold letter banner that reads GOOD LUCK. They ask me a million questions about the trip—where I'll be stopping, what I'll be doing—and my answers are an equal amount of truth and lies. Stomach-churning guilt makes it hard to eat or drink, but my family makes up for it. By the time ten rolls around, Thomas is sleeping off six beers while Mom and Dad reminisce about the county fair photography contest I won when I was twelve.

I go to bed feeling like a liar.

I wake up feeling like one, too, but as Thomas drives us into the city, I finesse it. It's not a lie. It's a secret, which is just a truth that hasn't been told yet.

Thomas's hangover and the afternoon work call he has to get home for make him practically kick me out of the car as we pull up to Theo's. However, he manages to leave me with some parting words.

"Have a good time, kid," he croaks out. "Sadie and I have a bet on whether you let Theo stick it in. I say day three, she's got day ten, but I owe her some blue velvet couch she wants if you fall in love with him."

"Fucking hell, Mas."

"Have fun." His smile fades and he pulls off his sunglasses. "For real. I hope you find whatever you're going after. I'll be following along with the story."

I wave him off with a lump in my throat. He yells out the window, "Wrap it if you tap it!" and zooms off, cackling.

"Such a jackass—" I turn and my knees collapse. Theo's standing on the sidewalk, hands tucked into the pockets of his joggers. "Jesus!"

He smirks. "'Wrap it if you tap it'?"

"I couldn't even explain if I wanted to," I say. "Which I don't."

He looks down at his phone, illuminating the screen. "You're late."

It's 3:09. "We were supposed to leave at ten, so let's not start *that* conversation."

I wait for the long overdue apology, or an explanation, but Theo merely steps forward and takes the handle of my suitcase, brushing my hand aside. I block my senses to the fresh soap scent of him, that hint of firewood and vanilla. It's the sweetness that gets me most; Theo is all spice, no sugar. Strange that he wears it on his skin.

"Give me your other bags so I can pack up the car. We're leaving in five." Tension buzzes off him like electricity. Whatever he had to do this morning, it wasn't relaxing.

I let my backpack and camera bag slide off my shoulders, and he takes those, too, then walks toward the minivan he rented for the trip, parked in front of his house. I sigh. I'm still recovering from my disappointment when he told me we weren't taking the Bronco.

Paul walks out of the house just then. "Good afternoon, Noelle! Ready for our adventure?"

"I can't wait." It's ninety-nine percent true. The one percent is watching me, his expression unreadable.

"Shall we start the trip with a letter?" Paul pulls a slip of paper from the pocket of his khakis. My heart reaches through my ribs for that piece of Gram.

He hands it over. "Now, this one is out of order, so you'll have to forgive me. It seemed like the right one for our trip kickoff."

"I'm sure it's perfect."

I gingerly unfold the letter, struck again by the familiar loop of Gram's handwriting.

There's a sudden wall of heat behind me, the scent of Theo, his breath on my neck as we read together.

May 10, 1957

Good evening, my love,

Do you think I'm silly, writing this letter while you're in the room with me? I have so many ideas and I want to write them down.

Now that we've decided to elope, here's what we'll do: get married as soon as the year is over and then go on our honeymoon road trip. Should we get a map today? I'll show you all the places that sound most exciting, and you can tell me if I'm right or wrong (we both know I'll be right).

I'm dreaming about the beautiful photographs you'll take. Ones we can hang in our home when we get back to LA. Maybe I'll take some pictures of you—I'll steal your camera when we leave the courthouse. The whole trip will be crooked landscapes and close-ups of your face.

You always call my face precious, but it's yours that makes me happy. I am happy, even if it's not the wedding I thought I'd have. I believe you when you tell me it will be okay. Just keep saying it so I don't forget.

Yours forever,
Kat

By the time I finish, the words are dancing on the page. It's bittersweet to be doing this in her place. Her hope was so palpable here. What took it away?

"Well." I sniff, keeping my eyes pinned to the paper so neither of them can see my emotion, which is silly. My voice is threaded with it. "Good news: I'll be fulfilling the role of crooked landscape photographer."

"I doubt that," Paul says gently.

I hand him back the letter, averting my gaze from Theo. He hasn't said a word. Does he think I'm ridiculous? Or is it poignant for him, too?

When I chance a look at him, his gaze is penetrating, but not judgmental. Maybe it's in accordance with our truce; I don't know.

Clearing my throat, I say, "I'm going to use the restroom real quick."

I escape to do my business, patting at my face with forty-ply toilet paper in the mirror after I've washed my hands. With a stern, silent look at mirror-me to get ahold of ourselves, I let out a breath. It starts shaky, but ends steadier.

I can do this. I *want* this. Most importantly, I need it.

The bathroom feeds into the kitchen, and as I step into it, there's a rustling in the foyer. Fearing it's Theo, I slow, running my hand along the counter.

The footsteps recede quickly, so I pick up my pace. My fingers brush against something, then snag on its weight. It takes me five full seconds to recognize what I'm looking at, but when it sinks in, my heart skips a beat.

Our senior yearbook. I look over my shoulder to make sure I'm alone, though this isn't my secret to get caught with, then pull the book closer.

It flips to a page bookmarked with articles from our high

school paper, as well as one from Glenlake's. They're tennis articles about Theo.

But also about me.

My heart beats fast. I shuffle through the slightly smudged paper, my eyes scanning the profile our paper did on me, and the one they did on Theo weeks later. I counted the words in each of our articles and was pissed to discover his had one hundred more.

Why did he keep this? And why is it out now?

The pleasure that pours through my veins like a serotonin jet stream isn't just uncomfortable, it's concerning. It's bad enough that I'm curious about him. I can't think about the possibility that he might be curious right back. Mutual attraction? Fine. But mutual interest? That can only end in disaster.

This trip isn't about Theo and me. It's about Gram. It's about *me*. I have to squash this feeling.

I slam the book shut and put it back. I never touched it. Never saw it.

I'm absolutely going to forget it.

———

I DON'T FORGET IT.

Not when Paul insists he prefers the backseat, leaving me in front with Theo. Not when I find out Theo's programmed his phone to the van's Bluetooth, like a dog peeing on a tree. Nor when he reminds me as I'm covertly pushing buttons in an attempt to disconnect his phone, that we agreed to a truce and sabotaging his music isn't very truce-like. Not even when we have to listen to his old, moody '90s playlist full of songs I either loathe or don't know for the three-hour drive.

He was remembering me. He was remembering us, whatever us there used to be. What does it *mean*? There's nothing I hate more than a question unanswered, especially when I can't ask it.

I'm itchy and restless. Theo tosses me no less than forty irritated looks, though he stays contained in brooding silence. Paul is the MVP, wrapping me up in conversation until we pull up to our hulking cabin-style hotel in Groveland, forty minutes outside Yosemite Valley.

We check in and eat a quick dinner at the hotel's restaurant. By the time we're done, it's nearing nine and Paul's energy level has nosedived.

"I hate to cut the night short," he says as we exit the elevator on the third floor. "I'm not used to keeping up with you kids."

Theo has his hand on Paul's shoulder, guiding him down the hall. "It's fine, we have to get up early tomorrow anyway."

I've already set my alarm for six; we have to be out the door by quarter to seven to beat the crowds.

But after we say good night in front of our adjacent rooms, restless energy beats through me. I sit listening to the silence on the other end of the wall, staring at the camera bag with my freshly cleaned equipment, and think about the way Theo looks at me sometimes. The way his voice dips low. That crooked smirk.

At ten I give up and dig through my suitcase for my bathing suit. I only brought one, a high-waisted bikini I bought for a girls' trip to Costa Rica years ago. It's black, simple, a little sporty but shows a lot of ass, which is objectively my best feature. In hindsight, a one-piece may have been more appropriate, but I like my body in this suit.

Would Theo?

"No," I demand, glaring at myself in the full-length mirror. The gleam in mirror-me's brown eyes is defiant.

God. I can't even agree with myself. Maybe a dip in the hot tub will steam my brain cells into submission. Or kill some off.

Once I'm dressed, I slip on a robe and make my way down to the pool. The posted hours say it closed at ten, but the gate is propped open, so I slip inside.

Aside from the hum of conversation from the restaurant patio, it's quiet. At my feet, the hot tub bubbles, steam hissing into the cool night air. Above, the sky stretches into forever and nothing, an infinite number of stars shaken across it.

I yank at the knotted belt of the robe, but a voice nearby stops me.

"—push me out."

I freeze. That sounded like Theo.

"I know, Matias, but you—"

Again, the voice stops, clearly frustrated. It's definitely Theo; even angry—or, god, maybe especially that way—the timbre of it sings through my body.

"I've got my dad up my ass right now, I don't need you there, too. I told you this morning, I'm unavailable for the next two weeks," he says, low and tight. He sounds closer now, but I still don't see him. "You and Anton agreed to that—" Another pause, then a laugh. It sounds dead. "Yeah, I know what's going to happen, and that's exactly why I don't give a shit about the timing of this trip. I'm having my attorney look at everything, too. There's nothing else we can do right now, so let me do this. No more fucking calls, okay?"

There are footsteps now, incredibly close. I scramble to unknot my robe, my heart racing, but Theo rounds the corner just as it falls to the ground.

When he catches sight of me, he stops so suddenly that it looks like he ran into an invisible wall. He doesn't say anything, and I can't. I'm standing here with my ass hanging out, feeling naked in every sense of the word as his eyes sweep over me.

It's confirmed: he likes my body in this bikini. And my body loves that.

"Eavesdropping?" he asks finally, that tightness still in his voice.

"Keeping secrets?" I shoot back.

He's so tense. Even ten feet away, in the darkness and with a gate separating us, it's radiating off him. His shoulders are tight, his hand clenched around his phone like he's seconds away from throwing it.

Theo's life has always seemed perfect from far away. But I'm close enough now to see the cracks.

He pushes through the gate, slipping his phone into his pocket. His eyes run over me quickly and he swallows, then looks away.

"I had to check in with work," he says. His gaze flickers back to my face, dropping lower briefly. It's like the steam brushing against my skin: hot, but too insubstantial to really feel.

A cold shower would be ideal, but the hot tub will have to do. I slip into the water, letting out a sigh as it engulfs me. Theo watches from the edge, his hands in his pockets, the lights from the hot tub dancing across his face. It could just be the way it's distorting his features, but for a second he looks . . . devastated.

I remember the days I'd run to Gram's house after a terrible breakup or a professional heartache. There was something cathartic in knowing she'd open the door and instantly recognize I needed to talk. That I needed to shed a secret, or two, or ten.

I see it in Theo's face now; the weight of it, whatever it is.

"My gram and I . . ." I trail off, unsure. He's still looking down at me, his expression morphing from blank to hungry to miserable as the lights flicker under the roiling water. "We had a thing we did. We called it Tell Me a Secret, and every time we saw each other, we'd exchange a secret we needed to get off our chest. Sometimes more, depending on how big a disaster the day was."

Recognition of my offer smooths out his brow. His shoulders straighten and he exhales, deep and tired. Then he crouches, resting his forearms on his knees. "All right, Shepard. Wanna play?"

I raise a challenging eyebrow. "Do you?"

"Tell me yours first." It's bossy, too familiar, like he came up with the game himself and he's letting *me* participate.

But I started this, so I play along. I run my hand through a circle of bubbles, letting my expression turn threatening. "I want to throw your phone into the pool. If I'm subjected to any more Radiohead, I'm going to fling myself out of the car while it's moving." A smile—so tiny but *there*—breaks the straight line of his mouth, curves it into something lighter. My chest goes so warm. Must be the hot tub. "But also, you should get two weeks without whatever stress your job is giving you, if that's what you asked for."

His Adam's apple bobs, and I follow the sinuous motion. I hate that it's sexy. I hate that *he's* sexy, and that he's sad, and I don't like that I hate that. It scares me. I don't need this.

But I don't stop it, either. "Tell me yours."

"What do you have against Radiohead?"

I glare. "That's not a secret."

He grins. "Thom Yorke is a genius."

"Thom Yorke makes me want to throw myself out of a moving vehicle, and also, maybe try music from this century. Now tell me your secret, Spencer, or I'm going to push you into the pool with your phone."

He stands, and for a moment I feel so utterly exposed it takes my breath away. I shared something personal with him and he's going to *leave*?

I open my mouth to tell him where else his phone can go, but he gets there first.

"I can't wait to see you with a camera in your hand tomorrow." He says it in a rush, then looks down, exhaling slowly. "You'd better be as good as I remember. No crooked photos."

And then he walks away without another word, leaving me gaping after him.

Twelve

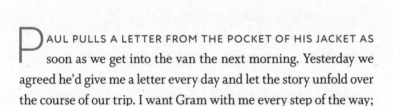

P AUL PULLS A LETTER FROM THE POCKET OF HIS JACKET AS
soon as we get into the van the next morning. Yesterday we
agreed he'd give me a letter every day and let the story unfold over
the course of our trip. I want Gram with me every step of the way;
stretching it out this way is like having her right next to me.

"Now we start with chronological order," Paul says, handing
the letter over.

Theo leans over from the driver's seat. I can smell the coffee
we drank together, the hotel soap scent that's all over my skin, too.

"This is after we'd started dating," Paul continues. "I figured
you didn't need to see any more of us fighting our feelings."

I turn, taking in Paul's fond smile, chest aching, before straightening in my seat. Theo's gaze snags with mine on the way, his expression unreadable. His jaw is dusted with a few days' worth of
whiskers. I swear to god if he grows a beard, I'll—

Blinking away from him and that dangerous train of thought, I
open the letter, tracing the words. "How long had you been dating?"

"Several weeks," Paul says. "We were still learning about each
other, but the deep feelings came quickly."

Theo thumbs at the letter's corner, his voice low in my ear. "Let's read."

I take a breath, imagining Gram's voice in my ear instead, saying these words out loud.

October 26, 1956

Dear Paul,

I'm afraid I was too honest with you last night. Not because I called you a pain—you know that's true—but because I talked about the type of man I'm expected to be with.

He's nothing like you. I'm sorry to say that's true. My parents have doted on me my entire life, and they want what's best for me. Only, they have a very specific idea of what that is—stoic, a rule-follower, devoted to service to his country. Someone who'll fit in perfectly with my father and brother.

I suppose I fought against the idea of us partly because you're a pain, but also because I heard my family's voice in my head every time I looked at you: he's not right for you, Kat. And yet, my own voice grew louder the more time we spent together. It's never done that.

This may end in disaster. My family may hate you. But I don't. I've never done a thing I thought they wouldn't like. You're the first thing I've been brave enough to go after just for myself, simply because I want it so much.

It's okay if this scares you. It scares me, too. But I'll do it anyway.

Love,
Kat

That last sentiment slices through my chest like a stone being dropped into water, settling deep. I think of my camera bag nestled in the trunk, of the pictures I'll have to take today. How is it possible to want something as equally as you fear it?

My gaze strays to Theo, whose eyes are still moving across the paper. His jaw ticks when he finishes, his gaze lingering on whatever words have captivated him before he looks at me. I can't read the emotion in his eyes, but it's heavy enough to snag my chest.

I break our connection, turning back to Paul, who's watching us with barely concealed amusement. "Gram ended up being a teacher, you know. She went to school—well, back to school—after my dad and uncles were older."

Pride shines in Paul's voice. "Yes, I heard through our mutual friends she'd done that."

That piques my curiosity. "Did you ever get in touch with her yourself?"

"She sent me and Vera a wedding gift, along with a nice note, which I couldn't help but write back to," he says fondly. "But before that and after, no, we didn't talk at all. Once we were in other relationships, it was best not to. I knew she was happy with Joe."

"Did it hurt, hearing about her life?"

"Right after we separated, yes. But after a while, and especially after my divorce, hearing about all of the things she was doing gave me hope that I'd get it right at some point, too."

That's something I haven't felt in so long—hope that things will shift into the shape I confidently sketched out when I was young.

"People rarely get it on the first try, Noelle," Paul says quietly. His eyes slip past me to Theo. His arms are crossed over his chest, his eyes locked on his grandfather's, searching. "There's nothing wrong with that. It doesn't make you less of a success story in the end."

Theo's lips press together as he looks down. The right side of his hair is a little flat, and there's a trace of a pillow mark on his cheek. He looks impossibly human right now; it taps a fissure into my heart.

Our gazes clash again, magnetic. It's too powerful to look away from, so thank god it's Theo who breaks the connection this time, shifting in his seat as he sticks the key in the ignition.

I wipe my palms on my thighs, folding the letter as the engine growls to life.

"Enough distractions," Theo says. "Shepard has some pictures to take."

THEO PULLS INTO THE PARKING LOT AT TUNNEL VIEW AN HOUR later. It's a popular viewpoint that overlooks El Capitan, Bridalveil Fall, and, in the distance, Half Dome, as well as an endless, lush spread of green. A few groups roam the parking lot, making their way to the stone wall that separates us from total majesty.

My brain is dreaming up photos instantly.

Theo's got my backpack unzipped when I get to the trunk, but he doesn't touch my camera. Instead, he stands there, arms crossed while I extract it from its case with shaky hands.

I take in his bodyguard-like stance and go back to last night—*I can't wait to see you with a camera in your hand.*

I hold it up for inspection. "Is it everything you thought it'd be?"

"And more," he says dryly, but there's pleasure in his eyes. Without another word, he turns on his heel and makes his way toward the lookout.

Paul removes his camera, winding the strap around his neck, and I nearly choke on my tongue.

"Is that a Hasselblad?"

He holds up the gorgeous camera as we walk, like he doesn't have four thousand dollars of extraordinary photography magic sitting in his palm. "My favorite. I've reverted back to film, mostly. I hardly use digital anymore."

"Where do you get your prints developed?"

"I have a darkroom at home." He nods to Theo. "Teddy set it up for me."

My gaze follows Theo, tracking across his shoulders, looser this morning. I get the feeling he'd do anything for his granddad. It's becoming an uncomfortable soft spot, the place where our kinship roots deeper with every detail Paul feeds me.

Paul pulls me out of my spiraling thoughts. "It's okay if it takes time for photography to feel right again."

"What do you mean?"

We stop next to Theo, who's perched on the wall. The wind ruffles Paul's hair back from his forehead, and he squints against the strengthening sunlight.

"After Kat left school, there was a time when I didn't touch my camera. I felt disconnected from my love for it. Disconnected from life, really. When I picked it back up, it took me time to get reacquainted. I had to figure out what I wanted to find through the lens." He squeezes my shoulder gently. "You're old friends who haven't talked in a while, Noelle. Get to know each other again."

I nod, fumbling with my camera as I move to the edge of the lookout.

Theo backs up toward Paul, making space for me.

"Don't choke." He gives me a crooked smirk. It's what he'd murmur when he passed me in the hallway on match days. Hearing him say it in a low voice was like hearing my opponent yell it across the court, except more delicious. Below the taunting tilt of the words was the assurance that I *wouldn't* choke. He may have thought he was better than me, but he knew I was really fucking good.

Want and fear have been battling it out, but with Theo's words, the want wins.

I check the ISO and aperture settings, adjust my shutter speed. Then, for the first time in six months, I put my eye to the viewfinder. My finger smooths over the shutter release, as light as the breeze that winds through my hair.

My mind goes blank, even as nerves dance under my skin. There are people around, but it's a hum of energy, a soft buzz until it's nothing. Until there's no sound but my own heartbeat.

The last time I did this, I was with Gram. Somehow, I'm doing it now, and she's here again. Or still.

I expel my emotion in the form of a watery exhale. Out of the corner of my eye, Theo rocks forward on his heels, but Paul cuffs his elbow.

It scares me. But I'll do it anyway.

I catch a solar flare in my lens and microscopically shift my weight on my right leg, leaning so it slices more fully into the shot. I press the shutter release. The gentle click of the lens sounds like a firework.

Like that, the anticipatory anxiety is gone. I take a few more shots. My arms crawl with goosebumps. I pull back to watch the hairs rise, the skin under turning textured, and wish I could capture that, too. Then I turn to Paul, who's lowering his own camera, beaming, and feel my smile spread across my mouth like the sun over the valley.

I shift my gaze to Theo. He comes up behind me, curving over my shoulder like he did in his kitchen. It's equally distracting, but not nearly as annoying, and that makes my heart beat with a thrill and fear.

"Let's see if these are TikTok approvable, Shep."

I press the playback menu and scroll through the pictures I just took, the ones I'll eventually share with thousands of people. Ones they'll hopefully love.

I wait for the voice in my head telling me I'll never amount to anything, but it doesn't come.

Instead, I hear my own voice, assuring me that, though these photos aren't the best I've ever taken, at least I *took* them. Maybe it doesn't have to be my best to still be enough.

WE SPEND THE MORNING EXPLORING THE VALLEY AND DROP IN to the Ansel Adams Gallery. Paul waxes poetic about his technical skill and use of previsualization, as well as his enduring conservationist beliefs. Theo catches my eye at one point, his mouth twitching.

Fanboy, he mouths, and I bite against a smile.

We eat lunch on the Ahwahnee Hotel's patio and the temperature climbs with the sun. Before my sandwich arrives, I'm peeling off my thin fleece pullover. I'm wearing a cropped tank underneath, nothing special, but Theo's eyes linger through the rest of lunch, sending a shot of electricity down my spine.

Not happening.

I drain my iced tea, but it does nothing to quench this specific thirst.

On our shuttle ride to our Mirror Lake hike, Paul insists on sitting across the aisle from us. I spend the entire time staring down at Theo's thigh nearly pressed against mine.

Thighs should not be so beautiful, especially smashed against a plastic seat.

Besides the continued struggle with my attraction to Theo,

though, the day has been perfect. I'm trying to remember the last time I felt this content, but I can't. There's no small amount of shock in the realization that some of that contentment is directly tied to Theo's company, though I don't dwell on the reason.

Paul's hiking sticks tap against the hard-packed dirt as we get onto the trail. "I can't believe I haven't asked this yet, Noelle, but have you ever been to Yosemite?"

I adjust my backpack, nodding. "A few times with my family. It's been years, though. I forgot how beautiful it is."

"It's my favorite place in the world," Theo says from beside me.

I turn to him, surprised at this voluntary share. "Yeah?"

He nods. The sun filters down through the thick canopy of trees, dappling his face and hair with afternoon light, caressing his shoulders. "I don't know how many times I forced my grand-dad to camp here—"

"At least twenty."

Theo gives Paul the smile he reserves for him alone—pure happiness, unabashed affection. "There's something about it. It's quiet, but not a heavy kind of quiet. Just peaceful. Feels like you can breathe here."

I stare at him, trying to work out exactly what he means. *A heavy kind of quiet.* I've felt it in grief, but I've also seen it in the low tones in which his dad used to speak to him, a firm hand gripping his shoulder, in the grim silence after Theo got a lit paper returned to him with a 93 written at the top. I have to make assumptions. He'll never tell me, but it still feels like he's revealed something.

"What's your second favorite place?" I ask.

"New Zealand as a whole. Milford Sound especially. I cried a little."

My mouth drops open. "No, you didn't."

He gives me a sly look. "I love that I could not tell you and you'll wonder forever."

"Your grandson is a total menace, Paul."

His laugh is jovial. "Sweetheart, I know."

I continue my line of questioning, curious now. "How many countries have you been to?"

"I've stalled out at forty-two. Haven't had much of a chance to travel the past couple years," Theo says, his mouth twisting with obvious displeasure.

I look over my shoulder at Paul. "And you?"

"Ninety-seven." He nods his chin at Theo. "He's trying to catch up with me."

"Forty-two is pretty impressive."

"Yeah," Theo agrees, but it's not smug. He seems in awe of it, and confirms that when he continues, "I realized early on what a privilege it was to be able to travel. Granddad drilled into my head that seeing the world is expensive, and it requires time people may not have. I can't do anything about the time part of it, but Where To Next was born from the idea that everyone should be able to afford a full-package experience."

"I love the off-season packages you offer," I admit. "Gram and I went to Scotland a couple years ago and practically paid pennies."

His attention turns keen. "Do you use it often?"

I lift a shoulder. "When I have the time and money. Before Gram died, I didn't have much of either. There's no way I would've gone on the trip without the off-season deal. Gram would've wanted to pay for my way, and it would've turned into this big argument of me not wanting to be a burden—"

Gah. Major overshare. I bite my lip to prevent further confessions, but Theo seems to have a one-track mind.

"Do you think it's a necessary feature?" he presses.

"Yeah, everyone I know has used it at least once. It's the biggest draw of your app, in my opinion." I eye him. "Why are you asking? Are you using me as some sort of one-woman focus group?"

He runs a hand over his jaw, distracted now. "Yeah, I guess."

We spend the next few minutes walking in silence before coming up to a portion of the trail where a creek is revealed, water rushing over huge craggy rocks. Behind it, a massive slab of mountain thrusts into the sky. My fingers start tingling, and my heart beats faster at the feeling in response. It's been so long since I've wanted to shoot anything so badly my fingers tingled.

"Can we stop real quick?" I ask, already popping the cover off my lens. "I want to get a few shots here."

"Go ahead," Paul says.

I scramble toward the edge, staying a safe distance from the drop, though it's not significant. It's just rocky, and the water below looks freezing.

But when I look through the viewfinder, the angle is all wrong. The pictures I took this morning weren't my best work, but I need to get up to speed quickly so I can capitalize on the attention and followers TikTok has afforded me. I want to make more videos. Need to, actually, and I want it to be with work that shines.

Which means I need to scoot closer so I can get this shot.

Theo's voice is sharp behind me. "What are you doing? You're going to fall in."

I slide an inch forward so the toe of my hiking boot rests on a rock. "I'm not. I know what I'm doing."

"Do you? Because you're way too close to the edge."

I peer through the viewfinder again. Almost there. If only

Theo would shut up so I could concentrate. "I know my body placement better than you, Spencer."

I inch forward. It's almost perfect, almost—

"Shepard, don't—"

But it's too late. The heel of my hiking boot slips on a wet patch of rock, and I'm falling.

Thirteen

Y OU'RE A FUCKING MESS."

I press my key card against the reader, my body throbbing from head to toe. "And you're overreacting."

Theo reaches an arm around me, pushing my hotel door open. His furious tension leaches from his chest into my back, but when he pushes past me into the room, it's with a gentle brush of his body against mine.

Still. He's pissed. The ride back to the hotel was deathly silent. Even Paul was quiet, beyond asking several times if I was okay.

As Theo stalks away, I focus on the mud streaking down his pants from his ass to his knee. He's missing the bottom three inches of his shirt. We used it as a makeshift bandage, so now he's rocking a crop top. His elbow is scratched but not bleeding, which is more than I can say for my knee.

I look down at it in dismay. It's no longer gushing, but it looks nasty underneath the shirt. The material is soaked through with blood. And my leggings are trashed, ripped from knee to mid-thigh.

Theo holds the first aid kit he got from the front desk over his shoulder. "Take your pants off."

"Excuse me?" I choke out, my shoulder clipping the doorway as I cross the threshold.

The look he gives me is incendiary. "We need to clean your knee and your leggings will be in the way. They're ruined anyway. Off."

My spine cracks, stiffening at his bossy tone, but I bite my lip against a retort as I watch him stride into the bathroom. He pushes aside all the crap I left out this morning, tossing the first aid kit onto the counter.

He has good reason to be mad; I had no business hanging off the edge of the embankment like that. What's worse, I didn't even get the shot *and* my lens is cracked, though thankfully I have a backup.

I drag myself over to my suitcase, digging around for a pair of shorts while my brain flashes through the past two hours: My foot slipping and the way I tipped forward. The horror of seeing the rocks ten feet below me with nothing to grab onto, knowing I was going to fall face-first into them. The feeling of being wrenched backward by my backpack, being thrown to the side from the force of Theo's momentum. The searing pain in my knee when it sliced against a jagged rock and the glug of Theo's racing heart underneath my ear when we finally stopped halfway down to the creek.

He'd gasped out, "Fucking hell. Shepard, are you okay?"

"I think so." My knee was already wet, on fire.

There'd been a brief pause while Paul called down to us. Then Theo's voice went sharp as a knife. "What the *fuck* is wrong with you?"

Turns out that was a rhetorical question. He ignored my breathless explanations as he got me up the hill, ripped his shirt like the Hulk version of Captain America, and bandaged up my knee. He ignored me during our hour-long ride from the park, and when Paul offered to grab water and painkillers in the gift shop downstairs.

That his first words to me in two hours are "you're a fucking mess" and "take your pants off" is deeply ironic. I *am* a mess. And it's not the first demand he's ever made of me, but it's the first one I've ever followed with such little hesitation.

I undress to the muffled sounds of Theo moving around in the bathroom. Something about it soothes me, that there's someone in there waiting to take care of me. That he's willing to, even after I messed up.

Maybe it's the adrenaline finally catching up, or the pain, but tears sting my eyes as I pull on my shorts. I take two gulping breaths to push the emotion back. I don't want to walk into that bathroom if I'm not calm. If I'm not calm, then I'm vulnerable. The thought of Theo seeing any more of my soft underbelly scares me more than falling down that embankment.

When I push the bathroom door open a minute later, though, I feel like I'm seeing *his*. He's braced against the counter, head hanging low. I nearly back out to give him more time to . . . I don't know. Collect himself.

The squeaking hinges alert him to my presence, though, and his expression straightens.

He pushes off the counter, clearing his throat, then freezes. "I—are those underwear?"

I look down, pulling at the cotton. "No, they're shorts."

"Says who?" he grumbles, turning back to the counter and grabbing one of the myriad packets littering one side of the sink.

"Target."

With a deeply impatient sigh, he gestures to the cleared space on the counter. "Hop up."

"Uh." I look down at my mangled knee. "I'm not sure I—"

Theo's hands are on me before I'm prepared. I don't know how I'd prepare for this, anyway: the warmth of his skin against mine above my waistband, the way his fingers dig into my back, his thumbs pressing hard into my abdomen.

I have to wrap my arms around his neck. I'll fall otherwise. It feels like I'm falling anyway.

He places me unceremoniously on the counter, his hands loosening but not immediately dropping from their bracketed position. His broad palms are the perfect width for the valleys of my body. I wish I could erase that knowledge from my brain.

My arms are still frozen around his neck. He reaches behind him, our faces inches apart, and grabs my wrists. He doesn't touch me like I'm delicate or fragile. He touches me like I can take it. My stomach tightens in tandem with the squeeze of his fingers over my wrists as he sets my hands on my thighs.

"Was that necessary? I think I've gotten thrown around enough today," I murmur into the silence.

He smirks. "Didn't know there was a limit."

Jesus. I look away, down at the spread of medical supplies. "Are you going to fix me up, McDreamy?"

"Who the hell is McDreamy?"

"He was on a show I've been bingeing that's on its, like, fortieth seas—" I wave my hand in the air impatiently. "You know what, it doesn't matter. He's a hot television doctor."

I look back up to find Theo's smirk has gotten bigger. His dimple winks at me, though his eyes are still stormy. "Hot, huh?"

"Settle your ego. You skew much more McAngsty."

He gives me a look that broadcasts his skepticism as he picks up an antiseptic packet. "McAngsty who saved your ass."

"I wanted to get the perfect shot."

The rip of the paper fills the bathroom. God, it's small in here. Theo's shoulders alone take up seventy percent of the space.

"And you fell down a hill," he says. "How's that perfection feeling now?"

It hurts like hell.

Theo looks at me like I've said it out loud, and his expression softens, just barely. He braces a hand on my uninjured knee, stepping into the vee of my legs.

"This is going to sting."

I stare at the starburst in his eyes, thinking *yes, it is* just before the vicious pain hits.

"Oh fuck," I gasp out, gripping his forearm. "Oh my god, that hurts."

"Breathe," he commands, and my lungs kick out an exhale on instinct. He's so close my breath stirs the curling hair beneath his ear. I squeeze my eyes shut so I won't look at him or my knee. The antiseptic burns almost as badly as the injury itself, nearly as much as the burn in my chest from realizing I could have hurt Theo, too. He drives me to the edge of my patience constantly, but I'd never forgive myself if something happened to him.

"I'm sorry," I breathe out.

There's a beat of silence. Then, "Don't do shit like that again, Shepard. We're going to be walking along much higher drops. I don't want to watch your body fall off the side of the Grand Canyon."

If we weren't close, I wouldn't have heard the tremor in his voice, but we're practically on top of each other. My eyes fly open. His head is bowed, focused on his work, his thick black lashes lying against the hollow beneath his eyes. A flush spreads across his cheeks.

I swallow, recognizing his fear. I felt it, too, when I was falling. I feel it now, knowing he cares, even if it's just that he didn't want me to die on his watch.

"I'm sorry," I say again.

"I know."

When he doesn't go on, I press, "This is the part where you forgive me."

"And if I don't?" He lifts his chin, pinning me in place with eyes that are dark, but edged in amusement.

"Then lie so I feel better."

Theo huffs out a laugh. "I forgive you," he says, just as he presses the antiseptic wipe against my knee again, adding pressure.

"*Shit.* Oh fuck," I hiss out, my eyes watering. "You're making it hurt on purpose, you asshole."

"Only if you ask nicely." His voice is electrified, arcing from his mouth right into the pit of my stomach.

I suck in a breath, picturing his hands on me. Not hurting me, but letting me know he's there, that he's got me.

The air changes, storm-like, awareness rolling in on Theo's hot exhale. For all of the ways we clash, I have no doubt we'd be good together like that, and he knows it, too.

"You're not supposed to like that," he growls out, frustrated, his gaze tracing my face like a touch.

Somehow his shirt has made its way into my fists. "Why did you say it, then?"

His gaze flickers up from my mouth. "Because I was trying to be an asshole."

"You don't *have* to try."

He's gotten so close. I don't know if I pulled him or he came willingly. He's between my thighs, but not the way I'd like. The slick material of his joggers brushes up against my skin, his hands shaping the curve of my legs as the antiseptic wipe falls away.

We were doing something before, but I couldn't say what.

Theo tilts his head. Our noses brush and my stomach spirals so quickly it makes me dizzy. He's going to kiss me, and I'm going to let him. Some foggy part of me remembers that this is a bad idea. That we don't like each other, and we had to make a truce to get along.

I don't think our truce included him running his hands up my thighs, his thumbs tracing the inside with the perfect pressure.

"What's that game called?" he murmurs. "From last night?"

"Tell Me a Secret," I manage, my heart in my throat.

His jaw ticks. "So, tell me one."

I don't want to admit it, but it's the elephant in the room. His thumbs are inches from the spot throbbing worse than my knee.

"I wouldn't stop you if you kissed me right now." I say it quietly in case he changes his mind, but his eyes darken, pupils dilating. He doesn't move, though his mouth parts like he can already taste it. "Now you."

His breath dances over my lips. "If I kissed you right now, I wouldn't stop."

My legs flex instinctively, trying to close to relieve some of the ache between them, but Theo's grip turns even firmer as he dips his head to run his mouth barely, *barely* against the spot where my jaw meets my ear.

"When you wear your hair up, I can't stop looking right here," he whispers against my skin. Another secret revealed, and I didn't even have to ask. "You've never caught me?"

"No," I moan. "Why are you messing with me right now?"

"Not messing, Shepard." His nose skims along my cheek until

his mouth is millimeters from mine. "Let's call it playing. Isn't that what we've always done with each other?"

Like that, he puts us on equal ground. I bite back a triumphant grin as my hands release his shirt and move to his forearms. His tendons dance under my palms as he flexes his fingers into my thighs, but he doesn't move otherwise. Why won't he *kiss* m—

There's a soft knock at the door. A rustle. Footsteps, and the sound of the door next to mine opening.

Paul. He told me he'd let me know when he dropped off my water and medicine, along with chocolate he promised would be more healing than Advil.

Paul, the grandfather of the man I'm about to kiss. Paul, who's pausing his life to accompany me on this road trip, telling me the secrets Gram either never got to or never intended to spill.

Paul, who clearly wants Theo and I to be a real thing.

My chest goes tight. I cannot mess this up, and getting tangled with Theo would.

"Hold on," I wheeze out, letting go.

Theo steps back immediately, and the sudden absence of his touch nearly makes me cry. It would've been a mistake, but it would've been a mistake that felt really fucking good.

I keep my eyes firmly on his face. He's hard and the material of his pants is thin and I truly can't handle any details. "We shouldn't do this."

He doesn't answer right away. His pulse thrums in his throat, below his impossibly tight jaw. "Okay."

"I want to," I say, in an attempt to reassure him.

One corner of his mouth pulls up as he rubs a hand up and down his cheek, then across his jaw. "I know."

"But Paul," I say, ignoring his smug tone. "I mean, you can see he's trying to play matchmaker, right?"

Theo lets out a breath, his expression softening. "Yeah, I can."

I run my hands over my thighs. Trying to erase his touch or preserve it, I'm not sure which. "We're attracted to each other, but that's all it is. It's not like we'd ever have something for real."

Not if he knew what state my life is in, anyway. I'm not too proud to admit that I've googled his past girlfriends. They're all beautiful, with accomplishments pages long. One woman worked for NASA, for god's sake. Maybe I'd be a fun distraction for him, a way to work out his stress while he's away, but then what?

More distressingly, I feel myself softening toward him, and it's only been a day. If I tangle those emotions with a hookup, it could get messy.

I don't need more messes in my life.

"Right," Theo says, interrupting my spiral.

His face is wiped clean of emotion. He grabs a Neosporin packet and Q-tip, applies a generous amount of goop onto it, then spreads it over my cut. My throat goes tight at the gentle touch.

"I don't want to upset Paul," I say, watching his careful work. The burn is gone, just an ache now. "I—I care about his friendship, and I don't want to risk his place in my life if things blow up between us."

His gaze meets mine briefly. "I get it, Shepard. The risk isn't worth the reward. My granddad already cares about you, and he's invested in all of this. I'm not going to mess that up for either of you."

Theo prepares several bandages, then presses them onto my knee. His movements are efficient now, not hungry, not lingering or rough, and I mourn the loss of it even though it's necessary.

When he's done, he helps me down, stepping away before our bodies can connect.

I lean against the counter. "Can we extend the truce to 'can look but don't touch'?"

His eyebrows raise. "You want to look, huh?"

"Nothing wrong with a little window shopping," I say. "Now that we've admitted we're attracted to each other, I mean."

Theo huffs out a tight breath. "Fine. I'm going to go check on my granddad, so I'll give you the opportunity to stare at my ass again."

"Again?"

"I felt you looking when I walked in."

I make sure he sees my 360-degree eye roll, but I do stare at his ass as he walks to the door. He catches me when he looks over his shoulder. The last thing I see before the door closes behind him is his smirk.

What he doesn't know is that I'm going to look *and* touch. But the only touching I'm going to do is with myself.

That's a promise.

Fourteen

THEO KEEPS HIS DISTANCE WHILE WE EXPLORE THE PARK the next day. It's for the best, considering our truce's amendment, but I find myself missing his irritating smirks, how close he gets to murmur dry asides. He walks just ahead of us on our hikes, but occasionally he'll angle his head to listen to my conversations with Paul.

So, on Monday, when I make my way down to the lobby for checkout, I'm shocked to find him watching my approach. The adrenaline of having his attention again snakes through my veins as his mouth pulls up.

He meets me halfway, taking my suitcase. "Saw your latest masterpiece last night."

The brush of his fingers against mine sets off tiny earthquakes, and my response is sluggish. "My latest—? Oh."

Last night I made Thomas sit with me via FaceTime while I crafted my next TikTok. It was only fair to hold him hostage while I muttered to myself, since it was his idea in the first place, but he abandoned me twenty minutes in. Thankfully Sadie kept me company, pumping me for trip details.

Making this video was such a different process from the one I made searching for Paul. Then, I assumed no one would see it. But I *knew* people would look at this. I spent over an hour erasing and reshooting and editing to make sure everything looked just right. I crawled around Gram and Paul's map spread on the floor to capture the stops, my knee still stinging but less intensely.

Eventually, I had a sixty-second video that gave the update people had been asking for. Now they knew I'd met Paul. They knew there were letters—I showed the first one I'd read—and additional pictures. They knew there was a map planning out the honeymoon that never was.

They knew I was taking the trip in her place.

I didn't mention Paul and Theo's part in it, but that didn't matter. People loved it, and my relief and hope were instant. The notifications started coming in as I was settling into bed. I turned off my phone so I wouldn't stay up all night tracking the numbers.

Which is why I'm rolling into the lobby twenty minutes late.

Theo doesn't look annoyed, either by my tardiness or the Tik-Tok. He looks amused. "I was wondering when you'd get around to making it."

His teasing puts me on edge. He's been so robot-like since our almost kiss that my response comes out defensive. "I had to think about it for a while. I wanted it to be—"

I don't say the word; it's not how I'd ever describe it. But Theo says it anyway. "Perfect."

"Just— I wanted it to be right. I wanted to do the story justice."

"The story that happened sixty years ago or the one that's happening now?"

It's such an astute observation that it throws me off balance. Now that he's said it, I recognize the feeling: living inside an important memory as it's happening, and being viscerally aware of it. "Both, I guess."

Theo hitches a thumb over his shoulder. "Well, you've got that guy's seal of approval. He's been reading comments all morning. Hope you're prepared to talk about it all the way to Death Valley."

I catch sight of Paul sitting in a plush leather chair, one leg crossed over the other. He has Theo's phone in his hands, reading glasses on, grinning down at the screen like it's Christmas morning.

It's a look so full of joy—and pride—that it makes my heart ache. It reminds me of Gram when she'd see my work.

I catch Theo watching me. His expression is a manifestation of the way my chest feels.

"What?"

His mouth parts, then presses together. Then the look is gone, replaced by the sly expression I've—shit—*missed*. "You said I could look."

I choke out a laugh. "There's a lot of nuance between looking and staring, Spencer."

"Sometimes I like to take my time."

I can't touch that, not even with a ten-foot pole. "Paul really likes the TikTok?"

"He's been calling it a Tic Tac, but yeah, he's into it."

The miraculous thing is, I am, too.

"I have ideas for more," I admit as we make our way over to Paul. My mind was racing last night. I stared at the ceiling for nearly an hour dreaming up the stories I could tell next. "I want to do a couple videos for our Yosemite leg."

"Then keep going," Theo says bossily. "And stop thinking so hard."

Paul grins up at me when we get to him, handing Theo his

phone. "Good morning! I saw your Tic Tac. It was just lovely. So many nice comments, too, though I didn't understand half of them."

"Social media vernacular is confusing," I agree, offering my hand to help him up.

He gives my hand a squeeze once he's standing. "You, my dear, are a storyteller. I've seen it in your photographs, and I see it here. You'll do more, right?"

The lump in my throat is so vicious that I can only nod at first. Eventually I get out, "Yes, I'll keep going."

My gaze slides to Theo. I've repeated his phrasing. He acknowledges it with a wink, and it tugs at me, a thread that's just been created between us. If I'm not careful, it'll turn into a web I can't get out of.

I turn back to Paul. "I told Theo this, but I won't include current pictures or videos of either of you unless you want that."

"Oh." Paul's eyes widen, his mouth twitching into a smile. "Well, I'm already a little bit famous, aren't I?"

"You're very famous by TikTok standards," I laugh.

"Tell the story how you want to tell it. If that includes the current version of me, I'd be honored."

"I'm okay with it, too," Theo says.

I arch an eyebrow at him. "It won't affect your reputation as the very serious cofounder and CFO of Where To Next?"

"You showing me, the cofounder of a traveling app, traveling?" he responds. "No, I think it'll be okay."

"Maybe you'll accumulate a fan club."

Deep in my bones I know people will go wild for him. I swear he was specially made for fantasizing over. Already I'm thinking of the ways my camera will love the planes and angles of his face, that body, and the way hungry, anonymous eyes will devour whatever I put up. It stirs something in my stomach. Not jealousy, but something sticky like that.

Theo shrugs, cheeks flushing. "Not my problem. If you're going to tell the story, might as well tell all of it. I'm not going to stand in your way."

Paul grins at the two of us, then takes me by the elbow as we walk out to the van, sharing his favorite comments.

Theo's already loading up the trunk by the time we get there, and instructs us to drop our bags so he can finish. Paul settles into the backseat as usual, and I take advantage of Theo's absence to add my phone to the Bluetooth, disconnecting his.

When he slides into the driver's seat and turns the ignition, Maggie Rogers's voice snakes out through the speakers. He looks at the multimedia screen, then over at me, unimpressed.

"I told you, more Thom Yorke and I'm going to throw myself out of the car. Allow me to introduce you to modern music."

He sighs. I settle into my seat, smug and singing along, as Theo puts us in reverse.

"All right." Paul claps his hands. "Where to next?"

WE MAKE IT TO DEATH VALLEY BEFORE SUNSET, HIKING THE quarter mile to Badwater Basin, a popular tourist spot. The landscape is monochromatic, an ombre of browns that fuse together to make something beautiful. In the distance, the mountain range looks painted on the horizon. Though it's evening, the air is still heavy with heat.

I walk next to Theo while Paul meanders ahead.

"So, which came first, Paul saying *Where to next?* or you naming your company?"

I know the answer already, but I want him to say it out loud.

Theo gives me a sideways glance, letting out a quiet laugh. "Of course you'd pick up on that."

"Yes, I'm a genius. Did you name it after him?"

There's a cornered look in his eyes, but he doesn't hesitate. "Yeah."

I let his silence hang for approximately two seconds. "I'm going to need more than that."

Theo's mouth curls into a barely-there smile before he squints out at the horizon. "It's what he'd say to me every summer when we were getting ready to take off somewhere. He always knew where we were going—he had to clear it with my parents first— but he liked to pretend we were going on this unknown adventure together."

"Why that moment, specifically?"

"It meant I got to spend time with someone who let me be me, without expectations. We got to go to places where no one knew us—all over the country when I was young, and internationally once I was older." Our arms brush, bringing goosebumps to my skin despite the heat. But it's not just Theo's touch; it's the emotion coating his voice. I recognize it in myself, the bittersweetness of recalling perfect moments you can't get back. "It was freeing to get away from my life. So, when Anton and Matias and I were thinking about names, it was the first thing that popped up. It felt right. I want everyone to feel that when they travel."

I fiddle with my lens cap. "That's kind of a pay-it-forward moment for you, over and over again."

Theo's features are painted golden in the light falling down on us. The tips of his lashes are honey hued, the blue of his eyes so clear, nearly bright. After my disastrous assistant stint, I prefer to shoot landscapes instead of people, but the urge to get this shot of Theo is intense.

He swallows. "I've never thought of it that way. But yeah. I guess that's right."

"You've done something pretty amazing with it," I say quietly.

"Yeah." His voice breaks, and he lets out a breath, running his hand through his hair before giving me a wry look. "You still ask a lot of questions."

I bite back a smile. Sometimes in class, he'd tally up all the questions I asked and slip the paper into my hand on his way out the door. I hated that touch as much as I wanted it. "Some things never change."

"True."

The air between us is thick, his sadness sitting on top of it. I bump his arm with my shoulder. "You can tell me to mind my business, you know."

"I know."

The basin stretches out in front of us, bleached-white salt flats shaped like polygons. The sun is starting to sink in earnest, and though I'm eager to take some photos, I'm disappointed our conversation is winding down. Theo giving a piece of himself to me feels like a gift, and I want to grab it with both hands. Ask for more.

He turns to me. His gaze traces the path of my ponytail pulled over my shoulder, moving up to that spot he touched with his mouth the other night. But it's not sexual; it's *familiar*. It makes me ache.

"No one's ever asked me that question before. I didn't realize how much I wanted to answer it."

I hear the *thank you* he doesn't say. I nod, too taken aback to come up with a casual response. He flashes me a quick smile, then wanders away, hands in his pockets.

I watch him for too long. I'm going to miss the sunset. My pictures. But I can't seem to step outside of our moment.

A gentle hand on my arm sends me crashing back down to earth.

"I didn't mean to startle you, sweetheart," Paul says when I whip around. His camera is cradled in his hands.

"It's okay, I was just . . . thinking." *About your grandson and how I seem to be sliding headfirst into something a little terrifying—*

Paul saves me from myself. "You shoot mostly landscape, right?"

"It's what I'm most comfortable with, yeah."

"Have you done much portrait work?"

"I—" I lift a shoulder. "I assisted a photographer for almost a year right out of college. I got burned, so I stepped away from it."

He hums, appraising me. "You truly do have a storyteller's heart. I recognize it in you just as I knew it in myself. I hope you discover that, and use it to make art that touches people." He elbows me, conspiratorial. "Even if it's just *you* it touches."

He lifts his chin toward Theo, turned toward the mountain range with his face in profile. The shape of him is lonely.

"I'm not sure I should interrupt," I stall.

"You're not interrupting. You're recording a moment." Our eyes meet and he smiles, a mixture of sadness and joy there. "Teddy's been my loyal subject his entire life. It's okay, I promise."

I bring the viewfinder to my eye. It feels too intimate to catch Theo in my lens, to bring him closer to me with a quick adjustment to the zoom. The angles of his face are so close I could touch them. I want to spread the heat from the air and the sun onto his skin, down his neck, into his chest.

I *want* him closer, even though he's safer at a distance.

With my heart flying, I press my finger on the shutter release. It's my first picture of Theo. But I doubt it'll be my last.

———

THE MEMORY OF THEO'S FACE IS STILL IMPRINTED HOURS later as Las Vegas comes into view, a neon blanket over the night-black valley below.

"I wish it wasn't so dark." Paul tsks, squinting out the window. "I've got a letter here. I should've thought of it when we were in Death Valley."

"We can do it now," I blurt excitedly. My hand shoots out, landing on his knee.

With a chuckle, Paul reaches over to the cardigan lying on the other seat, pulling out the letter.

Theo glances over as I smooth it out on my lap. "How are you planning on reading that?"

"I'm going to turn on the light and read it out loud."

"I won't be able to see the road if you turn it on."

This letter is getting read right now, come hell or high water. "That's an old dad's tale, you know. The car isn't going to crash because you turn on a reading light."

Even in the darkness, I can see his eyes roll.

"Here, I'll do you a solid and use my phone's flashlight. I'll even turn it down so you can still concentrate."

He sighs but doesn't argue. A win.

"Paul, what's the story with this one?" I ask.

"Oh, this one is quite self-explanatory. I can answer questions after, if you have any."

"She will," Theo says.

I toss him a glare, then clear my throat. "All right, here we go."

The van is silent save for my voice as I start to read Gram's words out loud.

November 17, 1956

Dear Paul,

Have you read F. Scott Fitzgerald? Probably not. Your nose is always stuck in a photography book.

There's a quote that reminds me of us: "They slipped briskly into an intimacy from which they never recovered."

When you told me you loved me last week, the—

I whirl in my seat. "This is when you told her you loved her?"

Theo snorts. "You say that like you didn't know it was coming."

"Excuse me, this is a huge moment."

He gives me a sardonic look. "We're on a road trip that's following the honeymoon they never had. Mentally prepare yourself for the rest, Shep."

I shoot an aggrieved look at Paul, who simply grins, then return to the letter.

When you told me you loved me last week, the happiness I felt was almost too much to bear. It's been just over two months since I met you, and you've quickly become the most important person in my life. Before that, it was my family, and now they have to share me with you, though they don't know it yet.

Which brings me to my next emotion—the fear, again. It's difficult to be in love and not share it with my family. But if I tell them about you, they'll insist on meeting you and your parents. I worry about the outcome. They'll talk about marriage and ask you too many questions. My father and brother might be horrible. They could ruin everything.

If it sounds too terrible (it would to me if I were you!), then I won't blame you for wanting to forget it all. We got ourselves briskly into this damn intimacy. We can get ourselves out, if necessary.

My heart hurts thinking about it. What should we do?

Love,
Kat

Theo's eyes flicker over to me, dark and thoughtful. Then they focus back on the road ahead of us, his right hand resting casually over the top of the steering wheel. The audacity of this man for looking so hot while driving a *minivan*.

I turn to Paul. "Well, we know you decided to continue on."

He nods. "I would've done anything for her."

At my delighted sigh, Theo groans, but it's indulgent.

"She called her parents soon after I read that letter. They weren't enthusiastic," Paul continues. "I spoke to them briefly, did the *sir* and *ma'am* song and dance, but their protective instincts were fierce. Kathleen was their baby girl, and I was a stranger whose intentions they didn't trust. We made plans to have dinner right after finals in December. They were going to be in LA to bring Kat back to Glenlake for Christmas break."

"Were you nervous after that call?" Theo asks.

"Not for myself. The thought of meeting Kat's parents didn't scare me. But I worried for her and her expectations. She wouldn't admit it, but she was hoping it'd go more smoothly than we feared. She sometimes saw her family with rose-colored glasses." He smiles. "She saw me with them, too. She thought the best of everyone she loved, and thought she could make it work through sheer force of will."

"But she couldn't," I say.

"No," he says sadly. "That comes with the next letter, though, unless you want to keep going now."

I smooth my thumb over the paper, shaking my head as I imagine Gram's hope—what it looked and felt like. How the fear probably mingled with it, making it more potent. Making it even more fragile.

"I want to wait." I love hearing it all slowly, little crumbs laid out for me to follow. I wish I could follow them forever.

Images dance through my mind as we move toward the ever-nearing lights of Vegas. Theo's knowing looks, the care he took with my knee, the kiss we nearly shared. Our moment earlier today when he shared the origin of his company's name. That break in his voice, the gratitude in his eyes right before he walked away. For *me*.

They're all tiny pebbles of intimacy under my feet, gathering so quickly they threaten to send me tumbling if I'm not careful. So much is riding on this trip: my tether to Gram, my relationship with Paul, my tenuous reentry into photography, and the story I'm telling on TikTok.

I need to be careful not to get too caught up in whatever this is—a distraction, a brisk intimacy. If I fall, it'll be scarier than my actual tumble down that embankment the other day. It'll be faster and will probably hurt twice as much.

Fifteen

I'm downstairs at the bar if you're up.

STARE AT THEO'S TEXT, PERCHED ON THE EDGE OF MY HOTEL
bed. It's nearly eleven, but I'm wired. I've been sitting here for an
hour, uploading Yosemite photos in preparation for my next Tik-
Toks. I lingered on a video of Paul and Theo at a picnic table, looking like a split screen sixty years apart—they have the same smile,
the same hunched motion in their laughter. Even their legs are
positioned the same—left straight out, right bent, foot balanced
on its toe.

It reminded me so much of Gram and me. I'd look at pictures of
us and laugh because we were mirror images, smiling our wide
smiles, that tooth-snagged one, our eyes nearly closed with the force
of our happiness. I sense the same pure joy in the connection between
Theo and Paul, and I can't wait to introduce them to the world.

But not tonight. Not with this text waiting for me.

I reread the invitation. Nonchalant as it sounds, that's exactly
what it is. I just don't know if it's an olive branch or something else.

I'm crouched over my suitcase before my brain catches up. I packed one semi-appropriate Vegas outfit, and I shimmy into it now—the black sleeveless bodysuit that dips low in front, revealing the subtle slope of my breasts, the jeans that lift my ass into outer space. I layer a couple of delicate gold chains around my neck, pull my hair out of its haphazard ponytail and finger-comb it into a hot, careless tousle. I even put on mascara, tame my brows into submission with brow gel, and use a cherry red balm to flush my cheeks and lips.

I look like I just had sex and had to quickly put myself back together. Mirror-me's grin is diabolical.

Theo said he wanted to look. I'll give him something to look at.

Instead of texting him back, I slide my phone into my pocket, slip into my strappy sandals, and make my way downstairs.

The bar is in an open-concept area not far from the check-in desk, curving sleekly around a towering display of liquor bottles. It's quiet, even for a Monday.

Theo's seated at the bar with his hand curled around a glass. He's watching a baseball game, eyes glazed with boredom. He looks down at his phone, illuminating the screen with his knuckle. Whatever he finds there—or doesn't—makes his mouth pinch with displeasure. His attention drifts back to the television.

Until it snags on my approach.

Surprise flashes across his face, his eyebrows pulling up. But he recovers quickly, and watching the awareness sink into his gaze sends white-hot power surging through my veins.

There's a confidence in the way his eyes drop down my body, a confession that he'd know exactly what to do with me. That I'd like it; he'd make sure of it. He traces the shape of my hips from twenty feet away. My breasts and neck from ten. By the time I'm standing next to him, his gaze is bouncing up from my mouth.

It pulls up under his attention. "Hello."

"Hello," he echoes in a smoky voice. "Couldn't manage a text back?"

"Figured it'd be redundant, since I made it down here so quickly." I slide into a seat, tilting my head to appraise him. The sweep of my hair over my bare shoulder pulls goosebumps onto my skin. "Unless you were checking your phone waiting for my response or something."

He grins, caught. "Such a little stalker, Shep."

I give him a cheeky wink. "What're you having?"

"Bourbon." His dimple pops as his mouth pouts into a smirk. "Two fingers."

I lift my hand to get the bartender's attention. "I don't respect a man who can't handle three."

Theo chokes on a laugh as the bartender approaches. If this were a tennis match, the point would go to me.

I nod toward Theo's glass. "I'll have what he's having."

He leans in as the bartender moves away, his shoulder grazing mine, breath brushing my ear. "Two fingers are enough to satisfy you tonight, huh?"

A quiet chuckle follows the shiver I fail to stave off. I dip my chin, leveling him with a look. "We're supposed to behave, Spencer. Don't get all riled up."

He grins. "Who's riled?"

Our noses are practically touching. He has the faintest scar just above the severe stroke of his right eyebrow.

A glass slides into my periphery—my drink. I pull it toward me.

Theo mirrors me, pressing his glass to mine with a soft clink. "Cheers, Shepard."

"What are we cheersing to?"

"Looking, I guess."

I can't help my laugh. "To looking."

With our eyes locked, he takes a slow sip. I follow, imagining the bourbon on my tongue is from him.

Theo breaks the connection first, setting his glass down and swiping his tongue along his bottom lip. I shove my hand under my thigh so I won't run my thumb over his mouth to feel the dampness there.

"Have you recovered from the excitement of today's letter?" he asks.

My chest warms at the question. Maybe he's simply moving us into neutral territory, but at the very least he cares enough to want to hear my answer. "Mostly. Is this boring for you, since you know their story?"

He shakes his head. "I don't really. Like I said, Kathleen wasn't a secret, but my granddad didn't go around dropping tons of details." His gaze moves up to the TV. "I like learning about it like this. On the road, I mean, with him."

His eyes move to me. He doesn't say it out loud, but I can read it on his face anyway: *with you.*

Another little pebble. My heart shimmies nervously. "When you say she wasn't a secret, what do you mean?"

"She was a point of contention between Granddad and my biological grandma, apparently. He met her right after he graduated." One side of his mouth quirks up. "It was supposed to be a one-night thing, but she got pregnant."

My eyes widen. "With your uncle?"

He nods. "They had to get married. I don't think Granddad was over Kathleen by that point, even though it'd been a couple years."

"I'm pretty sure Gram had met Grandpa Joe by that point." They got married New Year's Eve in 1959. If she'd stayed at UCLA, she would have graduated the previous spring. "So, not the best start for Paul and . . ."

"Anne," Theo says. "Not the best start and it never got better. They tried. Back then you did your best to stay in a marriage, but eventually it was too toxic."

"Paul told you all this?"

Theo pauses, taking a sip of his bourbon, a long, slow one. When he sets his glass back down, his eyes stay focused there. "My granddad told me some of it, and my dad . . ." He trails off, his jaw going tight.

I let my knee fall against his, just to watch the tension briefly flow out of him.

With a smoky-scented exhale, he shakes his head. "My dad grew up with parents who never loved each other. He held a lot of shit against my granddad, his feelings for Kathleen included, and aired all his grievances to me. He knew how much I idolized Granddad and he wanted to punish him. After a while the punishment wasn't very distinguishable between Granddad and me."

I rub a hand over my chest, wishing I could rub it over his instead. Is it the alcohol making him so willing to share right now, or is it me?

"He seemed hard on you," I venture. "The times I saw him."

Theo's laugh is humorless. "Still is. If I fuck up, it goes in his *told ya so* file. I remind him too much of his dad, I guess."

"What about your mom?" Theo's dad has always loomed so large that she's an underexposed image in the family portrait stored in my mind.

"She intervened sometimes, but my dad can argue a person into exhaustion, and she never had the stamina for that." His thumb arcs slowly across his glass. I can see the memories playing behind his eyes. "Now that I'm an adult, she lets us work it out ourselves."

I try to imagine how lonely that must be, to not have a reliable parent for comfort or support. It's not something I've ever had to deal with, and it leaves me scrambling for a response.

But he's clearly done with the subject. With a hard swallow, he pushes his glass away and runs a hand over his mouth, as if wiping away the words. "Anyway, that's my secret for today. If we're still playing the game."

"Always." Somehow, I don't think we'd ever run out of things to confess. It scares me as much as it thrills me. We have ten days left; how much could we fit in if we really cracked ourselves open?

His gaze sharpens at the sadness in my voice. "Tell me one of yours."

"I thought your life was perfect," I admit. "You drove me batshit with your perfect grades and that nasty serve—" He laughs, his eyes crinkling. That amusement breaks a wave of relief over my heart. "The spread in *Forbes*."

"You've got that page bookmarked, don't you?" The cockiness is back in his voice, in the upward curve of his mouth. His lips are so perfectly shaped for kissing, biting, sucking on.

"You wish I did."

Theo shakes his head, his smile quieting as the moment between us extends, then shifts. "If there's one thing I've learned, it's that the more perfect it looks on the outside, the messier that shit is on the inside."

I let him see the understanding in my eyes, even if I can't reveal my secret entirely. Then I lift my glass. "Cheers to that."

I'M NOT BUZZED, BUT BY THE TIME THEO CLOSES OUR TAB sometime after midnight, I'm soft around the edges. We moved on from the heavy stuff, pivoted back around to the tension that was brewing between us earlier.

Theo kept his hands to himself, but not his shoulder or thigh or knee, all of which pressed against me when he'd lean in to murmur some quip in my ear. When I swept my hair over my shoulder, his eyes zeroed in on that spot he claimed. I don't know why I never noticed him looking before; it was so hungry I felt it in my stomach.

Now, as he leads me out to the lobby, his palm curves into the small of my back.

When we step into the elevator a minute later, he presses the button for my floor, but not his. I slide him a look.

"I'm going to walk you to your room, since you're at the end of that long-ass hallway." He wanders to the other side of the car, hands in his pockets. Earlier, when he helped me with my luggage, the walk to my door took decades. "I'd be annoyed if I had to go looking for you because you got stolen."

Despite his innocuous words, my heart starts up at a furious pace. "How chivalrous of you."

"Only the best of intentions." His eyes glint underneath the lights. He looks wolfish, and suddenly I'm playing the part of Little Red Riding Hood. Only difference is, I'd *love* to get eaten up.

But I can't. I pinch my thigh, turning back toward the doors so I won't back Theo further into the wall he's leaning against.

The ride up is too fast and excruciatingly slow. The hallway is lined with plush carpet that muffles our footsteps; it's so silent that I hear Theo's soft exhales beside me. They're a little fast, and when I look over, his gaze moves up from somewhere south of my eyes.

The butterflies in my stomach migrate south expediently. "You're not coming into my room."

"I didn't ask to," he murmurs.

"Right. Because we agreed we weren't going there."

"Zero interest in that." He grins at my disbelieving look, a mischievous one I haven't seen in years. "I mean it. I wouldn't want to do anything you weren't enthusiastically into."

"It's not about enthusiasm."

"Right. It's about my granddad."

"It's about everything *except* my enthusiasm."

I shouldn't have said that out loud, though it's not a secret anymore. He looks at me like it was, and my body heats in response.

We're at my room now. I should shove my keycard into the slot, shut the door behind me, and double lock it. But I don't. My self-control is crumbling, and it falls apart completely when I turn and find him too close, looking down at me with eyes on fire.

"My brother made a bet with his girlfriend. I mean, my best friend. She's both things." I'm babbling. "Whatever. My pride depends on not giving in to this."

One of Theo's eyebrows arches in amusement. "What were the terms of the bet?"

Oh god, what have I done? My brain is lust addled.

"If we hooked up on a certain day, one of them would win money. Thomas already lost."

Theo moves in closer. His lashes lower with the meandering path of his gaze. The thick sweep of them over his skin looks almost sweet. I wonder what they'd feel like on *my* skin—on the back of my neck if he kissed me there.

"What was his bet?" he asks, his voice low.

"Three days. Sadie's is ten." I won't tell him about the other bet. It's not going to happen.

But this might: Theo's mouth on me. I want it so badly I'm nearly panting. I grip the door handle just for something to hold on to.

"What do you mean when you say *hook up*?"

"Why are you asking so many questions on a throwaway bit of information?" I ask, irritated with his pressing and his closeness.

"It's not throwaway and you know it. What does it mean?"

"Sex." I say it like we're in the middle of it.

His eyes darken. "So if we just . . ." He trails off, staring at my mouth.

"Kissed," I manage.

"Yeah," he murmurs. "Then it doesn't count. For the bet."

"No, it doesn't."

"And we're in Vegas, so what happens here—"

"Stays here."

"Yeah," he repeats, his voice going hoarse. Our gazes lock and he won't ask or push, but if I want it, then—

I let out a breath. "Just once. It could be our secret."

The silence stretches out unbearably.

When Theo's hand slips across my collarbone, resting there, every part of me pulls tight. And when he pushes me back against the door with the slightest pressure, I stop breathing altogether.

His thumb grazes the base of my throat, right where my pulse is beating wildly. For *him*, and he knows it. Everything he's doing is just a suggestion, the lightest touch, but he might as well be gripping me.

"Do it," I whisper.

"You," he demands, so I grab handfuls of his shirt and pull him tight against my body, lifting up to take his mouth.

He opens up for me immediately and at the first slide of our tongues, lets out the softest, most aching groan. His hand moves into my hair, the other cradling my cheek. And then he takes over, tilting my head exactly the way he wants it. Even though I started it, it's Theo in charge now.

He kisses like some people fuck: slow, deep, and dirty, with bitten-off noises that broadcast his need. The damp slip of our mouths, the occasional click of our teeth, the way we're tasting each other—all of it feels like we're doing this with our clothes off. His body on mine against the door feels like his body *in* mine in the bed just beyond the wall.

I turn wild at the thought, knowing I can't have it, knowing this is it. Our shared secret, a truth we're only telling each other. My fingers slip into his hair and tighten, and he groans so deeply I feel it between my legs. I press into him, where he's hard for me already.

"Fuck," he says against my mouth, dragging his hands down my body until they're at my hips. His fingers dig in hard, then he pushes, pinning them against the door. "Just kissing."

"Sorry," I groan.

He moves his mouth from mine, across my cheek, panting against the spot where my ear meets my jaw. "Your rules."

Right. Kissing, just this once. Dry humping is not on the approved list, but god, it felt good.

We have to stop, though. Eventually I'll remember why.

I rest my head against the door, staring up at the fire alarm blinking silently down at us. "Okay. Okay. That was—okay."

"Is *okay* your review, or did I kiss you into speechlessness?" he whispers into my neck. I feel his smirk against my skin.

I groan. "Oh my god, you have to leave."

He goes still before pressing a soft kiss to his spot. No one will ever be able to touch me there again. When he pulls back, mouth damp, his expression is unreadable.

"You have to leave," I repeat, "because I'm going to shove you into my room otherwise."

The naked lust on his face is devastating. I should have a street named after me for all this control I'm showing. "And we can't do that."

"No."

"Because of the . . ."

"The everything."

"Right." He blows out a breath, running a hand through his wrecked hair. "Okay."

"Yes, okay."

Tucking a strand of wild hair behind my ear, he says, "Okay to the other stuff, not the kiss."

"Yes, the kiss was five fucking stars, Spencer, now *go away*."

I push at his shoulder, laughing in exasperation as a smile spreads across his face when he stumbles back. His mouth is swollen, shirt wrinkled where I grabbed it. He looks like a mess, like he belongs in Vegas. He's all sin.

He walks backward as I stick my keycard into the slot. "You never answered my question earlier, by the way."

I pause halfway into my room. "What question?"

"Whether two fingers would be enough to satisfy you tonight."

It's a good thing he's too far to grab. "I'll let you know tomorrow."

And then I shut the door, locking it behind me.

Sixteen

IT WAS A TACTICAL ERROR LETTING THAT KISS HAPPEN. I CAN barely meet anyone's eyes the next morning when I join Paul and Theo for breakfast. Theo curls two fingers through the handle of his coffee mug at one point, and my imagination sets off down a long, dark, dirty road. When we load up the car to drive to our Airbnb outside Zion National Park, he catches my eye and smirks. Infuriating.

I do my best to ignore the vibes as we make our way into southern Utah. Paul hands over a letter, which is really a bullet point list of Gram's ideas to make their family dinner less horrible. It reminds me of her grocery lists, except instead of *milk*, it's *don't bring up war*. I laugh, missing her so much it hurts. I soothe it by telling Paul and Theo about the time I ran into a towering display of macaroni and cheese at Safeway and got buried under the boxes, and how hard Gram laughed as she was digging me out.

Theo's laughter sounds like hers did, incredulous and amused, and it's almost like she's here.

The landscape flies by as we drive through St. George, Hurricane, and a funny little town called La Verkin. We wind toward Springdale, the location of our Airbnb. On each side of us, massive rocks of brilliant red, rusty orange, and fawny brown rise up against the brilliant blue sky. It looks like someone took a paintbrush to every part of the earth and saturated it with beautiful, vibrant color.

It's going to be my favorite place this whole trip; I can feel it. Peace settles in my chest. I roll down my window so I can inhale it, too.

After we get everything unloaded, I'll work on editing my Yosemite photos. Tomorrow we'll go into Zion for the first of our three full days here, and Paul promised he'd let me have some time with his Hasselblad, which is generous considering I'll probably just ruin his film.

The cautious optimism blooming in my chest feels new. In reality, it's simply something I haven't had for months.

When we roll up to the Airbnb thirty minutes later and I catch my first glimpse of the home we're temporarily calling ours, the *cautious* part of my optimism flies out the window.

I jump out of the van, my hands clasped in front of me. The house is smaller than it looked in pictures, but the front porch is wide, with three pine rocking chairs lined up, colorful throw pillows sitting sweetly on each.

"Great, right?" I say as Theo and Paul climb out of the van, appraising it with varying levels of enthusiasm. Theo, of course, is largely unmoved, but Paul's face lights up.

"It's fantastic. What a find."

"And not too expensive, either." When I found it, I was so taken aback by the price that my fingers tripped over themselves to fill out the booking information.

We bring our bags into the house and spread out to explore. The main room is open concept, with the living room, kitchen, and dining room in one brightly lit space, decorated in a south-western style. The dining room table is made of roughly hewn, pale wood, big enough for me to spread my equipment out over later so I can get to work on my editing—and maybe finish my next TikTok. Out the large picture window, pink and red rocks sweep toward the sky. I press my fingers against the glass, gazing out at the incredible colors I'll get to capture tomorrow. I can't wait to wake up to that.

There's a long hallway that goes back to the bedrooms and, I assume, the bathroom. Theo heads that way, my and Paul's suit-cases trailing behind him.

Paul putters around in the kitchen, pointing to a French press. "Oh, this'll be handy for our early mornings."

"Yeah, I brought a bag of Blue Bottle coffee, we can use it—"

"Hey, Shepard?" Theo yells from the back of the house. His footsteps rattle the floor like an earthquake, and I brace myself for the problem. There's a raccoon family living in one of the bedrooms. The air conditioning is broken. A—

He strides around the corner, his eyebrows arched in surprise. "Want to tell me why there's only one bed?"

———— ~ ————

PAUL, THEO, AND I STAND AT THE FOOT OF THE BED, HANDS ON our hips.

"The listing said it was two bedrooms," I say for the fourth time.

Theo follows the script to a tee. "Are you sure? Because there's definitely only one bedroom. And only one bed."

With a sigh, I pull my phone from its haphazard tuck in the waistband of my leggings. I go to the app, clicking on the reserva-tion. "Right here. It says: sleeps four, one bedro . . ."

I trail off, my blood turning cold.

"What was that?" Theo takes my hand in his, pulling the phone up so he can read the listing details. The disorienting heat of his body and the reality of my mistake make me jerk against his grasp, but he won't let me go. "One bedroom, Shep. It says it right here. The other bed is a pullout in the living room."

His tone is mild, but all I hear is *you fucked up*. It's in my voice, not his, an unfair projection, but it curdles my stomach all the same.

I twist out of his hold, my cheeks heating. "I sent you this link before I booked it. You didn't say anything."

"I assumed it was fine," he says. "All I cared about was enough—"

"Rooms and beds for all, yeah, I got that. Would've been nice if you'd double-checked my work, is all." I press my hand to my hot forehead. I get flushed when I fail.

Enzo's voice blasts into my mind, screaming at me for missing the shot. Telling me I'm useless. Then I'm sitting in the cold acrylic chair in the HR director's office at work, my boss seated next to me while they told me they appreciated my contributions, but unfortunately—

It sounded so hollow. We all knew my contributions were few, especially the previous month when I was living in a fugue state. The flush on my face and the cold rush of adrenaline when they told me I was being laid off was the first emotion I'd felt other than numb grief since Gram died. What a way to break the ice.

This isn't the same. It's silly and small. But I wish I could rub the feeling off my cheeks so I don't have to think about the *real* mistakes I've made.

Paul wraps an arm around my shoulders. "It's all right, Noelle.

It's just for a few days. Why don't you take this room, and Theo and I can sleep on the pullout?"

"No," Theo and I say in unison.

"That's going to destroy your back," Theo continues. His gaze winds over to where Paul's arm is still encircling me, before settling on my face. He sighs, scratching at his jaw as he looks back at the bed. "I'll sleep on the floor."

"You can't sleep on the floor. *I'll* sleep on the floor."

He turns his stern eyebrows on me. "You're not sleeping on the floor."

I cross my arms over my chest, trying not to sound combative and mostly failing. Very thematic. "This is my mess."

"I could've checked the link when you sent it to me, and I didn't. We'll share this one."

"You don't need to make me feel bett—"

"I'm not doing anything." His tone is businesslike, very *get your head out of your ass.* I bet he's a badass in the boardroom. I bet no one pushes him around.

My throat goes tight. He's always been ultra competent, and in high school it was annoying but motivating. We spent years going head-to-head on everything—tennis, grades, endless verbal sparring matches—and I *always* kept up, even if he edged me out on occasion.

But this time I can't keep up. I have nothing to volley back, and that detonates whatever is left of my dignity. I'm raw from this fresh mess, small though it is. There have been six months of loss and stumbling, years of failure before that, and now I'm staring down the barrel of thirty and I still haven't found my place. Theo's willingness to own part of the mix-up is his own subtle brand of pity. It feels like a premonition.

What if I told him everything? That I'm jobless, directionless, so afraid to fail that I'll *never* have a chance at succeeding? Not the way he has, anyway. Would he react the same way he is now, with a conciliatory pat on the head? The thought makes me want to cry; it would be him giving up on me, and I don't know why it would matter so much if he did.

The room we're standing in is too small, too hot, too much, an unwelcome feeling that I thought I shook off when we started this trip, at least temporarily.

The thick silence is broken by a trilling phone. Theo pulls his out of the pocket of his joggers, checking the screen. From here I can see the name: Dad.

His expression pinches.

I'm already backing out of the room. "We'll figure it out later. I'll be out front if you need me."

But both men are in their own world already. Paul only nods, and Theo stares down at his phone as I ease the door closed behind me.

I can't help pausing when Paul's voice drifts out. "You don't have to take that. You know what he's going to say."

"Maybe he—"

"Your father's opinion isn't going to change. He wants you to do something that you know isn't possible." Paul's voice is as firm as Theo's was a minute ago. "What's most important is that *you* come to terms with what's happening. Leave him out of it. He doesn't have a say."

"You know that's not how it works with us," Theo says, voice low.

"Teddy." Paul sighs. "Why do you do this to yourself?"

I shouldn't be eavesdropping, but now I'm invested.

That's not true. I've *been* invested. I remember our game of Tell

Me a Secret last night, when I confessed that his life seemed perfect. I know now, even if he won't tell me, that it's not. But regard-
less of the messiness on the inside, he's built something amazing
with Where To Next. Maybe there's something to it, that even if I
feel messy and tied up and lost, it doesn't preclude me from eventually getting it right.

I just don't know how to get there.

The phone's ring cuts off. Theo lets out a sigh. "Okay, well, now
I missed the call."

"Good. He's going to upset you for nothing. Let yourself be
happy for a second, my god."

The silence behind the door is deafening, and Theo says in a
broken voice, "Don't say it."

"All right," comes Paul's quiet reply. "Just tell me what you
need."

"Alcohol. A metric ton of it."

"WOW, THIS IS . . . SOMETHING."

Paul steps across the threshold of the bar behind me, his eyebrows pulling up high. "Oh my."

Theo's the last to come inside. He looks around the Stardust
Cocktail Lounge, glancing at Paul. "This was really our best
option?"

"Noelle helped me search for *bar* on the internet, and this is
what it told me." Paul lifts a shoulder, which is cardigan-clad now
that the sun's gone down. "It ticked all your boxes, kid."

"I had one box."

"Then it ticked your box."

The parquet floor that stretches between us and the wall of

liquor bottles behind the bar is dull. I know without having to confirm that my shoes are going to stick to it all the way across.

Theo rubs at the back of his neck and sighs, eyeing the confused décor; there are several taxidermied animals mounted on the wall, including a tabby cat prowling on what looks like a foam core board toward a mallard duck, wings stretched mid-flight.

Peppered along the wood-panel walls are framed pictures of celebrities from the '80s interspersed with family portraits. A jukebox stands sentry in the corner, an old *Dirty Dancing* song playing. Overhead, a fan turns lazily.

But there's a good crowd in here, and everyone seems happy, which is sorely needed.

Paul leans in conspiratorially, a smile on his face. "Good enough, right?"

"It's awesome," I admit as we make our way to an empty table.

Sure enough, the floor sucks at the soles of my sandals. I nearly lose my left one, but I eventually win the war and get to my seat. Theo sits next to me, and Paul settles across from us, picking up the handwritten menu lying on the table. Which, yes, is also sticky.

We order food and a round of drinks from our waitress. Once she's gone, Theo turns his attention to me.

"Have you recovered from this afternoon?" he asks in that wry tone. But I've spent enough time with him now to hear the subtext. There's genuine concern there. I may be seeing his cracks, but his wellness check makes it clear he's seeing mine, too.

"I should be asking you that," I deflect.

Theo's eyebrows jump in surprise. "Eavesdropping again?"

"It's a small house."

"Sure is," he murmurs, his mouth pulling up slightly.

"Too soon," I say with a glare, but it lacks heat.

Across the table, Paul's eyebrows raise slowly, and he pulls out his phone, tapping at the screen to show he's minding his business.

"Is your dad causing waves?" I venture. Theo confided in me the other night; maybe he needs it now, too.

He leans back, eyeing me. "You really were listening."

My cheeks heat as our waitress returns, setting down our beers. "Small house, I told you. Is he trying to get involved in your work issue?"

"He was our first investor and is still . . . enthusiastic." Theo's choosing his words carefully. He takes a sip of beer, and his mouth comes back glossy, a speck of foam clinging to the peak of his top lip. "Just wanted to give me advice, you know. Real caring shit."

"Advice on your work issue?"

He looks down at the table, his mouth flattening. "Yeah, Anton likes to give him all the insider info, even though he's not technically involved. They've got a cozy father-son vibe."

My heart drops.

Theo must see my concern, because he frowns. "Wipe the pity off your face, Shepard. It's not a big deal. He has opinions. Sometimes I have to hear them. Doesn't matter to me."

"Teddy," Paul says quietly.

"I don't pity you," I insist. "They're shitty, your dad and especially Anton. It's *your* business, no matter how much your dad invested early on. He should stay out of it, and Anton should respect your place in the company."

The grief in his eyes is there and gone, but I see it because I'm close enough to. Because I've felt it, too.

I just don't know *why* it's there.

The arrival of dinner breaks up our conversation. Paul and I exchange a look and we make the same wordless decision simultaneously. The rest of this night is going to be lighter. We're going to recapture our peace. I'm going to make Theo forget. Maybe even smile.

And I'm not going to think about why I want to be the one to put it there.

Seventeen

I PULL MY HAIR INTO A PONYTAIL, WAVING MY HANDS IN front of my flushed face. "You're an absolute machine. I can't keep up with you."

Paul has expertly led me through five songs, singing along with all of the classics we've queued up. Despite our attempts, Theo's merely been a spectator, nursing his first beer while his granddad and I tear up the dance floor. But that smile is there, the dimple popping every time we make eye contact, which is nearly constant. His eyes are often warm, sometimes heated, as he watches me with avid interest.

"Oh, I love dancing," Paul says, pulling me out of the snare of Theo's dusky eyes. "One more song and then I'll hand you over to Teddy."

"Granddad—" Theo begins, but Paul holds up a hand.

"You owe Noelle a dance. I hope you've been taking notes on how it's done."

Theo laughs, shaking his head. "You're such a pain in the ass."

But Theo's smile quiets when I slip my hand into Paul's, and he frames us up. My heart feels too big for my body from that look on his face, from thinking about Theo's arms around me.

The jukebox clicks quietly, indicating it's queuing up the next song. When it comes on, I gasp. "*Oh.*"

"What is it?" Paul asks as we begin to sway.

I can't breathe through the aching. "Gram's favorite song."

Paul makes a soothing sound. Theo's expression turns intent, and he curls his hand around the back of his chair, like he's going to get up. But he doesn't; Paul's got me.

Etta James's "A Sunday Kind of Love" wafts out of the jukebox. Gram and Grandpa Joe used to dance to it all the time. Now, with Paul's paper-skinned hand gripping mine, the slight stutter in his otherwise graceful steps, I'm overwhelmed with emotion for the grandparents I was never prepared to lose. It hits me like grief often does, a wave that drowns me.

But breaking the surface is relief mixed with the joy of being here with Paul. With Theo. Being pulled into the orbit of their relationship is like living mine all over again with Gram. It hurts, but it's a gift, too.

A tear slips down my cheek. Paul turns us just as I'm wiping it away, and Theo stands up, determined now. Paul chuckles under his breath. The transfer between grandfather and grandson is seamless, and suddenly I'm in Theo's arms. It's instinct to wrap my hand around the warm nape of his neck, to press in against his chest and let him take my right hand in his.

I close my eyes, rest my cheek against his shoulder. I swear I feel the sunlight on my back from my grandparents' backyard when Thomas and I would look in the kitchen window, spying on their impromptu dances.

"I miss her," I whisper.

Theo's hand tightens around mine. "Tell me something."

I'm sinking into the warmth of him now. My thoughts turn honey-like, sticky and slow. "A secret?"

His cheek brushes my temple as he shakes his head. "Something about her that made you happy."

"How much time do you have?" I quip, smiling when he laughs softly. "I loved watching her dance with Grandpa Joe. Anytime a song came on, she'd grab his hand and make him dance with her. Even in public. I can't tell you how many restaurants they made a scene in."

His voice lowers, amused. "Did it embarrass you?"

"No. God, I loved it. They cracked themselves up dancing in the middle of, like, Glenlake Pizza. After Grandpa Joe died, I'd be her dance partner, which she thought was the best thing. Her laugh made me so happy." My nose tingles with unshed tears, and I close my eyes, trying to remember the exact cadence of her laughter. "It feels like I'm forgetting it."

For a moment, Theo simply leads me in a slow sway. From the table, Paul watches with a small, sad smile.

"Was it loud?"

I pull back, frowning. "Was what loud?"

He looks down at me, his eyes shining with mischief. "Her laugh. Was it loud?"

"Oh, absolutely."

"And did it get kind of high-pitched at the end?"

Where is this going? "Actually, yeah. A little bit."

"Then you can't forget, because that's what yours sounds like," he says. His words clutch at my throat. I stare up at him, gaping, as he moves us to the melody Gram's laughter drowned out more than once. "I could hear you down the hall most days, Shepard. Your laugh shook the walls until it went into dog whistle mode."

His words have a bite to them, but his expression is so soft it makes me want to pull his mouth down to mine. "Are you trying to distract me from my sadness by roasting me, Spencer?"

Theo raises an eyebrow. "Is it working?"

I roll my eyes, which are dry now. "It's very telling that that's your go-to strategy."

"It's very telling that it works on you."

My laugh bursts out, and I push at him, but he holds on tight. "You're ridiculous."

He grins, curving over me and pressing his rough cheek against mine. I want to tell him thank you, but the truth is, he probably already knows. It's buried in our bickering, in the small secrets we're giving away.

And anyway, I'm ready to move on. Our conversation falls away, the mood shifting from barbed teasing into something warm I sink into. Theo's body was made for mine like this; our rhythm is the same, everything lining up in a way that feels like comfort as much as it does lust.

Theo pushes me back, holding his arm out so I can turn under it. Then he grabs me and pulls me back home.

His smile is electrifying and beautiful. I've heard people talk about living in the moment, but right now I really understand it. I feel so viscerally *here*. And it's not that the messiness of our lives doesn't exist, it's just that right now it doesn't matter.

"I have a secret," Theo murmurs, his midnight eyes fixed on me, full of starlight.

"Tell me."

"Don't let it go to your head, okay?"

"Well, with *that* disclaimer . . ."

His grin is small, but it fades as quickly as it came. "You look so fucking beautiful right now."

The floor falls out from under me. "Oh." I swallow, desire mixing with something deeper. "I—"

Theo pulls me close again. "You don't have to give me one back. That secret was on me. Just couldn't keep it."

I don't know how to respond to that in a way that will keep us safe, but it doesn't matter anyway. Something vibrates in Theo's pocket.

His phone.

"Don't ans—" I start, but his hand is already fishing into his pocket. I don't need to look at the screen to know it's his dad; Theo's face says it all. His contentment bursts, a finger straight into the fragile, magical bubble we created.

"I'll be right back."

He's walking away before I can open my mouth.

Paul walks over. For a beat, we look at the door Theo just disappeared through.

I collapse into my seat. "'Not a big deal,' huh?"

Paul's expression is torn. "It's complicated, Noelle. Teddy tends to shut down when he's struggling."

"Yes, I've noticed. He's an icon among mysterious men."

Paul sits across from me, taking a sip of beer before settling his gaze on me. "It's hard for him."

I raise an eyebrow, like *go on*.

He lets out a sigh. "It's a symptom of the house Theo grew up in, unfortunately. And the house his dad grew up in, too. After Anne and I divorced, I traveled quite a bit, and I wasn't around as much as I could have been. It hurt Sam deeply, and he overcorrected with Theo. He pushed himself into every part of Theo's life from the time he was old enough to do so."

I think of my own dad, who never missed a tennis match, celebrated my wins with enthusiasm and commiserated my losses with frozen yogurt from Woody's and big, squishy hugs. Who's always let me be exactly myself.

There are ways in which I've competed against Theo without knowing, and ways I've won without realizing.

"Teddy has always been keen to earn his father's approval, because Sam holds back on praise," Paul continues. "Theo'd reach a goal, and there'd be five more waiting for him."

"Maybe him investing in Where To Next was a bad idea."

Paul lets out a frustrated breath in agreement. "I warned Teddy, but he needed the money, and his dad wanted to help him. Deep down, Theo translated that help into pride for his accomplishment."

"Are these all things he's told you?"

"A bit of it, but most of it I know because I helped raise the kid." He sighs, pushing away his beer glass. "Theo's not an open book. It must frustrate you because you are."

I shift in my seat, uncomfortable. God knows I have my secrets. My parents texted on the family thread this morning asking how the trip was going, and I could barely get my fingers to type a response.

Paul, oblivious to my inner turmoil, goes on. "I'm telling you this because Theo shares things with you."

I blink over at him, disbelieving. "Barely."

"More than you think. You have a bond because of me and Kat, but you also have your own. I see it."

The eager look on his face is why our kiss in Vegas has to be the first and last. There's an intimacy being built between us, though it's very much one step forward, two steps back, and Paul sees it. He's tied some hope to it, like *I* can somehow contribute to Theo's happiness. But I can't. I can't even contribute to my own.

Theo pushes the door open, pocketing his phone. Even with

the glower on his face, he's a light source. I lift toward him like a thirsty flower.

He walks right past us to the rickety bar with the equally rickety bartender behind it. I don't hear what he tells the guy, but a minute later a shot glass is set in front of him.

Theo drinks the shot. It's not a quick toss down his throat; it's a slow pour, like he's shoring himself up.

I can almost feel the burn in my throat, racing down my stomach, the acidic turn there from bad news and alcohol. I got drunk the day I was laid off, threw up in the bushes outside the apartment I had to move out of a month later.

I'm out of my seat before I can overthink it. Across the sticky floor before I can decide what I'm going to say. He helped me earlier when the grief got too heavy. Maybe I can do the same.

Theo gives me a sideways glance as I lean up against the bar, ultra casual, my eyes moving over the liquor bottle display. "You want to talk about it?"

He shakes his head.

"Okay, I expected that. I did see Radiohead on the jukebox if you're in the market for a mood-enhancing soundtrack." I pull two quarters out of my pocket, letting them rest on my palm. "On me."

He stares down at the quarters. "I don't need this."

"What? Money for your favorite sad boy music?"

"A distraction."

"I'm repaying the favor," I say, making a loose fist and jingling the change. "Literally and figuratively. You saved my mood earlier, I'm here to save yours."

He flags down the bartender and orders another shot. Finally, he looks at me, but barely. "My mood is unsavable, Shepard. Spare yourself and go hang out with my granddad."

His rebuff stings. It twists my concern into something uncomfortable and hot. Paul said he shares things with me, but it's not much. Sometimes he'll throw me a crumb, but what do I really know about him beyond things I learned ten years ago?

He's Theo Spencer, and any problem he has he can figure out on his own. I'm Noelle Shepard, who needs someone to come in and rescue her when she cries over a song that her grandma loved. The difference is clear.

He must see me shutting down as I realize that I'm not going to get anywhere with him tonight. His mouth presses into a thin line, and he looks down at the counter.

I push off the bar, waiting for a response I know won't come. "Come get us when you're ready to leave."

———〜———

IT'S FOUR A.M. AND I CAN'T SLEEP. THEO IS CURLED UP ON THE floor, facing the wall. He drank steadily for another thirty minutes after he stonewalled me, then stumbled out the door.

"I guess that's our cue to leave," I grumbled. The ride home was thick with silence.

I worried I'd have to help him get ready for bed, but he clanked and stumbled around in the bathroom before coming out with gym shorts on. I watched him while he wrangled extra bedding out of the linen closet and arranged it haphazardly on the carpet.

"You don't have to sleep on the floor."

He stopped, his back to me, and for a second I thought he'd capitulate. But then he shook his head, dropped to his knees, and wrapped the blanket around his body before stretching out. Five minutes later, he was snoring softly, and I was staring at the ceiling.

I fell asleep, but my restlessness woke me. For lack of anything better to do, I pull up TikTok and rewatch my videos, eyes filling at the pictures of Gram, the map, this introduction to their story I'm still learning.

I have to remember why I'm here. This is the story that matters, not whether Theo wants to pour his heart out to me. I've started to mistake our parallel paths on this journey for something it isn't. I can't keep doing that.

With a sigh, I kick off my covers and roll out of bed, grimacing when the mattress squeaks. But Theo is out like a light. His shoulders are bare, curving over the top of the blanket, hair mussed and dark against the white pillowcase. I grab my phone and the duvet from the bed. This room feels too small with both of us in here.

It's cold outside, the air like soothing fingers brushing over my flushed cheeks. I drop into one of the rocking chairs and lean my head back, staring up at the velvet sky.

The peace that settled over me driving here has gone and come back two times over. Now, tracing my eyes across the stars above, I urge the feeling back into my chest where that ache never really leaves me.

But the peace is gone now, in its place that grief that always lingers.

"Gram," I whisper up at the sky. "Where are you?"

The air is still. Not even a breeze.

She's not here, I know it. But in case she's somewhere, I start talking. "Your favorite song played at this bar I went to tonight, and it hurt thinking of you and Grandpa. But then a boy started dancing with me, and it hurt a little less."

I wipe impatiently at a tear. "I have unfortunate news there: I like him." I point up at the sky. "Don't tell anyone, okay? This is a secret. It's complicated and it can't go anywhere. Paul's his granddad—weird, I know, but stay with me—and he's traveling with us while Paul tells me your love story, the one *you* never told me." Wet emotion soaks into every word. "I like Paul, too. I don't have any of you left, and he's so nice. I get why you fell in love with him, although I'm still learning why you didn't end up together."

A star winks down at me. Realistically I know it's probably a plane, but I look for her everywhere, always.

"I'm afraid that once this trip is over, I'm going to go back to not knowing him." I don't even know who I'm talking about, Paul or Theo or both of them. "I'm really tired of losing people I care about."

It's so silent. It infuriates me that she can just be *gone*. That she left me like this, floundering for answers, talking to the sky.

I cover my face with my hands, my palms pressing against wet skin. "God. I don't know what I'm doing, Gram. Please help me."

Nothing. *Nothing.*

My eyes fill with tears. I want to scream. Instead I sigh, standing up.

But then my phone buzzes, slipping off the duvet wrapped around me. It clatters onto the wood porch, buzzing again.

I pick it up, illuminating the screen. It's an alert for a TikTok DM. Curiosity piqued, I open it.

> I watched the videos about your grandma. Omg, incredible! I also looked back on your feed and your older photos are amazing too. Have you gone to Yosemite yet? I'm looking for a birthday gift for my mom next month—she loves Yosemite and has been looking for the perfect prints to put in her house. Pls let me know if I can buy some!

My heart races. Is this a sign or coincidence? If Gram had the ability to communicate with me from wherever she is, would it really be through a TikTok DM?

The uncanny timing is undeniable, though. I'm so desperate for any glimpse of her, even this way, that I tell myself it's possible.

The urge to create something new sneaks into my veins. If Gram were truly here, she'd encourage me to do it.

It's why I creep back into the house to get my laptop, then sit on the porch for an hour, maybe longer, sending shots to my phone. I compile them into a sixty-second clip that showcases my best edited photos of our time in Yosemite.

Once that's done, I respond to the DM with a link to the video so she can see some of the pictures I've taken. I volunteer to send her additional watermarked photos if none of the ones in the video pique her interest, and I only pause for a beat before hitting send. The adrenaline and vulnerability hit me like a wave as it hurls through space to land in a stranger's inbox.

It's been so long since I've shared my work with anyone. I forgot what it's like, how terrifying it is. How it strips you right down to the bones. I forgot, too, how good it can feel to hear *I like what you did.*

A small step, but it's a step nonetheless, and the heaviness in my chest lifts, just a little bit.

There's one thing still weighing me down: I want to end the night with Theo smiling instead of shutting me out. It should've gone that way—me with salt on my skin from hours of dancing against Theo's body, my limbs stretched and tired, mind cloudless.

My thoughts drift to that video of him and Paul at the picnic table in Yosemite, Theo's head thrown back in laughter. I imagine what it would look like if I made him laugh like that, and how it would feel.

I want to memorialize it. Isn't that the magic of capturing moments like that? The ability to go back and visit that exact time again and again? I certainly will.

I stitch together that video with a couple others, including one of them hiking, Theo with his shirt slung over his shoulder, his backpack hiding most of his bare skin. At one point, he looks over his shoulder into my camera, and he doesn't smile exactly, but his eyes are warm.

The introduction to Paul and Theo is compelling, and it's only partially a testament to my talent. It's their bond. It sings.

Everyone is going to fall in love with Theo.

That's fine, I tell myself, caught in the lingering midnight blue of his eyes. As long as it's not me.

Eighteen

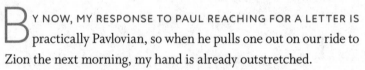

B Y NOW, MY RESPONSE TO PAUL REACHING FOR A LETTER IS practically Pavlovian, so when he pulls one out on our ride to Zion the next morning, my hand is already outstretched.

Theo's motionless next to me, his sweatshirt hood pulled over his head. I heard him in the bathroom early, when the house was still dark. He was trying to be quiet, but it was clear he was miserable.

I knew he wouldn't let me in if I knocked on the door. So instead, I stared out the window, tracing the blackened lines of the mountains, only closing my eyes when Theo padded back into the room, the floor creaking under his feet.

Paul lays the letter in my hand. "Here you go, my dear."

"Come back to you with questions?"

He grins, delighted by our routine. "You got it."

I turn in my seat—only to find Theo's face inches from mine, his eyes open and watchful.

"Jesus," I gasp out. "You were asleep two seconds ago."

"I was never asleep," he says, his voice rough. "I was trying not to die."

I hold up the letter. "Wanna read?"

He lets out a minty sigh. "It's literally the only reason my eyes are open."

I decide to let him get away with being grumpy; his hangover is punishment enough. I hold the letter between us so we can read it together, but my mind won't latch on. Theo has moved in close, his arm pressed against mine, chin dipping into the space above my shoulder.

"Can you . . ." I press my elbow into his side.

He shifts, barely, but I *feel* the minuscule smirk that twitches at his mouth. "Distracted?"

"With you mouth-breathing on me? For sure."

A quiet huff of air escapes his nose, and I bite against a smile. Amused-at-my-expense Theo is better than comatose Theo.

"Start at the same time," he says. "Ready?"

But I'm already reading.

December 15, 1956

My god, how were we supposed to prepare for that? That stupid list I made didn't account for what to do if our fathers started yelling at each other in the middle of a crowded restaurant. Or how to respond when my brother started interrogating you like you were the enemy! Asking you what your intentions were, Lord help me.

Your parents must hate my family. You must hate them, too, and my heart is breaking at the thought. I was lectured for the entire car ride back to Glenlake. I've never been talked to like that, not from them or anyone else.

Paul, they told me I can't date you anymore. They said I can't return to school unless I promise. I told them I would, but it's only because I'm desperate to get back to you. I can't believe I'm stuck here until the beginning of the year.

All I can think about now is how, in those weeks before our dinner, I'd worry about what was going to happen, and you'd force me to stop pacing. You'd put your hands on my shoulders, look me in the eye, and say "it will be okay no matter what."

I need you to tell me that right now. But you're not here. I'm alone, and I have to figure out a way to keep you and keep my family, too.

I have two weeks to figure it out and then we'll be together again. I love you. Please don't give up on me.

Love,

Kat

"Were you in LA when she sent this letter?" I ask Paul, turning in my seat. Theo plucks the letter from my hands and continues reading.

Paul nods. "Yes, she had a girlfriend in Glenlake send it to me so her parents wouldn't know we were talking."

"You must've been so upset."

"For her," he says. "I knew she must've been a mess. I hated to read that last line in her letter, pleading with me not to give up on her. She was the one with everything to lose if she didn't give up on me."

It's true. She had so much to lose if she chose him—her education, her relationship with her family, her access to Paul if they didn't allow her back at UCLA. I sense the corner she felt backed into to tell this lie, how sick she must have been, torn between her family and the man she loved.

I think about the hope she had before that dinner, the mixture of want and fear, and my throat crowds with emotion. I know that feeling, too—the plans you make, the dreams you weave in your head, only to have them break apart under the slightest pressure. It could be a terrible dinner, a family who doesn't approve. A mentor who makes you question yourself for years.

It could be a man who lets you lean on him, but won't lean in return.

Plans can be made and then just as easily broken. Hope can be created and fizzle away.

I wish Gram knew how brave I think she was for trying, even in the face of almost guaranteed failure.

And god, I wish she'd tell me how to do the same.

Next to me, Theo is silent, sensing my mood shift. He leans into me, just a bit, like he heard my thoughts. It's such a small movement, would be nearly imperceptible if I wasn't so hungry for it. But I am, so I feel it as if he wrapped his arms around me, and though I know I should, I don't push him away.

I LEAP OFF A SLAB OF ROCK, YELPING WHEN THE FRIGID WATER touches my skin. It swallows me whole, and I come up gasping. Across the way, Theo moves toward me, his naked shoulders glistening under the sun.

"Oh, holy shit," I laugh. "It's so cold."

We're spending lunchtime at a swimming hole one of Theo's friends told him about, not far off one of the popular trails. Apparently, it's not as well-known as several other places to swim—no one else is here.

It's an oasis. We're surrounded by cottonwood trees and smaller, scrappier bursts of verdant plants. Above us, the mountains tower into the sky. Voices echo everywhere, but they're distant and then gone.

After a morning of exploring some of the more popular, easygoing paths in the park, the frigid water is a welcome shock to my skin. The morning started out chilly, but now, with the sun hanging high above us, the temperature's creeping past eighty. The dichotomy of the heat in the air and the chill in the water is delicious.

Theo glides to a stop in front of me, his shoulders bunching with his short, treading strokes. "Always have to make an entrance, huh?"

I push my plastered hair off my forehead. "You have to admit it was splashy. Pun intended."

"The cherry on top would've been you slipping and cracking your head on a rock. This trip is missing a hospital visit."

My fingers instinctively go to the scab on my knee, my stomach twisting. "No need to make up stupid shit I could do, Spencer. I've already racked up a couple of actual instances."

He moves closer, his expression smoothing out into something lighter in deference to my tight tone. If nothing else, he pays attention. "What, like that time you fell down an embankment and nearly gave me a heart attack?"

"Or the fact that you're sleeping on the floor because I didn't read the Airbnb details closely." We drift to a shallow spot, my toes brushing against the rounded rocks below. Theo stands. It exposes his chest, that softly freckled skin, and he runs both hands through his wet hair, pushing it back from his impossibly handsome face. I clear my throat, blinking away. "You didn't have to sleep on the floor, you know. The pullout is big enough."

"Don't think it is," he says, his voice the same texture as the red rock I run my palm over to ground me, a velvet roughness. "I was too drunk to care about sleeping on the floor last night, but I'm paying for it now. My entire body is fucked up."

"That could also be the—and I quote—metric ton of bourbon you drank last night."

He groans. "Not my most brilliant moment."

My gaze drifts to Paul, who's across the way, propped up on a flat rock, book in hand. Though he has a clear line of sight to us, I feel alone with Theo.

I turn back to him. "Do you feel better now?"

I can't help my curiosity—or concern, though it'll probably be rebuffed.

His face wipes clean of its small smile, his eyebrows cinching back into the frown that's been his constant companion today.

My heart sinks. I start turning away in anticipation of him shutting me down. I don't want to look at his face when he does it. I don't want him to see how much it affects me that I can't get to him.

"Shepard," he says just as I start to swim away.

I glance over my shoulder, raising an eyebrow. He looks nervous, but something in his gaze is fortified.

"Can we play our game?"

It's my game with Gram, but the truth is, playing it with Theo keeps it alive. And if he's going to hand me a secret right now, he can call it ours all he wants.

"Okay," I murmur. "Tell me a secret."

He wipes a hand over his mouth. Delicate water drops shift all over his skin, clinging desperately to his eyelashes and hair, collecting in the soft hollows of his collarbones and rolling down his shoulders, his chest. They touch him everywhere I want to. I resist the urge to press my finger against every one, wipe them away so all he feels is *my* touch.

"I'm stressed because they're—uh, Where To Next's business model is shifting. We had investors come in last year and buy a majority stake of the company, and—" He lets out a dejected sigh. I move closer, the water lapping gently at my skin, and he watches my approach. "Any way I describe it will be a massive understatement, but to give you an example, the off-season deals will go away eventually."

"What!" I exclaim. "That's the best part."

Theo's expression twists. "I know. If the projections hold, then we'll recoup whatever losses we suffer with VIP packages and other elevated offerings. And if they don't hold, then the whole fucking thing goes down. I think it'll go one way, everyone else thinks it'll go the other." He runs his hand just beneath the water. "Anton and Matias got on board with it quickly. Really quickly."

"That hurt you."

Theo's eyes flash with surprise. "I—I mean, it could run the company into the ground, and there goes all our hard work. It also goes against the reason we came up with it in the first place. Travel should be accessible, not some series of Instagrammable moments that puts people on the outside looking in. This would make it unachievable for some of the people we've served for years."

His voice drops, so quiet that the birds singing above us nearly drown him out. "My dad thinks I'm too emotional about it. He keeps demanding that I do whatever they want just to keep—the peace." He clears his throat, squinting off into the distance. "Last night I told him he has to stop calling me. I don't want to spend the rest of this trip miserable over shit I can't control. It's bad enough I let him ruin my night last night."

Relief is as cool as the water against my skin, and pride as warm as the sun shining down on us. I get the feeling he doesn't set boundaries with his dad often.

"I'm glad you did that. No offense, but your dad's a dick."

One corner of his mouth pulls up. "Told you, it runs in the family."

Normally, I'd jump all over that, but I'm starting to see there's very little of Theo's dad in him. Paul's fingerprints are everywhere; it's just taking time to reveal itself.

"There's nothing wrong with being emotionally invested, you know." His expression softens with the realization that I'm not taking the bait. "It's not close to the same thing, but for me, caring about the pictures I'm taking means I'm doing my best work. Why is it a bad thing that you're invested? You built this business from nothing. If you're worried about its success, of course you'll want to fight it, whether it's business, emotion, or a mix of both."

His gaze moves over my face. "I do want to fight it."

"Then don't stop pushing," I say. "Maybe you can change their minds."

Theo looks down, then over at Paul, who's lying on his back now, hands resting on his stomach. His eyes are closed, and Theo's close, too, just for a beat.

"Yeah," he says finally. "It'll be fine."

It's hard to tell if he actually believes it, but I have no doubt it will be. If anyone can make miracles happen, it's Theo, even backed into a corner.

He circles around me, the tightness in his shoulders loosening just a bit. "Now it's your turn for secrets, Shepard."

I blurt out, "I'm proud of you."

I don't know who's more shocked by what comes out of my mouth: Theo or me.

"Oh god. I can't believe I said that. Out *loud*." I press my hand to my forehead, groaning. "Your head's gonna get so big it'll explode everywhere."

He grimaces, but amusement overtakes his surprise. "Graphic."

"It's true, though. I've . . . kind of followed your career a little bit over the years." His mouth curls in a wide grin, his dimple popping. I press my finger against it, pushing his face back. "*Shut up*, don't you dare bring up the LinkedIn thing."

Thank god he doesn't know about the notifications; he's already too smug.

"We fought a lot for supremacy in high school, didn't we?" I continue.

"Voted Most Likely to Succeed," he says, dryly. "Our one and only tie."

"But you won that, too, in the end." I'm being unbearably honest. But with his admission, he's showing me I'm strong enough to lean on. That maybe it's safe to lean on him, too. "I'm sure you're far too busy doing *Forbes* 30 Under 30 things to stalk *my* LinkedIn, but I'm not exactly killing it."

"You never list your titles, so I don't actually know what you do," he says. "You don't like your job?"

I don't have one. I could just spill it all right now, but that's too big. If I'm vulnerable in pieces, I won't lose myself completely.

"It's not what I want to do," I say instead. "But I've been too scared to do what I actually want."

"Your photography."

I nod. That's a secret, too. I'm handing them out now, but they're manageable ones. "I tried to make it work after I graduated, but I got burned and gave up. Or failed, depending on how you want to frame it. When Gram died, I didn't want to do anything at all." I blink, and a drop of water falls from my eyelashes. "Especially something that she never got to see me succeed at."

"I doubt that's how she saw it."

Deep down, it feels true, but it hurts too much to dwell on.

"Anyway, you've always been this bastion of success to me. You never second-guessed yourself. And trust me, I recognize that some of that is white man confidence."

He laughs. "I second-guess myself all the time."

"Well, from my perspective, to see you at the helm of this thing you built, being invested in it in every way, and fighting back . . . I don't know, it's impressive. You've always been impressive, which is your most annoying trait."

I expect him to laugh, but instead he just stares at me, his cheeks pink, looking leveled.

"There are forty other traits I could name off the top of my head," I say, suddenly uncomfortable.

He presses the heels of his hands against his eyes. "Goddammit, Shepard."

"At what point did I make a wrong turn?"

When he lowers his hands, his eyes are red from the pressure he put there. "You didn't."

I don't believe him, but he moves closer, gazing down at me with an expression so tangled I could never pull the strings of it apart to identify each emotion, even if I looked for days. For years.

He reaches out, peeling a piece of hair from my cheek, his fingers lingering. "We should yell it out."

I blink up at him. "Excuse me?"

"Yell," he says, laughing now. "It's a proven technique to release bullshit."

"We can't yell. Someone's going to think we're being murdered." I look over my shoulder at Paul, who's picked his book back up. "We'll interrupt Paul's chill vibes."

"Then we'll go underwater."

I stare at him. "Are you okay?"

"No. Are you?"

It's my turn to laugh. "No."

"Then get underwater and scream, Shepard."

But he doesn't give me a chance to do it myself. He takes my hand and submerges his body, yanking me under with him. His yell is a dull roar in my ears, muffled but powerful, like the first seconds of an earthquake, when it's just the low groan of the ground shifting underneath your feet. Right before it knocks you off them.

I yell too, first in surprise, then because it feels good. It's like my first plunge into this water minutes ago—the shock of it, then the numbness that brings relief. The water rushes into my mouth, pushes back out with the force of my breath and voice. With it, I push all of the grief of the last six months, the frustration of the past however many years, the disappointment and pressure I've put on myself. For *what*?

We come up gasping, staring like we're seeing each other for the first time. Water runs like tears down his cheeks and mine. Theo pants out, "Again."

I duck under the water with him, leaving my eyes open this time, drifting closer while we scream in tandem, bubbles rushing from our mouths. Theo's leg winds around mine, and he pulls me close, wrapping an arm around my waist. My heart races as I grab his forearms, as his hand cups my neck. His mouth gets closer, and for a second, I swear it brushes against mine. But it's just the water between us.

We come up wrapped around each other, water rushing off our bodies, gasping for air. I feel exorcised and electrified. Not fixed, but better. Like maybe I'm not the sum of my mistakes, my failures, my fears. Like maybe it's not too late to fight for what I want, if I can admit it to myself. That it's okay to have hope, to try, even if it doesn't turn out the way I expect.

I can feel myself at the precipice.

"Ahh," Theo says softly with a silly grin. It's the last vestiges of our joint tension riding out on his breath. I want to taste it on his mouth.

Instead, knowing we have an audience of one, I laugh and shake my head, reluctantly untangling my body from his. "That was the weirdest end to Tell Me a Secret ever."

"Do you feel better?" Theo's hand slipping from my neck is our last connection point, and the slide of his skin lifts the hairs on my body more effectively than the frigid water we're in.

I nod, unable to break my gaze from his. Beneath the surface, his knee bumps mine. Now that we've achieved emotional release, I'm hyperaware of how physically close we were. How close we still are. "You?"

"Right now, yeah."

Paul's voice carries on a sudden soft breeze, breaking our staring contest. "Take heart, you two. Nothing lasts forever."

Theo and I turn back to Paul, where he's lounging on the rock, camera in hand. "Is that a good thing or a bad thing?"

Paul smiles, a quiet one, as he brings the camera to his face and snaps a shot. "Both."

Nineteen

CAN'T LET YOU SLEEP ON THE FLOOR."

Theo looks over his shoulder from his crouched position. "What do you mean?" But his gaze drifts to the empty space next to me.

I've been pretending to busy myself with TikTok, reading and responding to comments from my videos. But so many of them are thirsty comments about Theo, and it just brings me back to him.

God, do I get it. If they could see him now, bent over the blanket he's trying to smooth out in low-slung gym shorts and a shirt so threadbare the golden hue of his skin shows in diffused patches, that thirst would multiply. They'd be screaming at me to tell him to get in this bed. They're already screaming at me to hook up with him, date him, fall in love with him.

I can't do that. But there's a lot of space between here and love where we could play.

"I can't let you continue fucking up your body in good conscience. I felt bad about it last night, and tonight it's extra absurd."

He stands and turns, hands on his lean hips. "Why absurd?"

I give him a look. His tiny smirk reveals he knows exactly why. I can't give what shifted between us today a name, but now it's as emotional as it is physical. I crave both things with him.

Maybe he craves it, too. He picks his pillow up and pads over, pausing at the bed's edge. He looms there, chin dipped toward his chest as our eyes lock.

"Are you sure?"

I let out a breath, pulling down the covers on his side. "Rarely, but about this, yes."

I'm wearing the shorts he mistook as underwear the other night, and his gaze goes dark taking them in, just before the room goes dark when he turns off the lamp.

Sight is replaced by sound: The brush of his skin against the sheet as he slips into bed. The rustle of the covers when he pulls them over both of us. The squeak of the mattress springs adjusting to his weight. The damp parting of his lips and his soft inhale.

It's been a long time since I've had someone I cared about in my bed, three years since my last relationship. Having Theo next to me, feeling the heat and weight of his body is unbearably intimate. That it's *Theo*, the boy who occupied so many of my thoughts a decade ago, the man who's turning everything upside down now, makes the moment surreal. It's so coincidental that I'm starting to think it can't be anything but inevitable.

"Good night," I whisper, lit up with awareness. I won't sleep for hours.

He lets out a breath. "'Night."

Even minutes later, my heart is beating too hard to close my eyes. It's the same sensation I felt leaping into the water, that heady rush of adrenaline. But I have nowhere to expend it, so it just keeps pulsing through my veins in an endless cycle of anticipation.

I shift my head the barest inch to see if Theo's asleep, only to find him looking at me, his eyes glittering in the darkness. The rush becomes a wave. I'm underwater again, but my scream's caught in my throat. "What?"

"I don't know," he murmurs. "You."

It's the way he says it, stripped bare, that has me turning fully. I press my lips together, waiting for him to go on.

He does. "You said I didn't have to sleep on the floor last night, but I stayed there because I wanted the alternative too much. To-night, I told myself if you said it again, I'd ignore it like I did last night."

"Why?"

"Because I want it too much," he repeats. "And after Vegas, we modified the truce—"

"Yeah, well, I think the truce is broken." We crossed a line earlier. Or maybe we stepped into a bubble where we aren't who we were ten years ago. We aren't even who we were two weeks ago. "I needed that earlier. The yelling with you, I mean. But I . . ."

"Tell me."

"I'm nervous to say it," I admit. Even that feels like too much.

"Tell me," he repeats, softly this time. "You're not doing it alone."

"It made me need this, too."

"What's this?"

He's pushing me, but the timbre of his voice is tight. It's as if he already knows the answer, and it's the same as his. "You, here in this bed. Us, letting whatever's happening between us just . . . hap-pen. We're both in a place where we need that, don't you think?"

His voice drops low, singing down my spine. "You know why I'd need it. Besides the physical attraction, why do you?"

"Too many reasons to count," I say, and he breathes out a

laugh. I close my eyes, pushing aside every responsibility and decision and conversation that's waiting for me back home. We have nine days left. The thought of really sinking into it, of not overthinking or worrying, is the pressure release I desperately need. "We don't have to name it. It can be whatever we need it to be while we're here."

"And my granddad?"

"If we don't have concrete expectations, will he?"

"Maybe." He pauses. "But possibly less so if we're chill around him."

"I wasn't planning on dry humping you in the van, so . . ."

"Were you planning on dry humping me in other places? Just curious." His teeth flash, almost predatory. "Besides hotel hallways in Vegas, I mean."

Remembering that—and the way he kissed me—has me sliding toward him. His features start sketching themselves out as my eyes adjust to both the darkness and his ever-increasing closeness. Finally I'm near enough to see his face in stark relief. His expression is stripped down to the naked need I feel. Whatever's in me is reflected in him, and it removes the fear.

I hold my breath when our legs brush. The heat of his skin is unreal, and so is the feel of his hand snaking over my hip. I press my hands against his chest, gratified to feel his heart beating as hard as mine.

"What are you looking for tonight?" he murmurs.

"Just you. That's as far as I've gotten."

His thumb grazes over the high plane of my cheek, and he presses the softest kiss to my forehead. I sigh out a breath. His fingers dig into my hip as he pulls me close, one heavy thigh covering mine.

"No sex," he whispers, his lips pouting over the words, barely grazing my mouth. "Not saying you want that, I just don't want to get caught in a compromising position if my granddad wakes up. But kissing . . ."

"Beyond encouraged," I breathe out, closing my eyes as his lips brush over mine.

His hand slides down my hip, and he moves his leg so his fingers can drift down my thigh, then cup the back of it. "Can I touch you?" he asks, burning a whiskered path across my cheek, to my neck, where he gently bites.

"Mmm," I sigh out.

"Hmm?"

"*Yes.*"

"You can touch me, too," he says against my ear. "Do you want that?"

I fist my hand in his shirt. It's so quiet I hear a seam groan. I want to rip the whole thing off. "Yes, I want that."

"Fuck, I do, too," he says just before his mouth covers mine. I still taste that *fuck* on his tongue when it slips against mine, and I gasp into his mouth when he wraps an arm around my waist and pulls my body tight to him, like he's planning to keep me for a while.

His hand moves up my side, fingers winding into my hair as we fall into an endless kiss. I press my palm against his lower back, feeling the surge of his spine as he rolls halfway on top of me.

The feel of his body is incredible. I've been watching it for days, striding down dirt paths and scrabbling gracefully up inclines, over massive boulders. I've secretly traced the contour of his thigh while he's driving, wondered how much the muscle arcing up toward his hip would give under my fingers if I gripped him there. I've watched the line of his biceps extend and bunch when he stretched his arms over his head with a rough groan after a long drive. I've studied the whole of him behind my camera lens. His body is all angles and planes and hard curves I've wanted to explore with my hands.

I do that now as he groans almost silently into my mouth, his tongue silky against mine, that slow, dirty give-and-take. I cup his cheek with one hand, letting the other explore the heat of his skin beneath his shirt, the softness of it stretching over lean muscle that shivers under my touch.

He takes my bottom lip between his teeth, then licks it to soothe the sting. I like the way he makes it hurt; it takes me out of my mind. It's the way we've always played with each other—a little rough, because we can take it. That he thinks I'm unbreakable enough to grip my hip that way, to grab my ass and yank me against his body makes me moan into his mouth.

"Your sounds," he says on a laughing groan. "You drive me so fucking wild, Noelle."

That wildness from him saying my name ricochets into my body, and I sink my fingernails into his skin until he hisses at the bite of it. I turn it sweet, skim my palms down his back, just so I can make it wicked again when I grip his ass in my hands, pulling him against me so tightly that for a second the breath leaves my body. He's hard everywhere, but especially between my legs, and I feel the pulse of him there.

Theo props himself up above me after a few minutes of drugging kisses, leaning all of his weight onto one elbow so his other hand can travel down, palming the curve where my neck and shoulder meet. There's no pressure there, but now I feel him everywhere—pressed against me from chest to ankles, measuring the fierce throb of my pulse with his thumb as he kisses me hard, deep, rough. The way I like it. The way I *need* it.

"Please," I gasp out.

He nips at my bottom lip. "What?"

"I don't know," I moan with a laugh. It's too much, not enough.

He rocks against me, exactly where it's too much. Exactly where it's not enough.

"You asked if you could touch me," I challenge. "So do it."

"I am," he laughs, scraping his teeth along my jaw.

"Not there."

He makes a noise in his throat. "Where?"

I could say it out loud, but I'd rather show him instead, so I reach up and grab his wrist.

He rolls off me, readjusting himself on his propped elbow. He doesn't stop kissing me; in fact, it intensifies as his fingers skim over my collarbone, down my breast. He shapes it with his hand, runs his thumb over my nipple, tipping his hips against the side of my body with a groan. It's a short detour to my stomach, where he stops, his pinky finger flirting with the waistband of my shorts.

"Here?" he asks. His smirk spreads across his mouth and mine, pressing into my lips.

"You're an asshole," I sigh, tortured. "Keep *going*."

His fingers are long, and he barely has to move his hand for them to slip under the waistband of my shorts, stopping just shy of where I need him. "Here?"

"You talked a big game during that two fingers conversation, and you're not living up to it."

He laughs, quiet and unguarded. It's so delicious I grip the hair at the nape of his neck and pull him down to me, kissing him deeply just as his fingers find the center of my need. They slip over me, then into me, and we both let out shaking groans. His thumb starts a torturous rhythm in tandem with the slow push and pull of his fingers. His tongue follows the same beat, sliding in against mine again and again.

He's pushing against my hip in short thrusts while he works me, getting harder with every minute he continues to build the perfect pressure. He listens for my cues, circling his thumb faster when I start to ride his hand in earnest.

"That's it," he murmurs. "That's good, isn't it?"

"Mmm." I grip his forearm as everything starts winding unbearably tight. "Can you come like this?"

"No, but it doesn't—"

"It matters, Theo," I say, my voice breaking. "Please. I need you to."

His body jolts against mine, either from his name or my request. "God, okay," he breathes out. "I—just let me get you there."

The intense mix of his touch, of his promise, of us finally doing this, pushes me right to the edge. "I'm there—"

His voice shakes with a heady mix of restraint and excitement. "Fuck yes, Noelle."

It's him saying my name again, curving over me to kiss me deeply, that throws me into intense, explosive relief. I release the smallest cry, my thighs closing around his hand, shaking as he gasps into my mouth. He doesn't stop, just slows his pace until I wind my fingers around his wrist, my kisses turning sloppy.

He sits up suddenly, pulling off his shirt. "I have to—"

I get a brief look at his broad chest before he puts the shirt down between us and lays back down, propped on his elbow again. He pushes down the waistband of his shorts, just past his hips so he can wrap a hand around himself. It's so dark that I can't see, but his mouth finds mine and a heady rush of lust interrupts my disappointment.

I feel the stroking bump of his hand against my hip and break off the kiss so I can bite at his jaw, replacing his hand with mine. His skin is hot, slick from his fingers in my body, from the plea-

sure he got touching me. He's so hard it must hurt, and the sound
he makes in the back of his throat when I tighten my grip tells me
it does.

"Show me."

He groans, his fingers curling over my knuckles, and he dem-
onstrates what he needs, the pace and the pressure that will get
him there. We do it together, quietly in this dark, strange room
we've made ours.

"Kiss me," he pleads after barely a minute. "Please."

I run my tongue over his bottom lip and he gasps, our pace
stuttering, then speeding up. He catches my lips, kissing me
deeply before pulling back to pant against the corner of my mouth,
my cheek. His other hand wraps into my hair, grips it as he whispers a soft *fuck* and pulses onto my skin and the shirt beneath us.

"That's it." I echo his encouragement from earlier, and he
wheezes out a laughing groan, our strokes getting slower and longer, his forehead dropping against mine.

We're both shaking by the time he finishes. Theo's warm
breath escapes his mouth in bursts, his heart pounding in his
chest pressed against my arm. Something deeper than pleasure
sinks into me when his lips press against my temple, his fingers
loosening their hold on my hair.

"That . . ." he murmurs, ". . . was my favorite shirt."

I turn my face into his chest, shaking with laughter. It's the last
thing I expect, but the first thing I need. It detonates any potential
awkwardness before it can build. I keep my nose and mouth buried against his shivering skin while he uses his shirt to wipe my
hip and stomach. I don't want to move. Ever.

When he's done, Theo's arms circle me. I shift onto my side,
sinking back into the cradle of his body. He lays his thigh over
mine, pressing a trail of kisses against my shoulder, up the slope of

my neck. Our fingers tangle together against my stomach, and I sink into the quiet connection of the moment. We've never touched like any of this, but it's this right here that makes me ache the most.

"Noelle," Theo whispers.

"Mmm."

"I love the way you say my last name with all your attitude, so I'm not saying stop calling me Spencer." He pauses and I open my eyes, holding my breath. "But now that you've started calling me Theo, don't stop that either, okay?"

I squeeze my eyes shut, inexplicably, exhaustedly happy. "Okay."

Twenty

"ARE YOU SURE YOU WANT TO STAY HOME? IT'S OUR LAST day here."

Paul looks up at me from his book. "Oh, yes, the past two days have really taken it out of me. I want to rest up for our next adventure."

Yesterday we spent the day on the Kolob Canyon side of Zion. Though we stuck to flat trails and Paul has the stamina of someone a dozen years younger, I believe him when he says he's wiped out.

But there's definitely a sparkle in his eye now as he tucks himself further into the corner of the couch.

God, that couch. If it were a person, I wouldn't be able to look it in the eye. I can barely look *Paul* in the eye. My cheeks flame at the thought of what Theo and I have done there the past two nights. My brain instantly offers memories of the confident, commanding way he kisses me with his hand bracketing my jaw, how he looks looming over me in the darkness. Those tortured, bitten-off sounds that escape his mouth when I suck on his neck, or bite the curve of his shoulder while I'm stroking him. How, last night, after a full day of not being able to touch, he filled his palms with me—my breasts, hips, ass—like he'd been thinking of the shape of me for hours.

"Shepard."

I jump. Theo's standing by the door already. From under the brim of his hat, his eyes sparkle with amusement, like he knows what I was daydreaming about.

I feel bad leaving Paul here on our last day in Zion, but not so bad that I won't take the opportunity to be alone with Theo. Plus, this means we can tackle a more strenuous hike; my body craves that burn.

"Okay, well, call us if you need us," I say.

Paul waves cheerfully. "I won't! Enjoy today's letter."

I pat my backpack, where it's safely tucked. "Can't wait."

"We'll be back by dinner." Theo opens the door, barely moving back so that when I step past him, our bodies brush against each other. He bites his lip, grinning, and I give him a droll look, grazing my fingers across the front of his gym shorts as payback. His hand shoots out to grab my arm as he shuts the door. Cutting in front of me, he backs me up against the wood, still chilled from the early-morning air.

"Guess how many times I said your name."

I arch an eyebrow. "Last night?"

His soft laugh brushes my lips like a kiss. "Right now."

"Couldn't have been more than twice."

"Four times." His eyes are fixed on my lips. I feel the bite of his teeth there, the slick slide of his tongue, the weight of him when I took him into my mouth last night. He had to be so quiet. His thighs shook so intensely, and when he came, his relief felt like my own. "What were you thinking about?"

I lick my bottom lip, satisfaction rolling through me when he follows the movement with an intensity I used to see on the tennis court. That single-minded attention waiting for a serve, for the chance to demonstrate his exceptional skill.

He's good at a lot of things. I don't hate it so much anymore.

"I was thinking about breakfast." I let out a gasping laugh as he crowds into my space, pinning my hips to the door with his. "Lunch, too. Wondering what we'll have for dinner."

He smirks. "You did look pretty hungry."

I flick his hat bill up so I can get a better look at his eyes. They're hungry, too. "You ready for this hike, Spencer? I'm going to push you. Might kick your ass."

His smirk turns into a full-out grin. "That sounds like a reward, not a threat."

"You say that now, but wait 'til we're on hour five."

"Again, that sounds like a reward." He ducks so his mouth is right there. Almost kissing me, but not quite. "But your threats always have."

Before I can process that, he rubs his thumb over my bottom lip, then grazes the corner of my mouth with his. The stubble on his chin burns my skin. And so does his hand when he slaps my ass with dirty enthusiasm.

I gasp. "Oh, you assho—"

He's already halfway down the stairs but turns back to toss me the van keys. "Let's go, Shep. Time for you to show me up."

———

"FUCK ME," THEO WHEEZES.

I look over my shoulder at him as a drop of sweat trickles down his nose. *I'd love to.*

Instead, we're hiking Angels Landing, a strenuous five-miler, with the sun blazing down, Theo randomly cursing behind me, and people passing us regularly on the trail. When the time comes for fucking, I sincerely hope it has a sexier ambiance. And less threat of death.

We're not at the terrifying part of the hike yet, but even this portion is rigorous. The trail is carved into the side of the canyon, and though it's wider in this series of switchbacks called Walter's Wiggles, the drop-off is straight down with only scrubby plants to stop the fall.

"Buck up, Spencer, you got this," I call over my shoulder. I'm winded, but my body is loving the familiar burn in my lungs, legs, and chest from the demanding incline.

Suddenly Theo's closer, nearly at my back. "Logically, I know that you wore those shorts because they're functional, but your ass in them is the only thing keeping me going right now." He reaches out to grasp my spandex-covered hip with firm fingers, his thumb digging into my ass. "Also, the fact that you're destroying me is hot."

Pride buzzes inside me. "Where's that competitive spirit?"

"Slid off the side of this trail after the twelfth switchback."

I laugh. There are twenty-one.

"And anyway, I've always liked watching you kick ass, Shepard. Even if it was mine."

"That's not true at all."

I appraise him. Despite his complaint, he looks like he could go for days. His cheeks are flushed, his forearms damp. But his strides are long and confident, and he's only slightly more out of breath than I am.

He grins, catching my lingering eyes. "Completely true."

"Not in high school."

"For sure in high school." I give him a look, and he holds up his hands, laughing. "Maybe you were annoyed by our competition, but I loved it. Either you were complimenting me in your ass backwards way, or *you* were killing it. Do you know how fun it is to see you get that homicidal glint in your eyes?"

"Oh please," I scoff, like I didn't inherit my focused murder eyes from my mother.

Theo's breath dances over the back of my neck as he gets closer. Probably a distraction so he can overtake me. "You saw me as someone to battle against, and I admit I saw you like that, too. But there were times when you felt like my only equal."

My foot catches on a patch of silky dust and I slide, only to catch myself against the wall. Theo's right there, half a second behind me, crowding me to safety. My heart races, both from the brief loss of control and from his words. From how true I want them to be *now*, not in the past tense.

"Okay, well," I say slowly, "that was a decade ago."

"You're kicking ass now, too."

My eyebrows raise doubtfully. "You're impressed because I'm a competent hiker?"

"It's very hot, don't underestimate that as a skill." I roll my eyes, trying to break free from his grasp, but he keeps me caught. He bends down so he can murmur in my ear, "Not just that, though. After I made you come last night—"

"*Oh* my god," I choke out with a laugh, pushing at his stomach. But he just smirks, not giving me an inch of space. A foursome passes us, the couple in back looking at us with amused smiles.

"I spent some time on your TikTok once you fell asleep. You're *good*, Noelle, and I knew it as soon as you picked up your camera in Yosemite. You had this look on your face—the same look you'd get when you'd volley a ball back and you fucking knew you were going to get that point. It's that *I've got this* look, and every single time you have that camera in your hand, it's there."

I swallow hard, staring up at him. There are people moving around us, feet shuffling in the dirt, breathless conversation, but it all bleeds away with his words.

"I admittedly don't know shit about photography, so take my opinion with a grain of salt. What matters is *you* know you're good, and it seems like you need someone to remind you that you know it." Theo's eyes track over my face. "So here I am, reminding you."

His words warm me, but it doesn't change the situation waiting for me at home: no job, no place to call my own. "I don't have my shit together the way you think I do."

I give him a piece of my secret to see what he'll do with it. Search his face for any sign of dimming interest, or suspicion.

But his eyes are clear, and it does something so intensely dangerous to my heart, flares it with hope and feelings I refuse to name. "Neither do I."

"You really, really do," I whisper.

He sighs, pushing back a strand of hair that's fallen from my ponytail. "Let's keep climbing."

THE LAST HALF MILE OF ANGELS LANDING IS HARROWING, SO we don't talk except to check in with each other. Theo stays right behind me as we traverse what is essentially just a narrow ridge of mountain with a thousand-foot drop. There are anchored chains to hold on to for most of the climb, but nothing else to protect us.

"You good?" Theo asks as we come to a section that's chainless, just a six-foot expanse of red rock with the valley swooping below us on either side. One wrong move and we're dead, literally.

I swallow. "Um."

Theo's hand comes to rest on my back, right under my cropped tank top. My skin is sticky with exertion and fear. "We don't have to keep going."

I force myself not to look down, instead focusing my gaze straight ahead, where the canyon seems to go on infinitely, the monolithic rocks curving into the horizon. It's so beautiful that my throat goes tight. "I want to get to the top. I'm just scared."

He lets out a shaky breath. "Me too. But I'm with you, I want to get to the top."

I take one step, toeing out to the unprotected path.

"Be so fucking careful, Noelle," he says, his voice deepening. "Take your time. Don't rush it, okay?"

"Okay." But the word is so quiet that the air snatches it away, and I don't know if he hears me at all.

We go silent, not even words of encouragement shared between us. The last portion is a straight climb up. Behind me, Theo's breath saws in and out, and the cadence of it, the fact that I'm hearing it at all, sends a supernatural calm through my body.

And then we're there. The earth flattens out and spits us onto a plateau. It feels like we're at the very top of the world.

I tip my chin up, hands on my hips, trying to grab my breath back. The sky is so close. If I could just reach my hand up, and Gram could just reach hers down . . . maybe we could meet again. It's the closest I've felt to her since she died.

I turn to Theo to say something profound, but he cups my cheek in his hand and presses his body and lips to mine. It's a soft, tender embrace. He's winded; his mouth opens over mine for a few gulps of air before he pouts his lips again, giving me one plucking kiss, then another.

"Holy shit," he breathes out. He inspects my face, devouring every curve and corner like he's reassuring himself that we didn't in fact fall to our deaths. Then he kisses me again, this time deeper. I grip his forearms, sinking into the feeling of him, the hard beat of my heart and the shaking fear and exhilaration in my muscles.

"Look at the view," I say against his mouth when we pull back for a breath.

His thumb grazes over the plane of my cheek. "I am."

He holds me in his gaze for a beat, and right then, I know he really sees me. Then he turns, dropping his hand from my face as my chest swells, curling an arm over my shoulders so we can take it in together.

The sky is an endless, sun-bleached blue, the earth split into two beneath it. The canyons on either side are an ombre of red, pink, orange, and white, topped with trees. They're massive, jagged, and ancient, layered from millions of years of microscopic, patient movements interrupted by cataclysmic events. It feels like life, those slow, steady moments of everyday routines, and the cracks made by life-changing things: love, death, other losses.

"God, I miss this."

I look over at Theo, at the wonder painted on his face. "What?"

He gestures out in front of us. "*This*. Traveling. Living. I don't know."

"You haven't been living?"

"I don't think so," he says, his eyes wandering over the view.

I don't think I have, either. It's certainly never felt like this.

I lean my cheek against his shoulder, scooting closer as his arm tightens around me. "All right, so what would Theo Spencer do if he were really living?"

His shoulder lifts in a sigh. "I'd do this, but for longer. Travel all over the place."

The image plants itself inside my head, though I have no right to think it: my sand-crusted skin pressed up against Theo's on some beach, a sweating drink next to each of us, tasting the ocean on his lips. Exploring new cities on the other side of the world together. Future things we haven't agreed to.

Theo brushes his fingers along my bare shoulder, bringing me out of my secret thoughts. "You gonna take some pictures?"

I give him a look. "Do you even know me?"

He grins. "Let me take a picture of you first. Memorialize your success at not falling off the side of the mountain."

"Just because I fell *one time*—" I try to sound annoyed, but his happiness is infectious, so I duck my head to hide my mirrored emotion, pulling my camera from my bag.

He frowns down at it after I hand it to him, until I take pity and show him where the shutter release is. "Just like this, so you can see through the viewfinder." I push the camera up to his eye and he nods, then drops it an inch, squinting playfully over the top.

He points to a few feet away. "Go stand over there. In front of that bush so you're not right on the edge."

I make my way over, unable to wipe the stupid grin from my face. Theo's adorable when he's clueless and lethal when he's playful. The combination of the two might destroy me.

"Noelle," he calls, and I look over my shoulder just as he takes a picture. I'm still startled by the sound of my name in his mouth, so distracted by the thrill it sends spiraling in my stomach, that I don't have a chance to school my expression. He grins knowingly. "Got you."

When he pulls me onto a slab of rock after I've taken my pictures so we can read the letter from Gram, he winds his hand around my thigh, securing me to him even further. He has me so fully that I worry how I'm going to untangle myself when this is over.

But that's not for me to worry about right now. Instead, I open the letters and read Gram's words from my spot on top of the world.

January 26, 1957

My dearest Paul,

I thought being with you without my parents' blessing would be terrifying. It's scary, but so much less so because I have you.

I don't know what's going to happen. We have until the school year's over before we discuss our next steps. Eventually, I'll have to tell my family, and I don't know if this happiness will last or if it'll be taken away again. I could write a thousand lists to help prepare myself, but just like with that damn dinner, it won't make a difference. Anything could happen in the future. Good, bad, who knows?

Tonight, after you dropped me off at home, I decided that I'm going to let myself be happy right now. I'm going to do this for me, for you, and not concern myself with what ifs or the future.

I'm telling you this so that if I start worrying or making lists, you can help me push it aside. Right here and now is exactly where I want to be.

Yours in this moment,
Kat

Twenty-One

I F THEO AND I DON'T HAVE SEX SOON, I'M GOING TO LOSE IT.

We spend one more night at the Zion Airbnb. With Paul just down the hall and us exposed in the living room, we're too paranoid to get into a situation we can't easily extract ourselves from. The trauma for all would be lasting and complete.

Still, it's hard to hold back, and we have to keep reminding each other not to take it too far that night when we're tangled up in bed together.

"Fuck, I want you," Theo breathes into the dark. He presses his cheek to mine as his hand makes magic between my legs. "We have hotel rooms in Bryce, right?"

I nod, too close to formulate words.

"Good. Tomorrow you're mine, Shepard," he whispers, catching my mouth with his to muffle my quiet moan as I come.

We spend Saturday exploring Bryce Canyon, and I endure endless glancing touches from Theo while Paul isn't looking. Somehow I make it through our late dinner with Theo's knee pressed meaningfully against mine, but I drag myself back to my room—which is next door to Theo and Paul's—completely dickmatized. I have Zion pictures to edit, a highly requested TikTok of Gram and Paul photos to upload, and DMs and comments to answer, but as soon as I'm done, Theo better make good on his promise.

But fate is clearly conspiring against us. That, and Best Western. The walls separating our rooms may as well not be there. I hear Paul and Theo's humming conversation as if I'm in the room with them, and all the plans I had go up in smoke. There's no way we're getting up to anything if there's a chance Paul could hear.

I'd be lying if I said I don't shed a frustrated tear or two, but it turns into reluctant amusement when Theo texts me later, after I've changed into my pajamas.

What are you wearing?

I reply: Did you hear me unzipping my suitcase?

Actually yes, comes his swift response. These walls are made of fucking paper.

Uh, yeah. So much for our plans tonight.

ALL our plans? We can still have some plans. We had plans in Zion.

I snort, typing: Paul was down a long ass hallway and we were quiet. We're talking inches here.

Yes we are. Eight of them.

My laugh echoes around my room. His comes when I text: Of course you've measured your dick.

That's an eyeball estimate, but you tell me.

I would never give you that satisfaction.

Still, when Theo knocks softly on my door later, I let him inside. Let him press me against the wall and kiss up my neck, along my jaw, hovering over my mouth until I make the quietest sound that screams my need. Only then does he kiss me, a handful of my loose, damp hair crushed between his fingers. We kiss like that, nearly silent, until my lips are bruised and my thighs are permanently clenched.

"Tomorrow's hotel better have thicker walls, Shepard." His voice is low and hoarse as he places his hand against my chest, right under my throat. He kisses me with an intensity that contradicts the tenderness in his eyes when he pulls back. "Sleep tight."

"I won't," I grumble.

SUNDAY NIGHT, I'M IN MY ROOM AFTER OUR DAY IN MONU-ment Valley, uploading photos. I click through to a shot of Theo facing the Three Sisters, a trio of tall, slim rocks rising from the rich red Navajo land. The breeze is catching his shirt, billowing it behind him. The next photo has Paul stepping into the frame, cradling his beloved Hasselblad. Theo's looking over at him, chin dipped toward his shoulder, an affectionate smile lighting up his features.

My favorite picture, though, is of Paul's hand cuffing the back of Theo's neck. Late-afternoon sunlight slices across the frame, illuminating their faces—and the obvious love between them. My chest aches; I care about these men, and our time is running out.

Sighing, I click to a photo of Gram's letter, held open by Paul, captured over his shoulder. Gram's elegant, loopy handwriting is stark against the paper, made nearly translucent in the light.

It reminds me why I'm here—for her, this secret. For myself and my grief. But I struggle to remember when Theo's near. At dinner, he sat close, and I felt the promise in every subtle touch he gave me. But when the elevator deposited me onto my floor, he only winked as the doors closed between us. I haven't heard from him since, and it's after ten.

I don't know the rules. We've admitted we want to see this

through, so what the hell? Is he waiting for *my* invitation? A *you up?* text?

"Fuck it." I grab my phone and type out what are you doing?

His response comes immediately: Open your door

My stomach bottoms out. I'm not proud of how fast I leap from my seat, but I manage to wrestle some control as I open the door.

Theo's standing there, slipping his phone into the pocket of his gym shorts. His hair is mussed, like he's been running his fingers through it, and his mouth curls up, his eyebrows set in a stern slash that goes right to the pit of my stomach. He steps closer, his hand circling my wrist.

That touch ignites me. "Were you already here or did you run when you got my text?"

His dimple carves out in his cheek. "Can I come in?"

"Unless you want to repeat the show we gave in Vegas, then yeah, you should."

He laughs, crowding into my space, pushing me back into the bedroom until the door closes.

I reach for his hips, bringing him close. All traces of his previous amusement vanish, replaced by the same hunger I feel. He doesn't tease me tonight, just cradles my face and slants his mouth over mine. As soon as our tongues touch, he lets out a low groan that's still louder than anything else I've ever heard from him. It sends a wildness careening through my blood. I fist his shirt, towing him back toward my bed, and he follows me with stumbling steps.

"What do you want tonight?" he asks, same as he has every other night we've been together.

I twist, pushing him down to sit on the edge of the bed. He goes without protest and wraps his arms around my thighs to pull me between his legs.

I curl over him, running my fingers through his hair, then gripping it just to hear his hot gasp against my collarbone. "I want you naked in my bed. I want you inside me."

There's a beat of silence where Theo's face stays pressed against my chest, but I hear his muffled "fuck."

His mouth moves up to graze my throat, sucking at the skin, teeth scraping lightly, then harder, like what I've said is finally sinking in. When he tips his chin back, the lamplight catches his eyes. His pupils are wide, blown out with desire.

"Get on my lap," he murmurs.

I crawl over him, settling my knees on either side of his hips. He grabs my ass and cinches me tight, kissing up my neck. With a quiet groan, he tilts his head, licking at my top lip, then kisses me slow and intense, in a rhythm I know he'll use when he gets inside me.

"Fuuuck me," Theo breathes when I start grinding against the hard length of him.

"That's the plan," I hum, kissing one corner of his mouth, lingering on his dimple pushed out by his smile.

"Is it?"

I graze my palm over his chest, where his heart beats fast and hard. "Have a better idea?"

He pulls back, his hands moving from my ass to my waist, making a fist in my tank top. His expression is twisted with desire, smile gone. "No. I don't."

Our mouths meet as his hands slip under my top, sliding over my skin. The feeling of his warm palms shaping my back, the incredible pressure of him between my legs and the way he pulls back to look at me, his expression in such severe pleasure—I could probably get there just like this.

But it's not all I want. I'm going to take everything I can get for the rest of this trip. It feels good to go after what I want and *get* it. Especially when the reward is Theo.

"Take off your shir—"

My buzzing phone interrupts my directive, but Theo's already pulling his shirt off, with that magical scruff-of-the-neck maneuver. I'm hypnotized by the smoothness of the movement and the nakedness of his chest.

A FaceTime request pops up on my computer, distracting me. I squint, trying to make out who it is. But I'm pulled away from my task when Theo grabs the hem of my tank top, whipping it off. I'm wearing a bralette underneath, but he looks at me like I'm naked.

"God, Noelle," he breathes, pressing an open-mouth kiss to each slope of my breasts.

I run my fingers through his hair, pushing away the thought of whatever call I'm missing, sinking into the wet heat of his mouth.

The ringing starts again.

"What—" Theo looks over his shoulder toward my laptop. "The fuck?"

I lean over, wrapping my arms around his neck so I don't fall over in my quest to see the screen.

The flashing name douses the flames we've been building, and my heart free-falls into my stomach.

"Oh shit, it's my dad." My parents have texted during the trip, and I've sent pictures regularly, but they're otherwise hands-off. Two calls in a row could be an emergency.

Theo's fingers close reflexively around me as I start to get up.

"I need to get it." I pry his hands off my ass, nearly falling off the bed in my haste to untangle us.

"You need to get it?" he repeats. He's intensely rumpled, his knees spread, very clearly hard with a swollen cherry mouth and finger-fucked hair.

I'm going to regret this. But I'll regret it more if it's an emergency and I ignore it.

"Sorry, I'm just not sure if it's—" I grab my tank top from the floor, pulling it on. "It's late and they don't normally call repeatedly."

His expression softens with understanding. "All right."

I sit down at the desk, angling the laptop so the bed isn't visible. But then I realize having a half-naked man in my room, visible or not, isn't ideal. Especially when that half-naked man doesn't know the story I sold to my parents.

"I—they can't see you. You need to go into the bathroom."

Theo blinks. "What?"

"Bathroom!" I wave my hands, panicked. The call cuts off, then starts almost immediately again. What the hell is going on? "Please, go. Now. And turn on the overhead fan. Um, in case it's a private conversation."

Theo wipes a hand over his face, dazed, but picks up his shirt. His gorgeous back disappears beneath the cotton material as he pulls it on, and my heart beats hard from the warring needs to have him and take this call. He looks at me as he closes the door, expression unreadable. A second later, the fan turns on.

With adrenaline-clumsy hands, I hit accept, stuffing earbuds into my ears.

My jaw drops at the scene greeting me: my family is crowded into the frame, laughing. My parents are seated at some restaurant patio table, Thomas and Sadie behind them.

"Are you joking?" I yelp.

"Beans!" they all yell in various states of drunkenness.

I place my hand over my racing heart. "You're drunk dialing me? I thought someone *died*."

Dad's face falls, and he mouths *sorry*, but Mom leans in, oblivious. "How's our favorite photographer doing? How's the trip?"

"It—it's great. It feels really good—I mean, it's really, um, it's been educational," I stammer, staring at the bathroom door. Jesus, I have an aroused Theo Spencer in there and I'm talking to my drunk *family*? "Listen, I—"

"Educational?" Mom repeats quizzically.

I shake my head. "I just mean I'm learning a lot. About photography and the areas we're visiting." *And Gram's long-lost lover, oh, and also his beautiful grandson, who's about to blow out my back.*

"What are your chances of coming out of this with work lined up?" She picks up a tortilla chip, crunching happily.

Oh my god. "Probably pretty good, Mom."

That part is true, at least. I've gotten more DMs from people inquiring about prints, and plenty of video comments raving about my photos. The traffic to my online shop, which I linked to my profile, is growing rapidly. It's not enough to sustain me, but it's more than what I had before.

It feels good. It feels *right*.

I swear a tear comes to Dad's eye. "I'm not surprised. Mom and I are so proud of how you've gotten back on your feet. I know it hasn't been easy."

Sticky guilt coats my throat. "Thanks, Dad. It's been nice getting back into it."

Thomas turns to Dad, sensing I need a bailout. "Can you and Mom go get another round?"

Dad frowns, confused. "But we're talking to Noelle—"

"We have some sibling matters to discuss."

"Love you, honey, see you Friday!" Mom calls around Dad's shoulder, then tows him out of the frame.

Thomas turns to me, eyes wide. "Oh my god, they would not shut up about calling. They've been bombarding me with questions, like I have a clue what you're up to." He pauses. "I mean, I do because of TikTok, but I can't tell them that."

A panic-inducing thought suddenly bubbles up. "You have to keep them away from TikTok."

"First of all, no shit. Second of all, you think they're going to somehow stumble across a video on a social media platform they don't even know exists?"

"Just please play defense for me, okay?"

"He's all over it," Sadie assures me.

"I am, don't worry," Thomas agrees. "But the chances of Dad finding out what you're doing via social media are slim to none, so chill."

"Right." I let out a breath, but it doesn't release the pressure in my chest. I've been so busy inside my bubble that I haven't let myself think of what I'll have to do when I step out of it. Telling Dad everything sounds as appealing as going home.

"You should show them to him, though," Thomas says. "After you tell him about this. They're really good, Beans. It makes me feel closer to Gram watching them."

"Yeah," I say, and we share a twin smile shadowed by our sadness. "Me too."

Sadie leans her cheek against Thomas's arm. "Are you good over there? Are you getting what you need out of the trip?"

My cheeks flush even hotter than when I was on Theo's lap minutes ago. "Yeah. I think so."

Something in my tone must tip Thomas off, because he lets out a honking laugh, effectively killing our tender moment. "You're fucking Theo Spencer."

"*No.*" I cut myself off, because, well, hopefully yes. "I'm— we're—it's complicated."

"So, you're exorcising your grief by getting railed by Gram's ex's grandson?" Thomas nods, impressed. "That's one way to do it."

"If that's true, you deserve it," Sadie says. "And I want details later."

I nod my affirmation, then turn back to my brother. "I'm not exorcising my grief that way, you dickhead."

"It's a perk, though," Thomas says with a smirk.

"If you hadn't called, it would be," I mutter.

Thomas blinks as Sadie hops excitedly in place. "Okay, well. TMI, but on that note, we'll let you go. I just have one request."

"What?"

"Sades and I made that bet about you and Theo, and her bet was day ten. Which is . . ." He trails off as he counts in his head. His eyes widen. "Fuck. Today. So you're gonna have to delay, Beans."

Sadie cheers. "Hell yes! I'm a genius. Noelle, go get your man."

I cover my face with my hands. "Oh my—"

"I'll buy you dinner if you wait a day," Thomas pleads.

"That'll cost more than what you owe me," Sadie argues.

He turns to her, placing a smacking kiss on her mouth. "Yeah, but I have to *win*, honey. Glory beats cash."

Sadie sighs and levels me with a look. "Fuck the bet. Don't delay on our behalf."

Everything inside me is craving a resolution to what Theo and I have been building. Now that I know everyone in my family is in one piece, I need them to go away. "Goodbye, you troublemakers. Take an Uber home, okay?"

"Duh," Thomas says. "Can't wait for your next TikTok, dude. Knock 'em dead."

The screen goes black, and I stare at my reflection in the laptop screen. Mirror-me looks windblown and off-kilter. But despite all of the uncertainty in every other area of my life, there's one thing I know for sure: I want Theo, for as long as I can have him, and he wants me.

The simplicity of it is calming. It frees my mind of all its other distracting thoughts, lets them drift away until only the honeyed ones remain. I stand, making my way to the bathroom.

When I open the door, Theo's leaning against the sink, his head bowed, eyes fixed somewhere far away. But then he blinks up, straightening, and his gaze heats immediately.

I reach out my hand. "Come on. We have some unfinished business."

Twenty-Two

"HOLD ON A SEC."

Theo's voice echoes around us. He takes my hand, towing me toward him, arms going around my waist. The feel of his body pressed against mine is complicated; I want to peel his clothes off and let him inside me. But I also want to lay my cheek against his chest, right over his heart, and sink into this quiet with him.

He tucks my hair behind my ear. "Is everything okay with your family?"

I groan. "They're fine. It was a drunk dial disguised as a check-in, those menaces."

"They seem great. From what little I ever saw of them."

My heart sinks at the held-back sadness in his eyes, and I curse my clumsy mouth. Not everyone has a family who cares the way mine does. I have no doubt they'd care about Theo, if it was like that. "They *are* great. Overbearing sometimes, but in a . . . gentle, herding type of way."

His mouth lifts in a sardonic grin. "Not in an *I'm going to insert myself into every aspect of your life and fuck you up* way?"

I run my fingers through his hair, following their path so he won't see the held-back sadness in *my* eyes. "No. They're pretty good at letting me be who I am."

Theo's chin dips, his eyelashes sweeping down as he closes his eyes, sighing. He leans into my touch, and I press myself closer, rubbing down his scalp, to the back of his neck where his silent tension lives.

"What do they think of all this?"

"What do you mean?" I ask, distracted.

"This road trip, what we're doing . . ." He trails off expectantly, eyes opening.

I don't know what to say, but Theo doesn't press, just waits. I can't admit it all; that would mean exposing myself completely. I'm ready to share my body, pieces of my thoughts and heart, but I can't give it all yet. I'm not sure he'll want it.

"Thomas and Sadie know everything, but my parents don't. My dad doesn't know about Paul. At least, I don't think he does. I haven't said anything about what I found. I was worried about how he'd react to it all, but I also wanted . . ." I swallow hard, fixing my eyes on the hollowed triangle at the base of Theo's throat, the faint freckles sprinkled over his skin. "I wanted to know more about Gram and Paul before I talked to him. And selfishly, I want to know her secrets before anyone else does. That was our thing, you know?"

"Yeah," Theo says quietly.

"I'm not ready to let it go. Because if I let it go, then I let . . ." *Her go.* I don't say it. I can't. It makes her death too real. I'll never hear her voice whispering the four words we exchanged nearly as

often as our most important three. *Tell me a secret* and *I love you.*
Two different things that meant the same.

I wish I could tell her about Theo. What a wild secret he is. I
trace the curve of his collarbone with my finger, watching goosebumps rise on his skin. What would she think of us? Is it too
strange that we're tied by her and Paul's interrupted love, or would
she think it was something like fate?

"What did you tell your parents?" Theo murmurs, bringing me
out of my thoughts.

"That this is a photography trip. Not a lie, exactly, but it makes
me feel like shit."

"And they support you?"

"Completely. My dad would cry happy tears if I made a living
from photography instead of—" *Staring at the walls of my childhood
bedroom for the past four months. Drifting from job to job I didn't give
a shit about before that.*

God. That's really what I've been doing.

"Instead of your corporate slog," he finishes for me wryly.

"Right." I can't hear more of my own lies out of his mouth and
don't want to think about who I am back home. I smooth my
palms over his chest, moving them up to circle around his neck.
"Anyway, they're fine. And we're getting off track."

His thumb brushes my cheek. "I don't mind talking about it.
We have time."

"Not much," I say. Four full days. Five, including our drive
home. "I'm done talking for now."

A smile curves his mouth, and I burrow my fingers into his
hair, pulling him down to me. Over his shoulder, I catch a glimpse
of us in the mirror. I watch the brush of his mouth against my
cheek, the fluttering of his eyes as they close when he touches my

skin. I watch, breath held, as his hand slides up to my neck, then my jaw so he can bring me back to him.

The kiss starts out tender, so soft it nearly hurts. He doesn't give me his tongue right away. It's like he's gauging whether we're ready to step into this different moment.

I part my lips against his, whisper, "Please," so he knows I need *this*—sinking into the physical connection that arcs between us. When his hand curves around my cheek and he lets out a quiet, pained sound, triumph squeezes my chest. It's a thrill to crack Theo open, even temporarily.

He tightens his arm around my waist and lifts me, walking me out of the bathroom with my legs dangling.

I laugh, wrapping my legs around his waist just before he stumbles to sit on the bed. Suddenly we're right back to where we started before that phone call interrupted us: my knees bracket his hips and we're grinding against each other, kissing in long, drugging waves that pause only when we have to catch our breath. But even panting against each other's mouths, our eyes locked while Theo's hands shape and grip my thighs, my ass, my waist—even that feels like fucking.

"Why'd you put your shirt back on?" I grab the hem so I can get it off him.

"Dunno, but I'm not letting go of your ass, so find a different way," he says against my throat.

The material stretches between my hands. "I'm gonna rip it off."

His teeth scrape my jaw. "It's my favorite shirt."

"Then let go. I'm trying to get you naked, Spencer. Cooperation will get you inside me sooner."

I'm unhanded instantly, and he helps me divest him of his shirt, then takes care of mine. I get stuck inside the material of my bralette when he tries to peel it off me, and he laughs, eyes crinkling. I've never heard his happiness so unrestrained. I tuck it away to remember later. He leans in for a kiss while my hands are over my head, the stretchy material binding me at the elbows.

"Get me out of this," I say without heat.

His smile grows against my mouth, and he bites at my lip, licks it, kissing me with surprising playfulness as he frees me. When he pulls back and looks down between us, his eyes tracing the curves of my breasts, his amusement turns smokier.

Our eyes meet as his hands gently grip me, his thumbs moving over my nipples. He leans in, capturing my mouth, fingers pinching roughly enough to pull a desperate sound from me.

"You like that," he says, not a question but a confirmation.

"Yeah," I sigh, framing his face to keep his mouth, grinding my hips against his.

He pulls out of my hold, ducking his head to kiss the slope of my left breast, right over my heart. Small, plucking kisses make a path to my nipple, where he licks, then sucks hard as his hand slides up inside my sleep shorts. He realizes immediately I'm not wearing underwear and the vibration of his groan against my skin is unreal.

"Lie down," he says hoarsely. "I'm hungry."

My stomach pulls so tight so fast that I almost fall off his lap.

I'm spread out on the bed in less than five seconds, and Theo hovers over me, kneeling between my legs, his fingers curled into the waistband of my shorts. A tiny grin pulls up his mouth. "Is that a yes?"

"Yes," I breathe out, lifting my hips so he can undress me. His eyes go dark when he tosses my shorts aside, taking me in.

My heart twists as Theo scoots back, adjusting into a position that looks like supplication—shoulders down, head bowed. His face lowers between my thighs and his gaze snares mine, then holds it as he opens his mouth over me.

Other guys have gone down on me, but no one's savored me the way Theo does, licking and sucking, stopping only to gasp out a breath every once in a while. His hand grips my thigh, holding it open so he can do his work.

"Fuck, Noelle." He pulls back after a time, watching the wet slide of his thumb over me, the press of his fingers as they move down to slip inside. His mouth finds me again, exactly where I need it, in a rhythm that gets me there so fast it's embarrassing. Then I'm coming, hands gripping his hair. He groans against me, eyes wild and latched on mine.

My throat stings as Theo crawls slowly over my body once he's brought me down, kissing my stomach, my breasts, my neck. I'm grateful the walls are thicker here, and that his room is on the floor above us. I don't have to hold back.

"I love your sounds when you come," Theo says, licking his lips with a smirk before kissing me. Against my mouth, he adds, "You're going to give them to me again in a few minutes."

"Always so sure of yourself." I push at the waistband of his gym shorts, watching avidly as he takes over, stripping down.

When he presses against me, both of us naked, we let out the same hungry sound. He's thick and hard between my legs. I shift so that he's right there.

His hips start to move, and he groans into my neck. "God, the feel of you. It's so fucking good. Let me do this before I get the condom."

I wrap my arms around his neck as he adjusts his body over mine, nudging my thighs further apart with his own. "You're really taking your time, Spencer. Come *on*."

"Mmm," he rumbles. "Feels like your body was made for me."

It was. My mind screams it as I snake my hand down between us. I wrap my hand around him, run it up and down his slick skin.

"Jesus, hold on," he gasps out, fumbling for his shorts. He pulls a foil packet out and, with one last searching kiss, sits back on his haunches.

This man is a work of art. Even putting a condom on, he looks beautiful, his expression taut with pleasure. When he smooths the latex down, he lets out a shaky breath. Our eyes meet and something deeper than lust passes between us. It's a sharp need, not just for the meeting of our bodies, but for the emotional threads we've woven together. Right now, it feels like we're creating something unbreakable.

I reach for him. "Come here."

He does, his hand wrapped tightly around his base before lowering his body over mine.

"Are you okay?" he asks, an echo of the same question he asked the other day after we'd yelled ourselves into temporary relief.

Maybe that's what this is, too. "Yeah. Are you?"

His head dips as he guides himself to me, as he strokes in just barely. "Yeah."

It's a gradual push and pull, each time getting deeper, but I want all of him. "You don't have to be careful with me."

He groans quietly. "Fuck. I know."

It seems to unlock something in him, though, and he thrusts all the way in, hard enough to shake us both. Hard enough to make us groan with the unbelievable pressure.

He rises to his knees, panting, one hand on my hip. The other goes to my chest, right below my throat. He brushes his thumb up the column of my neck, pressing in when he gets to my pulse point.

"Are you holding yourself back from your natural inclination to choke me?"

He laughs, incredulous. "What?"

"You always touch my neck when we're doing things."

"Things?" His hips start moving, too slowly, an unbearable drag.

I groan. "Kissing, touching, fucking now."

His expression softens into something achingly vulnerable. "I like feeling your heart beat fast for me." A secret revealed in the middle of our sex. "That's how I know you like me."

I look down the length of our bodies, to where he's inside me. To his hand, curled tight around my hip. I make a whole production of it, then drag my eyes back up to Theo's.

"I think it's obvious I like you."

He bites his lip against a grin, rocking into me. "You haven't said it."

My heart starts beating faster underneath his thumb. "Were you waiting for me to?"

His head kicks back as his pace increases, then slows again. He groans. He's holding himself back. He wants it to last, and that makes me want to break him into desperation. I *need* it.

"Because I do," I say, quietly.

Theo's eyes open, and he looks down at me, hips working, stomach clenched tight. "You do what?"

My nerves and need and arousal all mix together, making my voice shaky. "I like you."

He pushes into me so hard on the *you* that my voice breaks.

It's not a secret now: I like him, so much, *too* much, and maybe he'll ruin me. Not just because he's curled over me now, mouth crashing over mine, holding on to me so tight I'll feel it for days, but because he pulls back and says breathlessly, grinning, "I like you, too."

"I got that," I say, and he laughs, grabbing my hips to set a pace that's hard and perfect.

Our amusement bleeds away to rough groans, the sounds of Theo's body working into mine. His fingers dig into me, moving up to my breasts. He rests a hand on my chest, the heel of his palm pressing over my heart. It's the softest pressure there, the most intense pressure inside me, but his hand feels heaviest. It hurts the best.

I reach up and press my palm over his heart. It's racing. We're even. He smiles, like he wants that. Like that's what he was waiting for.

It's only minutes until I'm close. I tell him shakily, digging my fingers into his arms. His eyes get fever bright, and he curls over me, sealing our mouths together as he snakes his hand between us to get me there.

"Oh god." I groan, my eyes squeezing shut as my body pulls tighter and tighter.

"Yeah," he breathes against my ear, nipping at my skin. "When you come, I come. I can feel how fucking close you are—"

His words push me so hard over the edge of pleasure that I surge up against him, crying out. He presses his face into the curve of my neck, panting, until his pace shortens, stutters. The sound he makes as he comes stretches out my orgasm; it's so relieved, so wrung out.

The tension leaches out of Theo's body in waves, in the slowing undulation of his hips and the way our kissing turns from frantic to sated. Everything slows, and after an indeterminate stretch of time, Theo lets out a sigh, his final kiss so much like the first: tender, soft.

He lifts some of his weight off me, brushing my wild hair back from my face. I frame his jaw with my hands, pressing my thumb to his bottom lip. We stay caught in a gaze that says so much of what I can't out loud. His heart is racing from what we just did.

Did he feel it, too? That line we crossed? It didn't feel like simple sex. Then again, nothing between us has ever been simple.

My heart skips as he gets up to take care of the condom, and it's still unsteady when I come back from my trip to the bathroom. He's lying with his hands behind his head, eyes fixed on the ceiling. They move to me when I crawl in next to him, and his mouth pulls up proudly.

"You look wrecked."

I appraise him as I settle in. "Did I not work you hard enough? You should be passed out. Or incapable of speech, at the very least."

He brings me closer, wrapping me up in his arms and dropping a kiss on my head. "You destroyed me, Shepard. I'm just not ready to sleep yet."

There's a tenderness in his voice that pushes straight into my heart. I tilt my head back, searching for it in his eyes. It's there. He's not even trying to hide it.

"Me neither," I murmur. "Want to watch a movie or something?"

His response is immediate and accompanied by a smirk. "Or something. But a movie's good in the meantime." I huff out a laugh, and he rolls on top of me, biting gently at my neck. "We gonna fight over who gets to pick it?"

"Always," I say.

He freezes and then I do, realizing how that sounds. Like we have an infinite number of these days, when in reality we have a handful and then it's done.

His mouth parts, like he's going to say something, but instead after a beat, he grazes his lips over mine. He takes it deep within seconds, tangling his fingers in my hair.

Whatever he was thinking of saying, I'm glad he stopped. I don't have the right words, either.

Twenty-Three

WE GET TO OUR AIRBNB IN PAGE, ARIZONA, MONDAY AFternoon. It's an adorable boxy white stucco house, standing out starkly against the desert landscape. I release a happy breath, glad to be out of a hotel room and back in a place that feels like a home. We'll be in an Airbnb in Sedona, too.

"How many bedrooms this time, Shep?" Theo asks as I pull the van into the driveway edged with red rock gravel.

Unimpressed, I reply, "Three."

I checked after the Zion snafu. And once Theo and I started sleeping together, checked again.

He tosses me a wink that I catch in the air and pretend to flick out the window, but that only amuses him further, his dimple carving deep into his cheek. Behind us, Paul chuckles. We've kept things normal around him, but I can't help but think he's playing chicken with us. Theo told me earlier that he suspected Paul was awake when he snuck back into their hotel room this morning.

The thought of what we did last night—the sex, and the movie after it—has my body and heart pulsing in tandem.

Pushing that thought aside for now, I thread my arm through Paul's as we walk inside. The house is gorgeous and a bit of a splurge; it has soft white walls and wood-beam ceilings, with windows all along the back of the house that look out onto a wide patio and, beyond that, a valley surrounded by majestic red and pink buttes. The sunsets must be unreal.

"Don't worry, I got the bags." Theo's dry statement from the front door is punctuated by two thumps.

"Awesome!" I call back, grinning over at Paul, who laughs and pats my hand.

We explore the rest of the house together while Theo goes to the grocery store to grab food for dinner.

The backyard extends well past the patio, and we spend some time poking around back there, attempting to identify all the different plants, which sends Paul into a fifteen-minute monologue about the plants he's got his eye on for his own backyard. His excitement is so adorable that I could listen to him all night, but eventually we head inside. I insist that Paul take the master bedroom, mainly because he's Paul. Even though he and Theo have been happily sharing a room this whole trip, I want him to be comfortable.

But it doesn't hurt that the remaining bedrooms are on the other side of the house.

"Oh, I couldn't take this," he says, his eyes roaming around the large room, which also has an en suite bathroom.

"Of course you can, and you will. You're the guest of honor on this trip."

He turns to me, pulling me tight against his side. "No, sweetheart, that's you. It's been years since Theo and I have traveled together, and you made it happen. I owe you the world for letting me have this time with him." He smiles. "And with you."

I have nothing to say that won't end in me ugly crying, so I pull him into a proper hug instead.

The front door opens and closes, but it's been too long since I've had a hug like this—still strong but softened with age, with a whiff of old-school cologne—so I don't step out of Paul's embrace, even when Theo's footsteps stop in the doorway.

"Is she okay?"

When I pull back, I see the stricken look on his face. It wipes clean when he sees that I'm, in fact, just fine.

"Just having a tender moment." I nudge Paul gently, my chest aching from that hug and Theo's concern. "What'd you get us at the store?"

Theo's gaze lingers on me, then Paul, and I swear longing flashes in his eyes. But he blinks and it's gone. "I picked up steak and vegetables. We can grill it all together."

Once we've prepped everything in the kitchen, Paul stays behind to get the potatoes going. Meanwhile, I follow Theo to the grill, which is already heated up.

I set up my skewer station and get to work while Theo throws the steaks on the grill. They hiss, and for a minute, it's the only sound between us. Even the world surrounding us seems hushed, waiting for something.

Finally, Theo asks, "You okay, really? You looked a little . . ." He trails off, appraising me.

I spear a zucchini slice, then an onion, adding them to the skewer. I've made four in record time. "I can't *wait* to hear what word you land on."

He rolls his eyes. "You looked like you were trying too hard to be . . . not upset."

"I wasn't upset." I hand him the plate with my picture-perfect veggies. "Just achy, I guess. It's been a while since I've had a grand-parent hug. Paul's been filling a big void for me."

"You can borrow him anytime, you know. Even after we get back." He places the skewers on the grill, careful not to meet my surprised gaze. "Separate from me, I mean."

"Oh." I don't know what to say. The thought of having a rela-tionship with Paul without having something with Theo feels . . . incomplete. But Theo clearly wants me to know that our arrange-ment won't impact my relationship with his granddad once we get home. "I—"

"He really cares about you," Theo blurts, poking at the steaks. "I'm sure he'd love to keep seeing you when all of this is over. Even outside of telling you about him and Kat."

"He's become one of my favorite people, so I'd love that, too." I wish I could admit to the other things I want. It feels way too big for what we've agreed to, wanting to see *Theo* when we get home. Wanting to be with him. Date him.

The realization sinks into my stomach like ice: god, I really do want to date Theo Spencer. Eighteen-year-old me would be shaken to her core right now, but I *like* him, and I think, given the chance, I'd continue to like him. Maybe until it turned into something else.

Theo looks at me, his jaw ticking. His expression is searching, but he stays quiet. The tension between us grows tight, that thread between us pulling until it hurts.

I look down, heart racing as I pick up a cherry tomato, until the moment passes us by. "So, you wouldn't loan me your AP Lit notes senior year, but you'll loan me your granddad?"

A surprised laugh huffs out of his mouth. "You would've edged me out on that midterm—"

"I actually did."

"But there's no chance you'll take my number one spot with Granddad."

Gauntlet thrown. "You know I'm going to try now, right?"

"Why do you think I said it? I know you." It hits me when he says that; he does. He grins, seeing the realization on my face. "I *want* to see you try, Shepard."

I snort. "Why, so you can see me fail?"

"No." He sets down his tongs, facing me. Above us, the sky is starting to darken. The clouds are turning pink, painting Theo's face in the sweetest, softest light. I miss him already, his singular attention, the way he looks at me. "Because I'm pretty sure you'd tie for first."

He has to know what that does to me, to hear it, to know I could be in Paul's life like that someday. His faint smile tells me he does.

All of my feelings bubble up my throat, but I don't get a chance to say anything, and maybe it's for the best. Theo doesn't check to see if Paul's still in the kitchen before he leans down and presses his mouth to mine. I inhale, surprised, but he doesn't push it beyond the grazing of our lips, the brush of his nose against mine.

But Theo touching me—Theo doing anything—ignites my blood, so I grab a handful of his shirt and yank him to me. He laughs against my mouth, cupping my cheek so he can tilt my head for a better angle.

As with everything we do, it quickly turns intense, and Theo's amusement turns into an urgency I can taste. He wraps an arm around my waist, his hand fitting over the curve of my ass to pull me tight to him. I groan when I feel him growing hard, and his fingers tighten in my hair.

"Not the hair move," I complain.

He grins, kissing me so thoroughly my eyes cross, then squeezes my ass. Hard.

"You're an asshole," I pant against his mouth. "I hope you're hard all through dinner. I hope you watch me eating that dick-shaped skewer and it *tortures* you, because all I'm going to be thinking about is what time you're going to sneak into my room so I can tease you until you're begging for it. Then I'll hold out some more."

His shoulders start shaking under my arms and then he's laughing too hard to kiss me properly, so he pulls me into a crushing hug instead, pressing his smile into my neck.

"You are such a menace, Noelle Shepard," he murmurs, his voice thick with amusement. "What am I going to do with you?"

"I can think of a few things off the top of my head," I say silkily.

He growls, "I can, too."

Suddenly music is pumping out into the evening air. Theo and I spring apart.

"I found a stereo!" Paul calls. "Can you hear the music?"

"Uh, yeah," Theo calls back, his kiss-flushed mouth pulling up at the corners. "It's raging out here."

"What?" comes Paul's reply.

"Jesus," Theo mutters, shaking his head. He flips the steaks and skewers with a proficiency that's just as hot as the way he grabbed my ass, then takes me by the hand and pushes me away from the grill.

I resist, stretching my arm back toward it. "The food—"

"Can wait." He takes my outstretched arm and threads it around his neck, smiling when I follow with my other arm, my fingers winding into his hair. He circles his arms around my waist, his expression a dizzying mixture of stern and playful.

And then we're dancing. He holds me close for a few beats, and I let his body guide the movements of mine. God, we're good at this.

He either has Paul radar or he wants to douse the attraction that's arcing between us; he pushes me back right before Paul walks out with a serving dish.

I laugh as Theo spins me with the most beautiful smile on his face, then turn to Paul to make some pithy comment about his grandson's rhythm (which is actually phenomenal). But Paul's gaze is fastened on Theo, his face lit up with joy so intense he almost looks anguished.

The moment has nothing to do with me, but it still stirs emotion in my chest. The love between these two men heals something in me, just as much as it tears me apart.

The ache in my chest recedes as we sit down for dinner, when Theo slides his hand over my thigh under the table.

And later, when I look up at the sky, I swear I see a star winking down at me.

WE SPEND MOST OF THE NEXT MORNING EXPLORING THE VARious bends and curves carved out of massive red-hued rocks at Lake Powell. Theo drives our rented speedboat, sometimes racing over the deep blue water, sometimes puttering. He stops whenever Paul or I ask so that we can take photos, and we tuck ourselves into a less-busy section of the lake to eat lunch.

Paul digs into his bag with one hand once we've finished, holding up a finger with the other. "How about a letter? I forgot to give it to you two this morning."

"Yes!" I practically shout, diving out of my seat to get to Paul. He leans over with a quiet laugh and hands it to me. I run my thumb over the folded paper. No matter how many of these I read, I'll always crave more. "I feel like we're running out of time to hear the whole story. We only have . . ." Saying the number out loud is a finger against my bubble, so I don't. "We don't have a lot of time left together."

Some magnetic force in my body recognizes Theo's energy as he stands behind me. I sway back into him, letting my shoulder rest against his chest. I can blame it on the lake rocking us.

Paul eyes us, an inscrutable look on his face. "Why don't we make a deal?"

"Okay."

"We'll get through as much as we can over the next three days"—his expression softens when I wince—"but there's no need to rush it. You've enjoyed reading your gram's words, haven't you?"

"So much," I say thickly. "I knew a lot about her, but only through the lens of my own life, if that makes sense. Getting to know this part of her—her story with you—is like meeting her all over again." My throat tightens, and Theo's hand curls around my hip briefly, squeezing. "I just want every detail, you know? So I can keep feeling that."

Paul nods, understanding lighting his blue eyes. "The story will come. Let's do what we can here, and I'll tell you the rest when we get home."

A sense of foreboding gathers in my stomach. "I mean, I know the ending, but is it going to be bad?"

His expression softens. "Oh, Noelle, no. It's life. Some of it may be painful, but it's not bad, sweetheart. You and Theo standing here are living proof of that."

I nod, my throat too tight to speak now. Theo releases a breath, stirring the hair at my neck.

Paul winks. "That's our deal, all right? The story doesn't have to end when this trip does."

His words sink into me, pulling relief I didn't even know I needed to the surface. Suddenly my bubble feels unbreakable.

Timeless. I could stretch this story out for months if I wanted to. Get access to everything I'm craving: Gram's secret, Paul's friendship. Theo.

"It's a deal."

"Why don't you two read the letter, and I'll start us out nice and slow?"

"You're going to drive the boat?" Theo asks dubiously.

"Better than you could, too," Paul replies with a dimple-popping grin. "Don't forget who taught you how to drive one, Teddy."

I look over my shoulder, eyebrow raised, to see Theo's eyes roll. But he's grinning, the twin of Paul's. He's been looking happier the past few days; checking his quiet phone less, smiling more easily.

His hand traces down my forearm until his fingers tangle with mine. He tugs at my hand. "Come on, let's read this while Elder Speedracer's behind the wheel."

We settle into our seats, and I hold the letter up so we can read together. Theo's skin is warm with the scent of sunscreen and whatever level-ten potent pheromones he's constantly giving off.

I blink down at the letter, forcing myself to concentrate on Gram's handwriting instead.

April 2, 1957

Dear Paul,

I miss my mother. You'll probably think it's silly since I talked to her on the phone just yesterday. I miss her because I can't tell her all the things I want to say about you. I used to tell her everything. She'd want to know I was in love, wouldn't she? But if I told her, she'd go straight to my father.

I don't regret my decision to keep this from them. It's what has to be done, and the past few months with you have truly been perfect. But it makes me feel very far away from them. What will happen when school's over and I have to tell them? Who will I lose? I don't want to lose you, and I don't want to lose them. I'm still searching for a way to ensure this ends happily. I know there must be an answer.

Please tell me it will be okay no matter what.

All my love,
Your Kat

At the bottom of the page is someone else's handwriting. It must be Paul's.

It will be okay. No matter what.

"I feel the bad news coming," I say as the boat gains speed. "I know what happens, I know there's no way to stop it, but I want to anyway."

"Yeah." Theo's sigh is heavy. I look over just as his troubled expression smooths out. "She felt stuck. Like no choice was a good one."

His voice goes quiet at the end, and there's a familiarity there.

My camera is on the other side of the boat; I wish I had it so I could take a picture of him and show it to him later. Even if he feels stuck right now, my shot would show the miles of space surrounding him. The red rocks curving all around, the water below us, and the clear blue sky stretching endlessly above us. The sunlight glinting down on his hair, on his skin, making him golden.

I'd show it to myself, too, so I could remember this moment.

Somehow the choices I've made, whether they've ended up being good or bad, have all done their fateful work to put me right here for a reason.

My knee kicks out, pressing against his. He looks at where we're touching, then at me.

"It'll be okay," I say.

He nods and leans back in his seat, tipping his chin toward the sky.

A plane drifts overhead. From thirty thousand feet, the roar of the engines is barely a whisper. I tilt my head back to watch, pressing the letter to my chest. Absorbing Gram's energy and love.

There are people in that plane, living entire complicated lives I'll never know about, while Theo and I are down here, living the same one. For now, at least.

I reach over to take Theo's hand. His fingers tangle with mine, and I squeeze, holding on as tight as I can.

Twenty-Four

"NOELLE."

It's barely a whisper at the edge of my consciousness, but I bat it away. I'm dreaming, floating in cotton candy clouds, the sun hot against my back even though I'm stomach-up.

There's also something poking me, which makes no sense. Clouds are just air and moisture.

"Noelle."

That voice again, this time singsongy with amusement. I hear my own irritated groan, but it turns into something more honeyed when a warm mouth grazes the back of my neck. A shiver skitters down my spine, shaking me into awareness.

It's Wednesday morning, and we're in our Sedona Airbnb. I'm in bed, rays of light pushing through the closed ivory curtains. Theo is spooned behind me, his hand running from my hip to my thigh and back as he kisses along the curve of my bare shoulder. Traveling is disorienting, especially when we're moving from place to place, but there are perks. Being kissed awake is one of them.

"What are you doing?"

Silly question. I know a Theo Spencer seduction when I feel it. And I really, really feel it.

"Waking you up," he says. "It's after seven."

"Seven!" I try to sit up, but Theo slings his thigh over mine.

"Our tour doesn't start 'til ten," he says, his voice heavy with sleep.

We're going on a Jeep tour today, but that's not what I'm worried about. "Paul wakes up at the ass-crack of dawn. He probably—"

"Shh." Theo's lips skate up to my neck. He bites gently at my skin, drawing out a gasp. "My door is shut, and he's not going to go barging in there. He has no idea I'm in here, and I'm good at sneaking out by now."

"You've never stayed 'til seven," I sigh out.

"Feeling lucky today. And *very* motivated to stay," he murmurs, flipping me onto my back.

He hovers over me, naked, his hair everywhere, with sheet marks running down his cheek. I reach up to trace them, following the path until I get to his mouth. His eyes turn as soft as the early-morning light, as hot as the sun I was just dreaming about.

I love waking up with him like this—unhurried, quiet. The past few days Theo's been pushing his luck, waiting until the sun peeks over the horizon to leave me. But it's too good; not just the sex, but the after, tangled up together while we recap our day or talk about our favorite comments on my latest TikToks or watch a movie until we both doze off. I can't stop thinking about how I want this every day, without an end date in mind.

I swear I would've said it if my teeth were brushed, and for once in my life I'm grateful for morning breath. After Theo told me I was free to have a relationship with Paul separate from him, I've been wondering if that was a subtle reminder of our terms.

I've sunk so deeply into what we're doing now that it's been hard to remember what'll happen when we go home.

It's hard to remember that *this* isn't home.

I pull Theo down until most of his weight is on me, wrapping my arms around his neck. He burrows his face against my throat, pressing whisper-soft kisses there. His back moves up and down in a long sigh, and I echo the movement until we're breathing in sync.

A knock breaks the peace between us. Theo's head pops up, a dark wave of hair cresting over his forehead, his eyes flying to the door.

Paul's voice calls out, "Hate to bother you, but I just put a fresh pot of coffee out and cut up some fruit. Shall I make some eggs?"

I don't answer immediately, panicked, and Theo presses his hips into mine. "Your room," he mouths, graciously omitting the very deserved *dipshit.*

"Oh!" I squeak out, pinching his ass when he starts laughing silently. "Um, yeah, that'd be amazing. I'll be out in just a few minutes."

Theo frowns, pressing his hips forward again, sharing his ambitious erection. "Fifteen, minimum," he whispers.

"Two minutes, tops," I call, shooting him a triumphant grin even though my body is screaming for his again.

"That sounds fine, sweetheart, don't rush," Paul says.

"You're gonna get it later," Theo whispers against my ear.

"Oh," Paul continues, the smile clear in his voice, "and don't worry, Teddy. I'll make your eggs over easy the way you like them."

———

SO, THE CAT IS OUT OF THE BAG.

When Theo asks how long he's known, Paul gives him a look

over his readers and says, "Since the beginning. You've been downright cheerful."

I nearly choke on a slice of pineapple. Paul gives me a wink.

Theo's gaze moves to me, as if he's gauging what I think of that. But I want to know what *he* thinks before I determine whether I should worry. It's been a little over a week since that night in Vegas when I said we couldn't hook up. When I was sure whatever happened between us would ruin my chances to form a relationship with Paul. I thought the foundation of what Theo and I would create together would be too shaky. Maybe I thought the foundation of what Paul and I had was, too. But my relationships with both of them, separate from each other and intertwined, feel strong enough to take this, even if it doesn't last.

I lift a shoulder, like, *what can you do?* Theo's mouth pulls into a quiet smile, and he ducks his head, focusing on his eggs with his bottom lip caught between his teeth.

For his part, Paul seems unfazed, serenely crunching on multi-grain toast while he reads the newspaper.

There's no earth shifting. No avalanche of questions or concerned looks now that my relationship with Theo is out in the open. It gives me hope that maybe with time, all of my secrets will be revealed with this level of acceptance.

After breakfast, we go our separate ways to get ready for the day. But Theo corners me outside my door, giving me a long, lingering kiss.

"Gosh, you really *are* cheerful," I say smugly. "I wonder why that is."

"You knew why that was last night when I had your legs hooked over my arms," he murmurs back, pressing his hips into mine. One corner of his mouth pulls into a lopsided grin. "You liked that, huh?"

"I'd ask you the same question, but you barely lasted two minutes, so clearly *you* did."

He tsks. "Don't discount all the minutes before that. Besides, you'd already come. At that point, you were just along for the ride. Literally."

I grip the hair at the nape of his neck, just to watch his expression slacken with desire. "My point is, who knew all it took was regular sex to turn that perma-frown upside down?"

"That's not all it's taking, Shepard."

The timbre of his voice is so low I barely hear it. But the look on his face tells me I didn't mishear him.

"I'm feeling pretty cheerful, too," I admit. Our gazes lock and hold, and the warmth in his spirals down my spine.

It's not just the sex for me either, even though that part is the best I've ever had. It's all of it. I've never been less able to distinguish the emotional connection from the physical one. With Theo, one thing feeds the other. The sex is so good because the emotional connection gets stronger every day. The more he shares with me, the more I want him, and the more he touches me, the more secrets I want to reveal.

The truth is, I want him to know everything. Not just about what my life has been like, but what I want it to be. The hopes I have for it. When we get back on Friday, I'll be walking back into the life I left behind. But I'm realizing that I'm not only prepared to do something different, I *want* to.

Is it possible he wants to be part of that?

"Are you okay with Paul knowing?" I ask, testing him.

"Are *you*?"

"I think so. He didn't look like he was about to plan our wedding or anything." Theo's eyebrows raise, and panicked, I rush on. "There's no wedding, obviously. I just mean, it seemed like he had expectations from the start, and he isn't making a big deal out of them coming to pass. *Why* are you smiling like that?"

He's all perfect, shiny teeth. "I love seeing you flustered because you think you said something too revealing. Like you have a binder full of wedding shit with a picture of my face pasted on every page."

I roll my eyes. "Yeah, I've been adding to it since the day I met you."

"Freshman year, Cougar's bio class." This time it's my eyebrows that raise; I can't believe he remembers. Theo's cheeks turn pink. "You slipped on a puddle from the water fountain and nearly cracked your head on the doorframe. I saved you."

"You didn't save me, I *happened* to fall back into you. You seriously remember that?"

He grins. "A beautiful girl touched me—"

"One hundred percent accidentally."

"I didn't care. I knew right then high school was going to be awesome." He backs me into the door, smirking. "And now look at you. Touching me very much on purpose."

"Mmm." I let my hand drift between us, grazing over the front of his shorts. "A full circle moment."

Theo doesn't respond, at least not with words. Instead, he catches my mouth with his, kissing me until we're both breathless.

"I'm glad my granddad knows," he says against my lips. "Now I get to touch you whenever I want."

"Purposefully?" I tease.

He presses a kiss to my forehead, murmuring, "None of my touching has ever been accidental."

I close my eyes, my heart swelling, all the words I have left to say growing in my throat until it's so tight I'm nearly choking.

"You can have the bathroom first. Get in that shower before I climb in there with you," Theo says, pushing me back from the precipice.

"Whatever. Water conservation is extremely near and dear to my heart."

He grins, backing away down the hall. His eyes stay locked on me, so intent they feel like X-rays. Like he can see everything written all over me.

Am I that transparent? Paul caught on to us long ago, apparently. "When Paul said he's known from the beginning, when do you think he meant?"

Theo pauses, palm pressed to his bedroom door. "I don't know."

But something in his expression makes me wonder if he does, and he just doesn't want to say it out loud.

OUR TWO-HOUR JEEP TOUR TAKES US ON THE BROKEN ARROW Trail. The road is bumpy as hell, and Theo and I take turns asking Paul if he's okay. Finally, he tells both of us to knock it off, a giant grin on his face as the wind whips through his hair.

The rocking motion of the Jeep sends my body into Theo's again and again, a distracting mimic of the way we move together. At one point, he grins over at me, pressing his thigh hard against mine.

We stop at a stunning lookout abutted by red rock formations. The striations in them, which our guide reminds us show the passage of millions of years, make me feel like a speck of dust in the infinite stretch of time. How lucky that this is the moment I landed in. How temporary everything feels when surrounded by a landscape that was here long before us and will be here long after we're gone.

That day in Zion when we went swimming, Paul told us to take heart, that nothing lasts forever. Maybe these rocks will, but it's a beautiful and painful reminder that no feeling does, bad or good. No moment or mistake.

After I take some photos, Theo and I read the letter Paul gives us, a sweet one where Gram lists out the reasons she loves him. If she was feeling anxious, she didn't mention it, though Paul tells us at times she was wracked with it. I know a bubble when I see it. From this letter, it's clear they were in one.

Sedona is allegedly filled with vortices, magical, healing energy that comes from the earth itself, and I swear I feel Gram slipping her hand into mine. If everything else is temporary, at least the grief that clutches at me is, too. I let it wash over me so I can cling to the peace that follows. I close my eyes and tilt my face toward the sun, imagining it's her hand on my cheek, telling me that I'm exactly where I'm supposed to be. Doing exactly what I'm meant to do.

So, it shouldn't surprise me that when we stop at Bell Rock for another photo op and I step off to the side to check my email, there's one I never could've predicted.

It does surprise me, though. It shocks me so thoroughly that I nearly slide off the boulder I'm seated on. Theo, who's become my bodyguard against any surface I could fall off, shoots me a warning look. But his eyes widen with concern when he sees my expression.

He jogs over, Paul moving at a more placid pace behind him. "What's wrong? What happened?"

"I . . ." I stare down at my phone screen, then look back up at Theo. "This new boutique resort in Tahoe emailed me. They said they've been following our story on TikTok and are obsessed with it, and they love my photography. They're opening soon, and they asked if I could come up and take some promotional shots of their property and amenities, and create some content on my account."

"Yeah?" Theo reaches for my phone, then pulls back, silently asking for permission. I hand it over, and he reads the email, his eyes moving back and forth over the screen rapidly. Paul peers over his shoulder, pulling out his readers. I watch both men take in the information, their mouths pulling into twin smiles as they read.

"Noelle, this is wonderful." Paul moves around Theo and comes toward me, arms outstretched.

I leap up and step into his embrace, still processing what this means. It's an honest-to-god job doing something I love. I have no idea how much it'll pay—the email said we could discuss—and it's not like I'll be able to move out of my parents' house based on this alone. But it gives me a sense of validation that nothing else has in so long.

A leap of faith taken when I had no faith left has turned into this.

Paul squeezes me tight. "I'm so proud of you, sweetheart. And your grandma would be so proud, too."

My heart swells. "She would, wouldn't she?"

He grins. "Absolutely."

I pull back, splitting a look between him and Theo, who's watching the two of us. "I know it's just one job. It's not life changing, but . . ."

"A career in photography isn't easy, if that's what you want," Paul says. "But this is a wonderful step. You've made so many of them during this trip, and you should be proud of that."

It swells in my chest. "I am."

Paul looks at Theo, then back at me with a wink. "I'll meet you at the Jeep."

"Folks, we're going to head out in a minute," our guide calls.

Theo ignores him, stepping closer to me. He slips my phone into my hand, then cups my face in his. His thumb moves over my flushed cheek. "I have a secret, and I should've told you earlier."

"What?"

He shakes his head, grinning. "I fucking knew you could do this. You're so good, Noelle."

His confession is a shot of adrenaline to my heart. It starts beating double-time. "Don't go crazy with the praise, okay? First of all, it's not like you—"

He lets out a huff of insulted laughter. "What, I'm not me if I'm complimenting you?"

I give him a pointed look, running a hand over his T-shirt clad chest. "Take it down a notch with the conclusion jumping. You can compliment me, you've just got to put a little spice in it."

He course corrects. "You're so good, it's annoying."

I nod, satisfied. "Better."

"You're intensely weird," he says affectionately.

"A little soft on delivery, but otherwise perfect."

He rolls his eyes, grabbing my wrist so he can tow me closer. "You said *first of all* before, so what's the second of all?"

"Oh, right. Second of all, it's exciting, but it's small. And just one job."

For a beat, he appraises me. "You have no idea how amazing you are, do you?"

"I—" I swallow the urge to diminish this moment. I need this win, and I'm going to take it. I'm going to let him see me grab it with both hands. "I feel pretty amazing right now, actually."

His gaze turns warm and tender. I'm some soft candy melting in the heat of it. "You're good at this."

"Hell yeah, I'm good at this."

That warmth flares into something molten, and his grin grows from small to brilliant. "Let's go celebrate tonight. Just you and me."

"What about Paul?"

"Guarantee you he'll pretend to be too tired to socialize with us later," Theo says. "And I want you to myself, anyway."

My heart floats off into space. "Okay."

His gaze drops to my mouth. "I'm going to kiss the hell out of you now."

"Okay," I repeat, dazed.

He does, right in front of Paul and the family of four who's on the tour with us.

And, I suspect, in front of Gram, too, wherever she is.

Twenty-Five

"GOD, THAT WAS GOOD."

Theo looks over at me, his face shadowed as we cross the dark parking lot, hands clasped. "Request for you to say that later tonight, in exactly that same tone of voice."

I pull out of his hold, turning so that I'm walking backwards ahead of him. "I don't take requests. You're going to have to make me."

His eyes sweep down my body; I'm wearing the Vegas outfit since I have nothing else. He watched me all through dinner like it was the first time I'd worn it.

We get to the van, and Theo backs me against it until there's a millimeter of space between us. If I breathed, we'd be touching. I don't, just to watch his eyes darken.

"Shepard," he says in that velvet voice. It brushes over me the way his palm does, stroking up my neck until his hand is bracketing my jaw. "I don't know if you've noticed, but I've been making you nearly this entire trip."

You can make me for a lot longer than that. I raise an eyebrow. "You think so?"

"You do it right in my ear, so yeah." His mouth pulls up into a smirk. "I know so."

"Then we'd better go so you can get on it."

"I can't *wait* to get on it." He reaches behind me for the door handle. But instead of moving us so he can open it, he leans down to brush his mouth against mine, then parts his lips, inviting me to do the same. I taste the wine we had on his tongue, the lemon tart we shared. It was Theo in dessert form: sweet with a bite.

It's been more than a year since I've been on a date, and none have ever felt like this—like it's the start of something I'm desperate to name but can't, whether it's too soon or because we don't have enough time left. As Theo kisses me with the moon peeking down at us, I know he feels it, too. It's in the pace of his mouth moving over mine, the way he leans into me like he knows I can handle the weight of us, the way his hand tightens in my hair. It makes my kiss turn desperate.

Nearby, a car alarm chirps politely. Theo pulls back first, breathless, his lips glossy from me.

"Let's go home," he says, his voice barely a rumble.

"Yeah," I say, wishing home meant somewhere less temporary.

But then my gaze snags on a neon sign in a storefront window across the lot. The PSYCHIC/TAROT sign blinks.

It's nearly ten, so it stands out. Maybe that's why I straighten, pressing my hands against Theo's chest to move him out of the way. Everything else around the storefront is dark, but a soft, warm light leaks out of the gauzy curtains, painted pink by the neon in front of it.

Theo's arm winds around my waist. "What shiny thing just caught your attention?"

"Psychic." I blink away from the sign and up into Theo's face, awash in skepticism. "Let's go see."

"You want to go see a *psychic* right now?" he repeats, but I'm already walking, my sandals clicking against the pocked asphalt. He mutters, "Oh, Jesus," but his footsteps aren't far behind me.

It's as if there are hands pushing at my shoulders, curling around my hand as it covers the chipped gold door handle. Before Gram died, I never thought of myself as spiritual, but since I lost her, I've been searching for ways to find her again, to hold on. Right now, I *know* I need to be here.

A bell jingles softly when I open the door. I expect to get hit with a face full of incense, but instead it smells vaguely of jasmine, like the bushes Gram had planted in her front yard. The space is small but clean, nothing like I imagined. One wall is an abstract mural of a desert landscape, an eye hovering in the middle of it, the rest a soothing sage. There's a long, beautiful pine table in the middle of the room with an iMac, a deck of cards, several candles, and a shit ton of crystals and rocks. A deep green velvet chair sits on one side, two orange tweed chairs on the other.

"Hello?" I call tentatively.

Theo stops just behind me, his breath stirring my hair as he sighs. "Shepard, what the hell."

A woman pushes through a set of yarn-woven curtains separating the front room from the back. Like the shop itself, she paints a surprising picture. She's young, maybe a few years older than us, with long, curly brown hair. Her skin is damn near poreless, cheekbones high, with the most arresting green eyes I've ever seen. She's wearing funky patchwork jeans, a cropped lavender sweater, and pink platform sneakers. She looks like someone Sadie and I would see at a bar and strategize about making our friend.

"Hey, folks, super sorry, but I—" She stops, taking us in, and puts a hand to her chest, stunned. "Wow, okay, I was going to say I'm by appointment only and I'm booked three months out, but . . ." Her eyes drift over us, sharp and far away simultaneously. She laughs. "Yeah. Wow, come on in."

Theo lets out a quiet snort, then a grunt when I dig my elbow into his side. "I don't want to interrupt you if you're really not available. We were having dinner across the way, and I saw your sign."

"I got distracted and forgot to turn it off, but now I'm feeling like that was the universe doing its thing." She waves her hand, the thick gold cuff on her wrist wobbling with enthusiasm. "Seriously, come in, come in. I'm Flor, by the way."

"I'm Noelle and this is Theo."

"Hi." His tone broadcasts this wasn't his idea, but he pushes at my hips, following me into the room. We sit, and he scoots closer immediately, closing the three feet of space between us. When he catches me watching him, he raises his eyebrows like *what?*

"Close enough?" I murmur.

"Better view from here," he says, tapping the desk, but his eyes stay locked on mine, and his dimple flashes.

A shuffling sound snaps me out of my trance. I look over to find Flor seated in the green velvet chair, a deck of tarot cards in her hands and a wide grin on her face. "I love this for me. Can I get your birthdays, place of birth, and time of birth, if you have it?"

I rattle off my information, and she writes it down, nodding. "Born at 12:12 a.m., got it. A midnight baby, cool."

"That's the only reason I remember, honestly."

"What about you, my skeptical friend?" Flor asks, appraising Theo.

He tells her, then winks at me. "And I was born at midnight, on the dot."

I roll my eyes. "Of course you were."

Theo reaches over to take my hand while Flor works on her computer. She hums, her attention drifting toward us sometimes, other times off into space.

Finally, she says, "Okay. In the interest of transparency, I have plans in a bit, so I can't give you an intense reading, but I'd love to do a quick session for both of you. You down?"

"How much is this going to cost?" Theo asks.

She spreads her hands in front of her. "I'm doing this for my own curiosity, friend. You can tip if it resonates, but this reading is selfish."

I lean forward. "Selfish how?"

"The energy between you two is pretty intense. It feels old."

"Old?" Theo echoes, insulted.

Flor laughs. "Old, like multigenerational. Like lots of forces and people worked to get you together. You're very, very connected, and that's rad."

Theo catches my eye. It's obvious he's struggling to believe this, though a faint blush spreads across his cheeks.

But her phrasing tickles my curiosity. I'm determined to leave myself open to her message, whatever it is. When she says multigenerational, does she mean Gram and Paul?

I'm not so high on myself that I presume to know everything about how the world works. It's true that I don't know what after death looks like, but I *do* feel Gram sometimes, in the stars above me at night. Right now in this room. What if Flor can feel that, too? What if she feels all of the things that had to happen to get us here?

"You go first," Theo says to me, his fingers lacing tighter through mine.

I turn to Flor, my heart beating heavily. "Okay."

She shuffles the tarot deck. A card falls out almost immediately, and she picks it up, humming again. As more cards join the first on the table, varying emotions cross over her face like a passing storm.

"Mmm." She nods, as if someone's just whispered in her ear. "Got it."

Theo's gaze is hot on my cheek, but I focus on Flor. There's an energy building between us, a vibration in my chest. Fingertips against my neck.

Her eyes meet mine, and it's like a lightning strike into the center of me. "It's been a lot, huh?"

My throat tightens so quickly I can only let out a choked noise. Beside me, Theo angles his body toward mine, his knee pressing up against my leg.

"You've had these massive expectations for a very long time, and they haven't been met. It's worn you down to the point that you swung the pendulum all the way to the other side. You went from all the expectations to none." Flor looks down at the cards, tapping one, and I lean in. The card is a beautiful swirl of green, white, black, and yellow, with a skeleton that hangs over the word *DEATH*. My heart drops. "You had guidance, though, someone in your life who showed up for you when you couldn't show up for yourself, and that kept you afloat in a space that wouldn't have been sustainable otherwise."

I nod, barely, playing with Theo's fingers anxiously.

Flor leans forward. "That guidance isn't with you anymore, right?"

"Right," I whisper as goosebumps bloom on my skin. That's not a coincidence, it can't be. "It was my grandma. She died six months ago."

"Yeah, so, most times the death card means transformation,

but sometimes it can mean earthly death," she says. "In your case, and especially with the other cards I pulled, I think it's both. Your grandma's death cracked your world down the middle. It put you in the shadows that were lurking around the corner anyway. A soulmate doesn't have to be romantic and can serve a very specific need in your life. You can have one your whole life or many." At this, her eyes flicker to Theo, like she's making sure he's listening, before landing back on me. "She was one of yours. She was rooted in every aspect of your life, so when she died, those roots pulled up and left everything a fucking mess. I don't blame you for retreating, friend. It's heavy."

I brush at my suddenly wet cheeks, flushing with embarrassment.

"Maybe—" Theo starts to say, but I shake my head, my eyes locked with Flor's.

"Keep going."

"Here's where it gets a little magical," Flor says with a wink. "Like I said, the death card also means transformation, and I pulled the wheel of fortune card, too. You're in the middle of all this. It's an intense time of change for you. Everything feels upside down, but that's just your perspective shifting. You're seeing glimpses of the way things could be, aren't you?"

It comes in snapshots: The beginning of this trip to now, my camera in my hands, Gram's letters. Paul and his cardigans, his kind smile and even kinder words. Theo and his X-ray eyes. The moments I've captured on film and video. That email from the Tahoe resort. Home. Theo's house and the spaces I could fill—his kitchen for dinner, his bed some nights.

That last visual sinks its claws in. "I do. But I question if it's real."

Flor places her hands over the cards, as if absorbing their energy. "That's normal. You're in build mode, and that feels scary. But give yourself credit for your bravery. That's what's going to carry you through. You think you've given up, but you haven't. You're just resting before you build the rest."

Sometimes hope hurts when it grows too quickly. Right now, it's so big inside my body I want to scream. Instead, I let out a breath. "Thank you."

Flor gives me a warm, guileless smile, like she didn't just strip me down to my bones in front of the man who's stripped me nearly that far.

"All right, now it's Stern and Silent's turn." Flor sweeps my cards up and starts her shuffle over again.

Theo leans over, whispering, "You okay?"

I nod. "It's just intense. You'll see."

He makes a sound in his throat, full of doubt, but then Flor murmurs, "Wow," and his penetrating gaze darts to her.

"What?" he asks, edgy.

Flor inspects the spread, her eyebrows arched high. "Well, it looks like your world is crashing down around you." She pins him with neon eyes, placing her fingers over two cards. "Does that resonate?"

She says it like she already knows it does. It's telling when Theo doesn't respond.

Her appraisal is brief but keen, and she holds up the card. It's a stone tower, aflame, with people falling out of it. "This card means crisis and transformation. Something's happening or happened that's shaken the foundation of everything you know. I also pulled the ten of swords—" She pushes it across the table, the corner catching in a wood grain. The pop it makes sounds like thunder against Theo's silence. "These swords have found their target.

Could be you, could be a relationship. There's a sense of betrayal, right?"

"Did I get the two worst cards because I don't believe in this or what?" Theo asks, but his voice is unsteady.

"They're not the worst cards," Flor argues. "I mean, listen, does anyone *want* these cards, especially together? Knee-jerk response would be no. But this is destroying what no longer serves you so you can come back stronger, in a different way. You're preparing for a transformation."

Theo releases my hand, pointing between the two of us. "How can we both be transforming?"

Flor lifts a shoulder. "We're all constantly transforming, sometimes in little ways and sometimes in big ones. It's possible the universe wanted you together while you went through this. I can't say for sure."

My gaze drifts over to the mural, to the painted eye that's been watching us from the start, and a shiver works down my spine. I turn back to Theo, whose hands are now laced between his spread knees. His brows are drawn tight, but otherwise I can't read his expression, and I wonder if any of this makes sense to him. Is it about his relationship with his dad? About his job? Are the cards saying he should give in to what Anton and Matias want? Where To Next's uncertain future clearly hurts him, but maybe the transformation is literal—the company will shift, and his growth will be tied to that.

It sounds like a good thing, but Theo's frown deepens.

"My point is, this is going to happen no matter what. It's *happening*." Flor leans forward on her elbows, the tower card falling to the ground, and presses a long fuchsia nail on the table in front of him. "The cards are inviting you to let it go and let something new and better grow. You've been placed with resources in your life that will help you move on, but you have to allow that resource to help you."

There's a long, drawn-out silence. Finally, Theo clears his throat. "Got it."

I place my hand on his thigh, palm up, but he doesn't take it, so I curl my hand over his leg instead, wanting to comfort him somehow even if he won't grab hold of it himself. There's an invisible wall between us. Whatever this means to him, he's processing it. Alone.

Flor crosses her arms, her expression kind. "I hope this helped."

"So much." Part of me wishes I hadn't pushed so hard, though. The light, sexy mood Theo and I built over dinner is gone, and I don't know if I can get it back. "Thank you for taking the time to do this."

"Totally selfish on my part. That connection, whew." Flor fans her face. "Nearly blew me over when you walked in."

I laugh uncomfortably, digging in my purse for cash so I don't have to look at Theo. It's one thing to feel the intense connection. It's another thing for a total stranger to feel it and make it a thing.

When I find what I'm looking for, I stand and extend the money toward Flor. "We won't keep you; I know you said you had plans."

Theo pushes my hand away, placing two hundred-dollar bills on the table. "Thanks for your time," he says woodenly, his eyes lingering on the tarot cards before drifting down to the one on the floor.

He turns and leaves, his shoulders coiled.

I turn to Flor, hesitating. "I'm sorry, he's just—"

There's no good way to end that sentence. I don't know what he is. Skeptical, so he wants to get out of there? Shaken, so he has to leave?

She waves me off. "I get it all the time. It's hard for people to hear what needs to be done, especially when it hurts."

My hand is on the doorknob when Flor says, "By the way, when I said he had a resource to help him move on?" Our eyes meet and she smiles. "I meant you."

Twenty-Six

T HEO IS WAITING ON THE CURB WHEN I STEP OUTSIDE, HIS
chin tipped up toward the sky.

"Are you okay?"

He blinks out of whatever trance he was in, blowing out a breath. "Can't say I've ever had a date end that way."

"Are you okay, though?" I press, inspecting him for signs of distress.

His expression blanks out. "I'm fine. I'm not getting twisted up about a few cards randomly pulled out of a deck." He steps closer, taking my hand. "You good? It got heavy in there for you."

I shift from foot to foot, feeling silly suddenly. Inside that room, everything was intensely real. Now, with conversation from nearby restaurants floating in the still air, with Theo looking at me like everything's fine, I wonder if I overreacted. Maybe I assigned too much meaning, not just to his reading, but my own.

My cheeks flush. I tuck a strand of hair behind my ears, looking past his shoulder. "I'm good. Let's get back?"

Theo's eyes narrow, but he nods. When I start to walk, he pulls me back until I'm pressed up against him. "Hey."

"What?" My heart is pounding. I don't know why.

His voice dips low. "I don't believe in that stuff, but if you're upset about anything she said, you can talk to me. You know that, right?"

I stare up at him, the moon shooting silver through his hair, teasing me with how he'll look years from now.

A million words sit in my throat, and these are the heaviest: *you can talk to me, too.* But he won't, and because of that, I can't give him anything more than a shaky "Yeah."

The ride home is mostly quiet, and we step into an equally silent house ten minutes later. Theo heads for the kitchen. "Want a drink?"

I kick off my shoes by the door. "Sure. I'll be right back."

He grabs a bottle of wine, opening a drawer for the bottle opener. "I'll take this out to the patio. Meet me there."

When I slip into the bathroom, I lean against the door with a sigh. The small window above the shower lets in a slice of moonlight, and I breathe in the darkness, remembering the energy I felt earlier. The words Flor gave me.

Am I so desperate for change that I want to believe what she said? Is it pathetic to lay so much hope at the feet of the progress I've made these past two weeks, with my photography and how I'm processing Gram's death, and even Theo? So many times now I've thought of the bubble I've been living in here. It's expanding every day, and maybe there's a chance it'll survive when all this is over. But I'm starting to worry I'm headed for a painful reality check when I get home.

Frustrated, I flick on the light—and yelp when I see my reflection.

There's mascara all over my face.

"Oh, for *Christ's* sake." I wet a washcloth and wipe at my cheeks until the streaks are gone. The skin underneath turns pink, then red. Now I look pissed.

But I am, a little. Theo brushed off that whole thing, and I *do* want to believe it, whether it's ridiculous or not. I want to believe that I'm capable of being brave enough to keep trying. I even want to believe I'm the person he might turn to when he needs help. Isn't that what people who care about each other do?

And I do care about him, deeply. Has this trip intensified a feeling that would never survive outside of this, or is it real?

Suddenly I'm questioning everything.

I make my way back to the kitchen, slipping out the door to the patio, which Theo left ajar. He's sitting on a sleek L-shaped couch, facing out toward the dark horizon. When he hears the creak of my footsteps on the deck, he looks over his shoulder.

"I gave you a big-ass pour," he says, holding the glass above his head as I come up behind him.

I relieve him of the glass, taking such a deep gulp that I'm breathless when I'm done. Theo raises an eyebrow as I skirt the couch and plop down, keeping a few inches of space between us. "Thanks for telling me I had mascara all over my face."

He double takes at the tone of my voice. "It wasn't that bad, Shepard, and we were headed home anyway. You looked like a beautiful raccoon."

God, this asshole. He makes my chest hurt. "I looked ridiculous."

"All right, point taken," he says, his mouth pulling up. "I'll be sure to alert you next time."

I nod, swigging again.

"Noelle." When I look over at him, he's watching me carefully, his expression morphing from amusement to concern.

"Theo," I volley back.

"What's wrong?"

"Nothing."

For a beat, the only sound between us is crickets chirping. Finally, he says, "Tell me the truth."

Those words hit me somewhere deep. It's a more intense version of Tell Me a Secret; the stakes are so much higher.

I'm afraid the bubble is going to pop when I least expect it, and I've been through that before. I never want to feel that loss of control again, so I put my finger to it, and I pop it myself. This is my life, and if it's ugly and he hates it, he was going to walk away eventually anyway.

"You don't believe what Flor said, but my reading was spot-on. The big expectations that turned into none, Gram being my guidance when I was floundering, and how I just . . . felt uprooted when she died."

I take him in as I set my wineglass down—the stern set of his eyebrows, the concern glowing in his eyes just below, the way he's leaning in toward me, ready to catch every word. And there, written all across his face, how he cares for me.

"I don't have a job," I say. "I lied to you when I said I did. I got laid off five months ago, and I'm pretty positive it was just a more humane way to fire me. I mean, it wasn't my dream job by any stretch of the imagination, but I've never had that. That photography assistant job decimated my self-esteem, and the rest of my professional career has been underwhelming. Then I can't hold on to some mediocre job I didn't even like?"

His eyebrows fly up to his hairline, and he sits back, his mouth parting.

I continue, gaining steam. "I couldn't tell you, so I let you believe this was a vacation instead. I didn't have a choice at the time. All we ever did was battle against each other to be the best, and thankfully we didn't see each other for years, so you had no idea how easily you leapfrogged me. But then you caught me at my lowest moment while you were at your highest. I mean, god. *Forbes?* Really?"

Hurt flashes across his face, but he schools it immediately. "That's why you didn't tell me? Because you thought I'd look down on you for not being successful? When who the fuck knows what that really means, anyway? You look at me and think that's the only way success looks, but I promise you it's not."

"You cofounded an *entire* company, Theo."

"It's not that straightforward," he argues.

I can't help thinking of Flor's words earlier: *your world is crashing down around you.* But if he doesn't believe that, it can't be true.

"I've been living in my childhood bedroom turned Peloton studio since January, if you want to talk straightforward. For better or worse, I wanted to save face in front of you. It's not like I knew when we met up that first time that eventually we'd be . . ." I gesture between us. "Whatever this is."

"Whatever this is," he repeats blankly, running a hand over his jaw. "Right."

"I've been job hunting, but it's so bleak, and I'm still scared of pursuing photography. It feels safe here, but what happens when I go home?" I let out a breath. "What if I fail again?"

"You're already not failing," Theo says. "That thing with the Tahoe resort—"

"What if that's it?"

"What if it's *not*?" he shoots back. "You're talented. You *know* you are. And holy shit, fine, so you had to take a breather after one of the most important people in your life died. So you got laid off from a job you hated anyway, and you haven't quite found your place. You tried to make a go at photography years ago and it didn't work *that time*. Do you think that's an indictment on who you are as a person, that you're struggling? Do you think that I'd look at you now and think *she's going through a rough time, so nah, she's not for me?*"

I shrug helplessly. "Historical data goes against me. You dated a woman who worked for NASA."

"And you mean more to me in two weeks than she did in nearly a year, you little Google stalker," he snaps out, genuinely affronted.

My heart takes off as that settles between us. He sees my eyes go saucer-wide and lets out a frustrated grunt.

"I said it earlier today and I'll say it again—you have no idea how amazing you are. I'll give it up to that psychic, because she had one thing right: you've been through hell losing your grandma. Maybe I didn't know her personally or see your relationship play out, but I know what you had with her. I recognize it in my own relationship with my granddad." His voice wobbles, and he clears his throat over it. "The way you talk about her, the way you're honoring her by taking this trip. Hell, the way you made the decision to just *go* and allowed me and Granddad to tag along. We're getting to create memories together while you're still grieving the fact that you don't have any memories left to make. You don't fucking know, Noelle, the scope of what you've done."

Just like that, my eyes are leaking again, and this time he reaches over to wipe the tears away.

"Have you been reading the comments on your videos?" he asks, his eyes locked with mine. "The ones where people say they've called their grandparents, their parents, their people to tell them they love them because they've realized how lucky they are?

The ones where people say this story you're telling is helping them with their own grief?"

"Yes," I whisper. Those are the ones that heal me the most.

"You think that's not success? You think I don't look at you and wonder what you see in *me*?" His thumb moves down to my cheek, and he follows it with his eyes. "You think I don't watch you taking pictures or editing them on your computer with that scrunchy little face you make"—he grins when I let out a choked laugh—"and sit in awe of the work you do? How people connect with it? Because I promise you, I do. If you could see yourself through my eyes, your head wouldn't fit through the door."

It's not my head that's grown, it's my heart, suddenly too big for my chest. It presses painfully at my ribs, struggling to get out so it can plop itself in Theo's hands.

"Don't put yourself up against me," he says. "I'm going to be the one who doesn't measure up."

"That's not true," I say, insulted on his behalf.

"It *is*." There's something searching in his voice, in the way he looks at me. He inhales, as if he's going to say more.

But instead he lets out a pained, frustrated sigh, then grazes his lips over the corner of my mouth, moving to the other side. I close my eyes, parting my lips to let him in if he wants it.

"I hate that you felt like you had to lie to me," he murmurs. "But just so we're clear, I want you, Noelle. Don't think that there are conditions to the way I feel about you."

I pull back, as breathless as if he'd been kissing me for minutes or hours, instead of just teasing me with his mouth. "I feel the same way."

His gaze turns intent. "Yeah?"

"Yeah."

He sighs, dragging his mouth along my cheek, until it gets to my ear. "Tell me a secret."

"I don't want to be done with this in two days." As soon as that last confession is out, the relief pours through me like adrenaline. "Tell me yours."

He pulls back. "I don't want to be done with this at all."

Firecrackers in my blood. It's the only way to describe the feeling, and I suddenly have to be closer to him, so I crawl into his lap. I cradle his face and bring him to me, laughing against his surprised inhale, then licking up his groan. He adjusts to the change in mood flawlessly, cupping my ass to pull me closer.

Theo's kiss turns intense immediately, and I take it, because I can. Because we battle, but at the end of the day we're doing it side by side.

"I need you," he says against my mouth.

"Can we go—"

He has me in his arms, striding toward the door, before I can say *inside*. He closes and locks the patio door behind us, then carries me to his room, tossing me onto the bed.

"I knew you wanted to throw me around," I say as he crawls over me, biting softly at my neck, sucking at my skin. He moves up to my jaw, the corner of my mouth, before nipping at my bottom lip.

He props himself up on one elbow, tangling his free hand into my hair. For a moment, he just looks down at me. I wish I had my camera so I could capture this moment, even though I know I'll never forget—it's the beginning of something I don't see the end of.

"I meant all of that," he says. "I want to keep seeing you when we get home."

I run my fingers through his hair, melting when his eyes fall closed, his mouth pulling up. "I do, too. And I'm sorry I lied."

"I understand," he says hoarsely, then kisses me so deeply, with an urgency I'm not sure *I* understand, though my body runs wild with it.

Our clothes are gone in minutes, and I grip his hair while he settles between my legs, licking at me until I'm begging for him to make me come. He pushes me over the edge with brutal care, so hard I have to muffle my sounds with the back of my wrist. And when he crawls back over me, panting from all his tireless work, I take the condom he pulled from the pocket of his jeans and put it on him, watch as he leans back and takes himself in hand, stroking up and down through the wetness he created.

"Fuck," he whispers, mesmerized.

"Really wish you would." I push my hips up, trying to pull him into the clasp of my body. The need I have is so big it aches. I want it to hurt when he fills me.

He grins and I reach up, pressing my thumb into the crevice of his dimple. He curves over me, still pressing right where I need him, but not sliding in. His tongue slips past my lips, tangling with mine as he rocks his hips. I cup my hands around them to feel the way his body works, muscles playing under hot skin. Then I dig my nails in, smiling in triumph when he groans against my mouth.

"You can take me, can't you," he pants out, and it's not a question. He just wants to hear me say it.

"Yes," I whisper.

The give-and-take we have is so good. He knows I can handle what he gives me and throw it right back, and it stokes my craving, that he wants all of me, even the parts that are still broken or healing.

A hungry look curls into his expression as he lines himself up, his chest rumbling out an *mmm*. He doesn't see the relief on his face when he sinks all the way inside me, but I do. It's a secret he doesn't even know he's told me.

But I know, as he curls his hands around my shoulders and fucks me until I'm crying out quietly against his skin, it's also the truth, simply set free.

Twenty-Seven

"JEEZ, SHEPARD, I THOUGHT YOU WERE GOING TO PULL OUT a shiv and stab me in the heart as your grand finale."

I laugh, winding my arm through Theo's as we leave the hotel's on-site tennis court, where we just played three sets. "Would've been unnecessary bloodshed. I proved my point when I wiped the court with you."

He looks over his shoulder to make sure no one's around, then gives my ass a punishing squeeze. "You barely beat me in the last two sets, and I kicked your ass in the first."

"Still beat you," I gloat.

"I'm never going to hear the end of this, am I?" he groans, squinting against the early-morning sun.

"Unlikely. But you can challenge me to a rematch when we get home." My heart beats hard, and not just from my victory; it's the first time either of us have talked about specific post-vacation plans.

It's time to start making them, though. After spending the night in Palm Springs, we're driving home in just a couple hours, though I'm trying not to think about it. I won't be wrapping myself around Theo tonight, listening to his heartbeat as I fall asleep, or waking up to him tomorrow morning, getting the sleepy, vulnerable version of him.

"You were on your phone early this morning. Everything good?" he asks as we approach the elevator.

I shake my melancholy thoughts away. "Oh yeah, I got a reply back from The Peaks Resort. They want me in Tahoe as soon as possible, and I said I could come up anytime next week. They confirmed Thursday was perfect."

Theo's eyes widen. "Really? That's quick."

"I have absolutely nothing else going on, and I get to stay there for free for a night—or two, if I wanted."

We step into the elevator, and he backs me into the wall, gripping the handrail on either side of my hips. His neck is damp with sweat, cheeks flushed, eyes bright as they move over my face.

"Want to come with me?" I tease.

Storm clouds enter his eyes, chasing away the light. "Uh, I don't think that's possible. I'll be deep in shit next week."

I tug on the hem of his T-shirt. "No kidding. I'm just daydreaming. I know I can't ask you to escape real life so soon after getting back to it. They're probably going to superglue you to your desk."

"I—" A muscle tics in his jaw as the elevator dings; we've arrived at our floor. He looks over his shoulder, and says, faintly, "Yeah."

The change in his mood is so abrupt that I grab his wrist as we exit the elevator. "Hey, wait."

"I'm good," he says, anticipating my next question. "I just . . ." He runs an agitated hand through his hair, looking at me. "I guess I'm not quite ready to think about being done here."

My chest goes tight. "I'm feeling it, too."

"We've got close to an eight-hour drive, though, and I don't want you getting home too late. Let's get packed up and go."

"Okay," I say, but he's already walking away.

———

PAUL GIVES US A LETTER AS WE SETTLE INTO THE VAN.

"Remember," he says. "The story's not over. We have time."

Theo hasn't fully rebounded from our weird elevator conversation earlier. Still, I get a small grin as he leans on his armrest, ready to read the letter with me.

But I'm not sure *I'm* ready. The date of this letter was just days before the one Paul gave us when we started this trip two weeks ago. I sense the end approaching, and I don't want it to, as surely as I don't want to drive home today.

Theo's hand covers mine, his thumb tracing a line over my knuckles. A touch of reassurance.

With an exhale, I read.

May 6, 1957

Dear Paul,

I don't want to worry you, but I spoke with my father today and he wants me to meet a friend of Robert's who lives here. The expectation was clear: he wants me to go on a date with him. It seems they're tired of waiting for me to find someone myself. I told him it wasn't possible, that I'm too busy with school and I'll find someone when the time is right. My father didn't have much to say after that, but my brother asked all sorts of questions about who I've met since last winter. Since you.

I think they're suspicious.

I have a wild idea. I've been thinking about it for quite a while, but I've been too scared to say it out loud. I have no idea what you'll think, or if you'll even want it.

What if we elope?

We could get married when school ends, keep it a secret until it's done. Maybe my parents will accept you once you're my husband. And if they don't, there's nothing they'll be able to do anyway.

It's a risk. They would be very angry. But I think eventually they'd forgive me.

I wish

I love you.
Kat

I trace the crossed-out *I wish*, rubbing at the ache in my chest. The anxiety in Gram's letter transfers to my already unsettled stomach. She cut herself off before she could complete the thought, but she let Paul see her worry, her hope and despair in those crossed-out words.

"The elopement was her idea?" I ask.

Behind me, Paul says, "It was, but I'd thought about it, too. When she brought me the letter, I was relieved. It seemed we had the perfect solution to an imperfect situation."

A tangle of emotions wrap around me. I look over at Theo, his face reflecting what I'm feeling: curiosity, concern, a hint of sadness. I know only some of it is related to Gram and Paul's story.

If I hear the rest now, it'll be my last game of Tell Me a Secret with Gram. It makes me want to bend over in my seat and cry. But I also want to know. I need that closure before I get the closure from this trip.

And maybe I need the reassurance that after things end, life goes on. Sometimes even beautifully.

I turn back to Paul. His eyebrows raise, his age-worn hands folded in his lap.

"Can you tell me the rest?"

Paul's expression softens. "Of course."

Theo squeezes my hand and starts the car while Paul begins.

We wind through Palm Springs as he tells us he suspects Robert's friend tipped Gram's parents off about their relationship.

"There's little other explanation for why her parents rushed down to LA and pulled her from school," Paul says, settling into his seat as we merge onto the freeway. "I have to assume she sounded different after their call. I'd overheard enough conversations with them to know it was a possibility. She thought she kept our secret well, but I worried they'd hear it in her voice—the anxiety, the extended pauses before she answered questions. Secrets get harder the longer you keep them."

In my periphery, Theo shifts in his seat. I look over at him, questioning, but he only shakes his head.

"Robert's friend was local, and her brother was terribly overprotective of her. Robert never admitted it to Kat, but I believe he had his friend follow us after that call," Paul says. "Unfortunately, I believe the day he chose was the day we got our marriage license."

The van jerks as Theo repeats, incredulous, *"Marriage license?"*

My jaw drops to the floor. "When you said you'd made plans, you *really* made plans."

Paul laughs wryly. "We did. Even though it was all very fast, we were determined. *Too* determined. In hindsight, we wanted to make it work so badly that we didn't see the holes in our plan." He sighs. "Kat had never stepped out of line, and she loved her family dearly, despite how heavy-handed they could be. I knew she hated keeping that secret, but I underestimated her fear of how it would alter their relationship. I was so distracted by all the logistics that I didn't see that she was struggling with the decision itself."

I imagine her trying to figure out which way her life would go. Which way was right, and how much it was going to hurt either way. "So what happened?"

"Like I said, we went to get our marriage license. It was just before finals. Kat was a nervous wreck, looking over her shoulder every moment, but when we got that license in hand, she seemed relieved.

"Two days later, there was a knock at our fraternity house in the middle of the night. It was Kat's friend, Gail."

"Damn," Theo murmurs.

"She told me that Kat's family and Robert's friend had shown up at her dorm, saying they knew about the elopement. Her parents made her pack up her things," Paul says. "The timing was too coincidental, and Robert's friend being there when they got her still makes me think he was the culprit."

"Screw that guy," I mutter. Paul and Theo chuckle in tandem.

"Gail escorted Kat to the bathroom, and Kat told her where all of our letters and pictures were. She was able to write me a quick note telling me what happened. She told me not to worry, we'd figure it out, but of course I was worried sick."

"How could you not be?" I say, feeling sick myself. "Was that it? You never got to see each other again?"

"Oh no. I was furious and determined to figure it out. My parents urged me to let her go, but that, of course, made me dig my heels in even further." He looks at his grandson, a soft, sad smile on his face. "Stubborn pride runs in the family."

"Granddad," Theo says, a warning in his voice. I look between the two men as they seem to have a silent conversation.

Finally, Paul looks back at me. "Kat's friend in Glenlake was able to act as an intermediary for us. We sent letters, had a couple of calls. I held on to our marriage license, just in case, but she got more hopeless, even as she insisted she'd figure something out. Her parents were very good at persuading her, telling her she'd find someone new, that they'd never accept me. She'd had a wonderful relationship with them up to that point, so their opinion mattered."

"So did yours," I say.

"Yes," he says. "But so did *hers*. I offered to talk to her parents, to assure them, but it was too late. Too much time had passed, too many lies and secrets in our relationship. I never would have gained their trust."

"Wasn't there a chance they'd come around?"

"Maybe they would've tried in their way, but what if Kat's relationship with her parents eventually deteriorated beyond repair? What if Kat lost them?" Paul shakes his head. "I couldn't have lived with that. I loved her, but I didn't want her to sacrifice, even though she was willing to. We would've fallen apart under that pressure. Hell, we already had. It took me years to recognize that truth, but once I did, I could see it from the start."

"She was a strong woman." Why am I arguing? I know how it ends. If Paul and Gram had ended up together, Theo and I wouldn't even exist.

"She was," he says, equally kind and firm, "but she was also twenty at the time, when women were either dependent upon their family or their husband. I loved your grandmother and I always will, but that relationship wasn't to be. It taught me the lesson I needed then, and for my first marriage, too."

Theo's eyes catch Paul's in the rearview. "What lesson?"

"When it's right to fight for love, and when it's right to let it go. Kat and I were built on an already crumbling foundation. Pushing for that relationship would have ended in disaster, and in the end, we both knew it."

"So, did you break up for good in that letter I found?" I ask.

"No, I drove up to Glenlake," Paul says. "It was midsummer by that time. We met at a park near her house and talked about what we should do, though we knew by that time. We just had to say it out loud. It was hard and very emotional. For a while I wasn't okay, and I suspect she wasn't either. I sent her the letter you found in hopes that we'd both heal. And we did."

My throat goes tight; even if she felt like she failed, she ultimately found her happiness. She doesn't need to be with me now to tell me that. I think of her and Grandpa Joe dancing in the kitchen. My dad and his brothers. Our raucous Christmases and Gram's wide, happy smile.

I'm going through all the stages of grief at once. Listening to Paul and Gram's story hurts. But knowing how it played out soothes the sting of their heartache.

"It took time," I say finally.

"Healing always does," Paul says. "Remember, nothing lasts forever. You have to hold on to the good things, knowing you may be on borrowed time with them. And with the bad, recognize that eventually it will pass."

"Any regrets?" Theo asks, his tone searching.

Paul shakes his head, gazing at his grandson. "None. Any failure I felt at the time turned into opportunity down the road. The pain led me to my first wife and our boys, to you, and ultimately to Vera."

We all sink into the silence together, considering that.

I let out a breath. "This is going to take some processing."

"Undoubtedly," Paul replies. "It took me years. Give yourself time."

Miles pass before we speak again. My mind is spinning with thoughts of Gram, of this trip, of the men in the car with me. Theo's zoned out with his Radiohead, and Paul's reading in the backseat, humming quietly, when I realize something.

I turn to Paul, raising an eyebrow. "You said we could take our time with the story, but you finished with time to spare."

"Well, I got the feeling you wanted an excuse to keep seeing me." He winks, and it's so much like Theo's mischievous one that I can't help laughing. "But truly, *I* wanted an excuse for you two to keep seeing each other."

"You are such a pain in the ass," Theo mutters.

He raises an eyebrow. "But you worked that out, didn't you?"

I catch Theo's eye, my face flushing. I guess we did.

The rest of the drive passes too quickly. I try to hold on to the last hours I have before I step back into real life, but it slips through my fingers like sand, and suddenly we're pulling up to Paul's house. Mine will be next. My parents texted to let me know they're out to dinner with friends and won't be home when I arrive, but they can't wait to catch up. I hate that I'm coming back to an empty house; I've become so used to not being alone.

I don't want to let these two weeks go. I have no idea what to expect now, even though there are things to look forward to: that Tahoe trip, the momentum I've gained with my photography, Theo. The changes I've dedicated myself to making. I'm not the same Noelle I was when I left.

Theo unbuckles his seatbelt, raising a questioning eyebrow at me. "You want to stay over at my place tonight?"

"You have no idea how much I wish I could, but I should probably be there when my parents get home."

"Of course," he says, though he doesn't try to hide his disappointment.

I hang back while Theo and Paul embrace. Neither of them let go for a long time, and when Paul claps Theo's back and whispers something in his ear, Theo squeezes his eyes shut.

"Best trip of my life," Paul declares. Theo looks toward the house, wiping at his eyes. I step toward him, but Paul intercepts me, his expression soft. "Thank you for this opportunity, sweetheart. I can't tell you what it's meant to me."

I swallow hard, pushing down the emotion that's moving up from my chest. "Thank you for telling me your story. I'm sorry it was painful, but I guess I can't be sorry for how it turned out."

His smile is wide. "It's exactly as intended, Noelle. I promise. Oh! There is one more letter I'd like to show you. Let's make a date."

I catch Theo's eye as Paul pulls me into a tight hug. The affection on his face flattens me. "Yeah, a date sounds perfect."

THEO PULLS MY SUITCASE FROM THE VAN WITH A GRUNT. "YOU free this weekend?"

I blink out of my blank stare at my parents' house. "All yours, Spencer."

Theo sets the bag aside and pulls me into his arms. I sink against him with a sigh.

"I'm going to miss you in my bed," he says. "Kicking me in the middle of the night, making your annoying snuffling sounds."

I give him a derisive look. "First of all, you've been in *my* bed. Second of all, you talk in your sleep, so you don't have room to talk."

"I do not talk in my sleep," he insists, cheeks turning pink.

"You sure do." Sometimes he sighs out a nonsense phrase; other times it's a whole conversation from another dimension. I'll never admit it, but I have a recording on my phone.

Theo's eyes narrow. "What do I say?"

"Oh, didn't I tell you? I know all of your secrets now." He laughs, a little uncomfortably, so I take pity on him. "I'm joking. It's gibberish."

"Right." His shoulders drop and he tightens his hold on me. Against my hair, he murmurs, "I'll be around all day tomorrow, so just come over whenever, okay?"

"You gonna let me take Betty for a joy ride?" As I say it, I'm imagining that: the wind in my hair and Theo's, my hands all over the steering wheel. His hand high up on my thigh, watching me because the sight of me driving his Bronco makes him—

"Absolutely fucking not." Theo extinguishes the fantasy before I can finish it, pulling back. "But I'll drive you. We'll go somewhere private, and you can meet me in the backseat."

"Zero chance of that if I don't get my hands on her stick shift."

That dimple pop is so unfair, as is the smug smile it brackets. "You can get your hands on *my* stick shift."

"Somehow not as compelling."

His grin turns wicked, but it drifts away as he cups my jaw, running his thumb over my bottom lip.

"I had a good time with you, Shepard," he says.

What a wild understatement. This has been the best two weeks of my life. "It was okay."

He laughs, aware that I'm full of shit. "I'll expect to see a Tik-Tok detailing all your favorite things about me before bedtime tonight."

"No problem, it'll be like five seconds lon—*gah!*" He grabs me around the waist with a growl, lifting me, and I let out a shriek that sends birds flying from their tree perches. "Fine! It'll be a ten-parter, okay?"

"Two parts dedicated just to my massive—"

"Ego, yes." I wind my arms around his neck, digging my fingers into his hair.

"Gonna be a menace to the end, huh?" Theo says softly, eyes warm and happy.

I lift an eyebrow, my heart suddenly pounding. "What end?"

Something flashes in his eyes—I swear it looks like fear—but then it's gone, quick as a camera flash. He adjusts my position so our noses graze, then brushes his mouth over mine, keeping it soft and ending it just like that. A promise of something more.

"Bye, Noelle," he whispers.

"See you, Theo," I whisper back.

I watch him drive away, standing next to my suitcase. There's nothing left to do but to go inside. Step back into my old life.

I can't wait to make it brand-new.

Twenty-Eight

ALMOST IMMEDIATELY, THE TRIP FEELS LIKE IT WAS A LIFE-time ago. The only tangible reminder I have is intense tan lines.

And Theo.

I show up at his doorstep early Saturday morning, both because I spent the night before tossing and turning in an otherwise empty bed and because I'm trying to formulate how to tell my parents what I've spent the last two weeks doing in a way that doesn't sound completely unhinged.

I'm worried about telling Dad. Worried about how he'll take Gram and Paul's story, how he'll take that I traveled with Paul and lied about it. I'm less worried about how he'll take my actual relationship with Theo, but he's such an integral part of the entire tangled web. Will he think less of him?

There wasn't an opportunity to talk to my parents when they got home Friday night, at least not about anything serious. I met them out front as they poured out of an Uber. They showered me with enthusiastic greetings, and I recapped each of the stops I'd made, showed them a small selection of photos I set aside as proof I'd been working, and mentioned the online shop I'd gotten up and running while I was away, as well as my upcoming trip to Tahoe. Mom's excitement ratcheted up to a twelve at that news. Dad insisted he wanted to talk more when it wasn't so late. I sent them to bed, relief and guilt warring in my mind.

I want to tell them everything. I need to. But I need time to figure out how to make it sound less like a secret.

When Theo opens his front door Saturday, though, his hair damp from a shower, he banishes every thought I have but one: I'm absolutely head over ass over head again falling for this man. It's terrifying and thrilling. All my emotions have chasers.

He pulls me into his arms, his hand snaking down to cup my ass, and presses a quiet "I missed you" into my neck. The door closes behind me, and he pushes me against it, kissing me hard, with an edge of urgency I've felt since I left him. We don't even make it upstairs.

We spend all weekend together, falling back on the same habits we picked up during our trip—middle-of-the-night movies that are interrupted by either sleep or sex, dancing around his back patio while dinner sizzles on the grill, and, of course, my covert recording of his sleep talk. He's surprisingly restless, his words gibberish but emphatic, and several times I wake him up with soft kisses on his neck, a hand moving up and down his back to bring him out of whatever strange things he's dreaming. He sighs, pulling me close, and I don't sleep again until the tension leaves his body.

We do other normal life stuff, too, and that's almost more exciting than anything else. I drag him to the farmers' market on Saturday. He grumbles about it but buys me a bouquet of wildflowers when I'm not looking and indulges me stopping by every vendor for free samples. We go out to dinner, and he finally takes me for a ride in his Bronco. He doesn't let me drive it, but it's only a matter of time. Even though I don't get my hands on Betty's stick shift, Theo makes it up to me when we park in an empty lot near Ocean Beach and I straddle his lap in the backseat.

Maybe all of this should feel mundane after the adventures we had, but it doesn't. It feels like *life*, one I could have and be proud of. One I'm actually having.

Sunday, I take Theo on a hike in Tennessee Valley, my favorite with Gram. I can tell it means something to him that I brought him here, and I talk about her all the way to our final destination—a coved beach at the end of the trail. We set up a blanket to eat lunch, and afterward I lay my head in his lap, looking out at the water while he absently runs his fingers through my hair.

"I promised Thomas and Sadie I'd have dinner with them tonight," I say, watching a cloud shaped like a flat heart drift by. "Want to come?"

He eyes the water, his thumb moving over my temple. "Wish I could. I need to get ready for tomorrow."

"Lots of emails to catch up on?"

"Yeah," he says absently.

I reach up, running my nails lightly over his cheek until his attention returns to me. "You want to do a double date thing with them sometime?"

Theo must hear the hesitation in my voice; his eyes get sharper, then soften. "Of course. When things settle down."

I nod and close my eyes, and if his thigh tenses under my cheek, I try not to notice.

When I leave that night, he cradles my face in his hands and kisses me with surprising intensity given how laid-back our day has been.

"You okay?" I ask.

"Yeah. I . . . This week I might not be around much. I'm not sure. So if I don't answer you right away, it's just because I'm dealing with things."

I can only imagine how stressful his week will be, and I press myself closer. "If you need to talk tomorrow, take a break and call me, okay? If things get weird at work or whatever. I'm here."

For you, I add silently.

Theo clears his throat, pressing a final kiss to the corner of my mouth. I expect some acknowledgment of my offer, but he simply says, "Thanks for a great weekend."

I brush it off, grinning as I slip out of his hold and out the door. "You're only saying that because you got laid about forty times."

"Saying it 'cause it's you," he shoots back with a beautiful smile. I watch it fade in my rearview as I drive away, until I turn the corner and he's gone.

My heart doesn't stop racing, even as I pull into a metered spot near Thomas and Sadie's apartment. I have to lay my forehead on the steering wheel and take several deep breaths so it won't be written all over my face.

Unfortunately, my brother knows me like the back of his own hand, so when he throws open the door to his apartment and takes a good look at me, he bursts into laughter.

"Shut up," I grumble, stepping inside.

"What is wrong with you, Mas?" Sadie asks, pushing him aside to fold me into a tight hug. "Hey, darling girl. How was everything?"

"Really amazing."

And then I burst into tears.

⌒

I'VE JUST SPILLED MY GUTS TO THOMAS AND SADIE—EVERY DE-tail of the trip, every grief-ridden and healing thought I've had about Gram, that intense psychic reading, my fear of telling Mom and Dad what I've been up to, and, sans sex details, what's happened with Theo.

"The really questionable thing is," Thomas says, leaning forward to uncork the emergency wine he grabbed for us as soon as I started crying, "I knew you were going to fall for Theo and I still made that bet. I have to buy a *couch*, dammit."

"The really questionable thing is betting against me, period." I let out a breath, then groan. "God, I have no idea why I cried like that. I'm actually fine."

Sadie rubs my leg. "Permission to psychoanalyze?"

"Granted." I sniff, accepting the glass Thomas hands me. He snakes his arm behind Sadie's shoulders, his fingers just long enough to squeeze my shoulder, too.

"I know you're fine, but you've also had a really emotional couple of weeks," Sadie says. "Do you feel like you ever got a chance to process your gram's death?"

I go back to that first month, where I essentially shuttled myself between work and my apartment. How I couldn't look at pictures of her or hear her voice in voicemails. How I stopped going out with my friends because they'd ask how I was doing in that specific "you're grieving and I'm uncomfortable but have to ask or I'll look like a dick" tone of voice. Those months I spent staring at my camera, at the walls of my childhood bedroom, at the views from the hikes Gram and I took together.

"No." For the first time I realize it's true.

Thomas stands and moves around the couch, settling in next to me and ruffling my hair.

Sadie continues, "A while back, I ran across an article about this thing called grief trips. When you lose someone, you travel— maybe to their favorite place or a place that brings you peace or somewhere brand-new to shake yourself out of your routine—and you get to process that way." She leans forward, catching my eye. "That's what this was for you, I think. You had this story unraveling with Paul, these emotional letters, and it was a way for you to focus on your grief in a controlled way. And at the same time, you had some joy in your life with Theo."

"That doesn't explain my outburst."

Thomas smacks my leg. "We're your safe space."

"We're a place for you to unload," Sadie adds. "Your parents don't know what happened, so you have to wear a mask with them. With Theo, it's this new, bright, exciting thing, and you just spent a weekend together after a *really* emotionally heavy trip, so you want it to be magical. It's a normal response. You're purging some of the stuff you've had to compartmentalize."

I let out a breath, gulping down a mouthful of wine. "I guess that makes sense. It's been a lot. And I truly have no idea if Dad is going to be upset about where I've been and why, or if he'll understand. This trip was mine, but the loss is all of ours, you know? All of the details I got are. He's in a better place now than he was six months ago, but how do I know that his grief can handle it?"

"You won't know until you tell him, and the sooner you tell him, the better," Thomas says. "You know how he is. He idolized Gram and Grandpa Joe's relationship, so the thought of you palling around with some guy Gram almost married right before Grandpa may be weird. But he also knows how special your relationship with Gram was, and the fact that you're getting back into your photography is sending him to the moon. While you were gone, he wouldn't shut up about how proud he was of you for starting up again."

My eyes start to fill. He flicks my cheek lightly to stop it, like he did when we were kids and I'd get all wound up to cry. I smack his hand away, like *I* always did. But his distraction works.

His eyes drift toward the clock meaningfully. It's eight. By the time I get home, our parents will be in bed, and that's by design. "For real, Noelle. You should talk to him tomorrow. Dad loves you and he'll support you, even if he doesn't understand at first."

"I don't want to hurt him. With the story, I mean."

He appraises me. "You're the one who's the most invested. At the end of the day, Gram had a happy life with Grandpa Joe, and that's what'll matter to Dad."

"Ugh, you're right. I'll talk to him tomorrow," I say. Thomas lifts his eyebrows. "I *will*. I promise. No more delaying."

"Let's move on to the next item of business," Sadie says. "Are things serious with Theo?"

Even hearing his name makes my stomach swoop.

"It's early, but . . ." I lift my shoulders helplessly. "It kind of feels like it's headed in that direction. I mean, don't go ordering that couch, Mas, but—"

Thomas scoffs. "You're just saying that because you don't want to admit it."

"I'm saying that because you can't be in love with a person after a matter of weeks," I argue. And even if I feel it, it's not something I can say out loud right now.

Is Theo getting there, too? Does he want that? In so many ways now, I feel like I know him. Like we get each other, and the connection we're building is headed for something that can really *only* be love.

"You just spent a cumulative . . ." Sadie trails off, counting in her head, her lips moving silently. "Three hundred and thirty-six hours, give or take some time for sleeping—"

"When you were doing that separately," Thomas adds. "Plus you've known this guy for years."

"Great point," Sadie says, beaming at my brother. "That's a lot of quality time. It's reasonable you'd catch intense feelings."

Thomas nods, elbowing me in the ribs. "Yeah, and it's possible anyway. I fell in love with Sadie right away."

Her cheeks pink up, even as she rolls her eyes. "No, you didn't."

"Uh, yeah, I did."

They start to lean around me for a kiss, but I push at both their shoulders. "No, no, no. Kiss on your own time. And not right now, either. I'm hangry."

"It's your own fault for wanting to come over so late," Thomas mutters, but he leaps up, heading for the kitchen.

Sadie and I stand together. She wraps her arms around my waist, squeezing me tight. "I'm so excited for you. You've got a lot of exciting things coming around the bend."

I rest my cheek against her temple. "Yeah. I think I do."

~

I SPEND MOST OF THE DAY MONDAY EDITING PICTURES, UP-dating my online shop with new prints, and organizing orders that have been placed. I'm nowhere near a point where I can make a living doing this, but it's a goal worth driving toward.

I still have to create my end-of-trip TikTok, but I'm not in that emotional space yet, so I answer comments and DMs instead, fo-cusing on the ones where people tell stories of their own grandpar-ents, their moms and dads, siblings, or found family members who've impacted their lives the way Gram did mine. The way Theo and Paul have, too.

A swell of pride sits on top of the more obvious emotions as I respond to the messages—grief, always, and nostalgia—knowing that my work has started these conversations, that people connect with it. That they see themselves in it. It's what's always drawn me to art; that it can be simultaneously so personal and so intensely universal.

The house is quiet with my parents at work, but it doesn't feel lonely like it did before. I'm focused, barely stopping for lunch. Before I know it, the sun is slicing through my window, glinting against the metal back of my computer.

After grabbing a snack, I settle back at my desk, picking up my phone to check if I have a text from Theo. I FaceTimed him early this morning to wish him luck. He was quiet, maybe a little distracted, but who could blame him? Walking back into a shitstorm after two weeks off could fell even the most stoic person.

"You okay?" I asked, suddenly feeling like I'd asked him that a lot lately.

He nodded, running a hand over his bare chest. "Yeah, I'm good. I—I'll check in."

But he hasn't, and now as it creeps closer to four, I feel a sense of foreboding I can't explain.

Maybe it's that I texted Dad earlier, telling him I wanted to make sure we had dinner together tonight. He promised to pick up In-N-Out on the way, our favorite meal. I stared at that text message for minutes, guilt shadowing my productive day.

I drum my fingernails on my pale wood desk, then text Theo: How's it going? I'm having dinner with my parents tonight, but I can come over late.

I have no idea what Theo's day looks like or if he'll be up for it. Surely he's talked to Anton and Matias. Did his two weeks away give them the distance to see that they want to work together to find a happy medium? Or is Theo conceding to it all?

I wish I knew. I want to be that resource Flor claimed I was during his reading. A safe space, an open ear. If he's having a bad day, I want to pour him a glass of wine and let him unload. And if he's had a good one, I want to celebrate it.

My phone dings, and I grab it eagerly, assuming it's Theo's response.

Instead, it's a LinkedIn notification: Theo Spencer, who you follow, is in the news.

I frown, hitting the banner, and an article from a well-known tech site pops up.

TRAVEL APP WHERE TO NEXT'S
COFOUNDER AND CFO EXITS BUSINESS

Adrenaline crashes through me, the words swimming in front of my eyes. It takes several frantic moments for what I'm reading to sink in.

In a surprise move today, popular travel app Where To Next announced that cofounder and CFO, Theo Spencer, has exited the business.

"We are so appreciative of Theo's invaluable contributions over the years," cofounder and CEO Anton Popov said in a press release by the company. "We wish him the best. Nathan Mata, current SVP of Finance, will be stepping into his role. We expect a seamless transition so we can continue providing our valued customers with unforgettable experiences, and are excited about the future growth of WTN."

The next couple paragraphs go on to talk about the history of the business—*which is Theo*, I want to scream—and the current state of the business.

At the end is this: *Spencer could not be reached for comment.*

"Fuck, fuck, fuck," I whisper, dread pulling at me, making me clumsy and sluggish. Did they blindside Theo with this, too? The thought makes me want to throw up. I can only imagine how he's feeling.

There are footsteps down the hall, heavy and purposeful, and my brain spits out *THEO*, though it can't be. He must be at home.

The door swings open—no knock—and my dad stands there instead. He holds up his phone, my TikTok account on the screen. His expression is tight, cheeks pale.

"Noelle," he says, in a voice I rarely hear from him. "What the hell is this?"

Twenty-Nine

STARE AT THE PHONE IN DAD'S HAND.

"I can explain," I manage to get out. My heart is on fire, and my mind has taken off in about five different directions, trying to figure out what the hell's happening.

He steps into my room. "Start explaining, then."

Another wave of adrenaline hits as I push back from my desk. I need to go see Theo. "I can't."

"*Noelle*." Dad lifts his hands, exasperated.

"I mean, I can't right now. I'm going to. I was going to explain everything tonight, actually." As I say this, I'm pulling a sweater over my head, marveling at the spectacularly shitty, ironic timing of everything. "But I—something happened and I need to go."

Like that, his expression changes from irritation to concern. "What's going on? Are you okay?"

"I honestly don't know," I sigh.

A stricken look crosses his features, and I recognize it immediately: the knee-jerk catastrophizing we've started doing since

Gram died. It's hard to conceptualize that sudden bad news could be right around the corner until you get it yourself. Then, the reality that life can change in an instant never leaves your mind.

I hold up my hand. "It's not me. There's an emergency with . . . a friend."

The fear is replaced with understanding—and curiosity. One blond eyebrow raises. "Is it your friend from this weekend?"

Friend. The word felt like a lie coming out of my mouth, and it sounds like one coming out of Dad's. He needs the truth, and I want to say it out loud. "You know what, no, he's not my friend. It's Theo, who I"—I gesture to his phone—"well, I'll tell you more later. The short story is that I'm dating him and I'm pretty sure I'm in love with him and something happened and I need to go see him in the city."

Dad blinks at my outburst, then wipes a hand over his mouth. The frustration is still there, tightening the corners of his eyes, but I see that ever-present kindness, too. "Wow, Beans, okay. That's a lot to process."

"I know." I let out a breath. "I swear when I get back, we'll talk. I'll lay out exactly what happened and answer any question you have. But Theo needs me, so I really have to go."

"Take a deep breath," Dad says. "Don't start your car until you're calm."

"I'm calm." I stuff my shaking hands in my pockets, heading toward the door.

He steps aside but touches my arm to stop me. "I love you. Okay?"

"Okay." My eyes fill and I lean into him, placing my cheek on his chest. His heart thumps beneath his chambray button-up. "I love you. I'm sorry."

He drops a kiss on top of my head, then pushes me gently. "Go on. I've got to watch all these videos anyway. I only got through the first few."

Oh god. I compartmentalize that and run to my car, backing out of the driveway at a speed my parents' next-door neighbor will probably post about on the neighborhood online message board. Doesn't matter to me. Theo's alone, processing this news, and he doesn't have to be.

I get to the city in record time. When I park at his house, I squint up at the living room windows. There's no movement.

My heart pounds against my ribs as I climb out of my car. I head toward the front door, but then I hear it—sad boy music, drifting out on the light breeze from the backyard.

"Shit," I mutter.

There's a slender alleyway between his house and the next one, so I make my way down it. The music gets louder the closer I get; it's a *really* sad song, which is saying a lot considering it's Radiohead. When I get to his gate, I reach over and unlatch it, swinging it open.

Theo is slouched in a chair at the patio table. His left hand is circled around a drink resting on his knee, and his cheek is propped on his right hand. He's staring out at nothing. If he hears me, he doesn't acknowledge it.

It's an achingly solitary picture.

"Hey," I call quietly, closing the gate behind me.

He looks over and my heart falls all the way to my feet. His hair is mussed, eyes subtly rimmed red. His expression is blank as he watches me slide into the seat next to him.

"You saw," he says.

"Yeah, I did." I swallow against my helplessness seeing him like this. So leached of emotion, no trace of that dimple.

"I'm surprised you're here."

I frown, confused. "Why wouldn't I be? You just got horrible news." His gaze bounces away, but he doesn't say anything, so I press on. "You must be in shock."

A humorless huff bursts from his mouth. "*Shock* isn't the word for it."

"What is the word?"

For a moment, he doesn't say anything. Then he inhales sharply and starts talking, blasting past my question. "It's like every time I think I've done something worthwhile, every time I think I've gotten to a place where it's safe to say, okay, *this* is success, I've *finally* done enough, it's still not fucking enough."

"Enough for wh—"

He sets his drink on the table and leans forward, scrubbing both of his hands over his face with a frustrated grunt. "And I can't even deal with the fact that I've been pushed out of my own company by myself. They had to put that fucking statement out right away, and my dad's been calling me all afternoon. I'm never going to hear the end of how I wasted that first fifty K he gave us, even though we've grown it so exponentially I can't do the math off the top of my head." His laugh is humorless. "I guess it's not *we* anymore. I need to stop saying that."

I scoot closer, laying a hand on his arm. Our knees press together, and my body wants to take it further, curl up on his lap. No matter how close I get, though, there's a distance between us, shaped like his profile as he looks away.

"Talk to me," I say. "Tell me what happened. Are they even allowed to ambush you like this? Just tell you it's over? Can't you fight that, like, legally?"

Theo's silence extends, long and tight. Finally, he says, "They didn't ambush me, Noelle."

"What do you mean? The article I read said it was a surprise."

"Sure, to the general public. Not to me."

Unease drips into my veins. "I'm not really following."

He stares off into the distance. "This exit has been in the works for weeks, and our arguments over the direction of the business for months longer than that. Like I told you, they want to take the company in a new direction. Our investors want it, Anton and Matias want it, everyone wants it but me because I can't let go of the idea that it's already what it should be. And I pushed so fucking hard—" Again, he wipes at his face with his hand. "The investors wanted me gone, and Anton and Matias ultimately agreed. When I decided to come on the trip, they'd just given me paperwork to buy me out of my equity. I knew what I was coming back to. It wasn't a surprise. I mean, Jesus, even the psychic knew."

A finger snaps in my mind and I'm back in that room. Sitting next to Theo with that painted eye gazing down at us. Remembering what Flor said: *This is going to happen no matter what. It's happening.*

I remember him calling it bullshit after, then holding me when I cried over how real it felt to me.

I remember the way I confessed everything.

"Wait, did you know what you were walking into today?" I say quietly, as a hurt I can't properly identify winds itself around me.

"I wasn't positive it would be today, but . . ." He trails off, shaking his head. "No. Yeah. I knew it was over."

Memories from the previous two days stretch between us in the ensuing silence—me at his door Saturday morning, the way his hands gripped me while he whispered that he'd missed me after less than twenty-four hours apart. The ebb and flow of our conversations, and the quiet we shared, where this information would have fit perfectly. How I talked his ear off about my anxiety over my Tahoe trip this week. The way he listened and reassured me, all while holding on to his own anxiety with tight fists.

I think back to what Flor told Theo, my heart starting to beat fast: *You've been placed with resources in your life that will help you move on, but you have to allow that resource to help you.*

I was there, not just on the road with him—when he was sitting on all of this, too—but in his house, his bed, his life. His *real* life, and he didn't tell me.

Something in my heart fractures. For him, and myself.

"Theo," I breathe out. "Why didn't you say something?"

He looks down at my hand, still curled around his arm. "I didn't know what to say to you. I thought maybe I'd figure out how to break it to you before the statement went out, but that didn't happen, obviously."

How to break it to me? I shake my head, lost. "I mean before. All those times I asked if you were okay, all those times we talked about your work and what it meant to you? We spent the entire weekend together—"

He averts his eyes, setting his jaw stubbornly. "I didn't want to mess it up with this."

I stare at him, long enough that he finally looks at me. "It wouldn't have messed anything up. I *want* to know things, including the things that hurt."

"Even the things that show you I'm not the guy you think I am?" he says, a challenging glint in his eyes. They're so dark I can't make out the emotions lurking there. It makes him seem like a stranger.

I frown. "What does that mean? Who do I think you are?"

"Not the guy who got fired from his own company, that's for fucking sure."

There's a beat of silence while I process exactly what he's saying.

"Hold on. You think I would *judge* you for that?" Theo simply appraises me, and his silence sounds like a *YES* screamed between us. My blood heats. "I don't know if you remember, but I aired all of my dirty laundry to you. Now it feels like you were just patting me on the head—"

"I didn't pat you on the head," he snaps, straightening.

"Well, you sure didn't share any of this in return, apparently because you thought I'd think you were a failure. So, not sure what that says about me," I shoot back, my throat tightening. He opens his mouth, his brows flattening into that stern line, but I press on, averting my eyes. "I mean, clearly there's no comparison between us. I lost a menial job I couldn't stand, and you lost the company you founded and led to multimillion-dollar success, but—"

"*That's* why I didn't tell you," Theo bursts out, and when our eyes lock, something cracks inside my chest. "That right there. God, Noelle, can you blame me for not wanting to admit this to you? You hold me up as some paragon of success. You spent our entire trip talking about the *Forbes* shit, about the great work I'd done and how you looked up to it. How would you have felt if I'd been like, 'Hey, by the way, my entire life is blowing up and I'm about to be unemployed'?"

"I'd say, 'Yeah, me too!' I'd feel like you were telling me something *real*." I drop my hand from his arm. This conversation has shifted so quickly that I'm dizzy. "Are you kidding? You didn't want to tell me because you think I'm some fangirl who couldn't handle you not being perfect?"

"Our entire relationship, from the time we were fourteen, was about you thinking I was good enough based on what I'd achieved." Theo stands up, pacing away from me. "Do you know what it was like to grow up with a dad who, every time you did something you thought would make him proud, decided that actually, he wanted more than that? Who moved the goalpost every fucking time? He made me feel like a failure, *always*."

"I don't know what that's like, and I'm sorry," I say, tears springing to my eyes. My dad is waiting at home for me, confused and angry, but even through his disappointment he supports me unconditionally. I hate that Theo doesn't have that.

His mouth twists. "Then there was you, who got pissed every time I did something, and it made me feel it was enough. Like it was actually too *much*. You had nothing to gain from acting that way, and that's how I knew it was real. I fed off that, Noelle. I had your voice in my head long after high school ended."

I'm so shocked that he thought about me at all, never mind carried my voice with him, that I can only mouth words in return.

He runs his hands through his hair, blowing out a breath. "When we started on this trip, though, and you kept talking about all of my achievements, what I was doing, that damn profile—I was about to lose everything I've worked for these past six years. Can you understand why I wouldn't want to tell you?"

"No," I choke out, standing, too. "I can't understand. Yes, I admire all of the things you've done, and yes, it pissed me off as much as it made me proud. But given our situations, why would I, of all people, judge you for that? I have no right to, and even if I did, I wouldn't."

His jaw locks. "Our situations aren't the same."

His words, said so stonily, hit their mark. "Right. Because my job was shitty and yours was important."

Surprise flashes in his eyes—and panic. "That's not what I meant."

"What did you mean, then?"

For a beat, he doesn't say a word. Then he looks away, the panic receding into what looks like defeat. "You know what? It doesn't matter."

The frustration of him slamming down the wall again makes me want to scream.

"Of course it matters, Theo. What you say or don't say matters to me, and you're standing here holding back again. Why aren't you giving me a chance to see all of you? To prove that's enough for me?" I take a step toward him but keep the space between us. If I step any closer, I'll want to touch him. "I laid out everything with my job—and more. I trusted you with that, and you gave me all these sweet words back about how stumbling wasn't an indictment on my character. So was that bullshit?"

He has the audacity to look insulted. "No."

"Are you sitting there laughing at me? Thinking that I'm not worth your time because I'm in a rough spot?"

"*No.*"

"Then why is it so pathetic for *you* to stumble? Why can't you trust that I l—like you the way you are?" My emotions are running faster than my mouth can keep up with, and my stomach free-falls at what I nearly just admitted. "Why do you think you're such a special case, that when something bad happens to you I'll walk away, when you sat there and told me you wouldn't do that to *me*? Do you think I'm that big of an asshole?"

"No, Noelle, I just—"

He takes a step toward me. I hold up my hand, backing into a chair. I can't think clearly when he's near, and suddenly I'm desperate for the boundary. As we kept getting closer, I slowly stopped protecting myself, while Theo was doing it the whole time.

The realization *hurts.*

"You kept me at arm's length because you didn't trust me, and you did it with intention every time I asked you if you were okay, every time I invited you to be real with me or when I was fully transparent with you." My mind flashes to the times he stopped himself mid-sentence, how he circled around the full truth, those flashes of anxiety and fear he'd shut down. "I let you know me, and you didn't do the same."

He swallows hard, his pulse moving rapidly in his throat. I've kissed that exact spot so many times, when his heart raced for other reasons. But now everything feels like a lie.

"Don't say that," he says. "You know me."

"How can I, if you only want me to see the Theo Spencer who has all his shit together? You kept this a secret from me, thinking I'd walk away if I knew the truth."

He laughs humorlessly. "God, you are so obsessed with secrets."

"What does *that* mean?"

"That whole trip was about that, wasn't it?" he asks, eyes flashing. "About uncovering your gram's secret love life, when in reality it was probably something she dealt with and moved on from and didn't think was necessary to drag up with you. Then you started poking at mine, wanting to play that game—"

"It's not a game. It's me wanting to know you. Share with you, be vulnerable. You poked at me, too, don't act like I was the only one trying to uncover secrets. When I did the same, you downplayed it or shut down completely. So, why is that?"

He sighs impatiently. "Not everything is a conspiracy to lie. Why can't this just be me trying to get through my life before I talk about it?"

"Because I'm in your life!" I exclaim. "You can't feed me one story, then tell me the same story doesn't apply to you. You can't say you want to be with me, be there for me, and not let me do the same. That's not what I want in a relationship."

Panic crosses his features again, but like clockwork, he shuts it down, crossing his arms.

I take several calming breaths before trying again. "I'm not your dad, Theo. I'm not anyone else in your life who expects you to be a certain way, then tells you you're not enough when they think you can't deliver."

"That's what you're doing right now," he says flatly.

"It's not. I'm only asking you to let me be there for you. To be open with me. To trust that I'll like *you*, not Where To Next Theo or 30 Under 30 Theo or Gold Star Son Theo. You've given me some of that the past few weeks, but I want it all. I'm greedy, okay? I just want *you*, and all of the good and bad stuff that comes with it."

Even now, as I'm practically begging for it, he's not giving it. He just watches me, the only sign of life that heartbeat ticking in his neck.

"These past few weeks have been everything to me, and so much of that is *you*." My voice breaks on the *you*, and he looks away, eyes shining in the waning light. "I don't know how to tell you any other way that I want to do this. But I showed you everything, and you were hiding things from me, and now you're shutting down. I don't want to fight a brick wall over and over again."

Nothing for a beat, then he exhales my name, looking down.

"I think you're scared, and when you're scared, you're frozen." I search his face, willing him to meet my eyes. "Ask me how I know."

There's such relief in admitting that I was right where he is, and that I'm coming out of it. For a second, it washes away the ache in my chest. If Theo could just break through, if I could help him get there somehow, then I could reach out and touch him.

But he has to be willing to let me in, and he's not there yet. Suddenly I'm scared he'll never be. That we'll lose this.

My throat closes at the thought, but I push past it. "Maybe I do care too much about secrets, but it's just because it makes me feel close to the people I . . . care about." Shit. I keep getting so close to the edge, and Theo isn't going to be there to pull me back this time. It's not just a busted knee I'll walk away with. "I want that with you, but I'm scared to give you more until I know you're ready to give me an equal amount in return."

"Yeah, I got that," he says shortly, running a hand over his jaw with a sigh. "I'm not used to—I can't do that right now. You're pushing too hard, okay? I'm dealing with all this other shit, and this is too much."

I lift my hands helplessly, my eyes and throat crowding with tears. "So, should I go?"

He opens his mouth, then closes it, his lips twisting into a tight purse. Finally, he says, "It's better if I'm alone."

Those words are like pressing a detonator connected to my heart. I pick my phone up from the table with a shaking hand. "Right. Of course. If you change your mind, you know where to find me."

I'm halfway across the yard when I hear his soft, emphatic "fuck." My footsteps stutter, but he doesn't follow me, so I keep going. I push through the gate, biting my lip hard so I won't burst into tears until I'm in my car and driving away.

Tell me a secret. A whisper from somewhere, but it's a taunt, not a request.

I'm so tired of playing this game. And now I have to face the secrets I've told with all of Theo's sitting on my chest.

Thirty

I T DOESN'T MATTER HOW OLD I AM—SEEING MY PARENTS SIT-ting together on the couch triggers my fight-or-flight response.

They watch me walk into the living room, Mom with her bad-ass velvet blazer on and a neutral expression. Dad is seated on the edge, hands clasped and hanging between his knees, a slight frown marring his affable features.

I take my seat in one of the cream linen wingback chairs across from them, mirroring my dad's posture. "Hey."

"He—" Mom takes in the state of my face, eyes widening. "Honey, what's wrong?"

Apparently, I did a terrible job of touching up the sobfest I in-dulged in from the end of Theo's street all the way across the Golden Gate Bridge.

"Did that kid hurt you?" Dad's eyebrows crash together, and he's halfway off the couch before I raise my hand, trying to hold back laughter despite how wrecked I feel. What's he going to do, go to Theo's house and hug him to death?

Actually, god, that's probably what he needs. But you can't hug a brick wall.

"I'm okay." I clear my throat when my voice catches. "It just wasn't the conversation I expected."

Mom doesn't look convinced. "We can wait—"

I shake my head, pressing my palms together and catching them between my knees. "No, I owe you an explanation, and I'm ready to give it."

"All right," Dad says slowly. "Well, as you know, I found your TikTok."

"I didn't even know you knew what TikTok was."

"I didn't," he says. "I was in the kitchen at work earlier and overheard these young dudes talking about some series they'd been following. Is that what you call it? A series?" He doesn't wait for my answer, just waves his hand. Dad prefers more tactile entertainment—the crisp pages of a book, ink transferred onto his thumb and finger from a newspaper. Social media holds no appeal for him. "They started talking about a trip, and named off a few locations, which were *your* locations. So I said, 'Hey, my daughter's traveling a similar route, let me see that video,' you know, thinking maybe it was someone in your photography group."

My heart simultaneously expands with love and shrinks with shame.

"It was you, though," he says, his gaze searching.

"I'm sorry," I whisper.

"Well, hold that thought. After you left, Mom and I watched all the videos. And then spent some time reading the comments and . . ." He trails off, clearing his throat the way I did moments before. For the first time, I notice that his eyes are a little glassy. Mom looks at him, a soft smile on her face.

"Were you crying?" I exclaim, starting to stand.

He holds up a hand, his eyes reddening further. "What you did with this is powerful stuff. All of the comments about people's families, about your talent. I want to say right off the bat that we're so proud of this work you did."

"It's incredible," Mom agrees. "But we're trying to wrap our heads around why you said the trip was something it wasn't. Why didn't you just tell us what you were doing?"

"It's a long story," I warn.

"You're clearly good at telling them," my dad says. "Why don't you start from the beginning?"

With a deep breath, I do. I start with how I found the photos and letter. I tell them how afraid I was to break the fragile skin of Dad's healing by bringing up a love story that wasn't his parents'. I admit I wanted to have one last secret with Gram, and talk at length about the connection I felt to her while I was there. I tell them—haltingly—how attached I grew to Paul. To Theo.

When I'm done, my throat is raw from talking so much, from crying earlier, and I swallow hard. I wish I had a drink. Water, or better yet, vodka.

Dad lets out a heavy sigh. "Thank you for putting all that in context. I don't love that you lied, but honestly—" He cracks a smile, and all of a sudden he's laughing. Mom's grinning, too, and I split my gaze between the two of them.

Did *they* have vodka? "Um, are you okay?"

Dad wipes at his eyes. "Yeah, it's just—it's kind of funny, because I knew about Paul."

All of the air leaves the room. For a second, I can't hear anything but the heartbeat in my ears. "I'm sorry. What?"

"It's not a secret, honey. Mom mentioned it in passing a time or two when us kids were older, in a nostalgic *look how it turned out* kind of way." He sobers up, leaning forward. "Given your relationship and that little secret game you two had, I understand that this may have felt like she was hiding it from you, but I don't think that's ever what it was. It was just a chapter of her life that had closed."

"But didn't that—for you—" I let out a breath, frustrated with my scrambled brain. "Her and Grandpa's relationship meant so much to you. I thought if you knew, it might bother you."

"Not at all. Part of what's so epic about their love story is that they chose each other, Noelle. They made the decision to make it work." He lifts a shoulder, looking over at Mom, who he shares a private smile with. "Every relationship comes with a tipping point, where you decide if you're going to let it go or hold on tight. Sometimes you have multiple—"

"Speaking from experience," Mom pipes up, digging her elbow into Dad's side.

He grins at her before continuing. "There's nothing wrong with either scenario. In fact, both decisions are incredibly brave. But I think it's miraculous when two people decide together that they're going to hold on. Gram and Grandpa did that for sixty-some years, and they loved each other deeply through every minute of it."

Theo's words drift through my brain. *You're so obsessed with secrets.* I created an entire separate path because I thought Gram and Paul's relationship was one. I went on their aborted *honeymoon*, for god's sake.

"So I made this whole thing up?" I'm asking myself as much as I am my parents. "I could've just asked you, 'Hey, do you know about a guy named Paul?' and you'd have said, 'Yeah, as a matter of fact I do' and all of my questions would have been answered?"

"Well, no. I couldn't have given you the story Paul did. If you'd asked me, I would've given you the information I had, which wasn't all that much, and you'd have moved on. Look at where this other path took you."

Two weeks of reading Gram's words and hearing about her first-hand from Paul, feeling that connection between us strengthen. Two weeks of rediscovering my love for photography, and finding Theo.

None of that would've happened if I hadn't dug deeper on my own.

My parents scoot apart, and Dad pats the space between them. I stumble over, letting myself be pulled into the circle of his arms.

His tone is soft and soothing, his bedtime story voice. "All our grief is different, and you faced yours in a way that you needed to, which was keeping one of the main tenets of your relationship with Gram alive. That grief never goes away, but it can grow into something that you can handle, or even grow from. Look what you created from it—your own story woven in with hers. That's something she would love. She would be so proud of you."

"Dad," I groan, my eyes flooding. My heart is breaking and healing all at once, in waves. She would be proud. She'd probably frame all the complimentary comments about my photos. And the ones that called her a babe, too.

He shakes me gently, and I look up to see his eyes are wet like mine. "Mom and I are proud of you, too. Whatever you needed to do to come home with that smile on your face, it was worth it. I can't be all that mad that you lied to us anymore, because look at what it brought you."

I close my eyes and I swear I see it play out like a movie behind my eyes, using all of the images I've captured. It's beautiful, even the painful parts.

It's not a mistake I made. It's my life.

My mind drifts back to Theo. Him in that backyard, alone. Me, walking away.

"Hey, and think about it—you have that job in Tahoe this week,"

Mom says, interrupting my thought. "That wouldn't have happened if you didn't go, and I'm sure there'll be more where that comes from."

"Of course you'd mention the job," I say without heat.

"I love you, but I'd also love my Peloton room back."

I laugh, wiping at my face. "I'm working on it."

"Love you, Beans," Dad says, and they both lean in to hug me tight. It mends something torn inside of me.

"Thank you," I whisper, kissing their cheeks in turn.

Their support is endless, and somehow it just makes me ache that much harder for Theo. I want him to have this, too, from me. I just don't know how to get through to him.

I DON'T HEAR FROM THEO ON TUESDAY, AND BY WEDNESDAY I'm restless. I leave for Tahoe tomorrow, but I'm afraid if I sit around, I'll end up at his door, begging him to open up. Literally *and* figuratively.

Somehow, I wind up at Paul's door instead.

His eyebrows shoot up in surprise, then relax as he smiles. "Noelle, come in."

For the third day in a row, I start crying, and his smile crumbles. He lets out a soft tut of concern, gathering me into a hug.

"I missed you," I say by way of explanation, resting my chin against his cardigan-covered shoulder.

That's only part of it. I miss Theo. I miss being in our bubble, listening to Paul's voice telling stories. I miss the magic of that life, even as I recognize I'm building something special in this one, too.

He pets my hair, leaning a soft cheek against my temple. "I missed you, too, sweetheart. Please come in, all right? Let's sit."

He leads me to the living room, and I try not to look anywhere that'll remind me of Theo. Not at the gallery wall with all the pictures of him, younger with a smile more easily handed over; not at the back deck where I walked out on him playing gardener, displaying that beautiful back my fingers have since traced every curve and dip of. It's even hard to look at Paul right now—it's Theo's face in sixty years.

"I'm sorry I just showed up. I should've called or something."

Or at least made sure Theo wasn't here, though part of me desperately wants him to be. Other than a baseball game playing quietly on the TV, the house is still.

Paul sits at the end of the couch, angling to better face me as I plop down.

"It's absolutely fine. I do have my poker buddies coming over later, but we have time."

I nod and run my hands over my thighs. "I don't know if you've talked to Theo . . ."

"Yes, of course," he says, his expression turning somber.

"I didn't come here to pump you for information, or even talk about him." I swear disappointment flashes in Paul's eyes as he nods. "I . . . actually, I was hoping I could read the last letter you mentioned."

His face brightens. "Ah, I was waiting for this."

He reaches under his coffee table, where a stack of photography books lie. He pulls the top one out and opens it to a page that has a gorgeous landscape photo of Zion. Angels Landing to be exact, where I was so high up I felt like I could reach Gram. A shiver runs down my spine; on top of that lies a letter, though it doesn't look nearly as timeworn as the others.

Paul nods his head toward it, and I take it, unfolding the three pages carefully.

"I'm not sure if you remember me telling you Kathleen sent Vera and me a wedding gift and a note?"

It takes me a second to pluck the memory out of my mind. "You mentioned it the first day of our trip."

"Yes, exactly. Now, some of this won't be relevant because it's her gossiping about our old college friends. But I would love it if you'd read the part where she talks about you."

My breath catches in my chest. "She talks about me?"

"All her grandkids," he confirms, his eyes twinkling. "That part lasts for an entire page. There's a paragraph devoted just to you."

I make a mental note to take a picture of Thomas's paragraph and text it to him. But first, with Paul's hand on my shoulder, I read mine:

> *Then there's Noelle. Now, I'm going to tell you a secret: I know we're not supposed to have favorites, and it's easy for you since you have one grandchild. But if I did have a favorite, it would be my sweet girl. I look at her and my heart feels like it'll burst. She's my shadow, always following me from room to room. If I'm sitting down, she's in my lap. People say we're alike, but she's so much braver than me. She's so curious. Gets in everything! And when she really wants something, she never, ever gives up. I feel this with all my grandchildren, and I don't want to wish away the years—every minute is wonderful—but I can't wait to see what she does when she grows up. I know whatever it is, it'll be spectacular.*

The words are blurred by the time I finish, and I bend over the letter, holding it to my chest. Over my heart. I'm being stitched together, but damn, it hurts.

Paul sweeps his hand over my back while I cry, not just for the loss of Gram, but for the love she gave me in the first place. For the belief she always had in me, even when I didn't have any in myself, and for the realization that I'm finding it again. To see it in her own words, like it's a secret being whispered directly to me from her, is as perfect as it is painful. It's exactly what I needed, and somehow she knew that.

If there's anything I can learn from Paul and Gram's story, it's that I can fall and get back up, I can let go and it still won't be too late to hold on to something else, as long as I keep trying. That eventually the peace will come exactly when it's meant to.

I hate that Gram is gone; I'll never get over it. But I don't have to dig up any more secrets to keep her near, because she's *everywhere*. She guides me when I guide myself.

Paul's voice cuts gently into my thoughts. "I wrote her a letter, too, as a thank-you for the gift, but also so I could gush about my own favorite grandchild."

I wipe at my face, letting my hair curtain between us so I can pull myself together. Though I said I didn't want to talk about Theo, the truth is I'm hungry for any crumb.

He takes my silence for what it is: a request to keep talking. "I don't remember the exact wording because it was a while ago and my mind isn't what it used to be."

"Yeah, right," I scoff, laughing soggily.

The amusement in his voice is clear as he continues. "I told her all about Teddy—how smart he was, how focused even at five. But more important than that, how much he smiled. How loving he was."

I push back my hair, looking at him. He's watching me closely.

"I've seen that five-year-old boy for the past several weeks, even with his unfortunate work situation," he says. "I watched you two grow closer every day and build something that is very special. I know it feels hard when he tries to push away, but what you have is worth holding on to."

It's such an echo of what my dad said that it stuns me. *Let go or hold on.*

"He doesn't trust me," I whisper.

"He trusts you. He doesn't trust that what you have won't be taken away from him." He shakes his head. "If this is worth it to you, Noelle, then be patient with our boy. It takes him three times as long to admit to his own happiness because he never knew he was allowed to have it."

The words sink between us, wrapping around my heart, which hasn't stopped aching in days.

"Okay," I say finally. It's a promise I don't know if I can keep. It's worth it to me, but is it worth it to Theo? I still don't have that answer.

Paul moves us on to other, less wrought subjects, plying me with coffee and cookies. By the time I stand to leave, the sun is hanging low in the sky.

"I didn't mean to stay so late," I say as we walk to the front door. "I'm leaving for Tahoe tomorrow to work with that resort, so I need to pack." I give him a wry grin. "Again."

"Will you let me know how it goes?"

I pause at the threshold. "Is that okay? Even if things don't work out with Theo?"

He gives me a look, pulling me in for a final hug. "You were hers," he whispers. "So, now you're mine, too."

I'm so busy crying as I drive down the street that I nearly miss the flash of red turning the corner. But then I see—it's Theo behind the wheel of Betty, headed toward Paul's. Our eyes meet through our windshields, and electricity arcs between us. I'm so flustered that my foot stomps the gas, and I lurch past him. I don't slow down, but watch in my rearview mirror to see if he'll stop. He doesn't, so I don't either. It feels like my heart is attached to his bumper; it pulls and pulls as his taillights move further away.

Then I turn the corner and he's gone.

When I pull into my parents' driveway, there's a text waiting for me. It's from Theo.

I want to be the person you said you need.

I wipe at my cheeks, searching for what to say. In the end, it's simple: You already are, Spencer. I just need you to trust that. And me.

I wait for his response, but it doesn't come.

Thirty-One

T HANK YOU SO MUCH FOR EVERYTHING, NOELLE," EUNICE, the resort's marketing director, says as she ushers me back into the lobby. "I can't wait to see the final product. The shots you just shared are beautiful."

"It's not hard to do when you're working with a view like this." I gesture out the floor-to-ceiling window, which looks out to a massive deck, a sparkling pool, and beyond that, the towering trees and craggy mountains that make Lake Tahoe so picturesque.

"Seriously, though." She pushes her black bangs out of her eyes. "When I tell you my boyfriend and I stayed glued to our phones while you were traveling, I'm not exaggerating. We fell in love with your story, and your photography is so captivating. Not to mention your social engagement is phenomenal, so you were an easy sell to my boss."

I've read comments saying similar things, but to hear it in person is wild. I'll have to pinch myself later when no one's around. This day has been surreal.

I wish I could share it with Theo. Yesterday he texted me: **good** luck in Tahoe, Shep. You're going to blow them away. I sent him a shot of the sunset falling behind a thick copse of trees, but only got a hearted picture in return.

Blinking away from the memory, I say, "That's really nice, thank you. I had such a great day with you."

"Right back at you. You've been a rock star." Glancing down at her watch, Eunice frowns. "I have to get going, but I wanted to check with you about something. It's half business, half personal."

"Of course."

"I have a friend in San Francisco who's opening up a coffee shop. He's looking for someone to shoot his space and menu for all his social platforms," she says. "I'm not sure what your schedule is like, but would it be okay if I passed your information over to him?"

I work hard to keep my cool, getting out a "Yes, that'd be great."

Meanwhile, inside my body there are firecrackers going off and car alarms blaring. That I could have a potential job as I'm finishing this one is . . .

It's everything I was too afraid to reach for before. Theo's voice echoes in my head, smug and proud: *I told you so.* I'd give anything to hear it in person.

"Amazing!" Eunice chirps. "Well, then, I'll let you get to the rest of your night. Thanks again for everything. You'll be in touch with the final images? And let's rereview your sponsored content schedule on Monday."

"That sounds perfect."

We exchange our goodbyes, and I walk to the elevator, restlessness growing in my chest.

It means something that Theo is the first person I want to call right now, doesn't it? It's *his* support I want. He's given me so much in response to everything I've told him, and I know that's real. I hate that he didn't tell me what he was going through, but he didn't hold himself back from me completely. I saw enough of him to fall in love. That's real, too.

Paul told me it takes Theo three times as long to admit to his happiness, because he didn't know he was allowed to have it. Now, I realize it must take him half as long to admit to his perceived failures, because that's all he heard about.

I think of all the years I had Enzo's voice in my head, telling me that I wasn't good enough to be a photographer. That was after only a year of working with him, and the result was devastating and lasting. Theo's dad has been telling Theo he isn't enough his entire life. How deep must his voice be in Theo's mind? In his heart? Did he hear that in *my* voice, too?

I think of my own family, who accept all my failures, perceived or real, with love and support. Who don't judge me for it. When I went to Theo on Monday, I failed to recognize that, aside from Paul, he's never had someone who accepts him for who he is. Who loves every corner of him, both bright and shadowed.

And then I think of his text from the other day: *I want to be the person you said you need.* I told him he already was, to trust that. But there's so little he's been able to trust, and now, not telling him *why* he should trust that feels like a grave error.

I exit the elevator, my heart thumping. I'm supposed to leave tomorrow morning, but there's so much I need to tell him and none of it can wait.

My camera bag bounces against my hip as I speed walk down the hall, bursting into my room. I make a beeline for my phone, ignoring the texts from my parents, Sadie, and Thomas for now.

Instead, I pull up the text thread between Theo and me and start to type.

I meant it when I said you're already the person I need, but I didn't tell you why and I want you to hear how amazing I think YOU are.

I pause, embarrassingly out of breath from my dash down the hall and from fear and exhilaration, waiting to see if any text bubbles will pop up. There's nothing, so I continue.

So much happened today. I took kickass photos. The marketing director loved me. She's giving me a referral to someone in the city who may hire me. It was a pinch-me moment, a perfect one except for one thing—you're not here for me to share it with. You were the first person I thought of calling. You're the one I want to tell everything to. I don't regret sharing what I did with you, even if it seemed like it on Monday. You make me feel safe. I just want that feeling for you.

My knees are shaking along with my hands. I sit on the edge of the bed, chewing at my lip. Still nothing. I take a deep breath and dive back in. God, this is so long. It's turning into a—

A letter. A *love* letter. But I'm going to say the most important things right to his face.

I was supposed to come home tomorrow, but I'm driving home right now and I'm going to show up at your door. I know I said I was scared to give you any more of my secrets until you gave me something back, but these aren't secrets. It's just the truth. You have 3.5 hours to decide if you want to open the door when I knock.

He still doesn't respond. No bubbles to indicate he's even seen it, either rolling his eyes or with hearts in them. I need to see his face to determine which way this is going to go.

My bag is packed in minutes, fueled by the frantic pace of my heart, and I tow my suitcase behind me as I throw open the door.

"Fucking hell!" I shriek at the tall body in the doorway, reeling back. My heel catches on the edge of the suitcase and I'm tipping over backwards—

But Theo reaches out. He grabs me by the arm, holds on tight, and pulls me until I'm steady on my feet.

"Not the reaction I was hoping for," he murmurs.

"Are you kidding me?" I pant out, dropping my purse and lowering my camera bag so my hands are free to check if he's real. I press my palms to his chest, feeling the heavy, fast beat of his heart behind his ribs. "I was about to drive back to you!"

He smiles, but there's anxiety behind it, the corners of his eyes tightening. "Beat you to it."

"That's so you," I croak out around my thick throat.

"You invited me up here, remember?" he asks, stepping closer. "Or has that invitation expired?"

"N-no. Not expired." Even with my hands on him, it's hard to believe he's here. "How did you find me?"

"Thomas and Sadie."

Oh god. Thomas is going to be smug about this forever.

Theo's expression turns solemn. "I have so much to say."

"I do, too." My fingers curl into his soft gray shirt, encouraging him to come closer. He does, the movement as tentative as the hope on his face. "I texted you a novel, basically."

"I saw it right after I parked."

"Theo, I—"

"Me first," he interrupts, but it's so gentle that my eyes flood. "Since I came all this way."

"Typical of you to try to take first, but—" I break off with a smile when he laughs. "Go ahead."

Theo sobers immediately. "I'm sorry for what I said on Monday and how I shut down. I'm sorry for not explaining myself better when I said our situations weren't the same. I didn't mean our job losses, Noelle. I meant what happened after them."

I nod silently, so he knows I'm really listening.

He makes a frustrated noise from the back of his throat. "You have a strong support system, and I'm used to being alone. It's . . . it's been better for me, historically, to be that way and now my default is processing bad things by myself. It's hard for me to trust that it won't be used against me. I didn't think you'd want me if you knew what had happened, so I thought I was delaying the inevitable by not telling you."

"I *do* want you. No matter what."

"I know. It took me a while to get there. I had to process what you said and realize that you want to be with me, even with the shit I'm going through." He lets out a soft breath that stirs the hair at my temple. His words move over my heart the same way—a cool whisper that brings relief. "I'm sorry I kept you waiting."

"I'm sorry, too," I say. "For not recognizing that it might take you longer to trust me with something this significant and pushing you to share before you were ready. I made an already shitty situation worse."

"You were hurt."

"So were you. My pain doesn't supersede yours." Emotion swells in my throat at the look in his eyes—a powerful affection I recognize but want him to name. Theo waits, as patient as I should have been with him, his hands sweeping up my arms. "Clearly we still have a lot to learn about each other and how we respond to things, but I want to learn your—" I shake my head. "I'm not going to call them secrets anymore. Your truths, I guess, when you're ready to give them to me."

"Funny you mention that." His eyes dart past me, further into the room. "Can I come in?"

I push back against him as he steps forward, tilting my chin back. "Can you give me a proper hello first?"

He raises an eyebrow. "Is that the price of admission, Shepard?"

"*Yes*," I say impatiently, smiling when he laughs quietly.

But our amusement is short-lived. He cups my jaw, his fingers fanning over my cheek to bring me to him. His touch ignites me, and this close, he can see it. His mouth curls up right before it brushes against mine.

I let out a quiet, needy sound, fisting his shirt in my hands. He sighs out my name, kisses me softly once and then again. I push in closer, but he keeps it light. Patient.

"Hi," he murmurs against my mouth.

"Hi," I manage to get out.

"Today went well?"

My eyes fill. Of course he'd ask about that. "Yes, it was amazing."

I get his dimple, a brilliant, proud smile. "I knew it would be."

"It makes it more real now that I've told you." A tear starts to fall down my cheek, but Theo's there to catch it.

"I'm about to know the feeling," he says with a private smile I wonder at. But he just kisses me again, lingering like he wants to make sure this is real. "Let's go talk."

Leaving my luggage at the door, he leads us to the couch, setting down a bag I didn't notice before.

"How are you feeling about work?" I ask.

He slides me a look and pulls out a folder, then circles my wrist to pull me down onto the couch.

"It's a lot, but I'll be fine," he says. "I had an oddly civil talk with Anton and Matias and a rough one with my dad."

"What happened?"

"I told him about the trip Granddad and I took with you. He wasn't thrilled about our family business being splashed all over the internet." I grimace, but Theo just shakes his head, looking surprisingly unruffled about it. "I knew he'd hate it. But *I* didn't.

Those two weeks meant everything to me—and to Granddad—and that matters."

My heart squeezes at the steel in his voice.

"Anyway, he moved on from that to focus on what happened with my job. He's having a harder time letting go of the dream than I did, but I told him he has to. I'm not going to talk to him until he does. His voice can't be louder than mine in my own head, you know?" His gaze locks with mine. "And I've got people in my corner who'll help drown it out, anyway."

I scoot closer to him, my chest tight. It's a massive step, and I can see in his eyes that he knows it, that some weight has been lifted by finally erecting that boundary. "I'm so proud of you."

"You didn't say that like you were about to throw up like last time," he says, grinning. "Progress."

I roll my watery eyes, then appraise him, letting my gaze run over his face. "You're really okay?"

His voice is pitched equally low when he says, "Better now."

We get caught in an extended moment that weaves between us, a thread added to all the ones we've made these past weeks. Invisible. Unbreakable.

There's so much more I want to hear, though, so I nudge us out of the moment, running my hand up his thigh. My fingers brush against the folder in his lap. "Tell me what you've been doing with all your newfound freedom."

"I, ah," he starts, scrubbing a hand over his jaw with reluctant amusement, "I actually spent yesterday trying to figure out how to make a TikTok."

My eyes widen. "What? Why?"

"I wanted to make one for you." His expression turns self-conscious. "It's harder than it looks to make something as good as yours, so I eventually gave up and moved to plan B."

"What's plan B? Actually, I'm not even sure I understand plan A."

He laughs softly. "Plan A was a video where I basically laid my heart on the line. Plan B is the same, but hopefully with less trolls in the comment section."

My throat is so tight, my heart so impossibly full. "No promises."

Theo grins, a hopeful thing that quickly dissolves into a gentle curl. "I went to see Granddad on Wednesday. Well, you saw me, so you know."

"Yeah."

"We had a long talk." He runs a hand through his hair, leaving it mussed. "Very long. So long that he ended up canceling his poker game. He had a lot to say, which won't surprise you."

"Zero percent surprised."

His eyes move over my face like he's taking a mental snapshot. "You and Granddad both gave me a lot to think about. How I view my success, how others view it, what I think I deserve and how I sabotage myself because of how I grew up." I reach over to take his hand, and he looks down as his fingers weave through mine. "But it wasn't until Granddad took me into his darkroom and showed me the pictures I want to show *you* that I really understood what I was at risk of losing if I didn't get my shit together."

My hand tightens around his. "You weren't going to lose me."

"I could've," he says quietly. "Maybe not right away, but eventually. I want to be that guy for you, but I want to be it for *me*, too. We both deserve to be with someone who wants us exactly as we are, don't you think?"

"Yes," I whisper, my eyes filling.

"Did you ever notice how my granddad took pictures of us?" he asks suddenly.

I frown. "Vaguely."

"He took a lot, the stalker, because he knew what he was capturing before we did."

"What do you mean?"

His smile is so tender it looks like it could break, and I hold my breath, not wanting to disturb it. "Let me show you."

Thirty-Two

M Y EYES DROP TO THE FOLDER IN THEO'S LAP. HE PUTS A hand over it, his veins road-mapped underneath his skin. I've had that hand all over my body, and now I feel like it's holding my heart.

"There were things I held back," he says. "The stuff with my job, but other things, too. I want to tell you now, if that's okay."

"Okay," I say faintly.

He opens the folder and my gaze locks in on the top picture. It's Theo and me at Tunnel View overlook, the day I took my first photo. I'm in profile, my camera cradled in my hands. It's clear I've just lowered it, and I'm gazing out at the view in wonder. Theo's several feet away, watching. His expression mirrors mine, but he's looking at me.

"Here, I was thinking about how proud I was that you took that photo even though you were scared," Theo says, his voice low in my ear. "I thought about how scared I was that I walked away from a wreck I'd have to face in two weeks. I wished I could be brave like you, and I wish I'd told you that."

"Theo—" I croak out, but he shakes his head, placing the first picture down.

"There's more."

The next one is us in Death Valley. We're standing close, mirroring each other. Our shoulders are curved in toward each other. I'm gazing up at him, eyes wide, totally rapt. Theo's hands are in his pockets, his body leaning into my space. It's like he wants to reach for me, but won't let himself.

"This is when you asked me about Where To Next's name," he says. "Granddad said it, and I *knew* you'd ask me about it. You're always paying attention. I didn't realize how much I needed to talk about it, but somehow you did."

His expression got so soft when he told me that his trips with Paul were woven into the foundation of the company. It was clear how much it meant to him.

"I'll never forget when you said Where To Next was my pay-it-forward moment over and over again," Theo says. "You saw my intent the way no one else did, even Anton and Matias, and it hurt to know that was going to get taken away from me. You understanding what I wanted to do in the first place took some of that away, and I wish I'd told you that in the moment."

I'm fully crying now, but Theo doesn't stop. It's like the floodgates are open and everything's pouring out at once. It's a purging of secrets.

The next picture, we're in Zion at the swimming hole. We've just breached the water after yelling, and we're looking up at Paul, so close our shoulders are touching. Underneath the water, our legs look tangled.

Theo's thumb smooths down the corner. "This day, I played around with just telling you what I was going through. I could tell that you were going through something, too, and part of me knew you'd understand. But when I was talking about the company changing, you said you'd followed my career and that you were proud of me for fighting for this thing I believed in . . . I couldn't say that I *couldn't* fight it. It was already done. I felt like a liar, but I didn't want to let you down."

"You wouldn't have."

"I know that now." He leans over to press a kiss against my hair, brushing at my wet cheeks with a knuckle. "But I was scared. I didn't want to run you off. I didn't trust what we had yet."

We shuffle through more shots Paul took of us, and the realization is a lightning strike to my heart.

He did hold his biggest secret back, but he gave me so many smaller ones. The truth is laid out here. There are quiet moments where we're hiking next to each other on dusty red trails, Theo's hand hovering at my back. We talked about mundane details of Where To Next, my photography, bickered over high school shenanigans. There's a shot of Theo looking right at the camera, his undiluted affection for Paul written all over his face. He let me see every tender part of their relationship while putting his vulnerability on display. He let me share their love, knowing it would heal me, too.

There's a photo of the two of us dancing on the back patio in Sedona, the night before I confessed everything to him and he confessed right back. It wasn't about his situation, but in telling me the way he saw me, he exposed his own wishes. In hindsight, I can see how much he wanted to believe those words for himself, and how much he probably needed to hear them.

I trace my finger over our tangled bodies. "It did hurt that you didn't tell me about losing your job. But you didn't hold back entirely, and it means everything that you trusted me enough to do that."

"I do trust you," he says quietly, then picks up the last picture.

It's the one Theo took of me at the top of Angels Landing in Zion. I'm in motion, turning toward him. The photo is a little blurry. I teased him about it when I emailed it to him at his request, but I loved it then. Mixed in with all the others now, I love it even more. In the photo, he's just called my name, and my eyes are lit up with *everything*. I'm telling on myself so badly.

Theo smiles, like he knows. "This one is my favorite."

"Tell me why."

"Remember how determined we were to get to the top?"

I laugh. I can still feel how shaky my knees were crossing the chainless section of the path, and yet how oddly calm I was with Theo right behind me.

Our eyes meet, and he lets out a breath. "Remember how we did that together?"

I nod silently, not trusting my voice.

"You got up to the top first, and all I could think about was how beautiful you were. You asked me what I'd do if I had time, and when I said I'd travel, I didn't add the most important part." He shifts, curving his hand around my leg. His eyes are a deep, fathomless blue but so clear. I can see everything in them. "I didn't say that I'd spend it with you, but I wish I had. It was the first time I'd thought about what I could do once I'd left my company in a way that made me happy, and that was because of you. Because of what we could do together."

Theo sets the picture on the table with all the others. A stranger could look at these and know how we feel. It was right there, growing between us every second, when we acknowledged it and even when we couldn't.

"Noelle."

He says my name so quietly, it's barely a sound. The same emotion that's welling in my chest is threaded through his voice when he gestures to the photos and says, "This is the way I fell in love with you."

I knew that's where he was headed, but hearing it out loud is still stunning, so I fall apart. Just a little. "It's the way I fell in love with you, too."

"I could see that." A slow, almost shy smile spreads across his face like honey. When I lean forward to kiss him, I can taste it.

"I love you," I say, and he says it back, framing my face in his hands. He gives me each word soaked in relief.

"I wish I'd told you all of this sooner," he says, pushing my hair back from my face. "You make it easier to try to be brave, but I'm not always going to get it right. I can't be perfect."

"Haven't you been listening to me? I don't want you to be perfect. After all our battles, Spencer, you should know that it actually pisses me off."

He laughs against my neck, kissing up my throat, to my ear, along my cheek, until he places the most careful kiss on the tip of my nose. His eyes are wide open. Mine are, too.

"Can I tell you why I love you?" I whisper.

Pulling back, he nods. The unease in his expression breaks my heart. But it fortifies me, too.

"First of all, you're the best grandson ever. You'll do anything for Paul, and it's clear you're obsessed with each other. And even though he's yours, you stepped aside and let me have important moments with him without hesitation." I say all this watching his anxiety melt away, turning into something so hopeful it makes a tear run down my cheek. "You're so selfless that you're going to share your title of favorite grandchild with me."

His smile is luminous. "Slow your roll."

"You catch me when I fall down hills, and you only yell about it a little bit. You have really terrible taste in music." I hold up my hand as he starts to protest. "That's not a plus, but it's worth mentioning. I want the bad parts with the good."

Theo laughs, but his eyes are suspiciously glassy.

"And last but not least, you held me up when I was at my lowest until I could climb out myself." I swallow reflexively a few times while Theo gazes at me with the smallest, most beautiful smile. I'm glad no one's here to take our picture; we must look ridiculous, so in love. It's the best moment of my life. "You didn't try to fix me. You just supported me until I believed it. I want to be that for you, Theo. Not because it's a tit for tat thing or because I need your secrets to feel like we're even, but because your happiness is important to me, no matter what it looks like."

"I want that, too," he says hoarsely. "You have no idea how much."

"I do. It's how much *I* want it."

With a relieved exhale, he pulls me onto his lap and tangles his fingers in my hair, bringing my mouth to his. We've given each other so many words that now there's nothing left to do but this. The pressure of his kiss is immediately intense, and I sag into him, wrapping my arms around his neck, feeling his heart beat hard against my chest. One of his hands moves down my back, and he cinches my hips tight against his until I can feel all of his need.

"I love you." He groans while he says it, tightens a fist in my hair to keep me exactly where he wants me—right here with him.

I laugh against his mouth. "Yeah, you do."

He grins, pulling back. He's close enough that I could count each of his eyelashes individually if I wanted to spend my time doing anything but getting naked.

He gives me his stern eyebrows, but now I know all of his softness. They're as effective as ever, but in a different way. "Your speech was better than mine, Shepard."

I arch an eyebrow back. "It's not a contest, Spencer."

Our grins are mirrors of each other—euphoric love with a pinch of competition. That's just who we are.

But shockingly, Theo concedes. "Okay, fine. This time we both win."

He's right. We both do, for the rest of the night and long after that.

Thirty-Three

A Year and a Half Later

CAN'T WAIT TO FALL FACEDOWN ON THE BED AND SLEEP FOR forty-eight hours straight," I groan as I lug my suitcase up the stairs, my arms and legs screaming against the weight of three weeks' worth of clothes, toiletries, and gifts packed to the brim.

"That sounds less fun than other things you could be doing facedown on the bed," Theo says from behind me.

I give him a look over my shoulder, but he's too busy staring at my ass. When I don't respond, those deep blue eyes make their way to my face. He grins unabashedly at being caught.

"We've been traveling for nineteen hours, Spencer. If you're planning to do anything other than sleep, I invite you to start talking sexy to your hand now."

After flying in from Milan with a stopover at JFK, carrying all of our stuff upstairs is the equivalent of climbing Mount Everest. I heft my bag onto the landing with an exhausted huff.

Theo drops his suitcase next to mine and immediately pulls me into his arms for a lingering kiss.

"Nooo. I smell like airplane and airport and staleness." Despite my protest, I melt against him, looping my arms loosely around his waist. He steps in closer, deepening our connection.

He lets his hands roam, stroking absently over the curve of my lower back, his fingers splaying wide, up along the valley of my waist until he finally reaches up to cradle my cheeks. I'm surprised at the intensity of his touch. We've been stuffed on an airplane together for nearly a day, and traveled all over Italy for three weeks before that. But he's kissing me like he's either memorizing me or this moment.

I've had a lot of time over the past year and a half to catalog his moods. I watched the melancholy he had to shake off with the change of his job status and the distance it brought to his friendship with Anton and, to a lesser extent, Matias. I intimately know the spark that returned when he decided to try again nine months ago, and now I regularly see it when he's on a call with the travel nonprofit focused on local community impact he's been working with. I recognize the calm affection he reserves for Paul when they're bantering, the disgruntlement I have to distract him from after a phone call with his dad, and the warm amusement he shows my family.

Sometimes it's frustration when I push him too hard to share before he's ready, and I have to give him space. I love the quiet pride in his eyes when I come home from a job. My TikTok engagement grew exponentially after our trip, and it's afforded me opportunities I've only dreamed about.

But this mood of Theo's is my favorite: when we're in the middle of a moment he clearly wants to remember. He'll pull me into his arms just like this, kiss me for a minute or two or five. He makes sure I'm breathless before he pulls back. Sometimes he'll tell me how happy he is; other times he'll simply press a kiss to my forehead.

He does that now, then sweeps his thumbs over my cheeks and says, "Welcome home."

The first time he said that to me when I moved into his place a year ago, he got the goofiest smile on his face. It's become his thing—every time I walk in the door, he'll call it out to me, even if I just walked down to the corner store. And when I get up the stairs, he's wearing that same smile, dimple shamelessly on display.

I never get tired of hearing or seeing that, and after three weeks away from home and all the people we love, it feels like a moment *I* want to memorize, too.

"I love you," I say. My life with Theo is like finally slipping into a space that's shaped just for me. My path to get here was long, and often disorienting as hell, but the payoff was worth it.

I wish Gram were here to see. But somehow, I think she knows.

"I love you, Shepard," Theo murmurs against my lips.

I check my watch over his shoulder—it's after nine, but I'm starving. "Did you say Thomas and Sadie dropped off groceries earlier or did I dream that?"

"They were here," he says cryptically, his mouth curling up as his gaze moves beyond me. I start to turn, expecting to see them standing behind us with confetti poppers, but Theo palms my cheek and brings my attention back to him.

I lean back, still in the circle of his arms. Underneath his sun-bronzed skin, his cheeks are flushed. His eyes are bright, a little wild, which I assumed was from overtiredness. He barely slept the entire ride home. In fact, he kept *me* up with a nearly constant bouncing knee that I threatened to put out of commission permanently.

"Are they . . . still here?" I venture.

He laughs. "No."

"Are you worried they went through our stuff or something? Mas is nosy as hell, but Sadie knows to keep him away from bedrooms and vibrator stashes."

"No," he repeats. "I just don't want you to look behind you until I tell you that I did something while we were gone. Or I had Granddad and your family do something while we were gone, with my direction."

"What?"

"You've been meaning to put up new photos on the wall, right?" He nods his chin over my shoulder, and I start to turn. Again, he directs me back to him.

I push against his palm with my cheek, but he holds fast. "Oh my god, let me *look*!"

He laughs, his chest shaking against mine, pressing closer. I can feel the beat of his heart. How fast it's going. "Holy shit, you're impatient. Let me set it up."

"I'm going to be old and gray by the time you do."

Something shifts in his expression, from amusement to hope so raw it wraps a fist around my heart. "I can't wait to see that." Before I can respond, he continues, "You wanted to put new photos in the frames on the wall, but you've been so busy I wanted to take that off your plate. I thought it'd be cool to come home to it already done."

"You chose the pictures and everything? All on your own?"

He nods, biting at his lip. "I picked some that I know are your favorites. Kind of a mixture of trips we've taken, shots of our families, that kind of thing. I even got a few from Italy."

Everything inside me melts. "You really are the best, do you know that? If it didn't benefit me so much, it would be annoying."

He doesn't even return with a smug quip. Instead he grins. "Okay. Now you can look."

I turn. The wall is big enough that it can handle close to twenty frames in various sizes. I start from the top left and work my way across. There are new photos from our road trip with Paul, replacing some of the ones that were there before. Photos from weekend trips we've taken, dinners out with friends, one of Paul and my dad, who have turned into hiking buddies, my favorite snapshot of Gram and me, and—

Nestled in the middle are four framed pictures of Theo and me, ones I haven't seen before. It takes me a second for my brain to realize what I'm looking at, but my heart catches on right away, beating furiously.

In the first picture, we're on a private boat tour in Positano and I'm facing away from the camera, my hair flowing out behind me. Theo is in the foreground, faced toward the camera, a small smile on his face. He's holding a piece of paper that says: WILL.

The next picture, we're at dinner in Florence and I'm gazing out toward a cobblestoned square where a band is playing. Again, Theo's holding up a piece of paper, a little smirk on his face. It says: YOU.

"Oh my god." Tears are already falling from my eyes. I move on to the next one.

We're at the beach in Taormina and I'm staring out at the ocean, hand shielding my eyes. Theo's a few feet behind me, wearing only swim trunks, looking gorgeous. I can still feel the heat of his skin against my palms when we came back to our hotel and got tangled up in bed. In the picture, Theo's sign says: MARRY.

In the last picture, we're in front of a coffee shop in a narrow, picturesque alleyway in Rome. Theo has me wrapped up in his arms and my face is tucked into his neck. He's looking at the camera, his eyes filled with so much love I can't help letting out a sobbing laugh. I remember that moment, when he pulled me into a hug so sweetly affectionate. I closed my eyes and soaked it in and thought *god, my life is so good.*

There's a ring pinched between Theo's fingers in the picture, and a piece of paper is held up against my red dress. It says: ME?

In the reflection of the framed glass, I see Theo behind me, kneeling.

I turn around, my hands over my mouth, and stumble to him. He's holding the ring from the picture between his thumb and forefinger.

"Are you kidding me?" I cry, kneeling down with him. If we're doing this, it's going to be together.

He smiles, his eyes crinkling at the corners. I love him. I want to watch those lines deepen with time, until he's old and gray, too.

"I know we don't use the word *perfect*, but the past year and a half has been as close as I've ever had," he says, his voice going hoarse as he fights against the emotion welling in his eyes. "And I know we don't do secrets, either, but it's not a secret that I want to spend the rest of my life with you, right?"

I let out a wet laugh. "No, you've been pretty obvious."

He grins, a tear slipping down his cheek. "No one loves me like you do, Noelle. I wake up every morning thinking it can't get better, and then it does. It's never going to be perfect, but we can spend the next sixty years or so making it really damn good, if that's what you want, too."

"Sixty years, huh?" Even two lifetimes don't feel like enough.

"At least." He runs a finger over my wet cheek, then asks quietly, "Will you marry me?"

I throw my arms around his neck, and he teeters with a laugh, wrapping his arms around my waist to keep us steady.

"I will marry the *hell* out of you," I say, pulling him to me for a kiss that's all him laughing, me crying.

"I love you," he whispers once, then again as he slides the brilliant diamond onto my finger. I say it back, against his mouth, his cheek, right up against his ear so he never forgets this moment and what he's given me.

After a few minutes of dizzy, euphoric making out, Theo pulls me to a stand.

I gaze at the pictures, imagining someone finding them someday. Wanting to know our story. "How did you do all this without me knowing?"

His hand moves up and down my back in soothing strokes as he appraises them. "I worked it out in advance with someone, depending on where we were—sometimes it was days in advance, like with the boat tour, and sometimes minutes, like that picture in Rome. I gave them my number so they could text me the picture afterward."

"Who printed them out? Who put them up? My whole family was involved?"

Theo nods. "Thomas and Granddad got them printed. Everyone, including your parents, came and swapped out the old pictures with these."

That explains the FaceTime call I got from my family two days ago. They were all giddy to the point of hysterical laughter. I chalked it up to a boozy brunch, but now I know they were just beside themselves with excitement.

"You are all so sneaky, oh my god." I press my hand against my forehead, feeling the cool metal of the ring against my heated skin. "How am I ever going to beat this?"

Theo turns to me, pulling me back into his arms. He gazes down at me, pure happiness and unabashed affection written all over his face. "It's not a contest, remember?"

I stare down at my ring, mesmerized, before blinking up at him. "Is this real? This is my life?"

"Shepard," he says, grazing his lips against mine. "It's ours."

His glancing touch turns into searching kisses, and I push him back toward our bedroom, yanking at his shirt. He lets me pull it over his head, laughing, bringing my hand up to his mouth so he can kiss my finger right above the ring he just gave me.

We've had all kinds of sex many times over—frantic, slow, intense and rough, the makeup kind after a fight, the sneaky type in places we could get caught—but engaged sex is going to be my favorite. I can already tell by the way he grips my hips tight in his hands, by the need in his eyes.

Theo backs me into the wall next to the bedroom, dipping his mouth to my throat. He presses it right over my steadily beating pulse and smiles against my skin. "Where should we go on our honeymoon?"

I consider it, but only for a second. Then I smile, wrapping my arms around his neck. "How about a road trip?"

Acknowledgments

When I was a teenager, my grandma found a story I'd left up on my computer. When she told me she'd read it, I wanted to dissolve into a puddle of angst and humiliation. But she assured me she loved what I'd written, and said something that stuck with me: "Finish writing it. I want to see how it ends."

I never finished that story, nor did I finish the dozen that followed it. But I did finish this one with her encouragement echoing in my head. I think that if she'd been able to hold this book in her hands, she'd tell me just how much she loved the ending. But more than that, she'd tell me how excited she was for the beginning of this thing I've been dreaming about for so long. I want to thank her first, because the spark of this story began with her.

My endless gratitude goes to my incredible agent, Samantha Fabien. The way you understood this story and Noelle's journey from the beginning, and your unwavering belief in me, still feels a little unreal. I'm so grateful for you—and our grandmas for conspiring to bring us together! Many thanks also to the larger, equally wonderful Root Lit family.

To my amazing editor, Kerry Donovan, thank you for loving Noelle and Theo as much as I do and for taking a chance on all of us. I feel so lucky to have access to your guidance, skill, and deep well of knowledge. To the rest of the Berkley team who've helped make this a real, actual book—Mary Baker, Megan Elmore, Christine Legon, Dache' Rogers, Fareeda Bullert, and Anika Bates. Thank you to Emily Osborne for the incredible cover direction and Anna Kuptsova for her stunning cover artwork. I'm so appreciative of all of you!

I dragged a million people along this journey with me, so please bear with me. Firstly, to Anya and Kate, whose nicknames I won't put here because sometimes we're not publicly embarrassing—who am I without you? I never want to find out. Thank you for holding my hand, for laughing with me until I cry and crying with me until I laugh again. Our friendship is the best friendship in the world.

To Sarah T. Dubb, Risa Edwards, and Livy Hart, this book would quite simply not exist without you. Thank you for your encouraging words in the margins and for pushing me to be better every day. To Alexandra Kiley, Maggie North, and Sarah Burnard, thank you for giving me such thoughtful, encouraging feedback while I wrote this, and to Jen Devon and Ingrid Pierce, thank you for being amazing cheerleaders along the way. You are all incredible humans with fierce talent. What a combo!

Ongoing gratitude to those who read, reassured, and hyped: Mae B, Kate Robb, Aurora Palit, Sofia Arellano, Rebecca Osberg (#BTeam represent), Ambriel McIntyre, Nicole Poulsen, Carla G. Garcia, Tasha Berlin, Caitlin Highland, Jenn, and Ashton. My deep appreciation also goes to the Berkletes, who I one hundred percent could not survive without. Special shout-outs to Sarah Adler for lending an ear in the early whirlwind days, and Alicia Thompson, who is an excellent hand-holder and an even better friend. Many thanks to the Hopefully Writing and #TeamSamantha slack groups, who have been such great support systems. To Esther, the first person to highlight these finished words: thank you for helping me check off a bucket list item. I'm surrounded by so many people whose generosity somehow exceeds their immense talent, and I think about the jackpot-hitting luck of that every day.

To Mom and Aunt Teri, who, along with my gram, introduced me to romance books—that turned out to be pretty life-changing! Thank you both (and Maddy!) for celebrating with me every step of the way. You can read this, but maybe let's not talk about it after. To Dad, who will only ever read this page, thank you for being proud of me no matter what. To my extended family—the one I was honored to be born into and the one I was lucky enough to marry into—I love you all!

To my husband, Steve, you've given me the space and time to make this happen, and have supported me through it all in true #1 hype man fashion. Thank you for showing me what a love story looks like so I could turn around and write one (and also for telling everyone I wrote a book as soon as we step foot in a bookstore, every time). To my little hype boy, Noah, thank you for allowing me to experience the most rewarding, unconditional love. Thank you for wanting to help me write my next book, too. Someday you'll figure out why that would've been awkward. I love you both more than anything.

And to you, reading this: I never thought I'd be lucky enough to have people hold my book in their hands, so thank you for making this dream completely, fantastically, finally real.

you,
with a
View

JESSICA JOYCE

READERS GUIDE

Questions for Discussion

1. Secrets are a main theme of *You, with a View*: Noelle wanting to discover a piece of her gram's life that wasn't revealed during their game of Tell Me a Secret, the elements of Paul and Kathleen's relationship, and Noelle and Theo revealing their own over the course of the road trip. In what ways do you think secrets can bring people together? Conversely, how do they pull people apart?

2. Noelle is grieving both her gram and a career that hasn't lived up to her expectations; Theo is grieving his job and the lofty plans he had for his company. What are the different kinds of grief a person can experience? What do you think is the difference between grief that holds you back and grief that helps you grow? How did you see their grieving play out in Noelle's and Theo's lives over the course of the book?

3. Throughout the story, Noelle struggles with what she views as her lack of success in adulthood. Did you think her view of success, both her own and others', changes by the end? How do you define success in your own life?

4. Noelle has a close, supportive relationship with her family—did you have a favorite secondary character in *You, with a View*?

5.   What do you think of Paul and Kathleen's story? Even though they didn't have a happy ending with each other, do you think they still got their happy ever after? Have you learned any lessons from failed relationships (family, friends, love) in your own life that have helped lead you to stronger future relationships?

6.   At the beginning of the book, Noelle connects with Paul and Theo when her TikTok goes viral. Once she starts documenting their road trip, she connects with strangers via comments and DMs about the impact of her work, viewers' important relationships that mirror Noelle's and Gram's, and even Paul and Kathleen's story. How has social media connected you to someone or something meaningful or important?

7.   Describe your perfect road trip: What places would you visit? What kind of music would you listen to on the way? Who would you want to bring with you?

8.   Have you ever visited any of the places Noelle, Theo, and Paul travel to in *You, with a View*? Did you have a favorite scene on one of their trail hikes?

9.   Noelle's passion for photography comes out in many ways in this book. What was your favorite photograph taken by Noelle or someone else in this story? Do you have any hobbies that you've returned to at different points in your life?

10.   Noelle grows close to Paul as they travel on Kathleen and Paul's planned honeymoon road trip, and as they share their memories of her beloved grandmother. Was there one letter that Paul shared with Noelle that you think was most meaningful to her?

Keep reading for a preview of
Jessica Joyce's next romance!

Prologue

HATE THINKING ABOUT THE WAY IT ENDED, BUT SOMETIMES I think about the way it began: with me walking through the door of someone else's house without knocking.

This has always been a typical move of mine, wandering latch-key kid that I was in my early years. But in every other way, the beginning is an atypical day.

When I let myself go there, I watch it in my head like a movie. I let it feel like it's happening now instead of thirteen years ago, where the real moment belongs, where fifteen-year-old me is turning the doorknob on a house I've burst into hundreds of times before. I find no resistance, because by my sophomore year of high school—when this memory takes place—my open invitation into the Cooper-Kims' home is implied.

My best friend of five years, Adam Kim, is somewhere in here, probably still sweaty and gross from track practice. At least I went home and showered.

On the day it all begins, I greet Adam's three rescue dogs, Gravy, Pop Tart, and Jim, my ears perking up at the dulcet tones of a video game played at full volume, two male voices rumbling below it. I make my way toward the den with the dogs trailing behind me, the tags on their collars jingling, a sound that's as familiar as my own heartbeat.

Adam's house is warm and sun-filled, often noisy, with a lingering, faint vanilla scent I've never been able to figure out the source of. The first time I walked in here, something unraveled in my chest: it felt like home, not a place where two people lived with sometimes-intertwining lives. My house is quiet and often empty at fifteen, just as it was when I was ten and five and all the years in between. The times my dad and I do sync up are great; he asks me tons of questions and tells me what a great kid I am, how easy I've been, how proud he is of my grades, and he listens to every story that tumbles out of my mouth, his phone facedown on the dining room table while it buzzes and buzzes and buzzes. Eventually the phone wins, and I'm left craving more time.

It's why I've made a habit of making other people's houses my home, and why I love the Cooper-Kims' house best.

In this memory, I'm turning the corner to the den, wondering who Adam has over. I sincerely hope it isn't Brent; I keep telling Adam what a douche he is.

With the power of hindsight, I know what's going to happen seconds before it does, so I always hold my breath here.

I charge through the door and run face-first into a broad chest. It has so little padding it makes my teeth rattle.

"Whoa," a voice breathes above me, stirring the hairs at my temple. Warm, strong hands grip my arms to keep me upright.

I look up . . . and up, into a face fifteen-year-old me has never seen before.

Whoever this is, he's beautiful. He's tall (obviously) and broad-shouldered, with limbs he hasn't grown into. In this moment, I don't know that he'll fill out in a painfully attractive way—his chest will broaden and tighten to become the perfect pillow for my head. His thighs will grow just shy of thick, mouth-wateringly curved with muscle, the perfect perch for me when I sit in his lap.

But the eyes I'm looking into won't change. They'll stay that hypnotic mix of caramel and gold and deep coffee-brown, framed by sooty lashes and inky eyebrows that match the wavy hair on his head. They'll continue to catch mine the way they do in this movie moment—like a latch hooking me, then locking us into place.

"Oh. Hello," I say brilliantly.

His mouth pulls up; it's wide and meant for the toothy smiles I'll discover he doesn't give away easily. He's more prone to quiet ones, or shy, curling ones, like the one he's giving me now. "Hey."

I step back, my heart flipping from our crash and the warmth his hands have left behind on my skin. "Sorry, I didn't know Adam had someone over."

"Never stopped you before, Woodward," Adam calls distractedly, his eyes glued to the TV screen.

I roll mine, turning back to this stranger. "I'm that doofus's best friend, Georgia."

"Like the peach," he says, his voice lifting at the end. It's not a question, but a tentative tease. In my life, I've heard that joke a million times and I hate it, but in this moment, I like the way he says it, as if he knows how ridiculous it is and is in on the joke.

I grin, and in my mind when I'm watching this, I think about how open it is, how guileless and full of sunshine. "Good one. No one's ever said that to me before."

There's a beat where his eyes narrow, like he's trying to figure me out. I make note of how quickly he does, a tendril of belonging curling around me when he laughs. "You're joking."

"Yes," I laugh back.

He pretends to look disappointed. "So I'm *not* the first?"

"More like lucky number ninety-nine," I shoot back, and he grins. A toothy one. "Should I call you by the number, or do you have a name, too?"

"That's Eli—mother*fucker*," Adam shouts.

My gaze slips from the stranger's—Eli Joseph Mora, I'll find out soon—to Adam, whose tongue is sticking out while he furiously pounds on a game controller. A second one lies next to him, a decimated bag of Doritos next to that.

When I direct my attention back to Eli, our eyes click. I hear it in my head, feel it in my chest, both in the memory and for real. Whenever I let myself think about the beginning, I want to get out of this moment as much as I want to wallow in it.

Fifteen-year-old me smiles up at fifteen-year-old him. "Hey, Eli. I hope *you're* not the motherfucker."

"Not that I'm aware of," he says with a laugh. His eyes spark with amusement and other things, and the spark transfers to me, burrowing somewhere deep. It'll wait there for years while we go from strangers to friends to best friends. It won't catch fire until our junior year of college, when he joins me at Cal Poly after his two-year stint at community college.

"Who are you, then? Other than a stranger, until"—I look down at my watch, a Fossil one I bought with the cash my dad gave me for Christmas because he didn't want to get the wrong one—"three minutes ago."

"The new guy, I guess?" I notice his nose is sunburned along the bridge when he scrunches it. "I just moved from Denver, started at Glenlake two days ago."

He doesn't tell me now, but he will later—his parents moved him and his little sisters to Glenlake, a city in Marin County just north of San Francisco, to live with his aunt after his dad lost his job and they lost their house. He's sleeping on a pullout in his aunt's rec room. I always notice the way his shoulders pull up toward his ears, maybe wondering if I'm going to ask questions. He doesn't trust me with all of his heavy stuff yet, but eventually he'll trust me with a lot of it. I'm the one who'll hide my heaviness away.

"And Adam's already got you in his clutches?" I raise my voice. "You work fast, Kim."

Adam grins, but doesn't spare us a glance.

Eli looks over his shoulder at his new friend, then back at me, rubbing the nape of his neck. His expression is bashful, a little bewildered. "Yeah, I think he kind of adopted me."

"He does that," I say, remembering that first day of sixth grade when Adam and I met. How scared and lonely I was at a huge new school, where none of the pseudo friends I had in elementary school were all that interested in continuing our journey together. The closest friend I had, Heather Russo, told me when I got to her locker our first day to walk to the class I was so excited we shared, "God, we just started here, Georgia, we don't have to be together all the time. Stop being so needy."

Adam saved me from new-kid loneliness; it makes sense that he'd save Eli from it, though in the moment I don't know that he's lonely, too, or that Adam's house will become his home as much as it is mine.

"All right, Eli," I say, looking him up and down. He's got on Nikes that are fraying at the seams, gym shorts, and a T-shirt with a hole near the neck. I can see a sliver of collarbone pressing sharply against his golden skin. "I guess I'm kind of adopting you, too."

He lets out a breath, his eyes moving over my face. "Probably a good idea, since I've already got a nickname picked out for you and everything."

"I'll let you get away with that one, Ninety-Nine," I say, and my chest warms at the way his grin widens. It's an addicting feeling, knowing I'm in the middle of meeting a person I'll get to hang on to.

Adam looks at me over Eli's shoulder, his mouth pulling up, and I know he feels it, too: the three of us are going to be friends. Something special.

Years later Eli will tell me that he fell a little bit in love with me right then, and in this movie-like memory I always see it—the dilation of his pupils when we can't quite break eye contact, the flush along the delicate shell of his ear when I sit next to him on the couch minutes later, the way his eyes linger on me when Adam and I bicker over control of the TV, the steady bounce of his knee. The beautiful, shy smile he gives me over the pizza we have for dinner later.

He'll hold on to it for years, but eventually that spark will become a wildfire.

And then we'll burn it all down.

One

This wedding is cursed

OH, GOD, NOT AGAIN," I MUTTER.

To the untrained eye, this text message probably looks like a joke. A prank. The beginning of one of those chain emails our elders get duped into forwarding to twenty of their nearest and dearest, lest they inherit multigenerational bad luck.

In actuality, it's been Adam's mantra for the past nine months.

Adam is the brother I never had and I'm truly honored to be part of his wedding celebration. That said, had sixth-grade Georgia anticipated I'd be fielding no fewer than forty-seven texts per day from my more-unhinged-by-the-day best friend, I would've thought twice about complimenting his *Hannah Montana* shirt our first day of middle school.

The silver lining: I've taken a screenshot of each text and filed them away so I can present them to him via a PowerPoint-presented roast once his wedding is over.

My Spidey senses tingle with this text, though. It hasn't been delivered in aggressive caps lock, nor is it accompanied by a chaotic menagerie of GIFs (my kingdom for a Michael Scott alternative). Whatever has happened now might actually be an emergency.

Then again, the wedding is ten days away; at this point, anything that isn't objectively awesome is a disaster.

I pluck my phone off my desk and type out an exploratory what's the damage?

A bubble immediately pops up, disappears, reappears, then stops again.

"*Great* sign."

I wait while Adam molds his panic into thought, eyes on my phone instead of my computer. It's nearly four p.m. on Wednesday, the day before my PTO for the wedding starts, and I still have half a page of unchecked boxes on my to-do list, plus a detailed While I'm Away email to draft for my boss. I can't leave Adam hanging in his moment of need, though. What kind of best woman would I be?

No better than the largely absent best man? comes the unchari-table punchline. I slam the door on that thought. It's not like I've minded executing most of the best-people activities; actually, it's been a godsend for multiple reasons. It's just that it's so typical of him to—

I catch my own eyes in my computer's reflection, delivering a silent message with the downward slash of my eyebrows: *Shut. Up.* I'd rather think about curses than anything even tangentially re-lated to the subject of Eli.

Not that I believe in curses at all, but deep down, I do worry that Adam's been followed by bad vibes since he proposed to his fiancée, Grace Tan, on New Year's Eve. Their plans have involved a comedy of errors that have escalated from *bummer* to *oh shit*: the wrong wedding dress ordered by the bridal salon; names misspelled on their wedding invitations, requiring an eleventh-hour reprint; and the one that nearly got me to believe—their wedding planner quit three months ago because his golden retriever had amassed such a following on social media that he was making triple his salary as her manager.

For Adam, whose natural temperament hovers somewhere near live wire, it's been a constant test of his sanity. Even Grace, who's brutally chill, the perfect emotional foil for Adam, and an actual angel, has been fraying lately.

Then again, she wanted to elope. Every new disaster probably only further solidifies the urge to book it to Vegas.

Adam's texts shoot rapid-fire onto the screen:

Georgia

Our fucking DJ

BROKE THEIR HIP

LINE DANCING AT A BACHELORETTE PARTY

IN NASHVILLE

I seriously need to know what I've done in my 28 years on this dying earth that is causing this to happen

The possibilities are endless. I start to type, but he beats me to it.

That was rhetorical, Woodward, DON'T

I can see that Adam's shifting out of his panic fugue, and I physically feel myself shifting into fix-it mode.

Deep breath, nothing's burned to the ground, right? I text back. This is problematic but not fatal. We'll come up with a new list.

The bubbles of doom pop up again and I wait. Again.

Out of everyone, there's a reason Adam's come to me: I'm the one people run to when they need a shoulder to cry on, a brainstorm partner, a hype woman. The one who knows what to do when shit hits the fan or when a bottle of champagne needs to be popped. When their wedding planner peaced out, Adam called *me* begging for help.

I would've stepped up anyway, but my motives aren't completely altruistic. Dedicating myself to problem-solving Adam's wedding woes has been the only way to reliably stay in his orbit.

I'm a list girl. I learned the magic of them long ago—the way they can streamline tasks, dos and don'ts, expectations. Emotions. How they can take a messy, chaotic thing and make it manageable. They've been my coping strategy since I was a kid, the best way I can take care of myself. They quiet my mind and untangle my emotions so that I stay cool, calm, and compartmentalized. So *I'm* not a messy, chaotic thing, because that way loneliness lies.

Needless to say, it aggrieves me that there's no way to list my way out of what's been happening in my life: the friends I've built my social life around, who have been my family, are shifting into phases I'm not in—falling in love, cohabitating, building social circles with other nauseatingly happy couples—putting me on the outside looking in.

Really, though, it's fine. I mean, sure, I'm constantly kicking at loneliness, a feeling I've worked hard to avoid since I was old enough to know what that feeling was. Yeah, I can feel it peeking around corners anyway, curling up next to me at night in that empty extra space in my bed. Absolutely, watching my best friend find the kind of love I once thought I had, too, is a little soul-destroying, as is being knee-deep in my best friend's wedding festivities, knowing that in ten days I have to stand beside—

Anyway. I'm good. One hundred and ten percent okay.

My phone buzzes. I jump, shaking off the last thought. It came within inches of breaking a rule on a list I created when I crawled back from New York five years ago, dragging my obliterated heart with me: never think about *that* era with Eli—

"Hey!" I whisper-yell, flicking myself on the forehead. "Get it together."

I turn my attention to Adam's text: Can you help with a DJ list that isn't shitty?

That deserves a voice message. "Can I help with a *list*? Seriously?"

Like all the other times Adam's called me in for support, it's the serotonin hit I need to chase that lonely feeling away.

I just wish it would last.

Adam's text comes in as a Teams notification dings politely on my computer. My head swivels on instinct, ponytail sweeping across my cheek.

Nia Osman: hey, can I borrow you for 5?

Adam and my boss needing me plays tug-of-war on my people-pleasing tendencies, but only one of them is paying me. Adam's broken DJ is going to have to wait.

Nia needs to chat, I text. Take a deep breath, listen to your Calm app. I'll come back to you ASAP.

JESSICA JOYCE grew up a voracious reader who quickly learned how to walk and read simultaneously to maximize her reading time. Thanks to a family full of romance-novel-adoring women, she discovered love stories and never looked back. When she's not writing, you can find her listening to one of her chaotically curated playlists, crying over TikToks, eating her way through the Bay Area with her husband and son, or watching the 2005 version of *Pride & Prejudice*.

Ready to find
your next great read?

Let us help.

Visit prh.com/nextread

Penguin
Random
House